This
And he was dangerous.

The garden behind Cameron's house was just for her, for young Cammie, who had loved fairies, for the girl lost forever. Stark and male and big, the man had intruded into the feminine sanctuary.

"You may leave," Cameron said to him with all the aloof dignity she could manage.

He remained still. His eyes, those pinpoints of light, shifted from her, scanning the tall fairy garden statues. Cameron sensed he only moved when he wanted, when he was ready. He took a long swallow of his beer, his throat working, before he turned to her. "Nice."

"Didn't you hear me? I just told you to leave."

"Correction: you told me that I *may* leave. That means I have a choice." He walked toward her. Still holding the beer in one hand, he flicked her bell earring. His hand lingered, slid down to her wrist, and lightly circled the charms there. Though he was holding her loosely, the strength in those fingers could have crushed her wrist, silencing her bells—or her cry for help. His thumb brushed her inner wrist once, then settled into a slow, steady caress. The light, rough scrape of it seemed threatening, predatory.

"Your pulse is racing," he said softly. "What are you afraid of?"

Avon Contemporary Romances by
Cait London

SILENCE THE WHISPERS
FLASHBACK
HIDDEN SECRETS
WHAT MEMORIES REMAIN
WITH HER LAST BREATH
WHEN NIGHT FALLS
LEAVING LONELY TOWN
IT HAPPENED AT MIDNIGHT
SLEEPLESS IN MONTANA
THREE KISSES

ATTENTION: ORGANIZATIONS AND CORPORATIONS
Most Avon Books paperbacks are available at special quantity discounts for bulk purchases for sales promotions, premiums, or fund-raising. For information, please call or write:

Special Markets Department, HarperCollins Publishers, Inc., 10 East 53rd Street, New York, N.Y. 10022-5299. Telephone: (212) 207-7528. Fax: (212) 207-7222.

CAIT LONDON

Silence the Whispers

STILLWATER COUNTY LIBRARY
27 N. 4TH ST.
PO BOX 266
COLUMBUS, MT 59019

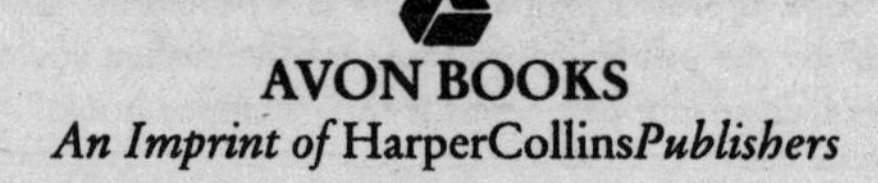

AVON BOOKS
An Imprint of HarperCollins*Publishers*

This is a work of fiction. Names, characters, places, and incidents are products of the author's imagination or are used fictitiously and are not to be construed as real. Any resemblance to actual events, locales, organizations, or persons, living or dead, is entirely coincidental.

AVON BOOKS
An Imprint of HarperCollins*Publishers*
10 East 53rd Street
New York, New York 10022-5299

Copyright © 2006 by Lois E. Kleinsasser
ISBN-13: 978-0-06-079088-2
ISBN-10: 0-06-079088-1
www.avonromance.com

All rights reserved. No part of this book may be used or reproduced in any manner whatsoever without written permission, except in the case of brief quotations embodied in critical articles and reviews. For information address Avon Books, an Imprint of HarperCollins Publishers.

First Avon Books paperback printing: July 2006

Avon Trademark Reg. U.S. Pat. Off. and in Other Countries, Marca Registrada, Hecho en U.S.A.
HarperCollins® is a registered trademark of HarperCollins Publishers Inc.

Printed in the U.S.A.

10 9 8 7 6 5 4 3 2 1

If you purchased this book without a cover, you should be aware that this book is stolen property. It was reported as "unsold and destroyed" to the publisher, and neither the author nor the publisher has received any payment for this "stripped book."

For Mom and Kaya

Prologue

HIS FATHER WAS MISSING. . . .

At dawn, early June's summer fog layered the English garden maze; tiny drops glistened on the shrubs as H.J. rushed into them, seeking his father.

The rain had left the earth cool and fragrant, the rolling hills were just starting to appear in the distance.

The well-trimmed trees and shrubs of the Somertons' Oklahoma estate surrounded a plantation-style mansion; the maze was directly in front of the sprawling wide porch, those wide curved steps, and it was due to be trimmed. As the gardener's son, ten-year-old H.J. knew that his father wouldn't be trimming at this hour, but where was he?

The damp mist seeped into his clothing and into his lungs as H.J. quickly ran through the familiar maze. But this time, he wasn't playing hide-and-seek with his sister or the little Somerton heiress . . . because Cammie Somerton had been kidnapped eleven days ago; she'd simply disappeared from her bed.

The two-million ransom had been paid immediately by her mother, but the child hadn't been returned. Now, eleven days since that May kidnapping, frantic searchers ran across the rolling hills and into the woods, and federal and state investigators were questioning everyone involved with the Somerton estate. In a few days, they would be questioning everyone in the town of Mimosa, going door to door. Not allowed inside the estate's perimeters, news reporters had practically set up camp outside the massive gates, marked by Somerton's "S" logo.

Paul Olson, the Somerton estate's gardener, had been questioned at the police station several times, and the investigators had been in the Olson house, searching the rooms, tearing them apart. And now the gardener was missing—after a restless night, he'd mysteriously left his bed and his family, at three that morning—supposedly to check to see if a garden hose had been turned off by a helper.

His wife had already asked everyone if they'd seen her husband, but H.J. had to do something. . . . If H.J. could find his father, then his family would be safe, and somehow all the trouble he sensed brewing would end. All the darkness that seemed to hover over his family would evaporate like the fog curling around his body now. H.J. didn't understand the rising fear in his mother's eyes, or the whispers at the Somerton mansion, the way the staff's eyes had followed him, the gardener's son.

The rising dawn had painted the plantation-style mansion a light shade of pink. To one side of the mansion, the fog layered acres of the Somerton ranch, which spread into green fields, barns, and grazing thoroughbreds, all enclosed by those white board fences.

To the other side of the mansion, Katherine Somerton's hot-air balloon was being prepared for flight. The heiress had to search for her daughter; everyone understood—she had to do something, anything, instead of feeling helpless.

H.J. understood perfectly: He had to find his father, the big man who was always there with his rough wide hands, his quiet gentle voice, and his love of his family.

A ten-year-old boy didn't cry . . . he had to be strong . . . *he had to find his father. . . .*

H.J. turned to see the massive balloon begin to lift into the rising sun, fog and darkness shadowing the big *S* logo and the basket below. As he always did, H.J. held his breath as the bright red-and-blue harlequin pattern of the balloon rose majestically into the blue-gray sky. The giant *S* logo slowly caught the sun, Katherine Somerton's signature script below it. A competent balloonist, Katherine Somerton was in the basket, her white scarf fluttering like a bright flag around her head as she rose up into the sunshine. In the shadows below her, her team, a small crowd of servants and her husband of one year, watched.

"Cammie, where are you?" H.J. whispered, fearing for the six-year-old heiress.

The ransom had been paid to the kidnappers, and Cammie hadn't been returned. H.J.'s mother had gently told him that not all kidnapped children were returned safely.

Fear pumped through H.J., and he shivered, cold in the fragrant morning air. *Was Cammie dead already?*

Today, H.J. was to have helped his father trim the hedge around the guest cottages, and just maybe—

H.J. ran up the stone pathway leading to the four guest cottages. Already experienced as his father's helper, the boy noted the untrimmed hedges. His father had planned to trim today, but he hadn't—

The boy stopped suddenly, scanning the cottages' doors.

One was slightly ajar—Hope rose and bloomed in H.J. . . . maybe his father was inside with Cammie.

Maybe Cammie was okay and safe and maybe H.J.'s dad was the hero who had found her.

His dad had always been a hero, the best, the man who could fix anything, knew everything, and understood the boy's disdain of playing teatime with his little three-year-old sister.

Everything was going to be all right and just the way it was before Cammie was kidnapped. . . .

H.J. was already running toward that slightly open door. Then he pushed it open and peered inside. "Dad?"

The living room was tiny and shadowed. H.J. pushed the door wider, and a rectangle of early sunlight spread into the room.

It fell upon Paul Olson lying upon the varnished boards of the floor, blood circling his head, the wavy blond hair matted with it. *He lay so still.*

At first, H.J. wanted to run away, but he came close to kneel beside his father. Maybe he could help, do something to stop the blood, maybe his father was just hurt and he'd be all right . . . . *He'd be all right—everything would be just as it was . . .*

But Paul's Olson's blue eyes were open and blank, and instinctively H.J. recognized death. "Dad?" he asked again, unevenly, as tears burned his eyes. "*Dad?*"

The boy swallowed as he looked down his father's body; the big revolver lay in Paul Olson's one hand, and the other gripped a note. Paper money was everywhere, all around his body, beneath it, on it.

H.J. shrank away, but then he had to know—

He eased the note from his father's big rough fingers and opened it slowly.

I'm sorry for what I've done. I needed money and kidnapping Cammie was the only way. I can't live with what I've done. . . . Paul Olson.

Then someone gripped H.J.'s collar, lifted him high, and tore the note from his hand. . . .

One

Twenty-eight years later

"WHERE IS THE REST OF THAT RANSOM MONEY?"

Hayden Olson stood in his St. Louis, Missouri, office, and watched the hot-air balloons glide past his window in the distance. In a harlequin pattern of bloodred and white against the clear June sky, the balloonists were practicing for a racing competition held later in the summer, but Hayden's mind ran back to the one balloon rising high in the Oklahoma sky years ago. . . .

Katherine Somerton had been an expert balloonist, and that fateful day—the day young H.J. Olson had found his father, suicide note in hand—she'd chosen to hunt for her kidnapped daughter, who had been missing for eleven days.

The kind, loving widow of Big Buck Somerton, married for one year to a new husband, Katherine would never know of Paul Olson's suicide note, of the ransom money scattered around his body. She would never know that her kidnapped daughter would be found three days later, wandering and dazed by search parties.

Because that day, when young H.J.'s life changed forever,

Katherine's balloon had exploded in midair, killing her instantly.

Locked in memories, Hayden ignored the paperwork waiting on his desk. He scanned the expansive fields of seedlings and trees, the greenhouses and shipping center of Grow Green Lawn and Garden. He dismissed the hum of the office outside his closed door and thought about Mimosa, Oklahoma.

A business trip to the chain's newest store in Oklahoma City would take him near the town that had turned against the family of the suicide-kidnapper, Paul Olson.

"I never want to see Mimosa again," Hayden said firmly as he turned back to his work as a top man in Grow Green Lawn and Garden company.

But seated at his desk, he watched another hot-air balloon sail by and knew that someday he'd have to return to Mimosa and reopen a past that his mother had begged him to leave alone—

Six-year-old Cameron "Cammie" Somerton had recovered and was now a grown woman, married and divorced, according to the newspaper clippings that Hayden had meticulously kept in that special file.

And the rest of the ransom money had never been found.

If that money were found, the trail just might lead to the answers Hayden had to have someday.

He flipped open the file on the upcoming grand opening in Oklahoma City and viewed the schedule his secretary had created for him, the contacts and her brief notes on the corporate suite in his hotel, the employees and manager, the grand opening specials. With his mind still on Mimosa and the Somerton heiress, Hayden tapped his pen on the thick file and stuffed it into his briefcase to review later.

That time, years ago, had remained locked inside him. . . .

Young H.J. had been helpless to stop anything, to protect his family.

That helpless feeling had eaten at Hayden for years, and there was nothing he could do to change the past.

Mommy? Mommy? Help me. I'm afraid. I'm cold, Mommy, and it's dark here. Why, Mommy? Why did they put me here? Mommy?

In the Oklahoma night, the echoes of the nightmare's whispers curled around Cameron Somerton as she struggled to leave their chilling grasp.

The child's whispers were always there, plaguing her, reminding her that those terrifying days in that damp hole had forever changed her.

Some people just know who they are, their role to play and how to live with themselves, the things they've done.

Others had to fight every day to get a grip on everything about them . . . or they could fly into pieces, never to recover.

Nightmares have a way of making the latter struggle harder for survival, for that oneness with who they are, how they fit into life . . . but most of all, how they could face day-to-day life, pasting the pieces into some semblance of normality.

Normality for Cameron Somerton was waking up amid a nightmare that left her cold and sweating and fighting to hold herself together. Every morning, she fought to push away that nightmare, to place herself step by step into a safe routine, to surround herself with air and light and color—and most of all, her good-luck pieces.

Because if she didn't, she'd dissolve into nothing.

She studied the dream catchers swirling softly above her bed and by her ceiling to floor windows. The dream catchers hadn't worked, because yet again the nightmares had come prowling.

In her remodeled barn, the ceiling fans stirred the fresh lemon scent of her cleaning aids, marking her obsession with cleanliness.

But then, she had lots of obsessions, and the town of

Mimosa seemed to understand; they knew she'd been traumatized as a child and that it had taken years of seclusion and care to bring her back into her life. They knew that as an adult, Cameron had hunted endlessly through the property and woods nearby for any kind of a mine, cave, crude basement, or old-fashioned storm cellar that would seem like a hole in the ground.

On the other hand, Cameron realized that one of the benefits of being an heiress was that people allowed her those little oddities that kept her pasted together, all the little pieces precisely in place. . . .

The downside of inheriting Big Buck Somerton's fortune was that there were people who wanted to take it away . . . and Cameron Somerton wasn't letting that happen.

This morning was for escape, a brief respite, a feminine ritual of spring plant gathering, of putting herself miles away from that mansion on an opposite hill and all that it represented. Today was for her "Other Self," and she'd dressed appropriately in everything that made her "Other Self" happy—the rose-colored lacy lingerie, worn tight jeans, a pink long-sleeve T-shirt, and pink tennis shoes with rose laces. Because her ritualistic, semiyearly plant hunting was emotionally freeing for her, and bad luck for the plants—they were going to die, after all—Cameron had also chosen her feel-good pink.

"The right lingerie and accessories are so important and give a woman confidence, isn't that right, Mother?"

Her Other Self needed this exquisite break from the grueling day-to-day burden of being the Somerton heiress, at the head of a giant corporation, managing a fortune and playing the role for which she had been groomed. Cameron worked very hard to keep the distinction between the woman with special needs of heart and soul and the heiress who served the many needs of others.

Every day, before that first mourning dove cooed, Cameron awoke to the usual nightmare, the whispers calling out for her mother to help her. Katherine Somerton had never come years ago, and she'd never come in a single nightmare. Sweating and breathing hard, her heart pumping, Cameron fought desperately to slide from the clinging threads of that nightmare into the brightly lit, airy space of the barn.

She absorbed the space, taking it into her, and pushed away the claustrophobia brought on by her trauma.

Routine helped—getting out of that bed . . . or couch . . . or chair—wherever she had finally fallen asleep to music—stretching to keep her body limber, then working out on her large body ball before stepping onto her treadmill and running until she heard only the racing of her heart.

Today, for one glorious selfish day, Cameron would leave everything and just live like everyone else.

When the pink-and-gold dawn started illuminating Cameron's ceiling-to-floor privacy windows, she was already dressed and waiting. She looked down her driveway to the state highway, then over to the small town of Mimosa to the opposite hill. Cameron looked past the grazing cattle and horses in the well-tended fields of the Somerton estate, to the mansion. As a child, she'd seen the white plantation pillars as gleaming, huge white teeth that could devour her.

But then Cameron liked to think that the gargoyles on her barn, the horseshoes nailed to it, protected her from that house and the memories of life without her mother.

She stood in front of the huge mirror that lent even more space and light to the remodeled barn, the perfect solution to a woman plagued with claustrophobia. Cameron prowled through the assorted jewelry in an abalone shell, then selected the tiny silver bell earrings and a matching charm bracelet, layered with bells, shamrocks, a cross, a rabbit's foot, a horseshoe, and anything else that she could attach for good luck.

She needed every bit of luck possible—because she was just possibly losing her mind.

The other jewelry in a locked drawer wasn't for today, not the diamonds and specially designed pieces she wore when she appeared as the heiress of the Somerton estate and millions. Those were only a small portion of her mother's jewelry, the rest locked in the safe at the mansion, or stored safely in Mimosa or New York bank vaults.

Cameron picked up the framed photograph of Katherine Somerton from the table beneath the mirror. In the ornate frame, the woman who had died long ago hunting for her daughter, smiled gently back at her.

"Hello, Mother. I love you," Cameron murmured, and traced the gentle blond waves surrounding the delicate, fair-skinned face, those clear blue eyes, sparkling with laughter.

Her routine included greeting the photograph each morning, the I-love-you, and wrapping Katherine Somerton's perfect love around her. "Everyone should say I love you every day, isn't that what you said? I'm trying to remember everything. But I wish you were here. I need you so much."

These special photographs were all she had to cling to since her kidnapping because Katherine Somerton's balloon had exploded in midair. . . .

Cameron held up the mirror beside her face, comparing mother's and daughter's features. Both were fair, though now Cameron's hair was darker, sun-streaked, and straight in a blunt cut, drawn back now into a smooth ponytail. Her mother's hair had also reached her shoulders, but it had been creamy blond and styled into waves around her face. Cameron's freckles contrasted her mother's pale, perfect skin; the eyes were almost the same blue shade, but Cameron's were more guarded and shadowed, her lips a little tighter. An almost imperceptible difference lay in the sharper slant of Cameron's eyes and Celtic cheekbones, her stronger jaw.

When she was twelve, Cameron had found these special pictures in a drawer of an old dresser she'd wanted to paint pink. Cameron had hoarded them, keeping them safe, until she could display them without fear. Then, when she'd finally asked her stepfather about the pictures, he'd said that he'd hidden them "because you were in such a state that it would have wounded you too much." And after years, Robert DuChamps had said he'd simply forgotten them.

And he couldn't remember where he'd placed the albums of the Somerton family either—but then, sentiment and tender consideration weren't Robert's strong point. Only a few pictures of Cameron and her mother had remained.

Cameron's hand shook as she replaced the framed photograph to the others surrounding it—pictures of a happy little girl atop her pony as her mother led it around the ring, that same little girl at a birthday party, hugging a clown and holding a big balloon, grinning at her mother. There were more pictures of that girl, dressed and standing beside her mother, both in their Easter best and wearing gloves.

Cameron glanced at the tiny gold cross, a necklace a little girl would wear, that hung from one corner of the mirror, mocking her. She'd worn it for years after the kidnapping, drawing protection from it, because those early years with Robert as her guardian hadn't been sweet.

She fought the darkness churning around her, the tightness in her chest and the panic that could bring, and swung her black hobo bag over her shoulder. She escaped into bright June dawn, lifting her face to the fresh air and sunshine, something she could never get enough of, preparing for a whole day of freedom, doing just what she wanted, even if it was only to take advantage of a one-day clearance sale on gardening plants far away from Mimosa. She revved her small Toyota pickup, put her hand on the stick shift, and pushed everything else away, her commitments, the mound of paperwork at her desk, and all the obligations of the Somerton heiress.

In passing down the long driveway from her barn to the highway, she glanced at the little farmhouse that had come with the property she had purchased just after her divorce, eleven years ago. Through the years, the farmhouse had only minimal attention, just enough to keep it standing, and before that, the old Riordan farm had been sold several times. Empty now, but still looking as if someone had loved it once—the little stone house nestled amid trees and borders of flowers, its vegetable garden in the backyard untended and overgrown within its sagging and overgrown picket fence.

"I really need to rent that, to put some life into it. A family who needs a break in these hard times," Cameron reminded herself as she drove out onto the highway and a whole day of well-deserved freedom.

The end to a perfect, glorious day of sunshine and freedom was a definite bummer.

Alone, parked beside the highway at eleven o'clock at night, Cameron's pickup was lower in the left rear, the tire going flat. Grazing pastures spread for miles around, the highway deserted, and the only company she had was that curious herd of cattle nearby.

She kicked the tire that wasn't flat, but too low to drive much farther. A lonely road at night was nowhere for a lady, or an heiress, to stop. But as long as that highway was empty, Cameron felt secure in her safety—

Headlights appeared on the deserted highway, like two bright eyes focused on Cameron.

The driver could be anyone—a friend, a good-natured passerby, a farm family coming home from a buying trip in Oklahoma City. Or it could be someone dangerous, and she might end up dead in the ditch's mud.

Cameron Somerton shook her head and pushed back her fear; on a deserted road, a woman traveling alone would be easy enough prey, and she was regretting her impulse to stop earlier at that cute little flea market, then the Eat and Gas Cafe.

The headlights came nearer, blinding her and heightening

her fears. She held her breath and waited to see if the car would pass by.

The echoes of her stepfather's warnings circled her, "You're worth several million, almost a billion, if you'd stop giving it away to charities, Cameron. You can't just go running around the countryside, acting like any other woman. You could be kidnapped—or worse."

"You'd better make certain nothing happens to me, Robert, or it will all go to charities," Cameron whispered to the damp night air.

She inhaled unsteadily, the fragrance filled with June rain, the new grass and good old Oklahoma eau de cow.

"If I hadn't stopped for that piece of pie at the Eat and Gas Cafe . . . if I only hadn't talked with Fancy . . . I could have been home by now." Long ago, down in that dark pit where she'd been held captive, Cameron had learned to talk to herself, to latch on to the sound of her own voice for safety.

The car's headlights trapped and blinded her as it pulled off the highway pavement and parked on the dirt shoulder behind Cameron's light pickup.

The nearby field's oil rigs were slowly bobbing in the moonlight, and on the slope of another hill, a rancher's herd of wild horses were grazing. Closer to the ranch's fence, the white faces of the small Hereford herd gleamed eerily.

The fragrance of the potted herbs, flowers, and shrubs in the back of Cameron's truck mocked her. Fated to die under her care, some of the pots had tipped and rolled, exposing their delicate roots. The plants weren't for the grounds of the estate, they were for her barn, where nothing but weeds seemed to grow.

Oddly, the instruction tags attached to the small trees seemed almost cheerful, catching the moonlight in tiny white squares. But they didn't flirt with the wind on one of those eerie nights covered in black velvet, the moon lonely above. The world seemed to stand still . . . and the only sounds were the frogs in a nearby pond and the occasional low call of a cow to her calf—and the hard, fast beat of fear in Cameron's heart.

She forced herself to act casually, to lift the box containing her small air compressor from between two rosebush pots. The thorns snagged her hand, scratching her.

But when the car's door slammed, she turned to face the man walking toward her. The roadside gravel crunched beneath his shoes, his stride long and purposeful—

She recognized that hard, blunt face, the neat, close haircut, the set of his shoulders within a white dress shirt, rolled back at the sleeves. Big and well dressed, he'd been hard to miss in the quiet ten o'clock hour at the Eat and Gas Cafe. He'd been at a corner table, a tired unshaven businessman, somewhere in his midthirties to forty. An expensive gold watch circled his wrist, and he'd frowned at the papers he'd drawn from his briefcase. The coffee cup at his side had already been refilled, so apparently he was preparing for a long night—or maybe a caffeine high didn't affect him.

And he hadn't been happy as he stared at her: His dark eyebrows had drawn together, a muscle had contracted in his jaw, his lips thinned between the lines bracketing them.

She'd dismissed him as one of the traveling salesmen who often passed by Mimosa, using Eat and Gas, the only place within miles of nowhere, to refresh for a long drive out into the world away from rural Oklahoma.

At nine-thirty that night, Cameron had decided to end the perfect day by stopping at the cafe for a turkey club sandwich and a raspberry milk shake. When Cameron had finished gassing up her pickup and parking it in front of the cafe, she'd gone into the cafe. Country music played in the jukebox; the trucker in the rear booth and the big tough-looking businessman who needed a shave were hard to miss in the empty room. She'd made her usual bathroom pit stop and had settled into her favorite front booth. Girl talk with her friend the waitress, Fancy Arnold, had been the perfect cherry on an otherwise glorious day away from heiress shackles.

When the businessman had left his table and everything on it to go outside, Fancy had lifted her eyebrows, her brown eyes sparkling within heavy shades of green eye shadow. While Fancy had continued her usual dialogue about how nice it would be to get a piece of something like that, Cameron noted the man getting something from the backseat of his BMW. He must have dropped it, because he went down between his car and her pickup for just a minute. When he stood, he walked toward the cafe's door with papers in his hand.

For just that moment while she was standing and preparing to leave, discussing the plants she'd just bought with Fancy—trying to nudge her friend into helping her plant them—Cameron had sensed that someone was studying her.

She'd turned slowly, checked out the big trucker in bib overalls, carefully feeding his Chihuahua by hand, then looked at the man dressed in a white dress shirt rolled back at the sleeves, a briefcase open on the table beside him.

His hard dark eyes had locked with Cameron's. It wasn't a casual, passing look, like experienced travelers take when checking out who is in their vicinity before settling back to business.

The look had been penetrating and had lifted the hair on her nape. It held contempt, as if he'd seen down to everything she was and didn't like it. Those narrowed eyes had seemed to rip down her, taking in her pink long-sleeve T-shirt and belted denim jeans. He seemed to grimace as he looked at her pink tennis shoes with the rose-colored laces.

And now that stranger was walking toward her, his headlights outlining that big powerful body . . .

Cameron gripped the handle of the air compressor and slid its box away. She knew a few defensive moves, and if he tried anything, one good swing at him might give her an advantage.

His white dress shirt gleamed in the moonlight, and he

stopped a few feet from her. Cameron realized she'd been holding her breath; it exploded with a "Stay right there."

"Are you going to swing that at me?" he asked, in a deep amused tone.

Through the years, she'd gotten used to amusement . . . a quirky heiress, tempered by the early disaster in her life, was allowed a lot of latitude among friends. "I might. I saw you at Eat and Gas. Are you following me?"

"The pie was good." He placed a hand on the tailgate of her pickup and scanned the plants. "That's a lot of plants. Are you in business?"

Cameron wasn't explaining the plants. She moved backward, toward the door of her pickup. If she could just get into the cab and lock the doors, she had a cell phone that could get his description out before she was killed. Her last words would be heard on the Mimosa hot line, and just maybe she could save someone else . . .

She glanced at her plants, worried for them. They could die in her pickup bed before anyone found them—found her.

Caution always paid, but the whole thing—her mind racing into deadly scenarios—was probably just her vivid imagination. Maybe. "Who are you?"

The pause was there, hovering between them, before he said very slowly, precisely, "Hayden Olson. Who are you?"

"Just someone who doesn't really want to get on friendly terms."

There was that quick, perceptive look and a silence as though he were circling her answer, then Hayden said, "Ah. I see. That's smart for a woman alone on a deserted road. But I could change that tire for you."

He crouched beside the tire, ran a knowing hand over it, and looked up at her. "How about it?"

"It's just low, not flat. I'm going to air it up." Cameron's hand had sweated on the handle of the air compressor, making it slippery. She changed hands, wiped her free hand on her jeans, and shook her head No. Her throat had tightened and though they were only a few feet apart, she sensed him quietly studying her—like maybe a murderer would, or a rapist. Or maybe a murderer *and* a rapist.

Her mind raced on to the potential danger. Her need to rescue everything, including the wilted and past-prime clearance-special plants, could be fatal. The pansy blossoms would shrivel, the azalea and rosebushes, the firebush, Shasta daisies, mums, and others would die, unwatered, poor little roots exposed. They would dry in the dawn before one of the ranchers drove by and noted Cameron's cold, raped body in the muddy ditch. . . .

Okay, so she had a vivid imagination. But then kidnapped and terrified at six years old had lasting effects.

Cameron straightened, drawing safety and confidence around her. She was wearing her good-luck shoes and underwear, her bell earrings were jingling, and her charm bracelet was definitely good luck. She had instructions on how to take care of those plants, and she was going to plant them.

"I'd really like you to leave now. I can handle this. I have an air compressor. And I know how to use it," she stated firmly. *One way or the other. You take one more step toward me and, Buster, you are going to have a real headache.*

He stood slowly and nodded as he studied her. "A lady should always be prepared, right?"

"I try to be. Please leave." He was carefully dissecting her features, one by one as if trying to see inside her, and she shivered. Did he recognize her from the newspapers?

The local newspaper had touted her contribution to a children's ranch and run her picture beside the article. Headlines of HEIRESS CONTRIBUTES TO INNER-CITY KIDS' SUMMERS couldn't be missed, and the paper had been at the Eat and Gas Cafe. The picture of her dressed in a designer cream slacks suit had been taken at her estate's office; the suit fitted her role as a pearl-wearing, well-groomed heiress.

Great. He probably knew who she was—an heiress worth plenty in the kidnapping and ransom business.

Hayden ran his hand through that thick, neatly clipped hair and frowned at her. "Anything could happen to you out here."

"Don't I know it? I can handle this, really."

Instead, he stood looking down at her. He took a deep breath, and the moonlight caught the set of his jaw. From the way his lips forced a tight, brief smile, she knew she was testing whatever patience he had.

"Now, it wouldn't be very gentlemanly of me to leave a lady stranded out here, alone on a deserted road, would it?" Hayden asked, after her heart pounded and a cow mooed.

"I'm quite fine, thank you." It wouldn't do to upset a murderer, either. Good manners could balance the scale. What had the hostage who had been successful in her own release said in her interview? Get their confidence, show them pictures of your family, make it personal?

Hayden leaned down a little toward her, and Cameron backed away a couple steps. He looked even more irritated, doing that breathe-in sharply, expelling slowly thing, as if he were counting to control his temper.

She really hoped he could manage his anger. As the person who could be most affected right now—on this lonely road—she had a definite interest in his ability to control himself.

His hands were on his hips now, and he seemed disgusted. "I'm not leaving you here . . . period. Give me that damn air compressor."

Whatever he was going to do to her, there was no need to curse. That was just plain insulting. The last words a potential murderee should hear should be something like "I'm really sorry about this. . . ."

A woman had her limits after all, her point of no return, the final straw, Cameron decided. "Say you're sorry."

Hayden blinked at that; his head went back, and he scowled down at her. "Why?"

"If you're a gentleman, you wouldn't curse in front of a

lady," she explained very slowly, just in case he was a well-dressed, dumbhead-murderer.

"Dammit," he muttered under his breath, and shook his head as if trying to dislodge her attempt to implant manners. "Look . . . just go get whatever makes you feel you have some sort of protection against strangers . . . and you can hold it on me while I check this tire."

He leaned down again and spoke very slowly as if she were the dumbhead. "But I *am* going to air up this tire, lady."

"Oh, no, you're not. I am using this air compressor until I can get to a station. You're not touching it."

Of course, she'd drive home instead of to a gas station. In small-town Mimosa, stations shut down at six o'clock on weekday evenings, seven on weekends.

This time his words were spaced, hitting the Oklahoma night like mallets. "You'd argue with a stranger—someone who outweighs you, say eighty or so pounds—on a deserted highway, *where anything could happen to you?*"

"Is that a threat?"

"This isn't going well," he said between his teeth, and this time his scowl added a flare to his nostrils; he was definitely taking deep breaths to control his anger.

"Git." It was an "old-timey" word, used by cowboys since forever, and she meant it.

"You know how to use that, I guess—the air compressor? You know about watching the pressure gauge?" Hayden asked quietly, studying her.

"If I said it, I meant it."

With another muttered curse, he pushed aside the pots holding the fuchsia azaleas and righted the pots that had turned over. In a quick movement, he reached to rub the ruffled leaves of the lemon-scented citronella, then the rosebush's between his fingers. He leaned over the side of the pickup and reached to push his hand down into the bed of plants.

"What are you doing to my plants?" Cameron demanded,

prepared to defend them. She had big plans for the citronella geranium, which was supposed to repel mosquitoes, and that poor little peach-colored rosebush needed someone to love it.

"They're dry. They're in poor shape . . . looks like the last of the lot. Tell your gardener to give them a little breather to recover before planting them. Those chives look wilted, like they've got aphids . . . tell him to dose them pronto." He studied her as the silence stretched between them, then said slowly, "That is a lot of mums. A lot of blooming plants. There's forsythia and more scented geraniums and lavender in there, too."

The words seemed to probe the night air, causing her to be even more uneasy. When it came to sensing probes, Cameron trusted her experienced instincts and her defenses shot higher. She reached up to wrap her fist around the small trunk of a flowering pear tree. If she had to, she'd protect it with her last breath. "So?"

Those eyes had narrowed on her, then he slowly shook his head and shrugged. "People who have hay fever and asthma would have problems with these plants—"

For an instant, she heard the whisper of an asthmatic desperately sucking air into her lungs. Cameron shivered; the sound came too frequently in her nightmares, that deep sucking sound, the terrified panting . . . Reacting as she always did when a dark memory slapped at her unexpectedly, Cameron shook her head, and the tiny bells at her ears did their thing, sounding happily over the whispers that disappeared into the night. "I know that. Did I ask your opinion?"

"You're used to giving orders, aren't you? Probably have someone take care of your every whim, dancing around you. . . . Odd that you'd know how to use an air compressor, or a regular jack, and that you'd—" Hayden stopped suddenly, inhaled as if drawing himself back, sealing himself off. He looked down at his dirty hands and grimaced, reaching to wipe them on the small bayberry bushes. "I'm not leaving here until you're aired up and on the road. Mimosa is just over that hill about five miles."

"I know where I am." She stared at him, waiting for him to leave. Whoever he was, he'd been around enough to know the distance to town. And that could mean—anything. He stood there, big and solid, unmoving in the moonlight, his hands on his hips. "Well?"

"Well, what?"

A survivor, Cameron was used to making compromises to get what she wanted, and Hayden Olson wasn't going anywhere. He looked as if he'd stand there forever, forbidding and harsh and thoroughly disgusted. "Back off. Go sit in your car. Don't start the motor, and I'll use the air compressor," she said finally.

He was pushing his luck by just standing there. *She* did have a slow-to-burn temper and it was straining at the leash now, despite the potential danger of the stranger. "Well?" she pushed.

With a deep breath and a slow shake of his head, Hayden Olson turned and walked back toward his car. The set of those wide shoulders said he wasn't happy. But then, neither was she.

He was one of those men who thought women were mindless and needed direction, and she'd had a lifetime of orders from someone just like him.

Cameron waited until he was in the car, the headlights still blinding her; she sensed his anger hitting her in waves. Hurrying to the task, she inserted the air compressor's adapter into the cigarette lighter, started the engine, and hurried back to attach the hose to the air valve. She crouched beside the tire and frowned as she noted that the air valve was a little loose and, when taken off, it revealed a piece of gravel wedged into it, depressing the small inner post. When she dug out the gravel and applied the air compressor, air hissed at her.

Okay, her tire had been a little low when she'd left the Eat and Gas, and she should have checked it then. But gravel didn't just get wedged inside an air valve by itself. Her fingers shaking, she flipped the jack's attachment down, locking it to the tire's valve, and turned on the machine.

While the air pressure rose, the BMW hadn't moved, and as soon as the pressure met the tire's standard, she unlatched the air compressor, got into her pickup, revved the motor, and spun out. She checked the rearview mirror to see if the murderer-rapist-kidnapper was following her, but the headlights swung around in a U-turn, the rear lights disappearing into the night.

"Well, I think I handled that nicely." She was shaking now in an afterreaction to the danger that hadn't happened.

Cameron settled into thinking about the past moments: Mr. Hayden Olson had seen the air jack in her hand; it was safety equipment no woman should be without.

Yet Mr. Hayden Olson had wanted to "change" the tire for her. Then, he'd wanted to use the air compressor, and he'd been reluctant to leave her to the task. Why? Because she'd find that gravel depressing the air valve?

He'd just turned around and headed in the other direction; that meant that he wasn't headed in her direction in the first place.

The tiny bells on her wrist seemed to jingle a warning as she lifted her hand to smooth her hair. Her eyes met her own in the mirror's silvery rectangle.

The pieces of Mr. Hayden Olson's interaction with her—at night, on a deserted road—didn't fit.

But then, neither did she . . .

Two

"DRIVES LIKE A BAT OUT OF HELL," HAYDEN MUTTERED DARKLY. In his rearview mirror, he watched the white Toyota's lights disappear into the night. "All alone on a deserted highway with a low, almost flat tire, and she's reprimanding me for cursing. Just some rich witch who's always had her way, been pampered all her life—"

But according to the newspaper on the seat beside him, she wasn't just any rich woman, she was the Somerton heiress, Cameron. And he owed the Somerton family a very big debt. *They'd taught him the first harsh rule of life—how to survive.*

Inserting the gravel into her air valve at the cafe was just a backup measure. Hayden had to have a closer look at the girl who had grown up amid every possible advantage, while his mother, his sister, and he had nothing but hard times.

Sins of the father. . . . But then the son of a kidnapper who had committed suicide wasn't allowed to forget anything, was he?

He'd had to talk with Cameron Somerton, to see if the little sweet girl, H.J.'s playmate of years ago, remembered him.

She hadn't. But then, he wasn't ten any longer; he was a man who looked like his father. Years could have easily dimmed her memory, and that grated, because he remembered so much.

Hayden flexed his hands on the BMW's expensive steering wheel, then reached for the package of wet wipes on the seat beside him. He wiped one hand, then the other, and finally the steering wheel, carefully erasing any dirt from the plants that might have clung to him.

Hayden took very good care of his possessions—he'd worked hard enough to get them, to place himself a galaxy away from his boyhood struggles.

Testing the plants' leaves and the pots' soil was automatic for a man who had been born of a gardener, who had put himself through college by landscaping jobs, and who was now an executive in a Missouri greenhouse and gardening supply company.

On a whim to see if the old Eat and Gas Cafe still existed, the place where his father had brought him as a boy, Hayden had dropped off a direct route to Oklahoma City on I-44 and connected with a southbound state highway. Two hours later, it had taken him to the cafe, and the pie was just as good as he remembered. The article on the Somerton heiress's donation to that children's ranch was hard to miss, touting her penchant for helping underprivileged children and other charity work.

Instead of tiny silver bells and good-luck charms, she'd worn pearls in her ears and around her throat in the photograph . . . and she was all class in that business blouse and slacks suit, handing a fat check to the administrator of the children's ranch.

In the picture, she matched that big Southern-style mansion and a chauffeur to drive her. But the white Toyota pickup wasn't a new model, she was an experienced stick-shift driver, and how many heiresses knew the value of an air compressor for a temporary fix?

And how many would demand an apology in the lonely middle of nowhere, where by just irritating a stranger, she could be killed?

Git. . . . Say you're sorry. . . . If you're a gentleman, you wouldn't curse in front of a lady.

Hayden heard the explosion of breath he'd been holding, and with it came a low curse—without an apology.

In the cafe, she'd clearly enjoyed her friend, the waitress, Fancy; Cameron Somerton hadn't been worried about anyone following her then. Weren't heiresses supposed to know the dangers? Didn't she know that anyone could spot her picture and kidnap her again?

And what the hell was Cameron Somerton, the lone heir of Big Buck Somerton, Texas oil and investment tycoon, doing out at night with no protection?

What the hell was she doing driving a stick-shift pickup when the Somerton garage was probably stuffed with luxury cars, let alone the grounds' service vehicles labeled by the flourish of that big *S*?

"Spoiled and rich and mouthy," Hayden muttered, recalling the tilt of her head, the way she called him on cursing, the way she looked ready to defend her plants. Most women would be wary of a stranger on a dark road, as she had been at first. Cameron, "Cammie" of long ago, had grown into an edgy, defensive woman. "Not her mother's daughter. Katherine was sweet—"

Damn her. She had him feeling guilty. He'd purposefully set up the meeting, causing that low tire, and she hadn't let him remove the evidence of what he'd done—and he couldn't just leave her deserted . . . something really could happen to her then. . . .

And she didn't remember him. Hayden frowned slightly into the rearview mirror. Cameron was taller, more angular, than her mother; her clothing and jewelry of tonight weren't the simple classic styles that had been Katherine's trademark. The heavy silver charm bracelet had jingled every time she'd moved.

But she was layered in pink, Cammie and Katherine's favorite color.

Hayden followed a slow-moving farm pickup overloaded with a giant round bale of hay. When he realized his mind was more on the Somerton heiress's mismatched oddities than driving, he passed the pickup and focused on the night road.

On the three-hour drive to Oklahoma City, his mind returned to Cameron Somerton and the plants she had chosen. Sickly now, but once full of blooms and scents, they would have triggered young Cammie's life-threatening asthma. Cammie's oxygen tanks were always at hand, her medications causing the local doctor to come to the mansion. *Life-threatening* echoed in the luxurious silence around him. "Her lungs are badly scarred from pneumonia and bronchitis, and any kind of smell that would be nothing to us could cause her to die. She'll have problems all her life, as long as she lives, poor thing," his mother had said years ago. "You be careful of her, H.J. Mrs. Somerton appreciates the care you take of Cammie because she really doesn't have any other children to play with. Her illness has taken away so much."

As Cammie's watchdog and playmate, young H.J. had often been cautioned about getting her too excited, making her run too fast, keeping her away from the fields and animals. She'd mourned not having a cat or dog, and her pony riding was always carefully monitored . . . always on specific days, the humidity and pollen counts checked carefully, the animal carefully groomed, and many times Cammie had worn her face mask to help filter allergens.

Then, there were the awful times, when she'd been bedridden, cautioned not to talk to expel the precious oxygen the machines pumped through the hose headgear and into her lungs—

A fresh wave of bitterness hit Hayden as he settled in to brood about that ten-year-old boy long ago . . . the boy who found his father on the floor of the Somerton guesthouse, a bullet in his skull and an apologetic suicide note in his hand.

And scattered around Paul Olson's body was five hundred thousand dollars of kidnapping money. . . .

Hayden's fists gripped his steering wheel as the past locked around him, and the need for closure. . . . He needed to understand how his father could possibly be a loving family man—and yet capable of kidnapping an ill six-year-old girl, then committing suicide, leaving his family to face gossip and harm.

Everything in Hayden told him that the answer lay in the money trail. "The rest of the two million was never found. Now I wonder where it could be?"

"What do you mean, I 'can't just do what I want for a day,' Robert?"

Cameron propped her pink western boots on top of her elegant desk in the mansion's second-story office. She studied her stepfather, the elegant and suave Robert DuChamps. In the morning after her clash with Mr. Hayden Olson, who had just happened to find her in the middle of nowhere, she hadn't slept well. Then she had picked herself out of her usual nightmares, desperately performed her morning routine on her body ball and the treadmill, then driven up the winding paved road to the Somerton estate.

It wasn't a place she wanted to visit, where painful memories lurked and curled around her, where guilt sucked away her breath.

As a child, she'd never played in the hallways or on the grounds; after Katherine's death, she'd been confined within special rooms. As a teenager, she'd lived in boarding schools and visited rarely, coming home for special occasions; she'd always been eager to leave. Then, as an adult, she relied on household staff to keep her apprised of the house and only used the necessary rooms to perform her role.

She came to Somerton House when business called—because she owed Katherine Somerton, a woman's whose honor and memory deserved to be carried on.

The man who could destroy Katherine's legacy by his gambling and womanizing had been her second husband, and someone that Cameron now had to deal with every day.

He'd been her guardian, but now as an adult, she'd taken the reins of Buck Somerton's fortune, and Robert DuChamps clearly resented her.

"You're in a mood. I can see there's no reasoning with you this morning," Robert stated in his cultured Southern-gentleman tone as he tapped his riding crop against his breeches.

But she knew his other side, the demanding harsh man deriding a child, the little Somerton heiress who had to play The Role.

"You're not afraid someone would kidnap me, are you, Robert? That someone else might want a share of the Somerton fortune?" she asked, taunting him, because now, she wasn't that little defenseless girl any longer. She'd grown up in The Game, and she knew how to hit back—just subtle remarks, but enough to remind Robert that she had inherited all of the Somerton fortunes on her twenty-first birthday.

She hadn't known how to use her power fully at first, but then survivors learn what they have to, don't they?

In the muted, elegant light of Katherine Somerton's study, the tall, stiletto-lean Robert DuChamps could have ridden out of the Old South. Sprawled in an elegant Queen Anne chair and dressed in his morning riding gear, the flowing white shirt, the dove gray riding pants and high, black polished boots, he remained handsome—to some women; his good bone structure, perhaps a blend of French and Spanish, had served him well. At his temple, small wings of gray in his straight black hair emphasized those black brows, those furious burning black eyes. His thin, well-trimmed moustache added that dash of the debonair Robert badly wanted to portray.

When others were around, he concealed his hatred of

Cameron, the heiress who controlled the estate's mansion, investments, and wealth—and therefore, everything about him, including his allowance.

Once, Cameron might have had Katherine's sweet gentleness, but her guardian until her twenty-first birthday—Robert—had tempered her with another element. Unlike Katherine, Cameron wasn't sweet, and she knew how to protect herself.

At thirty-four, she'd long ago researched everything about him, right down to his shanty-shack birth and racetrack gambling debts. Looking at him now, still handsome, his body toned by an extensive exercise room and visits to health spas, and a little nip-tuck around his jaw to delay an approaching "turkey neck," Cameron could see why Katherine, a small, gracious, but ordinary-looking widow, could be attracted to him.

But Cameron knew the real Robert DuChamps—and beneath the polish, he wasn't pleasant.

But he knew the real Cameron, too, and what she had done—the unforgivable.

Across the distance of the expensive hand-loomed carpeting, they faced each other—enemies each looking for the other's weakness, prodding, bound together by hate, money, and deadly respect for the other's power.

Robert had his riding stables, circulated with the nation's thoroughbred owners, and in front of the public, acted proud of his grown stepdaughter. After all, as Cameron's guardian, he'd done a good job of molding her into the heiress image, hadn't he?

Each knew there would come a time for a face-off, but despite her dislike of Robert, a part of Cameron remembered—and somehow clung to—the gentleness he'd sometimes shown her as a child. Children reach out to any kindness—when they're deprived of genuine emotion. When she'd emerged publicly, years after her kidnapping, she'd held his hand obediently at appearances, grateful for the small comfort in a fearful world. But in private, Robert had been cold and demanding.

Those first years after her kidnapping had been a harsh blur, the whispers plaguing her nightmares—and then at twelve, she'd found those photographs of young Cammie and her mother, and as she remembered more details of her kidnapping, the whispers came more furiously. . . .

Cameron looked down at the paper requesting Robert's latest planned purchase, a thoroughbred gelding that had placed in the Kentucky Derby. Katherine had always liked riding, but Robert had added another element to the Somerton estate, that of a respected racing stable. He raced the horses, but Cameron owned them, and that was something he resented—something she *wanted* him to resent, to know that anytime he misstepped, she could jerk everything he prized.

On the other hand, he could take away her entire life.

Locked in their standoff, each knew how far to push the other, and when to give just that little bit.

"Sure," she said, and quickly signed the purchase papers. "Just bring home the ribbons and the cups, Robert," she added, and watched his eyes flash angrily at that.

Cameron smiled her best sweet, innocent one at him. It was always nice to treat Robert like an employee, to put him in his place.

The flare of those nostrils and the tightening of his lips said that her barb had sunk home. "One day, you'll push me too far, little Cameron," he warned softly, because in their war, the barbs were quiet and deadly, echoing off the richly paneled walls. "No wonder you're divorced. No man would put up with your willful ways."

"You mean 'no man' that you would have arranged for me? Like you did William?"

"He seemed suitable, well bred," Robert stated tightly.

"Like you?" she asked again in that sweet, innocent tone with the underlying barbs. "How happy you must have been when we married—I was just twenty-one and had just inherited everything. You needed to keep me busy, didn't you? You needed someone you selected to romance me, just like you select studs for your mares, someone to keep me running, off on European trips, world cruises, and away from managing everything Katherine prized?"

"It's not unusual to select a potential husband for an heiress. I was acting in the best interests of everyone when I invited him to be a guest here."

"Except *my* best interests," Cameron returned flatly. "Try to arrange something like that again—another man for me, someone to keep track of me, to entertain me while you spend Big Buck's money, and you won't like the consequences."

"Don't you threaten me, you little—"

"Big Buck," she underlined, "earned his money the hard way, not by marrying an older, lonely widow. You knew just how to play Katherine, didn't you, Robert? But apparently not well enough, because she never took your name, did she? That must have irritated, to have Big Buck's brand on the woman you thought you owned? Wasn't that a little like having three in a bed, a woman still in love with her first husband? You didn't like being *Mr.* Katherine Somerton very well, did you?"

Robert's lips flattened against his teeth, his anger crackling between them. "Someday, you little witch—"

She was on that in a heartbeat, testing and pushing him to the very edge. "Someday—what, Robert? What exactly can you do that won't include yourself in this mess?"

The open door of the study swept wider in a soft swish against the carpet, and Madeline Fraiser entered the room.

At fifty, only sixteen years older than Cameron, Madeline was slightly plump, with a matronly figure she fought to control by regular trips to health spas. Just barely five feet tall, she wore a practical long-sleeve pin-striped blouse and black slacks, which clung a bit too tightly to her round hips. Her glasses were in their usual place on her chest, dangling from a gold chain lanyard. As Cameron's personal assistant and dear friend, Madeline worked on the Somerton estate finances, monitoring the corporate connections and investments and the expenses of the estate.

When Cameron was only seven, Madeline had stepped in to help Robert with bookkeeping, household, and money matters. She had also unofficially filled a semimotherly role, and affection ran deep between the women. Cameron smiled warmly at Madeline, the friend who had protected her and given her support and comfort through those hard young and teenage years. Madeline had been the one to come running to young Cameron's terrifying nightmares to quiet the whispers plaguing her.

Now Madeline carried a cup of her morning coffee in one hand and the usual stack of papers for Cameron's signature in the other. She glanced at Robert, did the little professional cool smile-thing that said he was there, and she was obliged to acknowledge him, but that was all he was getting.

Cameron really enjoyed Madeline's little smile and the way Robert inhaled sharply, clearly resenting the woman whose fingers were really on the Somerton purse strings. When arguing finances with Madeline, Robert always lost to her keen mind.

Madeline placed the papers on the big cherrywood desk. "When you have time, Cameron. I've researched retirement plans for the staff, and these might be the best." With the ease of long familiarity, she picked up the thoroughbred's purchase papers and sniffed, her usual reaction to what she considered "a waste of good money."

Cameron gave Madeline a warning nod and a look that said, "Just keep him busy and out of my hair."

Madeline nodded, and asked, "Did you sign that shareholder's proxy vote yet, Cameron? I can't find it anywhere."

"Yes, I went over that last night. I left it on my desk."

"Mm. I didn't see it. I'll take another look in the papers I collected. And the checkbook for the employee accounts?

You were personally going to give the head housekeeper a bonus check?"

Cameron frowned slightly; her forgetfulness was getting worse. Last week, she'd lost her schedule and address book, then she'd misplaced a locket that had been her mother's favorite. Lately, she'd forgotten to tell Madeline or Robert details about the arrangements for the Somerton Investors' Party at the mansion, a little family-style business and pleasure that had been one of Katherine's favorite social events.

Cameron reached to the pen holder on her desk for the matching pen, and stared at the cheap advertising ballpoint pen in her hand.

"Is something wrong, Cameron?" Madeline asked anxiously, as Cameron stared at the pen, trying to remember where she'd placed the expensive one that matched the pen holder.

She shook her head; there was no point in bothering Madeline with small details of a forgetful mind.

Cameron had started using index cards at her barn to remind her of daily chores, to reset the security alarms when leaving—because she'd come home more than once to an unlocked, insecure home.

Madeline made a check mark on her clipboard papers. "I talked to the real estate rental agent, and she doesn't think there will be a problem renting the farmhouse. She went over it and says that it's basically livable now, but it does need some work."

"Did you tell her that I preferred a family there, someone who would work with the gardens and the yard?" Cameron asked, distracted, as she opened the desk drawer and found the elegant pen that matched the holder. It was only one of a series of insignificant misplacements, of forgotten dates and times, of things she'd thought she'd done and hadn't, like registering those dates in her scheduling book.

Madeline shook her head and seemed puzzled. "No, I'm sorry, I missed that. Did you tell me that?"

"Yes, I—" Uncertain now, Cameron stopped. "I thought I did. Maybe not."

"Now about breeding Jack Russell terriers," Robert stated boldly. "They go with horse racing and thoroughbreds. I'll need a kennel built, and we'll need to see about a trainer for them."

Both women stared at him. "What?" Cameron asked, trying to shift into dealing with Robert, always cautiously circling her to get just that edge.

Madeline's wary glance at Robert, then Cameron, said she was expecting an explosion at any moment.

Robert locked in to argue. "I told you about that, Cameron. I was just introducing the idea to Madeline, to prepare her for the expenses."

Cameron couldn't remember any discussion about dogs or trainers.

"Whatever Cameron okays, just let me know the particulars." Madeline patted Cameron's shoulder, collected the papers, and left the room quietly.

"I don't know why she has to live here," Robert muttered. "I detest that woman. She's always around. She's got her fingers into everything I do. I'm not a child, and this damn allowance business has to stop. Katherine set that up when we married so quickly. She died before she could change it, and no doubt Madeline is urging you to keep it."

"She's been here, working with Somerton affairs and investments for twenty-seven years. You hired her almost right away after my—kidnapping—to come in and manage what you couldn't. I need her and she's efficient and I like her. She's here to stay, but you can leave here at any time, Robert," Cameron stated quietly. "But you're still going to be on an allowance. I don't know what you're complaining about. You get cost-of-living raises, you have your horses and the little extras that this estate brings you. You have the run of this house, don't you? A cook at the ready for whatever you want, Madeline to manage a very sizable investment portfolio for you, the benefits of Katherine Somerton's name so long as you don't remarry?"

It was an old argument, because Robert was always circling Cameron, trying to find ways to get the upper hand in managing the Somerton fortune. "I haven't complained about your 'guests,' the women you bring here, have I? By the way, the pool-cleaning service has been told to dispose of any underwear found in or around the pool. The housekeeping staff has been advised of the same of anything found in the sauna, or hot tub."

After a heavy silence in which Robert's hatred lashed out at her, he smiled nastily. "You'd like that, wouldn't you? Me leaving everything to you? To let you get everything *I've* worked for—put up with you for years to get?"

"You won't get anything if I die, Robert, and you know it. It will all go to my mother's charities—"

He stood and slammed his hand flat on the desk. "Your mother. . . . Well, we know the truth of that, don't we, Cameron-dear?"

The miniature ceramic frogs she'd placed on the desk—happy little things, designed to look free to leap as they wished—toppled as the desk shook. She meticulously placed them all into a row again and looked coolly at him. "You have what you want. I have what I want. You want to push this any further, and we're going to have trouble. Real trouble for us both."

"Then you wouldn't have those precious charities, would you? All that do-gooder work?"

"And you'd lose, too, Robert. Don't push me."

With a sweep of his hand, the flogs flew off the desk. "I made you what you are. I can take you down."

"Try. I go down, and you go down with me."

After Robert stormed out of her study, Cameron replaced the frogs carefully while settling her nerves. She stood and walked to the massive windows. She shrugged; her mind wasn't on Robert's complaints. She looked out at the rolling green fields, the white-painted board fences, the English garden maze below, and the guest cottages, just four in a row. In the rear of the mansion were the Olympic-sized pool and tennis courts, both rarely used. Beyond them, on a slight knoll, was a small, decorative, iron fence, enclosing Katherine and Big Buck's mausoleum.

As if she could touch the sky where Katherine had died, to hold just that bit of a wonderful, sweet, generous woman, Cameron placed her open hands on the glass. Tinted slightly against Oklahoma's summer heat, the glass was only a small barrier between Cameron and the wide blue sky.

She could almost see Katherine sailing in her hot-air balloon, her favorite pastime. Katherine Somerton was only five-foot-four, and she'd loved the freedom of the balloon, alone, high in the clear Oklahoma sky, where just maybe she dreamed of her only love.

But the last time she'd sailed, it was to hunt for her kidnapped daughter. Robert had reported her last words to the newspapers: "I can't just stay here and do nothing."

Then, hovering lower than usual in that wide blue sky, Katherine's red-and-blue hot-air balloon had burst, killing her.

Cameron smoothed the glass with her open hand and shuddered at the image the newspapers had carried.

Then she remembered again how deeply she had slept after eating in that cold damp pit with its unforgiving wooden door and its wooden beams and hard benches. She remembered how someone had lifted her into the dazzling daylight that day, when she was six; Katherine's funeral had been that same day, and she would never know her daughter had been recovered.

The darkness where Cameron had been kept had been so dirty, so cold, and she could still hear the whispers—*Mommy? Mommy? Help me. I'm afraid. I'm cold, Mommy, and it's dark here. Why, Mommy? Why did they put me here? Mommy?*

Cameron shook her wrist, and, amid the other charms, the

little bells jingled, a happy sound, and a reminder that she was alive, not imprisoned in the darkness.

While the gardener worked below on the estate, trimming the shrubs, his small daughters played in the maze, and Cameron traced their hide-and-seek antics. She opened the window to hear their shouts and laughter, as they reveled in a childhood she'd never known.

Cameron was never allowed that freedom, not unless it was during one of her fabulous and cold birthday parties, something society had prescribed for the child-heiress.

The day that Katherine died, the Somerton gardener had committed suicide, the note in his hand confessing Cameron's kidnapping. Then three days later, dazed and in poor health, Cammie had emerged—

Cameron pushed back from the window and with resolve sat at Katherine's big cherrywood desk; she studied the picture of the heiress smiling gently back at her.

"I'm doing the best I can, Katherine. I'm so sorry . . ."

Despite the warmth of the study, the echoes of a child's long-ago whisper chilled her: *Mommy? Mommy?*

She'd hear that desperate whisper forever, but Cameron forced herself to concentrate on the eternal paperwork. She had no choice; after all, she was the Somerton heiress, wasn't she?

Sophie Olson White carried in a big mixed bouquet into her son's office. As the vice president in Grow Green Lawn and Garden, his desk was littered with fall and winter sales catalogs, the tulip copy circled with black marker. Hayden continued frowning at his personal laptop when she placed the filled vase on his desk and adjusted the red snapdragons, white mums, and yellow miniature roses. The flower arrangement reflected her expert skills in the corporation's floral display room.

"What's wrong, H.J.?" she asked, using his childhood nickname.

In the third week of June, the morning breeze was cool, entering his office windows as Hayden stared thoughtfully at the bouquet. "Her pickup was filled with blooming plants. No asthmatic would choose forsythia, much less scented geraniums."

"Maybe she outgrew her illness. And there are wonderful medicines now." Sophie wiped her hands on the work apron she wore when working in the display room. She studied her son, whose eyes were brooding now and as black as her own. At sixty, she was slender; her hair was short and waving around the fine features of her face. Once blue-black, it had turned completely gray within two months of her first husband's death.

"That's not likely, not as I remember Katherine telling me about her asthma and its severity. Cammie's lungs were already badly scarred, her immune system damaged, and every day she took massive amounts of medicine—syrups, pills, inhalers. I'm not apt to forget your lectures, and Dr. Naylan's, about being careful not to let her exert herself too much . . . especially the part about keeping her away from anything that blooms. And I won't forget the one time I gave her a bouquet of wildflowers. I saw her desperate, sucking air and panicking . . . she almost died."

Sophie came to lay her hand on Hayden's shoulder. He'd been shattered by his father's suicide and scarred by the town that had turned against them; the kidnapping accusations and the loss of his hero, his father, had cost young H.J. dearly. In her heart, Sophie knew that Hayden would always be haunted by the memory, and there was nothing she could do to erase it.

On his desk, the laptop's split screen was filled on one side with a story about Cameron Somerton's donation to the Oklahoma ranch for underprivileged children, a respite from the inner city; the other side of the screen held an old article, courtesy of an Oklahoma City newspaper. The headline read, *The Gardener Did It.* "You're still brooding about her. It's been almost two weeks."

Hayden punched some keys and the screen filled with another article, *Gardener Suicide, Found With Ransom Money.*

"H.J.—don't." But Sophie knew that her son's scars ran as deeply as his love for his father.

"Something doesn't add up. I can't see a woman as wealthy as that wanting to do her own gardening work—or driving a stick shift by herself late at night. And she'd chosen blooming plants."

"Stereotypes were meant to confuse, H.J. She just doesn't match the heiress picture—or at least when you saw her."

"Dad didn't kidnap anyone, Mom."

Her son desperately wanted to disbelieve Paul Olson's suicide note, but then, it was the way of all children to see their father's as honorable, strong giants. Though she had remarried, the sweet memory of her first husband momentarily swept over Sophie. She still couldn't accept the fact that Paul had committed suicide—that pillow placed beside his head to muffle the shot in the guesthouse while she slept in their own home—or that he'd been involved in the kidnapping. Yet some of the ransom money was found around his body. The rest had never been found, and his family had been pushed to the limit about its whereabouts, interrogated fiercely by the local and state police, and by federal investigators.

They'd been condemned by the massive press dogging their every move, and ten-year-old Hayden had taken the brunt of it, often coming home bloody from fights. If they had stayed in Mimosa, he would have—Sophie didn't want to think about what could happen to a rebellious, defiant teenager in a town that had labeled his father a kidnapper.

As soon as the family had been clear of any implication, Sophie had packed her son and daughter into their old pickup with a few belongings and driven far, far away.

For years, the federal investigators had contacted her, checking on her whereabouts, her lifestyle, searching for that money. And every once in a while, a cold-case detective or a reporter intruded into their lives.

Hayden frowned up at her. "Katherine Somerton was reportedly very generous. Dad had said she was going to advance him the money to help out with my sister's operation. He wouldn't take it outright, or as a loan. You were already helping Katherine with her parties and cleaning, and Dad had planned to work off the medical debt by working extra hours. Now that doesn't sound like someone who would want a quick fix, does it?"

The logic was solid, unsettling in its truth, and Sophie had gone over every fact, had explained them to the investigators repeatedly. But nothing could be found of Katherine's agreement, of a loan to the Olson family for Gracie's lifesaving heart operation.

Sophie ran the flat of her hand across the delicate blooms and silently thanked God. She'd been lucky after those first hard years since Mimosa, and had settled into a job with good benefits, and Gracie had that operation. Happily married now and a mother of a boy and a girl, Gracie was a healthy, busy young woman, wrapped up in life.

But when Hayden played with his niece and nephew, it brought back memories of another child, sweet fragile little Cammie Somerton.

"H.J., you've got to let this go. Cammie was only six when she last saw you—it's no wonder she didn't recognize you at the cafe, or on the highway. Add those years on to the trauma she suffered, and I don't think that she would. Please leave this alone, H.J." Sophie felt like a deserter, but she'd fought the battle for her husband's innocence for years—and she'd lost.

Hayden's black eyes locked with Sophie's. "The rest of that money was never found. Maybe it's time that someone started looking for it again."

Sophie shook her head. "You can't start this all up again, H.J. I did everything I knew how to do—"

"I know you did. And you fought a whole system. But I'd like to settle this for myself, Mom . . . one way or the other."

"Oh, H.J. . . . you're walking into trouble if Robert DuChamps is still there. He never liked your father—and that's a mild term for it. If he recognizes you—"

"Cammie was a sweet kid. . . . She's changed, gotten tough, and DuChamps is probably the reason. I need to finish this for myself and at least try to follow the trail of money—we sure didn't have any of it. I want to know everything about her."

He stroked the small semicircular scar on his cheekbone, the gift of a carelessly placed garden rake to a boy who wasn't watching as he ran—the scar that little Cammie Somerton would touch thoughtfully, her blue eyes full of sympathy. *Does it still hurt, H.J.?*

Sophie stroked his hair—as black as her own was years ago. "You think she's the key, don't you? She was only a child when all that happened, H.J."

"So was I, and so was Gracie. I asked Gracie if she could remember going into the first grade—at about six—and she said she did. Trauma or not, if we remember, so can Cammie. She might remember something, anything. Yes, I think Cameron is the key somehow. I just have to find out how she fits. Robert wouldn't be dealing with someone he could hurt now, would he? Like a widow protecting her children?"

"I don't like this at all."

"Neither do I, but I'm going to finish it."

Sophie looked at the vibrant bouquet and remembered her first husband, fierce with anger at Robert DuChamps. *He's running around on Katherine. He goes right out of the door in the basement, right under his own wife's bedroom, and . . . The man hasn't done a lick of work in his whole lifetime. If we didn't need money so bad, I'd want to pack up and leave, but Gracie needs that operation.*

She studied her son. Hayden had taken her dark coloring, but his height and body build, those wide cheekbones, all belonged to his father, a man with blue eyes and wavy blond hair. She hadn't told Paul, and she wouldn't tell her son—that

Robert DuChamps had come to her one night, with his own offer, something a widow on hard times with two young children would find difficult to refuse. . . . "You have no idea what Robert is capable of, H.J."

"Don't I?"

His answer was tight, and Sophie understood that there was something her son had never told her. "H.J., did Robert ever do anything to you?"

Hayden stared grimly out to the wide blue expanse of Missouri sky, and inside Sophie, a tight cold wad of fear grew. "I want to know. That was a long time ago, but I still want to know."

"Nothing," he stated flatly, and she understood that Hayden needed to face Robert, not as a boy, but as a man.

Three

"MOMMY? COME GET ME, PLEASE, MOMMY? I'M SCARED—"

The childlike plea rang out, jerking Cameron from a much-needed sleep. Sitting upright, cold and shivering though her forehead was beaded with sweat, she stared sightlessly into the brightly lit, airy space of her remodeled barn. The dream catchers turned slowly above her, their feathers fluttering in the breeze from the ceiling fans—

As she focused on grasping reality and tearing the chilling whispers from her, Cameron struggled to place herself in her home. The tank top and men's boxer shorts she'd worn to bed clung damply to her; the sheet tangled around her legs. She kicked away the confining sheet and doubled her knees, gripping them as she trembled and forced herself to remember that she was a woman now—not a little girl, afraid and kidnapped in a dark cave with that one sliver of daylight to remind her of passing time.

The remotely controlled blinds were down at two o'clock in the morning, giving her absolute privacy. From her work space, the dead square of her computer's screen mirrored the lights suspended from the rough wooden beams. The wide paddles of the plantation-style fans cycled slowly. On continuous play from the ultramodern sound system, music throbbed softly through the barn.

In the kitchen area running along the opposite wall, the appliances' electronic clocks blinked in the shadows beneath the cabinets. Cameron's body ball and mat, the enormous treadmill were all in place, her weights on a bench, her exercise bicycle still in the shadows.

Everything was clean and neat and in place, but her.

She didn't fit. Cameron had never fit easily inside her life, despite playing the role of the heiress as best she could. . . .

The cream terra-cotta tile was cool beneath her feet as she hurried to the corner to use her bathroom sink, bending to splash water into her face. There were no walls in her bathroom now, retracted along their sliding rails to reveal a large, footed bathtub on a pedestal; a shower curtain could enclose the tub when needed. Since her plants always died, Cameron had settled for the woodsy decor of ferns and yellow buttercups on the tile, walls, and shower curtain.

She gripped the cool, cream-colored freestanding sink and stared into the lighted mirror. She tried to recognize the woman with the haunted eyes, her hair tangled on her damp cheek. "Cammie?" she asked unevenly. "Cammie, you're going to be just fine," she whispered desperately.

But as a six-year-old child, she hadn't been able to keep that promise, had she?

Somewhere in that cold damp dark hole, Cammie had died and innocence gone, Cameron had changed in those few days. And when she emerged, terrified and dazed, it had been to find her mother dead. . . .

A quiet gurgling turned Cameron, her hands gripping the sink like a lifeline. Her tropical fish swam through the large lighted aquarium, with its fingers of coral and seaweed. She focused on the tiny gold cross, dangling from the mirror, the framed pictures beneath it. "I'm here now, and I'm going to be all right. I'm going to be just fine," she said to comfort herself, to hear the sound of someone, anyone, speaking.

To work off the adrenaline still pumping through her, Cameron reached for her remotes and turned on the all-night radio station. The Oklahoma DJ was always good chatty company on a long night. She hurried for her cleaning tote, filled with disinfectants, brushes, and cloths, and began scrubbing the kitchen counters. Then she mopped the floor with a desperation born long ago in that filthy hole somewhere out there in the night—a place that she'd hunted for and couldn't find. Cameron hurried to clean the mirror, with its tiny dangling chain and cross. But it reminded her of the nightmare, and she hurried to vacuum the rug placed inside her doorway, to shove her clothing into the washer. She listened to the chug-chug, watched the steam rise, the soap bubbles churning, cleaning—but they couldn't clean her life, the guilt, could they?

Cameron reached for the fabric softener, lifted the bottle, shook it and frowned. She tried to remember; she'd just purchased a new bottle, hadn't she? Why was this one empty already?

Or was she so distracted that she had actually purchased the softener weeks ago?

Her hand shook as she replaced the bottle on the shelf. She took care to place everything in its exact place but for some reason, she'd placed her working notes on the catalog copy on the same shelf as her laundry supplies. . . . "I am really losing it. Robert would really like to know that, wouldn't he?"

Katherine's will had been specific: If Cameron were mentally unfit, Robert would control Somerton—and he wouldn't hesitate to commit her.

Cameron took the notes to her computer center, carefully placing them to her left side. Her favorite pen, a chubby style, wasn't in its usual place; instead, it lay on top of her mail.

She ran her hand over her closed laptop and fought to steady the panic sliding over her: A trusted friend, a rural mail carrier, often brought mail into the house. Phoebe Bertrum usually sorted the junk mail into the trash, then left the rest in a large flat basket inside the front door. Maybe she had brought it to the desk instead—

Cameron fingered through the mail; it was yesterday's, containing the paycheck she'd earned from her last copywriting job. The money was small, but it was something of her own, giving her pride and, for a few hours, focused her mind away from being the Somerton heiress.

"I can't and I won't lose it, Cammie," Cameron whispered forcefully. "I'm going to get myself under control and focus on Robert. He is *not* getting control of Buck Somerton's fortune again."

Then, to push away her panic, she turned on her treadmill, punching the electronic buttons, raising the elevation and the speed, until she was running—running away from everything—the darkness, the nightmares, and who she really was, a girl whose childhood had died there in that damp, cold pit.

When her lungs and legs could take no more, when her body was sweaty and her breath was the only sound she heard, Cameron settled down to a very private pleasure. She went to the photos that she'd found long ago, carefully slid one from the frame, and signed into her password-protected laptop.

Using it, she scanned the photo, ran it through her printer, and smiled back at the little six-year-old girl, a photo taken just before the kidnapping—her mother's first anniversary party, the night she had disappeared from her bed. "You're going to like this one, Robert," Cameron said softly, and settled back to enjoy thoughts about how he would react when he found it—

In their running battle, Cameron always liked to remind Robert of when she had been kidnapped, and that somehow, some way, she would make him pay.

"She's got everything a woman could want, and yet she's living in a barn away from a pampered life in that mansion. Now I wonder why?"

At the same time Cameron was fighting her fear, Hayden was also restless and brooding in his St. Louis apartment. He considered his laptop screen, the real estate ads for Mimosa, for sale and rentals, running across it. He closed the paper file on his desk, an assortment of dated clippings about the Somerton kidnapping, then Katherine Somerton's unusual death—the massive explosion of her balloon. Katherine's funeral was on the very same day that little Cammie Somerton had emerged from those woods, creating another firestorm of media attention.

The papers in Hayden's file were worn by use, and he had memorized almost every word of the articles: *Gardener Commits Suicide* and *Gardener's Guilt Kills Him* and *Suicide Note Admits To Kidnapping*. There were fuzzy newspaper photographs of his mother holding her two children, a ten-year-old boy and a three-year-old girl, protectively against her as she faced the press. After intensive investigation, Sophie Olson had been adamant about her own innocence and disbelieving in her husband's guilt. "Yes, our daughter needed surgery and money was tight, but Katherine was going to help us. My husband would not, repeat *not*, want to kidnap Katherine Somerton's daughter because he'd been refused by her. He loved me and his family. He would never, *ever,* do such a thing."

Hayden remembered that frantic scene well. His mother had tried to get her children to safety amid a barrage of reporters. A reporter had thrust his microphone in front of her face, and snapped, "There's been no evidence of that, Sophie. Where's the proof? And your husband was found with part of the money. What do you have to say about that, Sophie?"

His mother had stopped hustling her children to their old pickup and turned to the reporter. She'd straightened her shoulders and lifted her head. "Call me . . . *Mrs.* Olson," she'd ordered so fiercely that the reporters had stilled and stepped back.

Then one had regrouped, asking the question: "Do you

have any idea where the rest of the money is, Mrs. Olson?"

"If I did, it would already be in the hands of the police. I do not believe for one moment that my husband is a kidnapper—or that he killed himself."

As if one hungry beast, the reporters leaped on that statement. "Are you saying that it was murder? Who else was involved in the kidnapping? Do they have the rest of the money?"

In a storm of camera flashes and reporters pressing close with questions, Sophie Olson had coldly, silently faced them so fiercely that they stepped back. With a tight nod, she had hurried her children into their pickup. But tears glistened on her cheeks as she drove them to the gardener's home on the Somerton estate, just a small distance away from the mansion.

In front of their home had been the first time that H.J. had ever seen his mother break down—because Robert DuChamps had tacked an eviction notice to the gardener's door . . . and then things got worse.

Missouri rain beat on Hayden Olson's apartment window, placing that scene in Oklahoma into the past. Hayden looked at the framed picture of his family, his father looking proud as he stood with one arm around his wife and his hand on his son's shoulder. "Do the right thing, son," his father had often said when trouble brewed in young H.J.'s life. "Think about it and do what you have to do."

"Do the right thing," Hayden repeated, as a fresh battery of rain hit the window. "I think the right thing is to find the rest of that two million."

Cameron Somerton had chosen a barn to remodel, and according to the newspaper files, the open house soiree she'd held was at the old Riordan place. Hayden's mother was familiar with it, and the farmhouse which was in the current rental advertisements— "If you're ready to work off part of the rent and you're handy, this fix-up home is for you."

Anyone living in that house would have a good view of Cameron Somerton's life. "Real up close and personal,"

Hayden murmured, as he thought of the little girl with the pale unmanageable hair that had bobbed in ringlets, a girl he'd loved as a sister, safeguarding her in those desperate moments when she'd struggled to breathe—

"Life-threatening asthma and probably emphysema later. Given the wrong situation, one unguarded moment without her medications or filtered air, and she could die," the doctor had told him when Cammie was too sick to go out into the pollen-laden spring air. "Her mother is thinking about moving away, maybe to the desert areas, for Cammie's health."

But Katherine Somerton never got that chance, and grown now, Cameron Somerton hadn't recognized Hayden.

Maybe that wasn't important; she'd only been six when their lives had been torn away.

Her asthma won't go away . . . she'll never be totally well, the doctor had said, and yet Cameron's small pickup had been filled with blooming fragrant plants that had always set Cammie off. But in that fragrant night air, heavy with pollen, she hadn't used an inhaler. . . .

Hayden stared out into the stormy night and ran his thumb over the logo of his beer bottle. He'd worked until midnight, preparing to take his first vacation in years—albeit, a working vacation of just one month.

Then he dialed the number for the rental real estate agent handling property in Mimosa, Oklahoma.

The last day of June settled quietly around Cameron's barn and in the late afternoon, she was editing the advertising copy for Big Bear Catalog. The sound of someone driving up the farm road to her home caused Cameron to leave her computer and stand at the window viewing the front of her house, a stark barren patch of hard-baked dirt, serving as a driveway.

As she lifted her arms and started to stretch, the bells on the reindeer antler hat, a Christmas selection, tinkled. As a freelance catalog copywriter, she often received the party products from Emery Justin's office, testing them before writing the copy. Her suggestion of adding tiny sleigh bells at the end of each horn was ready to be e-mailed back to Emery. Writing the copy had been entertaining, leaving her with a feeling that she had accomplished something on her own—small and important to her pride, because she was judged on the quality of her work, not her inheritance.

With the beanie-type hat and fuzzy antlers on her head, Cameron reached to flick the tiny bells she'd attached with a safety pin. One bell jingled as she watched an older model Dodge Ram pickup slow at the big gate to her driveway and drive to the small stone farmhouse several yards from her home. The pickup pulled into a parking spot, then reversed, backing up to the front door. The driver—a big man—exited on the opposite side, blocking her view. According to Madeline, the man who had leased the house was "taking a break between jobs," which Cameron assumed meant that he was probably down on his luck and looking for work.

With a flip of Cameron's fingers, the bell on the other antler jingled as she waited for a good look at her renter.

Madeline had been tied up with the intricacies of tax sheltering and sent her usual brief, "Daily Status" morning e-mail. From its running, clipped tone, she'd probably voice-dictated the message while she was wrapped up in other details: "Real estate person called. . . . Renter coming—handy, he says, ready to work off rent money. Single male now, but says he is divorced with a family that may or may not come to visit. I take that to mean that he may have a live-in with kids—a Mr. Someone Olson from St. Louis with deposit money. The real estate agent knew you needed to be particular, so she placed a private call to the manager of his apartment building—apparently Mr. Olson is dating a woman with a little boy, so he's attached. I know you wanted a family, but the rental agent said he's got some gardening experience and said he'd fix the place up. I thought maybe he'd be okay for a six-month agreement, and I had Ray check the place over."

Cameron smiled at the reference to Ray Migina, Somerton's lead maintenance man, who had made the remark that Madeline tossed orders around so much that she needed a penis.

Madeline's rolling summary scrolled on: "Ray says the house needed work before a family moved in anyway, and it would cost a fortune in labor. All the windows need to be replaced, the plumbing, the septic tank problems, yada yada."

Cameron smiled at Madeline's note. As Cameron's personal assistant, the financial manager of the estate and main contact to an extensive network of Somerton financial concerns, Madeline was not only a good friend but thoroughly dedicated to her work and Cameron's welfare.

Madeline's note finished with: "You need to update your schedule on your date book when you're at the office. I stuck some dates in there you need—the publicity picture shoot for your donation of a special burn unit in the hospital. Call the caterer, will you? That prima donna won't deal with me anymore, but she likes you. . . . This farmhouse guy is probably on a budget, so I okayed lowering the rent in a trade-off deal. Six-month lease all signed and neat—but he paid in advance and the check cleared. Don't forget to sign your proxy vote on that airline merger deal. . . . Checking on how to set you up for balloon lessons. But I don't see the fascination, especially when that was the way your mother died. . . . Later."

"You do a good job, Madeline," Cameron said to herself. The overgrown azalea shrubs beside the farmhouse's front door prevented a good view, but Cameron saw that the new renter was unloading the back of the pickup.

The gurgle of air bubbles in the aquarium reminded Cameron to feed her tropical fish. In her Big Bear elf shoes, with their curled pointy toes and bells, Cameron padded to the aquarium to check her index card: she ran down the list of feeding times, then shook food into the water. Henry and Leon, her elegant black angelfish, floated majestically in her aquarium, while Zipper, the scarlet-and-black beta male watched them from his partitioned area. In an adjacent smaller tank, mama guppy was preparing to birth her offspring.

In her special world away from the shackles of the Somerton wealth and her duel with Robert Duchamps, Cameron smiled at the tiny female guppy with the black spot in her belly. She tapped the glass. "Hi, Mama. Feeling okay today?"

Everything was in place—as much as it could be in Cameron's world. She inhaled, glanced at the dying house plants she'd just purchased, and tried not to think about the rest of them, wilting outside in the hot midday sun.

Cameron wiggled her toes inside the elf shoes, the tiny bells jingled, and she tapped her alarm code, disabling it. She lifted the pots of dying plants to carry them outside. She placed the "poor babies" beside the unplanted trees on the front concrete porch and turned on the outside hose to water them.

As the wind chimes hung across the porch tinkled merrily, the azalea petals littered the ground around the bushes, the spindly tomato plants drooped, and the mums were steadily losing leaves.

With a defeated sigh, Cameron shook her head and slowly looked over to the backyard of the farmhouse.

A man was standing there, his hands on his hips as he surveyed the overgrown garden and fruit trees, gnarled and broken by wind and time. He rubbed a hand across his bare chest; his tanned shoulders gleamed, and in the distance, he looked familiar somehow.

Cameron hurried through her home to the backyard to collect the bird-watching binoculars she'd placed on the wooden picnic table; she returned inside. At her tinted privacy windows, she lifted the binoculars and hurried to focus them on the man. Through the lenses, she found the hard, broad face of a man she recognized— "It's him!"

She shoved her tripod for her telescope to the window overlooking the stone farmhouse and focused it on the man. Those hard features leaped into her lens, his two huge black eyes startling her. "It's the same guy!"

Fancy's small white Toyota pickup was soaring up Cameron's driveway, and the cab was filled with heads, probably her other girlfriends, Evie and Phoebe.

At first, Cameron had chosen them carefully to irritate Robert, who called them "classless tarts." The women were much more inventive when describing Robert. Cameron had grown to love each unique personality; they didn't condemn her for those odd moments when her fears surrounded her, the memories choking her. Brash, devoid of teatime manners and etiquette, fans of flashy cheap dressing and makeup junkies, their talk was bawdy, rude, and carried the weight of raw truth that Cameron desperately needed. And she saw something of herself in them; they had all survived the worst. Each woman had been seasoned by life's cruelty and didn't cast stones. Because they were the closest thing to a family that she'd ever had, Cameron had bought them all pickups, Toyotas to match her own, practical white for Oklahoma's hot summer.

Cameron picked up the binoculars and focused them back on the man, watching him as she waited for her friends to enter the barn.

Fancy and her friends didn't enter in a storm of chatter. Instead, the three women were walking across the old cow path toward the stone farmhouse. In tight jeans, sweaters, and high heels, they haltingly picked their way around the brush on the path. Apparently, they'd caught wind of a new man in the area and were hunting his availability.

"You guys are just bird dogs. That's disgusting. I know you've run through the local pickings, but have some pride." Cameron muttered as she recognized the flirtatious body language of her friends, and who was he again? Howard? Hayward? *Hayden?*

He wasn't acting like an "attached" man as he grinned back at the women.

Cameron punched the telephone button that was a direct lead to Madeline's cell phone, always at her hip carrier.

Madeline's "Uh-huh?" sounded distracted, and papers rattled in the background.

"The renter is here. Are you sure he's got a steady girlfriend?"

Madeline's pen sounded as it scratched across paper. "Said he had a family. Problem?"

"Could be. My girlfriends have him cornered, and he's not objecting. That doesn't sound like a man whose girlfriend and child might come visit him. What's his name?"

Madeline stopped shuffling papers, paused, then answered, "It says here, 'Hayden Olson.' "

When Cameron softly repeated the name she remembered from the night they met, Madeline's voice was no longer distracted, but taking on a protective mother-hen tone. "If there's a problem with him, I want to know."

"I'll let you know."

Madeline shuffled through more papers. "He's got good references. Seems stable enough. Since he paid in advance, the agent didn't push specifics. Says here that he has a long employment record with some gardening company—now that sounds good. She did make that private call, just to double-check—let's see, no problem as a tenant. Got another note here—Olson pitched in and helped the apartment 'super' repair stuff several times. Apparently, he knows his stuff. The super said Olson babysat for the little boy sometimes, so I see this as a family-type deal."

Hayden Olson. The same man who had stopped in his BMW that night, the man at the cafe, the man who just *might* have let out some air in her tire, and *might* have placed that gravel in her air valve. . . . *What is he doing in Mimosa? And now he's renting the farmhouse next door?*

Aware that Madeline was concerned, Cameron said, "You've got enough to do with setting up that investor's dinner at the house next week. Catch you later."

Cameron clicked off the phone and watched Fancy do that hand on jutting hip, head-tossing thing that said she was in full-throttle flirt mode. Evie, short and curvaceous, was all but drooling, her hands locked behind her hips, a position that showed off her large breasts to the best advantage. A beauty operator, Evie prided herself on her long nails, taking hours to do her own decals on them. Phoebe's dark straight hair with its red streaks swayed as she lifted her face and turned to point at Cameron's barn. Phoebe wasn't wearing her usual logo T-shirts, rather a red formfitting tank top.

Hayden nodded and stared at Cameron's home, frowning slightly. He couldn't see Cameron, of course, because she'd stepped back into the shadows and because her windows were of privacy glass. When his attention turned back to the three women, Cameron adjusted the binoculars for a closer look.

He was studying the leaves of an old twisted apple tree, touching them as he had tested the plants in her pickup bed. He'd lost that neatly trimmed expensive look, his hair longer than when she'd first seen him, and his jaw was dark with stubble. His bare chest and worn blue jeans added to his tough appearance.

Evie was on him like a bee on honey, grabbing that big hand and turning it to do her palm-reading trick. Apparently, by his grin, he liked his future, which probably included the women—they were all divorced and looking. When that was finished, the man crouched to tend a plant, and the women circled him. "Vultures," Cameron muttered darkly. "You're drooling, girls."

Fancy chose that moment to look up at Cameron's window and make a butt-patting gesture that said she'd really like to get her hands on his. Evie grinned and did a bump-bump movement with her hips, imitating sex. Phoebe blew on her fingers and shook them as if he were too hot to handle. When he stood and rubbed his hand across his bare chest, the three women seemed to lean toward him, then hurried after him into the house.

"Rats," Cameron muttered. "You're supposed to be *my* friends, coming to see *me*." The farmhouse's and her windows were opened, and apparently Cameron's friends were having a good time as the breeze carried their laughter up to her.

She answered the telephone absently, and still holding her binoculars, spoke to her ex-husband, William. They had been playmates in their marriage, and now as the best of friends, kept in close touch. He had been boyish and fun and brought with him a zest for life that Cameron had badly needed. But after the first months, they were more earnest friends than lovers. Their two-year marriage had given her a respite of light and fun that she would always treasure. "No, I don't think you should get an English mastiff. You're never home, William. . . . I know they're charming, but think of the piles they'd leave on your sailboat deck."

William was properly horrified, dismissing the dogs. He laughed when she switched the topic to his current girlfriend, one who always caused his tone to soften with affection. "Bring Arabella here anytime, William. I'd like to meet her. If you marry her, I'll be your best man."

"Yeah, I'd like that . . . if we get married. She thinks I'm a playboy and that I have potential that I've never used, and that disgusts her."

Apparently, William took working-class Arabella DiRoma's opinion of him very seriously.

"You do have all kinds of potential." Cameron watched the women emerge from the renter's house, still crowding close to him, their looks adoring.

"She's real sweet, Cameron, a homebody. She was waitressing when I met her, you know, and she says that she likes taking care of people and making them comfortable. She really enjoys life. I like to hang out with her, do little stuff like go to farmer's markets. It's amazing the stuff they have there. Did you know that people actually shop in flea markets for stuff to use? They really use those old plates and pots and pans for everyday cooking," he exclaimed.

"You're a work in progress, old man, and Arabella is good for you. You've changed my take on men, and that was hard to do after Robert's handling. I'll always be glad we met and married, that we had that time together away from here. You are the best thing in my life so far."

William was silent for a moment, and then he spoke quietly, seriously, "Arabella is eight months pregnant. My baby for sure . . . I was her first and last, she says, and she said she wants this baby. Did you ever want a baby with me, Cameron?"

"Gosh, no. What would we do with a baby? We're both so messed up—"

"Arabella isn't messed up," William stated firmly, proudly. "But if I marry her, my parents have threatened to disown me. That's not important to me, but—well, I guess I love the old things and want them to stop nagging me to drop her. Other than you, she's the best thing that has happened to me—like I'm going to walk away from her, or my baby. My folks say paternity payments are good enough. They even had one of their attorneys work up papers for her to sign—but she's never going to see them, not if I can stop it, and I will."

"But what do *you* think?" she asked William, as Evie tested the renter's biceps, and her wide-eyed, awed expression read like, "Oh, my, my. You're so big and strong, and I bet you're that way all over, too."

William continued his Arabella-debate: "But how would I support a wife and child? Everything I know is tied up with my family. Arabella is the domestic type, and she's already said she wasn't mixing with my parents' 'snob bunch,' as she called them. If my parents push this thing, don't bend a little, I'm heading out on my own. Got any ideas about how a playboy can make enough money to support a family?"

"Sounds like Arabella has good sense, and you can do any number of things well."

"She is not going to work, dammit. If we get married, I'm going to support her—somehow. I'd just like everything to be a lot smoother, you know? I won't have my parents insulting her, but I'd like our baby to know them, too. One thing I do know is that my money and likely inheritance is not one bit important to her—and she's not what they called her, 'a little gold digger.' "

"You're on the right track, old man." Phoebe was doing that picking a leaf thing from the hair on the man's chest and gazing up at him as if he were a Hollywood megastar. Cameron didn't doubt that Phoebe was probably offering her special little deliveries.

"I miss you, kid," William was saying.

"Then come see me. Your parents will come around, William."

"I hope so. You've got to get out of there, Cameron. Robert could actually lose it one day and hurt you."

Robert had already done that—but not anymore. "He's got too much to lose, and we both know it. I'm okay, William, really."

"I hate that bastard. No wonder you married me, probably to get away from him."

"I've never regretted it."

Still laughing, Cameron's friends made their way back up the old cow path to her house, and she ended the call quickly. "Get in here," she ordered as she opened the door.

Evie was flushed and excited. "Oh, he's gorgeous. Not a pretty boy type, but the real manly, studly kind, sort of a raw sexuality—"

"Oh, please. Spare me."

Phoebe twirled a long strand of her hair around her finger and grinned. "Not married . . . Has been though, so that means that he's interested. Said it didn't work out, but did not say anything nasty about his ex-wife, just that they wanted to go different directions. He's taking some time off, between jobs, wanting a little peace and the quiet of a small town. . . . Fancy had met him at the cafe, and—"

But Cameron already knew those details. "Thanks for the lowdown. You guys are supposed to be helping me plant. I've been waiting almost three weeks for you to have the time—but oh, no. There's never a right time, is there?"

Her friends dismissed her intentional guilt trip. "Boring. Big yawn," Evie said. "You should have come down and met him. We helped him clean up a bit. That place is pitiful, Cameron. You ought to have had it fixed up before moving him in. He's going to be real busy with that mess. The bathroom is horrible—by the way, I need yours."

Evie hurried to push the button that caused the sliding panels of the bathroom to move into place. "Gotta love this thing."

"I'm not planting any damn plants, because *you* don't like to mess in dirt," Phoebe said firmly as she studied her acrylic nails. "I just had these done. We just came out to check out the livestock. Word at the filling station said he was single and six-foot-three. That was all we needed to posse-up."

Fancy fingered the too-soft leaves of an African violet. "You've killed it already. Too much water. He said he'd get the place in better shape before having a party. *You* could have one here right away," she suggested with a grin. "One with music and slow dancing so I could get my hands on his body. He must have buns like rocks. I love the way his back moves—all those muscles. Wait a minute—"

She frowned slightly and studied Cameron. "You were in the cafe the night Hayden stopped by. We talked about him, remember?"

"I do now. Quite the coincidence that he'd turn up here, isn't it?"

"Happens all the time," Fancy said with the experience of one who didn't doubt life's little flukes. "Dibs, ladies, if he gets lonely one night."

But Cameron did doubt that particular fluke. The way he stayed a little too long, crouched between the vehicles, that gravel in her air valve, that U-turn of the BMW, were too many facts in a row. Especially for a man who turned up as her next-door neighbor.

"You guys are lechers. No way would I go to his party. I'm working."

The three women studied Cameron in her elf shoes and reindeer horns with the bells, her Party Girl banner, then burst out laughing. "Yeah, right. She's working."

Cameron could always count on her friends to dismiss her wealthy heiress position and treat her as though she were just like everyone else. Just like William, they had the ability to level her off her heiress-perch and periodically enjoy just being a normal woman and a friend. "Okay, I am. Tonight. At Al's Bar. I do work, you know."

"You work too much, honey. This part-time gig writing catalog copy and then filling in for Reggie when he needs a sub at Al's. And that charity stuff you're into—all those causes—would kill a horse. You need to play," Fancy said quietly as she smoothed back a strand of hair from Cameron's cheek. "You've got that dark and haunted look. Not sleeping well, hon?"

"Dreams. Bad ones," Cameron explained truthfully, and her friends' looks said they understood. Their arms circled her, and she leaned her head against Fancy's shoulder.

"Any kid locked in a hole like that and coming out to find her mother dead and then to top it off, raised by Robert, is going to have nightmares as an adult," Evie stated quietly.

I've been forgetting things. I'm afraid I'm losing it, Katherine. I'm so sorry for everything. . . .

"Maybe if you'd go live somewhere else, you wouldn't—"

"Her mom was thirty-four when she died, the same age as Cameron now. That's why it's getting to her," Evie said quietly.

"It's that tight-ass stepfather of hers. He'd drive anyone nuts. Prissy son of a bitch. Whatever you do, don't do that therapy gig again," Phoebe advised sagely. "You were in pieces when you came back last time. Those doctors get paid plenty for taking people apart. I could do better than they do and charge a lot less."

"Sure you could," Fancy said with a cheeky grin.

But Cameron knew that the professionals who had tried to

help her as an adult were missing important pieces to the puzzle of her life—and so was she; those pieces remained locked in the place where the whispers had begun, in that dark, damp hole.

Now, surrounded and supported by her friends, Cameron pulled herself together and smiled sweetly, hopefully. "So . . . I guess you guys aren't going to help me plant my stuff?"

"Um . . . No."

"Blast and double blast. Okay, then, come down to Al's tonight, and I'll slip you some free ones."

She actually paid for her friends' "free drinks," but they didn't know it. And she was very careful not to offend them. One of the biggest benefits of working part-time at Al's Bar, a typical country tavern, was that it really nettled Robert.

And that was what Cameron was all about now, pushing Robert's buttons—just enough to let him know that she wasn't that little frightened girl any longer, and to keep the balance of their war even.

When her friends had gone, still raving about her "hunk" renter, Cameron walked to the windows overlooking the rolling hills, fields and cattle and Mimosa. In the distance, just past that grove of blooming pink mimosa trees by her driveway, past the highway, and over the valley, the Somerton mansion stood like a pearl amid a sea of spring green, haunting her with memories . . . and with a guilt she couldn't admit aloud.

A movement past her windows drew her attention, and the renter was looking up at her barn, his hands on his hips. Then he began to move over that old cow path, coming toward her.

I might as well get this out of the way, Hayden decided. Her friends were an odd choice for a wealthy woman, a selection of misfits who suited each other somehow, loving each other and Cameron. She was even more of a mystery than the night he'd inserted that gravel into her air valve. He scanned the field of ragweed that would choke an asthmatic when in full yellow bloom. Weighted by wild honeysuckle vines tangled with thick grapevines, an old hog wire fence sagged between the posts; broken and overgrown, a weathered board fence rambled into tumbleweeds where young rabbits hid and watched.

An open bag of weedkiller pellets explained the dead and dying shrubs spaced haphazardly near the barn, where the soil should be rich. The plastic palm trees, an outsized hippo, and elephant completed the unique scene.

On the porch, wind chimes of every style tinkled gently from the rough cedar beam running the length of the barn. The late-afternoon sun caught and flashed on them, and on the assortment of old horseshoes nailed against the rough weathered-wood siding. Farther up on the shakes roofing, ugly gargoyles stared down at him, looking as if they were ready to pounce if he trespassed.

Hayden glanced at the assortment of plants, still in their plastic containers, sitting next to the Toyota pickup and across the porch. The makings of hanging baskets were scattered on the long concrete slab in front of the doorway. Sphagnum moss and potting soil were stuffed into one, a sad-looking fuchsia wilting inside it, the hairlike roots exposed to the air and sunlight.

Out of habit, Hayden crouched to use the trowel, easing the plant away, then potted it deeper into the soil. He turned on the outside faucet and the attached hose dribbled water into the basket as he crouched beside it. He paused as he heard a door slide open, and the faucet squeaked as it was turned; the water stopped, then light, quick footsteps sounded behind him and tiny bells jingled. The bells stopped when the elf shoes wearing them stood beside him. He wondered what the rest of her costume looked like; it was likely to be fascinating. But then, he was already fascinated with her, wasn't he? The heiress who didn't remember him? The woman of contrasts?

"Hi. Nice day, isn't it?" he asked quietly as he placed the finished basket into the shade.

Cameron wasted no time: "I own that farmhouse. Keep your distance, pay the rent, and do whatever fix-up jobs you've agreed to, and we'll be just fine. I thought you had a girlfriend with a little boy. Where are they?"

He dusted his hands and stood slowly, facing her. He wasn't prepared for the reindeer hat with the bells on the horns, or the Party Girl banner that ran diagonally over her T-shirt. He looked down to the elf shoes, now encrusted with fresh mud and rubble from the plants. "Nice shoes."

Her body shifted impatiently, the bells tinkled, and she took a deep breath, lifting the banner spread across her chest. "Your girlfriend? You're not attached to anyone special, are you? You rented that house under false pretenses, didn't you? Got the real estate agent to feel sorry for you, did you?"

A girlfriend with a little boy. If his relationship was being referenced now, that meant the Somerton dogs had been sniffing around his personal life. His relationship to the kidnapper of Cammie might be discovered sooner rather than later. For now, Hayden decided to indulge as little as possible, but still be truthful. "Hey, where did that come from? And you've been misled somehow. I did have a 'girlfriend' and she has a little boy. If it interests you so much, we called it quits almost a year ago. I'm just taking some downtime to relax a bit. I only said that I wanted to bring my family here when I could. I have them—a mother and sister, brother-in-law and a niece and nephew. You don't expect me to bring them into that run-down mess now, do you?"

Hayden decided that the guilty, caught-in-the-act flush looked really good on her. She shifted again, that restless movement setting off a tinkle of bells as she looked off into the rolling Oklahoma hills. "No, I suppose not. I'll have an account set up for you at the local lumber and hardware store. But my business manager will be monitoring it, so make certain that every bill carries an explanation of just what you're using and why. We have a pretty good handyman crew, but the chief maintenance man—Ray Migina—is busy now.

He'll be stopping by to see that the work is done properly."

"Okay . . . sounds good." Hayden studied her smooth, gleaming hair, the sun streaks in it, and thought of the pale curling fluff of Cammie Somerton. When the air was damp, her hair had spiraled into a huge mop. *She should have recognized me by now, but she hasn't . . . and that nettles.*

Cameron's blue eyes flashed up at him. "The night you were in the cafe and later, when you stopped to help me. You weren't going in my direction, and yet you showed up."

"It's easy to take a wrong road out here," Hayden said smoothly as he looked for something of Katherine in her daughter. Cameron was taller, more lean and leggy, and that cold, hard suspicion in her blue eyes wasn't Katherine's wide, warm look. Was she still wearing that tiny gold cross beneath her T-shirt? *I'll never take it off . . . my real dad gave it to me . . . I don't like Robert. . . .* Cammie had said.

"It wasn't a punctured tire. The valve cap was loose and somehow a piece of gravel had gotten wedged inside. *That's* what caused the low tire." She was testing him, suspicious of their accidental meeting and the cause of it.

"Really? That's odd." Hayden scanned the farmyard, the little stone house amid the rubble of overgrown brush and trees that badly needed pruning. Climbing roses needed trimming and a trellis, and there were beds of irises, lily of the valley, and tulips that needed cleaning, growing along the old picket fence. Beyond that lay a sloping hill, and then heavy woods.

Then he deliberately noted a real problem for an asthmatic, especially one with badly scarred lungs. Cameron Somerton might have forgotten him, but it wasn't likely that she could hide her physical reaction to allergens. "That's a lot of ragweed, a whole field of it. And there's honeysuckle growing all around here, some of it is breaking down the tree limbs."

Her words snapped at the still, late afternoon. "We have tornadoes here. Trees break in the wind. The field is yellow and pretty, and the honeysuckle smells good. I like it. You've got enough to do bringing that house up to par for your 'family' and taking care of the yard, so don't mess with anything else. Look, I've got work to do, and you should know that I like my privacy."

"Whatever the lady says," Hayden murmured. He reached for a hoe, left carelessly on the ground, and held it out to her. "This could be dangerous."

After another impatient breath, Cameron reached for it with her right hand and Hayden's thumb brushed the edge of her palm—it was smooth.

Memories of Cammie's little hand in his seared Hayden. She always noted the crescent scar high on his cheek, tracing it with her finger, her blue eyes sad upon him, the girl with the missing sixth finger, where only a small bump and surgeon's scar had remained.

He hadn't realized he'd been staring so intently, trying to see into Cameron, until she frowned and stepped back, gripping the hoe for protection.

But then an heiress needed to be wary, didn't she? And there were better techniques now to remove any imperfections of that hand, weren't there?

And this woman was definitely on edge, her lips set tight.

"You're staring at me," she said suddenly, frowning up at him. "I don't like being taken apart—dissected. If you have any problems, don't contact me—there's a property manager for that stuff. Our little neighborly chat is over."

On his way back to the farmhouse, Hayden remembered the smooth edge of her hand—where that little nub had been on Cammie's hand. It wasn't there, and Cameron Somerton wasn't allergic to all the spring pollen, the honeysuckle on the fence, the goldenrod that would turn a field into bright yellow.

The remainder of the kidnapping money had never been found, and the odds and ends of the Somerton heiress didn't match.

Hayden intended to put all the pieces together before he left Mimosa for good.

He paused and looked over Mimosa's picturesque sloping valley to the Somerton mansion, gleaming white in the late sun, thoroughbreds grazing on the lush fields once tended by his father.

As he had so often, Hayden lined up the sequence of events on that horrible day: He'd just found his father in the guesthouse. Katherine had gone up into the air to search for her daughter, and an explosion within the basket had supposedly killed her instantly—a malfunction, a possible leak in the propane system, which had been ignited by the pilot light, according to authorities. Robert DuChamps had evicted the grieving family of an admitted kidnapper, the deceased gardener. Seriously ill from her confinement, the six-year-old kidnapped child was recovered the day of Katherine's funeral—and as an adult, Cameron wasn't an asthmatic keeping her inhaler at hand amid summer air laden with pollen. Her clothing had the distinct scent of fabric softener and none of the pieces fit.

Odds and pieces, Hayden repeated mentally.

And he was very good at putting puzzles together. All he had to do was to find the missing pieces.

"You'll have to do better than this, sweet Cameron," Robert stated as he tossed the snapshot of six-year-old Cammie into a large crystal astray. Left beneath his bedroom pillow, the photograph clearly wasn't the original. This one was intended to remind him of the kidnapping the night of his first-year anniversary with Katherine.

He'd forgotten the pictures he'd tucked away in that old chest, ones he didn't want Cameron to see in those early years of her "recovery." Then, at twelve, Cameron had suddenly decided to paint that old chest—and life had been hell ever since. She'd kept them all those years, and as an adult, took her jollies in printing copies of Katherine and

Cammie and placing them where only he would find them.

Cameron's favorite hobby was pushing him, in small but meaningful ways that only he would recognize—like placing pink roses throughout the mansion, a reminder of the flowers Katherine had loved, that she had planted near Big Buck's mausoleum. . . .

Robert struck a match and lit the photo he was certain Cameron had reproduced. "She has her ways, and I have mine," he said, as the photo began to scorch, and then burn. "Sweet little Cammie. My, how you have changed. Forgetting things, are you? A little disconcerted at times, darlin'? Well, it's going to get a hell of a lot worse. Until you finally go off that deep end where you'll never be lucid again."

He looked out onto the Somerton estate, *his* thoroughbreds grazing, a colt frisking with his mother, tail high as he ran along the white board fence.

He deserved the Somerton empire for marrying Katherine, for putting up with an entire year of her whining ways, her constant reminders of her first husband's tenderness, his intelligence, how Big Buck Somerton had labored in the Texas oil fields to build his fortune.

Robert deserved the Somerton empire for raising Cameron, no easy task. She'd captured a bit of his steel and was now using it against him. He felt a mixture of pride and distaste for this woman he'd raised alone—except for Madeline's interference.

Then there was the constant, prodding desire for Cameron, to hold all that youthful strength and toughness against him, to take that saucy, defiant mouth, to own her in every way.

And he would, because those quick panicked expressions told him that Cameron was losing her grasp. "It's her own fault. She could have made it so easy. But she chose instead to defy me."

He glanced at Madeline passing by the doorway, her usual clipboard in hand, her short chunky body dressed in something that wouldn't flatter a corner fence post. He hated her, too, the woman constantly monitoring his allowance, who had bonded with Cameron in the years after the kidnapping.

When Cameron was finally institutionalized, Madeline would meet some accident—and oh, how he loved to think about ways to kill her.

Four

AT TEN O'CLOCK THAT NIGHT, HAYDEN SAT ON HIS PICKUP, his back against the windshield, his legs stretched out on the hood before him. The beer in his hand matched his brooding thoughts as he overlooked the winding night lights of Mimosa in the slight, rolling valley below. He traced the streets where young H. J. had once ridden his bicycle, where people had come to stare at his mother and whisper about her probable involvement in the kidnapping. After all, they said, how could a wife *not* know that her husband had lusted after another woman?

It was an answer that investigators and reporters had often demanded. During the media frenzy twenty-eight years ago, Robert had implied successfully that Paul had wanted Katherine Somerton, and when his advances weren't returned, the gardener took what he could—her child and her money.

After hours of cleaning out the old farmhouse, of fighting the old plumbing, and making lists of tools and necessities, Hayden inhaled the fragrant cool night and settled into his boyhood memories. He'd chosen the vista well, the place to overlook his past and brood about the darkness he could never forget. From the sloping hill where he'd parked his pickup, he could view Mimosa in the valley, the Somerton mansion rising a little higher on a hill to the west, amid its well-tended grounds, and Cameron Somerton's house-barn in the east.

A distance from Mimosa, a lonely country road wound to an old cemetery, unkept and overgrown with vines. At sunset and exhausted, Hayden had done his best to clear his father's grave, a distance away from the rest; the good people of Mimosa hadn't wanted a kidnapper and a man who had committed suicide resting among them. How pitiful that ceremony had been, attended only by the minister, anxious to be on his way, then by the three Olsons, huddled together beneath an umbrella. The stone was small and flat, the best the Olsons could afford then, the engraving weathered now.

But on the family plot behind the Somerton mansion was a decorated ironwork fence, with elegant carved angels guarding the door to the huge marble mausoleum; there, Katherine Somerton had been placed beside her first husband, Buck.

Katherine Somerton . . . Cameron Somerton . . . so different from her soft, sweet mother.

In the distance of night, Cameron's home was fully lit. "Not like Katherine at all," Hayden mused, remembering their earlier clashes.

Some small animal rustled in a small stand of mimosa, the pink blooms eerily holding the silvery moonlight as Hayden scanned the vegetation. As the Somerton gardener, Paul Olson had been careful to time any brush burns, and he'd eliminated the ragweed and the worst of anything that would irritate Cammie's asthma.

The hog wire fences around Cameron's barn were burdened by tough old grapevines, wild honeysuckle, and multiflora rose; ragweed would turn that field bright yellow, and mimosa trees bloomed in her backyard. "And she doesn't have a problem?"

Bitter memories churned inside Hayden as he traced the lines of Mimosa's streetlights. On the opposite hill, the mansion's lights glowed softly, as if their secrets waited for him, as twisted as that intricate garden maze.

His last sip of beer turned bitter as he thought of the sly innuendoes, the suspicion he'd found still lurking in Mimosa—that Sophie Olson, "the Gardener's Wife," knew something of her husband's crime, that she'd known where the rest of the money was. . . . Hayden had also discovered that few of the people who had been in town at the time remained. It seemed there were a lot of layoffs and buyouts immediately after the kidnapping—when Robert DuChamps started running the Somerton empire.

It would be only a matter of time before Robert recognized Hayden; he looked like his father, but harder perhaps around the eyes and mouth.

He was the gardener's son, a negative label that had scraped at the time.

Hayden listened to the call of an owl and the crickets chirping, and remembered his father and mother, the soft caresses and easy laughter, the way they looked at each other. Sophie had filled Paul's heart, and now as a grown man, Hayden understood those long, passionate kisses, the hungry sounds of a man who couldn't wait to have his wife alone. . . .

Robert DuChamps wouldn't be happy to have the gardener's son living beside the heiress, and Hayden wasn't backing off.

Where is that ransom money?

The lights remained fully lit within Cameron's barn, though she'd left earlier. She'd revved the pickup, reversed, and spun out, flying down the road onto the highway. "Like a bat out of hell," Hayden mused to the deer staring at him from the distance. "Go on, go on down to the pond and water. I won't bother you."

He'd learned quite a bit from Cameron's unusual and talkative friends, including that Robert was on a thoroughbred-buying trip to Kentucky, and that Cameron sometimes worked as a bartender at Al's Bar. "Now why would a woman with an inheritance like hers want to tend bar?"

Fancy's insight had provided one answer: "They don't get along, Cameron's stepfather and her. She does stuff to irritate him. That SOB deserves to be tossed out on his ear. I don't know why she's keeping him around, except for some misguided idea that her mother loved him."

Phoebe had quietly labeled Robert DuChamps: "He's a bastard. The luckiest thing she ever did was to marry William. He's a fun guy. Sweet. He visits sometimes."

Evie had dropped her flirting mode and been fiercely protective when adding, "Cameron is okay. She's a little bit odd around the edges—because of what she's gone through—the kidnapping when she was only six and the way her stepfather set up her husband. Cameron and William are like brother and sister now, enjoying each other, but they're both burned that Robert set them up. William is furious about how Robert treated Cameron, as a kid. William hates him. . . . We wouldn't want anything more unpleasant to happen to her. If you have to mess around with a woman, Hayden, do it with someone else."

Hayden's thoughts circled Cameron as he watched a small herd of deer move through the underbrush and emerge onto a rolling green field, grazing a short distance away from the cattle. "Other than her ex-husband, Cameron's friends are unusual for a society heiress, one who has a penthouse in New York, who attends art gallery events, and who hosts high-class charity events at the mansion."

He'd have to move quickly, gathering whatever information he could about Cameron and her life, before people discovered his real identity as the gardener's son, H.J. Doors would close then, people fearing the wrath of the Somerton fortune, of what Robert could do when protecting his interests.

Restless with his thoughts, Hayden knew that, tired as he was, sleep would be impossible. He took a deep breath, slid from the pickup's hood, and decided that this was a perfect time to start the ball rolling.

Fifteen minutes later, Hayden entered the tavern where he

knew Cameron would be working. Al's Bar was typical Western, dark and smoky, small chairs surrounding round tables. On a weekday night, business was slow. Evie and Fancy were doing the women-dancing-together thing, showing off a bit in their tight jeans and high heels, next to the jukebox. Cameron was behind the bar, pouring a pitcher of draft beer, her hair in a loose knot on top of her head, the ends spiking out to catch the neon lights of the beer advertisements. In a white blouse, she moved expertly behind the length of the bar, where several men were sitting on barstools. She smiled at one, flipped a glass high, and caught it in one hand, placing it on the bar. She lifted bottles in both hands and poured them into a glass, which she served to a young cowboy type; his body language said he wanted to get his hands under that blouse.

Cameron moved from behind the bar to take a tray with the filled beer pitcher and frosty mugs to a corner table. There, four men were evidently talking business with pads of paper and calculators. The heiress's jeans were tight, her hips swaying as she moved toward them. Tucked into her jeans, the blouse was thin enough to reveal her silhouette, the lightweight fabric flowing with her movements as she placed the tray on another table and lifted the pitcher to pour it into a tilted mug. She smiled at the men and chatted easily with them before setting the pitcher on the table and returning to the bar.

She had just lowered the waist-high counter partition closing off the bar when she saw Hayden. Cameron frowned instantly, slapped the bar towel over her shoulder, and opened the partition again, walking through it. She rounded the men sitting at the bar and came straight toward Hayden. When she stood in front of him, her hands on her hips, she asked, "What are you doing here?"

Whipcord-lean and long-legged, Cameron's body didn't resemble Katherine's small curvy build. Tonight, she'd used cosmetics heavily, accentuating the slant of her eyes, the fullness of those glossy lips. The effect reminded him of a mask, used to protect herself from anyone seeing inside to her emotions. "I can't be here? Do I need an invitation?"

"I thought we had an agreement: You stick to your territory, and I stick to mine. This is *mine*."

Up-front, cutting out her territory, warning him off . . . Cameron knew how to spell out perimeters, and she wasn't shy. But then, neither was Hayden, not when it came to something he wanted—like information about the remainder of the ransom money or tips that might help prove his father's innocence. "Did anyone ever tell you that you're not exactly the friendly type?"

When she moved, that restless impatient movement, Hayden noticed the bells at her ears and flicked one. "Why the bells?"

With a quick frown as if she had just remembered them, Cameron reached to touch that one, as if protecting it. She seemed so startled that Hayden relented a little—for the present—but her affinity for wearing bells and surrounding herself with good-luck charms was something he intended to explore. He flicked the other earring and watched fire light those blue eyes. "Lady, I've had a hard day, and I just want a beer and a little relaxation, okay? If you've got real objections, I'll leave. I can always pick up something and invite your friends over for a party. You could come, too, but not with that defensive attitude. Like I said, it's been a long, hard day."

The work had been nothing like the draining weight of his emotions, the harsh memories circling him.

"They told you all about me. I could kill them," she said beneath her breath and shot her friends a dark look. Their weak, too-innocent smiles said they understood her displeasure.

"So they said a few things about you, like you bought them pickups like yours—white Toyotas. That was nice. There's no reason they shouldn't say nice things about you, is there?"

"You must be something special, because they don't usually talk about me that much. But then, you were working it, weren't you? Showing off your muscles in your backyard?"

"Mm. You must have been watching. Were you?"

Hayden glanced at Evie and Fancy, who were now appearing worried. He looked down at Cameron. "Can I have a beer and company here, or do you want me to take the party to my place? Just a few friends, a little music, nothing loud or that would trash your very nice rental."

She caught the sarcasm, her eyes flashing beneath the heavy mascara, too heavy to be classy, and maybe that was another way she got back at old Robert, by looking cheap. "You saw the place before you rented it. I checked. You made a deal. You even paid the full six months in advance. Take any complaints you have to the property manager."

"Gosh, you're a real sweetheart. Am I having my beer here or at my house with my new friends?" Hayden asked, as Evie and Fancy climbed up to stand on the bar, dancing to the jukebox music. "They could do that at my place. The boards on the sawhorses would hold them."

With an exasperated sound, Cameron said, "You can have *a* beer here."

"Thanks. I'll leave a tip, Cammie." He'd purposely added the nickname to see if it would jog her memory, if she would remember a boy called H. J.

But she frowned and looked confused. "What did you call me?"

The nickname didn't seem familiar; her mother had called her that, never Cameron. "Cammie. I picked that up somewhere . . . must have been from your friends."

She was still caught by something inside her; the little bells jingled as she shivered just that once. "No, they call me Cameron. You must be thinking of someone else. I'm not a nickname person."

Hayden was silent, but he wasn't buying—she'd definitely reacted to the name.

Just then, Phoebe entered the bar. Dressed in a short leather vest, tight jeans, and red crocodile western boots, she grinned at Cameron. Then the other two women called to her, and she hopped up on the bar to dance with them, their bodies moving against each other and their boots catching the music's heavy beat. Cameron stiffened and glanced down at Hayden. "You're out for games. You like to push people, see how they respond, and just maybe you're in need of a little—but leave them alone," she warned quietly.

"Funny . . . that's exactly what they said about you." Hayden forced his eyes away from her angry flush, the way she lit up when prodded just that bit. The lady had all sorts of fascinating edges, and he intended to pick at each one until he got the answers he needed.

" 'Cammie'. . . . Jerk. . . . He left a dollar tip. Smart guy." The next afternoon, Cameron pummeled the hanging bag, putting every bit of her frustration into her kickboxing. Anchored to the floor, the bag vibrated with her hits. She was hot and sweaty, dancing around the bag, jabbing, kicking it. When her body and lungs protested the fierce, furious sport, she slowed; she tossed her gloves aside, wiped a towel around her face, and drank water. With more frustration to burn off, and still sweating, she decided not to change her black sports bra and spandex shorts just yet.

Cameron did a slow, stretching workout on her body ball, then looked through her binoculars to the old farmhouse. Her renter had already been to the lumber and hardware store, charging his lumber and repair necessities. Ray had checked on the purchases and agreed they were necessary. With his crew busy repairing and painting the estate's miles of white board fences, Ray had been relieved not to have added the farmhouse to his work list. Evie's and Fancy's friends who worked at the bank and at the hardware store had supplied Hayden's whereabouts of the morning: He had used his own money, fresh from a newly established checking account in

Mimosa's First National Bank, to buy a supply of garden tools, a rototiller, and garden tractor–lawn mower.

The telephone and septic tank trucks had already come and gone, and in front of the house was a pile of trash—old carpeting and linoleum. The Mimosa Flooring and Tile truck had arrived with two workmen, and Hayden had left for a time, returning with a new mattress and box springs set, wrapped in plastic. The two workmen had helped move the mattress set into the house and were now sitting on the front porch with Hayden, drinking coffee.

The indistinct rumble of male voices came through Cameron's open window—not that she was listening, of course. She picked up her binoculars and followed the men as they walked around the front yard, stopping periodically to examine the old trees and brush. They circled the old house, then spent the next half hour testing Hayden's new upscale rototiller and high-powered garden tractor-mower. An apparent male bonding indicated that Hayden wouldn't be a stranger in town for long. The men shook hands, and the workmen left.

Then Hayden looked at her house; he grinned and waved as if he'd been aware of her watching his movements.

"Jerk," Cameron muttered as she pushed the remote to lower the blinds. She walked to her computer, stared at the screen, and donned the Kiss Me Under the Mistletoe banner to be sold for holiday parties. "I've got better things to do than to see that you don't ruin Somerton property."

At twenty-three and just divorced, Cameron had moved from Somerton House and from Robert, and hadn't wanted anyone near her. She wanted the serenity of the old farm wrapped around her, the birds chirping, squirrels chattering, maybe the moo or two of a cow. Now, if she opened her windows for fresh air, all she got was revving saws and hammering.

Cameron propped herself in a big lounge chair, the modern shape curving to her body, and picked up the caterer's list of drinks and hors d'oeuvres for the investors' dinner next week. The charity fund-raisers had the usual guests, and one of Cameron's unofficial hostess functions was to introduce them to her wealthy investors; that reduced the constant, sly pressure to turn over more of the Somerton wealth to the charities.

But Cameron's mind kept returning to the new renter. He knew too much about her already, and he was hunting for something. He was definitely studying her, like when he flipped her earrings last night and the narrow, tense way he looked at her when he'd dropped the nickname Cammie into their conversation. She'd lied of course, but the name was inside her, a part of her, just like the whispers. *Oh, Cammie. . . .*

Distracted, she reached for the telephone when it rang. "Uh-huh?"

The masculine voice was warm and cultured. "How's it going, sweetie?"

"Oh, good times as usual."

Her ex-husband's chuckle caused her to smile, and she settled down to enjoy the light sexual banter, the teasing. William Van Zandt was always good for a distraction. "Missing me?" he asked in a tone that said he was half-serious and testing the waters.

"Always. But then, you're a sperm donor for another woman, so I'm definitely out of the picture."

"Yeah," he agreed almost dreamily, proudly. "How's old Robert? Leaving you alone?"

"Sure. Haven't had him foist a husband on me recently."

"You're pining for me, then," he pushed. "I've ruined you for any other man."

She smiled at that teasing arrogance. "Try again."

"That guy is a jerk," William stated suddenly, in one of those rare flashes of temper. "So was I. But I loved you, still love you, Cameron. I was thinking, maybe—"

"So when is your next regatta?" she asked quickly, to forestall William's predictable "getting together" probe.

Cameron smiled at the question because William would probably run if she acted interested. He was just balancing his life, before moving forward into a relationship so different from ones in his past.

Her distraction was effective, and William's long description of his playboy life rolled on for a good half hour. The only son of older wealthy socialite parents, he performed the necessary ritualistic functions because he loved them. The Van Zandts were always very proper, but seemed so cold when compared to William's outgoing, friendly, and caring nature. Getting his parents to accept working-class Arabella wouldn't be easy, but William was determined. "I miss you, Cameron. It's dull here. Come sail with me. Let's take a trip around the world, like we did on our honeymoon."

"Hey, I'm running Big Buck's kingdom, guy. I can't just take off when I want."

William continued to tease her: "I'm going to look like a lecher, going to Cannes and checking out the beach by myself. You could be my ruse. I could introduce you as the 'old ball and chain'. We'd have fun. Arabella would understand."

"Like hell she would. For a first husband, you were swell. Come see me anytime, William. And take care of Arabella."

"Too bad that I'm an only child with this whole heir business—without a sister like you. I miss you, sweetie," William said quietly.

"Ditto."

After the call ended, Cameron smiled. William always had a way of lifting her spirits, and lately, since she'd started forgetting and misplacing things, she really appreciated his calls. He had his own problems, but William seemed to know when she was upset, calling frequently and dropping in to check on her.

But then there was Hayden Olson, the man in the cafe, the man who found her on a deserted stretch of country road, and the man who had come to lease the farmhouse next door. *Who was he really?*

Cameron sat down at her computer, tried working on her copy and when it wouldn't flow, she ran an online search for Hayden Olson. If he had a home telephone in St. Louis, it was unlisted. While she was staring at the screen loaded with Olsons, Madeline called with Cameron's schedule for the day, and added, "You know Robert is not just buying a new thoroughbred, don't you?"

"Sure. He's probably got his next girlfriend spotted, right?"

"The guy has energy, you have to give him that. He's been circulating for years. This one must be more difficult to get than the rest, because he's visited her two times—a Virginia Ulbrech, wealthy, divorced, and in the right social class. Oh, excuse me—I mean, he's been thoroughbred shopping there twice, and he wants to bring her here. He called in this morning to ask if he could have an advance on his paycheck. 'Paycheck,' " Madeline muttered, as she shuffled papers in her office at the estate. "For what? Somerton is paying all of his bills, lodging, dinner, expenses. You'd think the guy would be happy with the fat check he gets every two weeks."

Cameron balanced Madeline's usual grumbling about Robert's excesses with the necessity of keeping him busy and out of Somerton business. "How far is he into borrowing from his allowance?"

Madeline tapped the calculator's keys. "Too far. He lost a lot in last year's Derby. And he's squiring this Virginia woman around, sending her presents like expensive diamond earrings."

"Give him enough to get him and his horse home." Cameron remembered Robert's dark looks at Madeline, and added, "Just deliver the message, Madeline. And if you have any problem with Robert, I want to know."

"The guy is a big fat problem, always has been."

Cameron phrased her words carefully, "If he threatens you, in any way, I want to know."

"There's the usual having me fired stuff." Madeline's voice

was very quiet and deadly, lacking her usual brisk business tone. "I know what he did to you, locking you in closets when I wasn't around. We had a few discussions back then. Maybe I was slightly attracted to him at one time, but when I saw how he treated you, I couldn't stand his guts. He knows if he touched me now, I'd kill him."

Cameron hadn't expected that quiet violence, which gave proof to her theory that Robert had already threatened Madeline. "Just let me know. I'll deal with him. I suppose he wants to bring his girlfriend to the party next week."

"Uh-huh. He wouldn't miss that chance to show off." Madeline's tone was distracted, and the tapping sound indicated that she was back to work on her calculator, as if she were already deep into managing Somerton accounts. "He's really trying to impress this lady. She breeds those Jack Russell terriers he wants and is bringing one with her. He's already called the staff with orders for quail dinners, expensive bubble bath and oils in his room. I guess she likes vanilla—good grief, she could just buy a bottle at the super market."

If he touched me now. . . . That was the first time Madeline had ever indicated that Robert would have tried anything with her; but then, he was likely to test all the women around him. Still, the thought angered Cameron, that a woman on Somerton payroll would be harassed by a lech. "Tell him to deal with me, and if he does arrange for his new girl to visit, have her stay in the guest cottage."

"But he always has them stay in the house—"

"Not anymore. And the dog doesn't come in Somerton House. You make a lot of these arrangements. Work this in when you talk to Mrs. Ulbrecht—the dog either stays on a leash at all times, or she can leave him at home, okay?"

With a groan, Madeline acknowledged the long-standing battle between Cameron and Robert, each one pushing the other with her in the middle. "Fine. You'll hear the squawks clear over to your barn. He likes to show off here, in the house, as if it were really his."

Cameron watched Hayden move out into the backyard, wearing only his jeans. "Just how tight is that lease for the farmhouse?"

"Very. He paid in advance. We weren't expecting trouble, and it's the usual lease form. . . . How bad do you want him out? Any specific reason?"

Cameron explained Hayden's "girlfriend with a boy" situation—that it didn't exist anymore, but that his family translated to just that, his mother and sister's family.

"My fault," Madeline said brusquely in the tone of someone who doesn't like to make mistakes. "I should have checked into this myself. I depend on the people handling our property to be thorough."

"You've got enough on your plate. He bothers me, that's all. He's a little too smart. He was at the bar last night, and thanks to my friends, he knows more than he should about me."

"Keep your enemies close, honey, that's what I always say. Tell your friends to tighten their lips." One of Madeline's many lines rang, and she said hurriedly, "Got to go. Incoming fax I've been waiting for. Let me know if you want the attorneys to work on getting him out. If he missteps, I want to know ASAP."

"Sure." Cameron smiled briefly with the image of Madeline's office on the main floor; it was big and busy, and definitely her very private territory. One of her quirks was that she cleaned the office herself, preferring that no one enter it without her in attendance. Cameron understood quirks and dismissed Madeline's as unimportant. After all, it was just another room in Somerton House. Cameron had never wanted to explore the house, not even as a child. It terrified her then, and as a teenager who visited infrequently, she preferred to stay in her room. She went there only when necessary now, did her business, and left—just that simple. Madeline was certainly free to keep private any room she wanted.

In the old garden behind the farmhouse, Hayden began to pick up limbs. Shed of his business shirt and slacks, and wearing worn jeans, leather gloves, and boots, he could have been any laborer. He wasn't stiletto-lean like Robert or William, built more to the broad, sturdy side, like a football player, and he had the wide hands of a workman, not the businessman he'd appeared that first night.

Those intense, quiet looks said that he was hunting something—what was it? But then, an heiress with an attached money bag was usually hunted for one reason or another, especially when she was unmarried. Would Robert dare to send another would-be husband after her, and had just picked another type? One more physical and challenging?

Of course, she was suspicious, an heiress had to be, especially one who had been kidnapped and fought her way free of Robert's grasp. Cameron watched a tractor with a machine fitted to the back drive up to the farmhouse. Hayden came out to meet the driver and pointed at different places in the backyard. The tractor revved, wheeled around, and planted the drill-like device in the ground.

Cameron picked up her phone and dialed Ray. She described the machine and Ray answered: "Yeah, it's a posthole digger. Lots of people use them to plant new trees. He bought a bunch of them at the feed and hardware store, using his own money. Bought the mulch they need, too. They've got to go into the ground right away before it gets too hot. He'll be watering from that old pump. It won't be long before that will need a new motor. He's already contacted the well people for a redo."

She thought of her hours of sweating to produce a tiny hole for a tree. "*You mean that I've been out here digging holes for trees when there was a machine that I could hire?*"

"You didn't ask, Cameron. I just thought you were working off frustration. Sometimes you just decide to go for it, and you don't want anyone interfering, like you are pitting yourself against something and need to work it out. You want me to send someone over? Hey, buddy—put those shingles over there, by the guest cottages!" Ray called.

Cameron watched Hayden make his way over the old cow path, heading her way. "Now what?"

"The last big tornado wind did some damage to two of the cottages and Madeline okayed the new roofs and shingles for the rest. That's okay, isn't it?"

"Sure. I'm fully confident in Madeline's decisions. I was asking about something else."

"You do that sometimes, talk in two streams, like you're someone else. I guess that comes from the kidnapping and handling so much big finance and duties in one day, and trying to keep apart from everything and sane the next."

Sane. Her whole life had been insane. "It's okay, Ray. Bye."

She jerked open the door before Hayden could ring the doorbell and repeated the question, "What now?"

Cameron was having trouble focusing with that wide chest, all gleaming and sweaty, little pieces of rubble clinging to the wedge of black hair in the center. Inch by inch, she took in his body as the wind chimes on her porch tinkled musically. The sun skimmed over his broad shoulders, following each curve of the muscles. When she did raise her eyes to his face, it was covered with stubble, his eyes crinkling at the corners and his lips curving just that bit to say she amused him. Hayden took his time looking down her body, the Kiss Me Under the Mistletoe banner diagonally crossing her chest. "Nice," he said appreciatively in that deep voice. "Real nice."

Cameron had forgotten she'd been testing the banner for wear and that she was still in her sports bra and spandex shorts. She must have trembled when her senses spiked, aware that Hayden's lingering look was definitely sensual, because her earrings jingled. For just that instant, when his nipples jumped on hard, tanned pecs, she thought of better ways of working off frustration than kickboxing and stretching on her body ball. "Why are you here?"

"Just being neighborly. Your trees are dying. If these are the same ones you bought when we met at the cafe, then it's been over three weeks—a long time to stay propped up against your barn. Do you want the guy with the tractor to come over and dig holes? He's right here, and he's cheap. He's going to plow my garden, and from the looks of that mess behind this barn, you might want to have him redo yours. I'd clean it up for you . . . maybe add a few stone paths, a birdbath?"

"Look. I like my privacy. Just stay on your side of the property, will you?"

"Take it easy. I just came over to let you know that I'm having a party tomorrow night. I won't charge admission. Your girlfriends are coming. You might as well come over. Beer and pulled-pork barbecue sandwiches—I mix my own pork rub and make the barbecue sauce from scratch—and the girls are bringing in some other stuff. It's just a little payback for the people who are helping me settle in. *Your* friends have helped a lot," he added.

"Conversation ended." Cameron knew he was taunting her—her friends had crossed her unseen picket line to Hayden. She closed the door firmly; she didn't like the way he was looking at her, too closely, as if seeing what made her tick. She ticked "odd," and everyone in Mimosa knew and accepted it.

When the doorbell rang, she jerked open the door. "What?"

"The banner is nice. It should sell well. I hear you write copy for catalogs and try out the gizmos. Pretty interesting job." Then Hayden reached to flip her earring, the tiny bell jingled, and he said, "I always liked Christmas."

She stilled the bell with her hand and frowned up at him. "Is that it? You like Christmas?"

"Sure. You didn't like the nickname 'Cammie,' did you? I'd have thought someone along your lifetime would have tried that one on you before."

The name stunned her, locked her mind, and she struggled to come up with an answer, "We're not going to be chums, you know. You can't just walk over here when you want."

"Okay, I'll remember that. I guess someone like you is used to having an assistant make appointments for neighborly visits." There was just that odd, quiet, searching look, then Hayden turned and walked back toward his farmhouse.

Cameron watched that easy, long-legged stride, that bare, gleaming muscular back, and closed the door, leaning against it. *Cammie . . . Cammie . . . It was a name she'd never forget.*

She had to be careful.

Then, because her eyes had locked on to Hayden's powerful back and tall body, her body was telling her that sex had been a long time ago. *But wouldn't it rub Robert if I were to take a lover—the man next door?*

Cameron smiled briefly at that whimsy. She might as well have the temporary pleasure of her body—because her mind was weakening, forgetting essentials—just small things, like replacing her old driver's license with the new, which was still in the opened envelope at Somerton House.

Today in the grocery store, a child had called for her mother— "Mommy? Where are you?" and the voice was so much like the whispers of her nightmares.

Cameron had reacted too frantically, her heart racing as she hurried between the aisles to find the child, her mother already at her side.

Cameron shook the bells at her wrist, holding them close to her ear. She had to keep the whispers silent, and she had to keep focused. If distracted enough, weakened enough, Robert DuChamps would again be her guardian—because she'd be in an institution.

He couldn't kill her. Oh, no, that would mean the Somerton fortune would go to Katherine's charities—dear sweet Katherine. . . .

The next morning, Cameron's double life started all over again as the Somerton heiress in charge of an empire and the odd woman who lived in a barn guarded by good luck horseshoes and gargoyles.

At dawn, Cameron walked to a place that called to her, Katherine and Buck Somerton's mausoleum behind Somerton House. Katherine's favorite pink roses were blooming, a big cabbage rose, bred from French and Old South stock. The angels at the door of the marble mausoleum seemed to watch Cameron as she opened the ornate gate and closed it behind her. "I'm here, Mother," she said quietly, and wondered if somewhere Katherine's spirit heard her, forgave her.

But then, Cameron had done the unforgivable, hadn't she? She'd lived, while another had died.

With a weary sigh, Cameron sat on a small bench and wondered why she was so drawn to this place, why it seemed quieter than anywhere else, where the scents were rain-fresh and clean, even in drought. The peaceful stillness settled softly around her as always, the birds chirping softly, the mourning dove cooing, as if everything waited for her, wanted her.

She knew what the stillness wanted, the hidden truths.

The angels looked at her, blaming her for living, while Katherine was dead. "I would change everything if I could," Cameron whispered, as tears flowed down her cheeks, and a thick braid of secrets and guilt coiled and tightened around her. "I'm the one who should have died."

A turtle with a high, rounded shell and a red marking on its head crawled slowly from the rosebushes, making its way to within a foot of her shoe. Its beady eyes stared at her, condemning her, as if it knew her secret guilt. "I'll find that hole. I've searched everywhere around here, hunted for years for it. I'll keep my promises to find it and remember everything. I won't stop until I do," Cameron whispered desperately to the turtle.

Uninterested in human drama, the turtle continued on its way. "But I know Robert was involved in the kidnapping, and just maybe Katherine's death. I just have to prove it, and proof may lie in that hole where I was kept. Okay, don't listen, Mr. Turtle."

A slight breeze slid through the rosebushes, bringing that delicate fragrance she remembered from long ago, the scent that always seemed to curl around her, soothing her. A bumblebee hummed and landed on a pink bloom, causing it to bob slightly. A black-and-yellow butterfly flitted along the stone path, then perched on the top of an angel.

This special place was so quiet, and its peace moved inside Cameron, giving her the strength to do what she must—

Her morning business session in Somerton House's office was its usual—busy. She went over every detail for the investors' dinner, she returned business calls; she checked the stock market, signed proxies and options, and went over Madeline's checklists.

Then, at noon, Cameron returned to her barn. She opened the mail Phoebe had left inside and settled down to work until midafternoon.

A sudden gurgling startled her, and Cameron stared at the fish in her aquarium—Henry's and Leon's beautiful fins moved only by the bubbles passing near them, not by life. Zipper's red fins swirled lifelessly and mama guppy floated near her nest—

Cameron started to shake, worried that she'd done something wrong. . . . Particles of food floated in the water. Had she overfed them?

Cameron checked the index card listing the usual feeding times and her checkmark said the last time she fed them was correct. But they were dead. Had she forgotten and fed them again? She couldn't bear to look at the aquarium, tears burning her eyes, and she turned away. "I'm so sorry. I'm so sorry."

She turned, unable to face the dead fish. Then hurrying, she snatched a sheet from the closet and hurried to drape it over the aquarium. Breathing hard, she held herself, rocking her body. "I'm losing it," she admitted shakily, "and I can't, Katherine. I've got to hold on, for you, for Cammie."

It's all right, the slow childlike whispers echoed from

long ago, *you're doing what you can. . . .* "But it's not good enough. It wasn't good enough, Cammie."

Don't cry . . . everything will be all right. . . .

"It won't be, and you know it. I'm going down, forgetting things, misplacing them."

It will be all right. The whisper soothed slowly, and she knew she had spoken, that the words were hers, long ago. . . .

"I've got to hold on. I've just go to," Cameron admitted to herself, needing to hear the sound of someone talking, reassuring her. She pushed her body to the computer, forcing herself to check the guest list one more time, the seating arrangements, all the little methodical things that needed to be done for the investors' party. She worked furiously, making lists to help her remember and keep control, until her eyes burned, her mind drained.

She couldn't breathe.

Panicked, she sucked at the musty damp air, clawed at the only door in that earthen pit.

No one would come. She knew she was alone forever and forgotten, trapped away from the sunlight that would appear as a golden slice between the boards of the door.

Somewhere beyond this place, people were laughing, and they weren't afraid.

And they weren't sharing the darkness with the dead.

Cameron tore herself from sleep and sat up, her body damp with perspiration and trembling as fading echoes of her nightmare blended with the loud party next door. She sat for a moment, pulling herself together and resenting the late-afternoon nap that she'd had to take, a respite from the tension and fatigue within her.

She'd opened the window for the cool, fresh air, letting it surround her as she'd drifted off, and now the music and voices next door said Hayden's party was in full swing. Evie's voice rose above the pounding music, "Hey, Hayden, we need more beer."

"Deserters," Cameron muttered as she headed into the shower. She'd have her own party without her friends, and when they wanted to replay the fun highlights to her, like rubbing against Hayden's fine body, she'd ignore them.

Hayden left the party for a few quiet minutes in his backyard. He'd really enjoyed the day, free of office duties, just working with the old gardens, planting the new trees. He walked to the hose he'd laid next to a newly planted tree, picked it up, and moved the slow drip to soak another one. The old apple trees were beyond saving, but he'd used a chain saw to cut them into winter firewood, which was piled at the back fence corner. He scanned the woods beyond his backyard. If he needed more wood, there was plenty of it there. A winter stay wasn't on his agenda, but then picking through aged rubble for a cold trail could turn into a longer hunt.

The heiress in the barn was too tightly strung, and maybe he'd been too curt with her. He needed her, after all, for those answers to the puzzle that didn't fit—and she was definitely the key.

Alcohol and fun was one way of loosening tongues, and his timeline was short—when he returned, Robert DuChamps would recognize Paul Olson's son, the likeness was too close. After that, things could get rough, because Hayden wasn't backing off.

As the past circled him, Hayden looked up at the silver Oklahoma moon, then over the fields to Mimosa. Fireflies had started their mating, tiny perfect flashes of light tracing their paths, and he thought of Cameron's sleek, curved body in that black sports bra and those tight shorts. For an unguarded moment, those blue eyes had widened, taking in his chest, and he could almost feel her smoothing his skin, her fingers digging in; she'd been aware of the heat flashing between them, just like those fireflies seeking mates.

In that brief moment with Cameron yesterday afternoon,

the physical jolt to his body had been hard enough to make him ache as he walked back to his house. Hayden had the distinct sense that lovemaking with her wouldn't be smooth or sweet—

A movement behind the barn drew Hayden's attention; he caught glimpses of Cameron between the trees and brush. She slid through the shadows, and the chance for a quiet moment with her was one Hayden couldn't turn down. He hooked another bottle of beer from the iced cooler on his back porch and walked up the old cow path.

She was having her own party, the radio picking up a fast beat as she danced on top of a wooden picnic table. Dressed much the same as her friends at the bar, those long legs were covered in skintight jeans, the short leather vest lifting with her arms to reveal the pale flesh of a smooth stomach. Her hands were open on her body, cruising it sensually, her head lifted to reveal that long neck, her face turned up to the moonlight, her eyes closed.

At the bar, she'd been all cool business, but this woman bent and moved like liquid heat, her hands lifting that smooth hair, her hips gyrating, those long legs opening and closing as her pink western boots kept time to the music. When she turned suddenly, her hands on her hips, her hair few out around her head, the tips catching the moonlight, and Hayden stopped breathing—this woman was so alive, so hot, so different from the cold, hard one he'd experienced. Her lean body flowed with the music, hips undulating, her shoulders moving as her hands hooked into her pockets. She fast-kicked around in a circle, still holding the country music beat.

If Hayden had ever seen pure passion in a woman, enough to stop a man's breath and harden his body, it was the Somerton heiress tonight, her hands open and moving sensually on her thighs and on her bottom.

In the dappled moonlight, Cameron spun around and around, her boots kicking to the fast beat, then suddenly she seemed to collapse. She sat on the table with her head in her hands, doubled over almost protectively. She reached to turn off the music and in the night, only Hayden's heartbeat and the party at the farmhouse could be heard.

Her hands held her head, her fingers spearing through that sleek hair. "Cammie? Cammie? Everything is going to be all right," she whispered to the moon. "We're all right. See? The fairies are here, just like you always wanted."

The hair on Hayden's nape lifted—*Cammie, she spoke to Cammie. Was she speaking to herself long ago—before she was kidnapped? Cammie had loved fairies.*

She lifted her arms as gracefully as a ballet dancer, sweeping them before her, and Hayden scanned the shadows to find tall garden statues of fairies, their concrete wings catching the moonlight, their bodies draped in living vines. Outsize, they seemed more like centurions, guarding the heiress.

Cameron had leaped from the picnic table, moving amid the statues. Her movements were graceful, and reflected the ballet and modern dance lessons an heiress would have. She raised her arms to embrace a fairy holding a bouquet of roses and her words floated to Hayden on the cool night air: "Where are you, Cammie?" she called softly to the night. "Tell me, please. Please, please tell me. . . ."

Cammie . . . Cammie. . . . She'd used that nickname, and yet had denied it earlier when Hayden had first tested her. If she remembered her nickname, why would she deny it? If she remembered her nickname, why didn't she remember him?

The moment was private and aching, and he should leave Cameron to whatever darkness rode her.

But he couldn't, not if he wanted to push her—the woman, he sensed, was the key to his father's suicide. . . .

Hayden moved out of the shadows and watched her hair catch the moonlight, spinning out around her pale face as she turned to him.

"Having a private party? You're invited to mine," Hayden said quietly, and immediately regretted his choice to push her now, because her cheeks were glistening with tears.

She looked as if she needed someone to hold her, that stark bleeding look of the haunted.

Five

CAMERON HELD VERY STILL, STARTLED BY THE MAN WHO HAD just emerged from the shadows. "What are you doing here?"

Hayden shrugged easily and held out a bottle of beer. "I just walked over to see if you might want to come to my housewarming."

"Just now? You walked over here . . . just now?" she asked through a tight throat. If he'd seen anything—Cameron had danced for herself, the kind of sensual dance to remind her that she was a woman, not a machine; then she'd danced for Cammie, using the ballet lessons she'd been forced to take from one of Robert's mistresses, just a little something to add the woman to the Somerton payroll.

Cameron had to separate herself as a woman from the child, giving them both individual places in her mind. Everything she did reminded her that there was a child, long ago, who needed to be remembered . . . and to remind herself that she was a strong woman with an almost overpowering role to play. Odd? Yes, but she'd survived, hadn't she? Her Other Self had survived, despite those early hard years with Robert.

The planes and deep shadows of Hayden's face were unreadable, his eyes steady upon her. Then moonlight caught the edge of one blunt cheekbone, gleaming and dangerous, his voice deep and rumbling across her skin, prickling it. "I came over just now."

The garden behind Cameron's home was just for her, for young Cammie, who had loved fairies, for the girl lost forever in that cold dark pit of earth and wooden beams.

Stark and male and big, the man had intruded into the feminine sanctuary. His rawboned features were too harsh for the statues, draped in concrete folds, vines, and moonlight. His shoulders caught a bit of that moonlight, the expanse broad and powerful; the early July's evening air seemed to tighten in her lungs, fear chilling her skin. *This man is hunting and he is dangerous. To me? What does he want?*

"You may leave," Cameron said with all the cool dignity she could manage.

He remained still, and his eyes, those pinpoints of light, shifted from her, scanning the tall fairy statues. Energy hummed between the statues, bouncing off them, as if they were whispering. In her nightmares, they *did* whisper, telling her secrets, but never the answers she needed to know, the pieces of a little girl in that hole long ago.

Cameron sensed that Hayden only moved when he wanted, when he was ready. He took a long swallow of his beer, his throat working, before he turned to her. "Nice."

"I think so. Didn't you hear me? I just told you to leave."

"Correction: You told me that I *may* leave. That means I have a choice." He walked toward her and, still holding the beers in one hand, flicked her bell earring. His hand lingered, slid down to her wrist and lightly circled the charms there. Though he was holding her loosely, the strength in those fingers could have crushed her wrist, silencing her bells–or her cry for help. His thumb brushed her inner wrist once, then settled into a slow, steady caress. The light, rough scrape of it seemed threatening, predatory. "Your pulse is racing," he said softly. "What are you afraid of?"

You, of course. Everything . . . nothing . . . of losing my sanity . . . of failing Katherine.

"Are you flirting with me?" Cameron asked, casually taking the beer as an excuse to draw her wrist away, just casual enough so he would know she wasn't afraid of him, this hunter with an ache she sensed deep within him. She circled the bottle with both hands and considered him, his motives—and hers.

She'd had years of sifting through others' emotions, trying to put them into a "safe" or "dangerous" box. Hayden was unusual, and that caused her to be suspicious, let alone the circumstances in which they had first met.

Most men backed away from her bristling chill, the fortress that gave her safety and kept away everyone but the best of friends, the people who understood that she was sometimes "odd."

Yet there was a link between Hayden and her, possibly a darkness within them both. Perhaps their kinship was the haunted linking with another similar soul, like magnets of opposite polarities drawn together.

He lifted his bottle and sipped it, then looked down at her. "Flirting with you? Hadn't crossed my mind."

That irritated. She was a woman, wasn't she? Other than being a little "odd," what was wrong with her? Cameron sipped the beer, felt the coolness beneath her thumb, using it to anchor her as excitement pulsed through her. While the heiress needed safety, her Other Self needed that edge to prove that she was still alive.

She slanted him a look, studying him, dissecting the angles, the moonlight catching on those broad, blunt cheekbones, the pinpoints of light in his deep-set eyes, steady upon her. They were both hunters, possibly equally matched, gauging each other, and the game between them could be exciting. The thought tantalized as she turned it.

That leaped within her, the need to play with danger, and her senses told her it lurked beneath that impassive stare—something else waited and hungered, and she sought to capture it. A few moments with this man, passing the time, wouldn't hurt. She toyed with the idea and wondered why Hayden "wouldn't think of it." "How curious. Most men might flirt with me, given the chance. I'm rich, you know. I'd be a good catch."

"I heard you'd been caught and didn't like it." Hayden walked over to the wooden table she'd danced upon and sat on the top, his boots on the bench. He scanned the fairies, the tilting birdbaths and ornate concrete benches and love seats, slanted a bit, because they hadn't been set properly. "What's the idea?"

"What idea?" She looked around at the statues, her friends who gave her comfort, who knew her deepest secrets and shared the nightmares that wouldn't go away; they'd listened to the whispers that terrified her. The fairies looked the same, but no one saw them as she did—something Cammie loved. This was really Cammie's garden, dedicated to the little girl who had been so terrified, who had become another person after the kidnapping.

Hayden lifted his beer, indicating the slanting, vine-wrapped fairy statues. "Usually people have some kind of layout, a theme? You have gargoyles and horseshoes and wind chimes in the front, a hippo, plastic palm trees, and that elephant, of course. But back here, you've kept to one theme—fairies and whimsy. Any reason for that?"

Cameron frowned and considered the statues. Hayden had latched on to the differences no one else had noted: the child part, the other part of herself who had died in that damp, airless place, had loved fairies. "My choice. There's nothing wrong with my fairies, or anything else I want around me. The horseshoes are a little bit of country bling-bling, that's all."

His "okay" came too easily. Then, "I heard your fish died today. Sorry about that."

"Things die around me," Cameron murmured before she

realized it, an insight she tried to cover by adding, "Plants most of all. I don't like getting my hands dirty, you see. I like other people to do my work for me."

He apparently dismissed her crisp snobbish facade, a shield for her genuine guilt and grief, and asked quietly, "Did you bury them?"

"The plants? You can see that they're still out front. I water them. My gardeners haven't had time. They're over partying at your place."

He smiled a little at that, too patiently, as if he recognized the diversion. "True, but I wasn't asking about your plants. I can see that they're in trouble. I said 'bury,' as in your fish."

Then his expression stilled and that odd quiet stare pinned her, as if he were searching for something inside her. Cameron tensed and shifted uneasily, glancing away to the tall fairies, her friends, her protectors, the ones she imagined whispering to her. What did Hayden see? *Cameron and Cammie together and apart, one and the same, yet different?*

"Do you need someone to bury your fish for you?" he asked. "I knew a little girl who liked to have a ceremony when hers died. They were koi and weren't supposed to die, but they did. I helped her—it seemed to ease her. We buried them beneath a statue, so she'd always remember where they were. She cried for days after that. I was just a boy who had earned some money doing yard work. I bought her a dime store goldfish. That seemed to help."

The story was sweet and poignant, a young boy trying to help a little girl, and Hayden was still watching her as if he were waiting for her response.

She thought of her mama guppy, ready to let the little black dot in her belly become tiny, almost transparent fish. And it was her fault the fish were dead.

Cameron turned back to him, anxious for him to leave so that he wouldn't see her fragile emotions now. She forced her voice to be crisp and cold. "That was a nice story. Aren't you missing your party?"

Hayden listened intently to the sounds of the party, the music and the laughter, floating in the night air. "They don't seem to be missing me. Did you take care of your fish? I'll help you," he offered again.

"I don't need your help." Her friends had recommended flushing the fish down the toilet, "out to sea," but she just couldn't do that. She couldn't even lift the sheet hiding the aquarium.

"Sure, you do. Bring them out here, and we'll find a nice place for them."

She couldn't bear to see them, let alone dip them from the tank. Yet his offer seemed too intimate, and if she did choose to take it, he would see her cry. Riding on emotions, Cameron might say something she shouldn't. "I can manage. Get back to your party."

Hayden shook his head and stood. "Whatever you say."

He seemed to be waiting, always waiting and watching her, studying her, taking her apart. "People say I'm odd," she said suddenly with clarity, her voice dropping truth into the softness like shards of ice; they wounded with the admission. "You might as well know it."

"So you say." His voice seemed to rumble in the night, a soothing tone. "I'd say that someone who was only six when she was kidnapped and held for two weeks only to discover her mother had died, might be a little odd around the edges. But then most people have experiences in their lives that make them seem a little odd. Or else they're lying."

She hadn't expected that insight, the last with a slightly bitter tone. "Who are you exactly, Mr. Hayden Olson, lately of St. Louis?"

"Someone with a mother and a kid sister. Someone who's taking a break to sort things out. Someone who has had a little too much to drink tonight."

"Does that sorting out have to do with me? You're looking for something. I can feel it. Just stay away from me." Then she had to ask suddenly, "Was it your sister whose fish died?"

He shook his head and turned to look at her as though he were trying to find something inside her. "No. Just a little girl who didn't have any friends. Someone like you . . . lonely. And I'm looking for a lot of things—everyone is, or they're lying about that, too."

Her whole life was a lie.

"I'm just fine," Cameron lied, disturbed now by a man who knew that tropical fish could be dear to her heart—when her ex-husband had laughed at her reaction. She handed the beer to Hayden and with his hands busy, moved in close to study him.

She considered the hard angles and planes of his face, and thought of how she'd first seen him, a businessman at work at a lonely cafe, dressed expensively, driving a BMW. In shape and attractive to women, he'd be perfect for her very special need to antagonize Robert. Her stepfather would hate Hayden immediately—a younger, intelligent man, a little hard around the edges, a very physical man.

"Thanks for the beer. I don't drink more than a glass or two. Ever," she said, remembering the sickening times she'd gotten drunk, trying to give herself momentary peace so that the whispers wouldn't come in her nightmares.

"That sounds like you might have—once."

"Maybe. It doesn't change things, everything is still there when you wake up." She'd trusted William enough to try drinking herself senseless so she couldn't remember, couldn't think about how she'd survived. On their private yacht somewhere off the coast of Greece, she'd become deathly sick. The results hadn't been pretty, but William had stayed with her, teasing her that she'd gone off on some tangent about the kidnapping, that she'd yelled at someone to stop whispering. Since she never wanted to revisit that weakness, Cameron never again drank enough to affect her control.

He smiled a little at the problems-still-there comment, as if he recognized hard-time hangovers. "What's with you?"

he asked quietly, as she came close, sizing his body against her height and curves.

He'd feel so good, heavy, hard, deep—

Maybe, for just that few moments, she might forget.

He was also gauging her, his heat soaking into her body. Needing just the feel of his body, Cameron leaned slightly against him, and that hard stomach met her breasts. She studied the brief wariness in his expression, before it tightened, and hardened. Cameron didn't miss that flare of his nostrils, the quickening of his breath upon her face. "You'd better go back to your party—"

His flat statement jarred the night: "I heard you don't get around."

Robert would be livid . . . the renter and the heiress, living side by side, intimate. . . . The idea churned again in her mind: a little hit on Robert's ego—her desire for another man, when her stepfather considered Cameron as his creation, his possession. . . . "I don't get around. Do you?"

"Been there, done that," he answered slowly, those black eyes pinning her. Her cheeks were warm, excitement pulsing through her. She always felt like this when she'd found something good to put over on Robert, scoring one against him.

Hayden flicked her earring. It tinkled a warning as he asked, "What do you want from me?"

Caution told her that she'd had her moment, that she'd better back off, because this man didn't seem to be the kind to be easily managed. Cameron stepped back and folded her arms. "You're doing a lot of work over there. Just make sure you don't wreck anything."

"You're free to come over and check anytime. That old storm cellar is a real hazard though, if you're planning to have anyone in that farmhouse with kids."

Cameron's body went cold, and she fought shaking. She'd hunted and found several of the "root" or storm cellars in the Oklahoma farming country, but none were exactly right, the one she remembered. According to the investigator's reports, every farm had been searched—every old cabin, excavation site for gravel, every hole in the ground.

Chilled by the ominous sense that somehow, this cellar might be the one where she'd been kept, Cameron's mind quickly circled the thought: Old storm cellars were dug into the ground, braced with wooden beams, and had sturdy wood doors to keep tornado winds outside. Early "root" or storm cellars were used to keep canned vegetables and root crops through winter's freeze and summer's heat. An old cellar like that would seem to be a damp and cold pit to a child. And where she had been kept, there was an old-fashioned canning jar with a glass lid and a wire to clamp it tight. . . . The investigation report had eliminated the old Riordan farm as being searched, and now Hayden had found one? "What storm cellar?"

Frowning slightly, Hayden hadn't missed her reaction. He caught the tinkling bells at her ears, the warm edges of his palms capturing her jaw. "You just flipped over. You were definitely flirting with me, and now you're terrified and pale and shaking."

She gripped his wrists, anchoring him, the man who might lead her to the place where she'd died, and where she came out so different. She'd know in a heartbeat if that was the place where she'd been held, where the whispers of her nightmares had begun. "I'm fine—tell me . . . I need to know. I *have* to know. I've hunted my whole life for where they kept me."

"The old root cellar is on the back of the property, dug into that hill in front of the woods. With that dried creek nearby, it may have been a springhouse at one time, cool enough to keep milk and cream in the old days. It has seen plenty of animal life. By the looks of the old iris and daffodil beds, some rosebushes, there was an old house near that hill before this one. . . . Is something wrong?"

For a moment, her throat was so tight with fear that she couldn't speak. Cameron looked at the woods to the rear of the property, thick and dark and overgrown with grapevines and brush, and scary to a terrified six-year-old girl, who had just awakened in them. "I . . . didn't know that it was there all this time."

She'd hunted for years for the place where she'd been kept—*and it could have been so close!* "I'd like to see it . . . to see what can be done to make it safe."

Is that where my life—where I changed? Is that where the whispers began?

"Now?" he asked quietly, placing the beer bottles on the table. "I'll take you. We'll need a flashlight. Let me turn off the party, or else they'll all be stumbling into that pit after us."

The pit. That's what it was behind the slats of that wooden door, a pit of dampness and darkness, devouring who she was, changing her.

"Where is it exactly?"

"Just past an old cistern that's been filled in. The cellar is built into the hill and pretty well covered with brush, blackberry bushes so thick—"

She'd been scratched badly, tiny scratches and tiny thorns. . . . She'd eaten the food the man had brought, and then she'd slept heavily, to awake with trees and sky over her, a meadow in front of her—and people in the sunshine. . . . "I want to see it—*now!*"

"Someone has dumped a lot of cans and bottles back there in front of it. You should wait until—You're shaking . . . and you're serious, aren't you? You really want to see it *now*? At night?"

Her fingers tightened on Hayden's arm; she wasn't letting him go, the man who could lead her to where the whispers began. "I said so, didn't I?"

He nodded slowly, considering her. "Okay, anything you say. You're the boss after all. Wait here. I'll end the party and come back for you. Or else they just may decide to join us, and that could get someone hurt, walking through the brush and mole runs."

Hayden was already moving toward the farmhouse, his stride long and brisk. She watched, trying to digest what she had just learned: The old root cellar behind the farmhouse could be the place she'd searched for years, to find her end and her beginning, and then the whispers would stop. . . .

Terror pushed through Cameron, chilling her. She should wait until daylight.

But she couldn't—

"I should have known." Hayden watched the narrow flashlight beam cut through the night, moving toward the rear of the property. Then with the last of the cars and trucks making their way down the driveway, he began to move quickly.

Cameron wasn't the kind of woman to wait for others; she was already moving through the brush toward the rise of hill where the old cistern marked the first home place.

She wouldn't like the excuse he'd used for killing the party. He'd found Phoebe on his back doorstep; she'd watched him make his way from Cameron's, and he hadn't corrected her impression, that knowing smile. "Private party," he'd explained to Phoebe as he urged her inside. "This one is over."

"Maybe she's due. You hurt her, and I'll kill you. But you seem like you're okay."

But Hayden was thinking of how Cammie had loved fairies, and how stricken Cameron had looked at the mention of the old cellar. He'd come across it while walking the old property, giving himself a break from restoring the farmhouse and collecting discarded trash. A bright patch of purple irises against the hillside had caught the sun, and curious about them, a possible indication of pioneer homesites, Hayden had walked to them.

The old cistern had been filled in long ago, the iron mounts for the drawing bucket detached and lying on the ground. The oak trees had been thick with leaves, and squirrels had leaped from one branch to another, scampering down the trunk. Rubble marked the pioneer home site, overgrown with brush, the stone walls broken, the roof sagging badly under the weight of broken limbs and vines.

Cameron's flashlight weaved through the night, the beam unsteady. She was already in the woods bordering the rear of the property and moving fast. With his heavy-duty flashlight in hand, Hayden hurried past the gardens that had just been tilled, the stacked apple wood at the back of the property, and eased past the barbed-wire fence.

In the night, one misstep could cause Cameron to break a limb, or cause her to fall down into the dangerous, rocky creek bed. Fearing for her, Hayden called to her, "Cameron, don't move. I'll be right there."

Her flashlight winked through the tree trunks, closer now. Hayden thought of her bare arms and midriff, the thorns in the thickets cutting at her. If she fell into one of the clumps of blackberry bushes, or hit her head on a rock, or—

Suddenly, her flashlight beam blinded him. "Turn it off," he ordered curtly.

"Where is it?" Her words came breathlessly and desperate.

"I told you to wait. Goddamn it—" He ran his flashlight beam over her. Her bare arms were scratched, but she hadn't seemed to notice.

"I would prefer that you did not yell, and that you did not order me, and that you did not curse," she stated firmly.

"Oh, well, hell—" Hayden stared at her face, the tiny scratches on it, the way rubble clung to her hair, and yet she commanded a quiet, intense dignity, so proper, just that sturdy bit of Katherine emerging. "Are you hurt?"

"I'm covered in thorns from one end to the other. But hey, guy. That's not your problem, is it? Just where is this old storm cellar?"

"The only way you're getting there tonight, lady, is if you hold my hand." He wanted her safe, this Cammie of long ago, trusting him.

Cameron, the woman, had other plans. "I don't hold hands."

"You will if you want to see that cellar tonight. Here, hold my flashlight." He picked up one hand of her hands, searched the scratches, and turned it, removing the worst of the tiny thorns. "You step onto a locust thorn and it can go straight through those pretty pink boots. Some of them are a good three inches long, and they mean business."

"I don't want to hear about it—the lectures, I mean. I've had a lifetime of those," Cameron warned quietly.

"I'll bet you have—if you just do what you want, when you want. And sometimes we don't get what we want, now do we?"

"Rarely." The heiress was back, watching him take her other hand and inspect it, repeating the process. "Are we finished yet? Can we move on?"

He straightened and studied her. Then he swept a hand gently down each arm, brushing away what he could, feeling the thin scratches run beneath his fingers. Then taking the flashlight from her, Hayden crouched to lift her boots, checking them for damage. Cameron braced her hand on his shoulder as she stood on one foot, then the other. "That's really not necessary. I'd certainly know if a thorn had gone through my boot or not."

Satisfied that no thorns had penetrated the boots, Hayden stood and brushed the rubble from her hair with more force than necessary, uncaring that he'd shown his frustration. "You know, you'd drive a sane man nuts."

"Great. That would be quite an accomplishment, wouldn't it?"

She sounded as if she'd already thought of trying that, and Hayden wondered about the man. Her ex-husband? Robert? Him? "You're frustrating as hell. Okay, let's go possibly kill ourselves, running around at night on a hillside. But then, you just couldn't wait, could you?"

"No," she answered quietly. "I couldn't."

Within his hand, hers was long and fragile, light and cold, as he made his way over the dry creek bed, the pale orangish stones filled with tiny fossils that he'd collected as a boy from another place. A distant memory soared by him: Cammie had been fascinated with the tiny fossils, a boy's prized rubble of long ago.

One glance in the moonlight told him that Cameron cared little for the danger of a turned ankle on the rocks, or a fall in which she could hit her head. She leaned forward, her expression intent, that long body tense. The top button of the black leather vest had come unbuttoned, and the pale softness of her breasts cradled no jewelry, no small gold cross that she said she'd never take off—*My real daddy gave it to me. . . .*

Cameron glanced at him, found that momentary lock on her breasts and as she breathed rapidly, they lifted within the leather confinement. She slid her hand away from his, rubbing it. "How much farther?"

I'll never take this off . . . my real daddy gave it to me . . . Cammie had said of the cross.

"Where did you go just now?" Cameron asked too quietly, warily. "You were someplace else."

Hayden shook free of the memory and nodded at the rocky bank, overgrown with brush. "It's beyond that brush."

Cameron was tearing up the incline before he could stop her. Following her quickly, Hayden saw her standing in front of the brush. She turned to him, the black leather peeled back now to show the profile of one moonlit breast, the taut peak, the soft underside. "Where now?"

He came to stand beside her, tracing the light over a mound of blackberry vines, loaded with thorns. "We can't make it through that tonight—"

"Why not?"

Hayden cursed as Cameron waded into the briars, her bare hands pushing at them. One reach, and he looped his arm around her waist, lifting her free and back to safety. She strained against him, stronger than he had guessed, and lithe in his arms. Hayden turned and clamped her to him, waited until she stopped struggling. "We'll come back when it's light with some tools to cut the brambles away."

"I'm not leaving here."

Lifted up to him, her lips gleamed, those Celtic witch's eyes slanted, their angry fire burning him. The scratch running across her smooth cheek alarmed him, her hair silky as it tangled against his cheek and his neck. She looked as if she'd fight heaven and hell to get to that old cellar. *What rode her so desperately?*

Her body was trembling, taut in his arms. "We'll wait," he said quietly, waiting for her body to give, to flow into his. "That cellar has waited for years. It's not going anywhere. Tell me why it's so important."

"Don't you get it? You know so much, hotshot. . . . I was kidnapped and kept in a pit. I've hunted for the place for years . . . this just could be it . . . where I ended, and where I began." She'd turned her passion to him, anger lashing out at him.

"Then I'll help you," he offered quietly, and bent to brush his lips across her cheek, where a thorn's scratch marred her smooth cheek. He wanted to smooth away that terrified desperation, to comfort her.

"Help me? *Help* me? No one can 'help' me. I remember a pit of some kind, no more than earth and beams, and I remember waking up in the woods, terrified. And I was different—and she was dead."

"Your mother?"

"My mother," Cameron said firmly after a heartbeat, as if she were trying to make herself believe some fact that had eluded her. She rested her cheek against his shoulder, and the weary softness of her body flowed into his.

"If I let you go, you won't try to dig through those brambles now, will you?" Hayden whispered into her hair.

"What do you care?"

"I care. You're with me, and I wouldn't be much of a good

guy, now would I, if I let you tear yourself apart? What would your girlfriends say if I let you do that?" he reasoned carefully.

"I take care of myself."

"Sure you do."

She bristled at that, turning on him furiously. "I've always taken care of myself. I do it every day, in more ways than you can imagine."

There was a river of emotion beneath that statement, and Hayden wanted to examine every bit of it. "Okay. What ways?"

"I think . . . I think the gardener killed her, too. He committed suicide in one of the guesthouses, and some money was found with him. . . ." She looked up suddenly at him. "You're holding me too tight—I can't breathe. What is it?"

"I thought I heard something in the underbrush," Hayden lied, because the image of his father, covered in blood, lying on that floor, had just flown by his mind, because Cameron had just added a twist—her mother might have been murdered. *Was it possible that his father was also a murderer? Could Hayden have been wrong about his father all these years?* "What makes you think he killed her?"

Her body trembled, and she pushed her face into his shoulder, turning it side to side as if trying to erase something—"She had to die. I *think* she had to die—I don't want to talk about it anymore."

She had to die. . . . Katherine had to die. . . . There was nothing in the articles about foul play, nothing but the balloon had exploded in midair. According to investigator's report, the propane system had malfunctioned—or Katherine had been so distracted that she had somehow mishandled the controls.

If Hayden pushed too hard, Cameron would back away, close up, and the access to what he wanted would be gone. A patient man, he decided to play for time. "Come on. Let's go back and take care of your scratches. We'll come back at first light."

I think the gardener killed her, too. Why? Had Katherine been murdered? How?

Six

***MAYBE THAT OLD ROOT CELLAR WAS WHERE SHE'D BEEN** kept—where her life had changed and where the whispers had begun. . . . She'd hunted for it all her life. Surely the search parties would have been over the old Riordan place. Hadn't they? How could they have missed the old homesite, or the storm cellar?*

After her shower, Cameron tried to control her excitement . . . after all, she'd personally been through every root and storm cellar she could find in the area—hoping to discover a part of herself left behind, that special part she couldn't replace. Now she'd found it—the damp, cold pit where the whispers had begun, and now as she remembered everything, maybe they would go away.

The cellar, no more than a hole dug into a sloping hill and reinforced with rough, sturdy beams was overgrown and hidden. Nearby, the old house place was only rubble, covered in vines and infested with mice. And somehow it had been missed by the search parties. How was that possible?

Cameron shuddered, remembering the rustling noises of the mice, free to come and go as they wanted, almost like the whispers of her nightmares.

She gripped the edge of her freestanding bathroom sink

and studied her image in the mirror. "Where are you, Cammie? I need you. I need you, Katherine. Tell me what I need to know."

After treating her scratches, she pressed a button, and the wall encircling the bathroom space slid away with a slight hiss.

She found Hayden right away and braced herself; it wouldn't be easy protecting herself, avoiding revealing too much, after he'd seen her desperation and her reaction. And it wouldn't be easy waiting until dawn; the hours would creep by.

He stood in the bright light of her living space, near the front door. His T-shirt was torn; a large L-shaped tear in the jeans on his thigh said he'd paid a price for coming after her. *No one ever paid prices for her—she'd paid them for others all her life.*

The burden was too much: someone else injured because of her—wasn't Katherine's death enough?

On edge, Cameron didn't want Hayden to see that she'd been crying in the shower. *It never paid to let people see her fears, she'd learned that much from Robert; her weaknesses could be used against her.*

Cameron moved to a softly lighted panel, touched a button, and the lights clicked off as familiar shadows surrounded her. Standing in front of the mirror with the cross and the family pictures, Hayden glanced at her, shrugged, and lit the candle arrangement. The flames flickered, dancing over the pointed crystals of her large Brazilian amethyst and tangling in the gold of the Mexican citrine.

Candlelight danced up the thin gold chain on his finger as he studied that small cross, rubbing it between his fingers. He let it drop to sway momentarily, then still, before he turned to her. "Nice. Are those pictures of you with your mother?"

She didn't answer, too aware of his stare taking in the luxurious towel wrapped around her body and knotted at her breasts. It was more than a casual look, more like a man who would take anything, everything, a tough, dangerous man who couldn't be bought. But in her experience, all men could be bought—couldn't they? For a price?

Cameron shook free of the towel wrapped around her head and finger-combed her hair. "You don't have to wait here."

He lifted an eyebrow. "But then, I can't trust you to wait until daylight, can I?"

She walked to the aquarium, the plastic skeleton in the colored gravel bobbing with the bubbles rising around it. The skeleton bumped gently against the tiny castle. It seemed almost real, the gurgling reminding her of the final sounds of death. Guilt crawled upon her. Mama guppy would never give birth—because of Cameron's carelessness, her forgetful mind. "Where are my fish?"

Hayden spoke softly, "While you were in that so-called bathroom, I buried your fish beneath that fairy with the rose bouquet. There's a clamshell marking them."

She closed her eyes, grateful for not having to do the task herself. "That was nice. But I don't need a babysitter."

"No, you're too old for that, and for that trick you just played, running off into the night where you could have broken that stubborn, pretty neck. But then, you're used to doing just what you want and getting everything you want, aren't you?" Anger seemed to explode from Hayden; it quivered in the shadows between them, raw, undiluted, passionate.

"What's it to you?" Her comeback wasn't exactly smart, but it was the best Cameron could manage—just out there in the night, within walking distance might be the place where she'd been held, where she'd changed forever. Maybe there she'd find what she desperately needed and the whispers would stop.

Hayden walked to her. "You're rich, you're spoiled, and you know how to stir up a man. But tonight, I'm not letting you break your neck. Do it on someone else's time."

Cameron considered her "someone else." Ray wouldn't

do, or her girlfriends. Robert would find ways to get answers from them; each had a weak spot, if pushed hard, and she couldn't endanger them, or their lives. And overweight and out of shape, Madeline wasn't up to climbing the backwoods, to helping clear away brush.

Hayden was in perfect shape. "I'll pay you to help me get inside that old storm cellar."

Those black eyes flickered, wariness replacing the raw anger. "You need me, don't you? Isn't that sweet? What are you looking for? It must be good to send you running like an idiot through rocks and woods and blackberry bushes—at night."

A perfect stranger might do, a man unattached to the area, someone who would move on in his life, someone who probably couldn't be bought . . . but maybe there was another way and one her body needed.

She'd only really known him for three days and yet, because of the drama enclosing her, it seemed longer. Should she dare step over that forbidden edge, trusting her body to him and slowing the hours until dawn?

Reacting to her instinct and testing his, Cameron reached to smooth his forearm—his muscles quivered beneath her fingertips, and she slid her hand over the deep scratches down his arm. She touched the tear of his sleeve tentatively, probing just inside to trace the scratch, to get closer to him. Then, as he tensed, she smoothed the intriguing length of his arm, tracing all that power, measuring it against her own body.

Hayden's hand caught hers, staying her; he was obviously trying to gauge her motives, to dissect her. That wariness only heightened the challenge, her need to push his limits. She could deal with a man uncertain of her. Manipulative? Yes. But then, she was what she had been created to be, and now her instincts told her to push the moment, to hunt the hunter.

He was studying her face, trying to see inside her again, but then his gaze moved slowly downward to her breasts. "Don't you wear that cross?"

"No. Never. I did wear it once, for years, as a child." Her breath came faster, the air heating, vibrating between them. *Would one night with this stranger ease her?* She'd heard that sex could be medicinal in extreme circumstances, and Hayden was just a passing stranger, a man who would move on, but who could give her what she needed tonight. According to Hayden, he'd "been there, done that," and he'd been married. He would know about moving on, after the moment. And for centuries sex had been used to gain leverage.

Cameron had learned early to play that leverage-and-power game, but she'd never used sex. Perhaps tonight would be her first time to try.

Who was she kidding? She just wanted to step into Hayden's arms, envelop herself in that hard, powerful body and push the limits of being alive and a woman until dawn.

"But you don't wear the cross now. Now you wear charms or pearls, right? Pearls to suit the heiress and charms and bells to suit yourself? The statues, the fairies in back, are special, aren't they? The gargoyles and palm trees in front are just to take people off the track, but the fairies in back—those really matter, don't they?"

He eased one of the bells from her ear, then the other, tossing them to the collection of jewelry in the abalone shell. Her bracelet followed, leaving her stripped of her defenses. To make a fuss over such a small thing could arouse his suspicion. But then, Hayden was already considering why she wore them: "I haven't figured these out yet, but I will. I'm not that much up on New Age. But that's a lot of dream catchers, and you burn sage and sweet grass, so that means you want to purify this—where you live. And that means there's something you don't want near you, something that isn't physical and probably dangerous."

He was probing, too alert, and digging into her private world, where secrets were hers alone—and perhaps Robert's. But for now, Hayden had to be stopped. Cameron stood back and crossed her arms, her bare wrist a reminder that he knew too much already and wanted more, and that he wasn't taking a sexual offering without questioning motives.

It all came down to motives, hers and his, and everyone else's. Cynical perhaps, but then Cameron had cause. "Are you going to kiss me or not?"

His finger slowly traced the scratch on her cheek. Then both big hands slid down her arms, to circle her wrists. His thumbs caressed her skin, slowly, seductively. "Think that would work, do you? Ways to keep occupied until daylight? Something to take the edge off whatever is running through you. It's tangible, you know, the high-voltage excitement, the hunger for whatever you need out there."

"You talk too much." Cameron moved close, testing the heat between them, the rigid stance of that male body, the stiff heavy prod at her stomach. Sex in the arms of a stranger—protected sex—might give her a little ease, trim off a little of the tension, and after all, what else did she have to do until daybreak? Fight the nightmares and the whispers? Wake up shaking and in a cold sweat?

Then there was Robert, of course. Hayden was just another tool to send Robert into a rage. Calculating? Justifiable? Maybe. She could smell the hunger, the heat of Hayden's taut, tall body, and almost feel him inside her, taking her away momentarily . . . "I like getting what I want. Objections?"

"Not right now," Hayden murmured as he slid the towel away from her body . . .

She wasn't sweet, Hayden thought, as he tugged Cameron to him, taking her mouth, but she was ripe and fragrant, and he had no doubt that she was experienced, her body moving into his, her curves soft in his skimming hands.

As his thumbs ran across her breasts, she arched with a sigh of hunger, too eager for him, too quick to lock her hands in his hair, to open her mouth to his—sex with him was feeding something other than desire.

Hayden forced himself back and eased her away from

him. "You're moving too fast. I'm an old-fashioned sort of guy. I don't want to take advantage of your emotional—upset, now."

She was shaking, on the edge, and trying to draw back into her cool, haughty heiress veneer. Her fingers trembled as they pushed back a strand of damp hair from her cheek, evidence that she was definitely affected, despite her calm tone. "Really? I hadn't noticed."

"What about a glass of wine? A little talk, that sort of thing?"

"All that takes time," Cameron reasoned, because she didn't want him prowling around her emotions; she only wanted the diversion of good, honest sex, to be exhausted by it until the nightmares, the whispering, the child's plea for help didn't come.

"Take time," Hayden ordered curtly as he bent to lift her towel and wrap it around that quivering, warm, fragrant body. She frowned slightly, confused just that bit and it pleased him. Maybe that was because he was unsettled after taking in the dream catchers over her bed, hanging in front of the windows, the index cards taped to anything that needed directions to operate, a reminder on her doors to set the electronic alarms, the yellow sticky notes on her mirrors and the flurry of notes beneath her refrigerator magnets.

Hayden considered her. At a guess, with all the cleaning solvents and devices, the assorted vacuum cleaners standing at the ready, the spotless appearance of the kitchen, the neatly arranged refrigerator, Cameron was more than a little concerned with cleanliness. Her work space was almost too orderly.

She'd said she didn't want to get her hands dirty, and yet, she'd torn through that brush without regard for them.

The contrasts of Cameron were enough to make any man wary.

"Are you one of those?" she asked finally, crisp enough to show her anger, as she moved to a well-stocked metal wine rack and slid a glass from the ones hanging upside down. She expertly opened a bottle, French and expensive—if Hayden recognized the shape of the bottle and the trademark correctly—then filled two glasses and took one to him. She looked up at him, her eyes shaded and mysterious—witch's eyes, he thought again, full of spells and secrets as she said huskily, "It's a long night, and if you aren't leaving—we might as well enjoy."

The transition from a friendship with a child to that of making love to the grown woman was taking some adjustment for Hayden—and that nettled, because she still didn't recognize him. "Do this often, do you? Deciding to have a man, just like that—because the mood strikes you? Why, what would your mother say?"

Cameron glanced at Katherine's framed picture. She would have no idea of what could happen to little rich girls, of the dangers lurking with a misplaced word, one step out of the social pocket—how angry Robert could get. Cameron wondered then what her mother could have found in Robert; but then a sweet woman like Katherine could have easily been misled by a younger, outwardly charming man who wanted her fortune. "You're the first. But it's been an odd night, and in a way, I feel I owe you."

"Sex is a big payment."

"I'm used to paying big."

"I'll bet you are." He finished the wine quickly, his body too revved for this game. "If it's okay, I'd like to use your shower. You'll be here when I get out, of course."

Without a comment, Cameron turned from him and stared out into the night, the lights of Mimosa winding like a dotted ribbon in the distance, Somerton House topping that opposite hill to the west. That high-priced telescope would give an excellent view of both. *You don't understand,* she'd said.

As her temporary lover, Hayden might get that insight, he might be able to understand all those little discrepanies she noted as "odd"—

But then, his body was reacting to hers for just one purpose. Hayden traced the way the towel clung to her bottom, that slight indentation between those soft cheeks, and admitted that Cameron's secrets weren't his only attraction to her . . . and she was trouble all the way—unpredictable, feminine, tough, fragile, with rivers of emotions running beneath the surface.

And he intended to explore everything about Cameron, the woman, the heiress, the secrets she held—like how her deadly asthma had mysteriously evaporated and how that scar from a missing sixth finger wasn't there. But the ache low in his body was telling him that its needs ran to heat and tantalizing woman, not to her secrets alone.

"While you were in the shower, the telephone rang. I answered, and they hung up, the call back number blocked."

"Thanks. Probably just some wrong number," she said tightly enough to warn him that she probably suspected the identity of the caller.

While Cameron waited for Hayden to shower, she punched the message machine's blinking light and Madeline's voice was crisp, to the point: "Robert is back. He's got that Cheshire cat look. She must have been good. His new thoroughbred is coming in later, a personal delivery . . . probably a very personal delivery. He wasn't happy about his 'guest,' Mrs. Virginia Ulbrecht, being placed in the cottages during the party next week. So be prepared for one hot call."

Robert's angry message was next, a boiling curse that Cameron had long ago dismissed. But she didn't dismiss his threat, because she knew just what he could do: "Someday you'll go too far, push me too far, Miss Heiress, and then, you're really going to pay."

Evie's voice was next, with Fancy's and Phoebe's giggling in the background. "Woo-hoo, so Miss In Denial finally decided to make her move—Hayden said something had turned up and we needed to take the party somewhere else— He had to get up early, my ass. Woo-hoo, and we know what turned up, don't we?"

"And just how big *was* it?" Phoebe called.

Cat calls from Fancy and Phoebe sounded closer, "Booty call . . . booty call. . . . Details. . . . Call. Give."

"Hey, I'm due one. It's been years," Cameron stated to the message machine. William's message had been placed from some party where she would have been the "Queen of the Limbo." A later, quiet message said that he missed her and that party life just wasn't what it used to be. "And I miss Arabella. That little guy really kicks now. It's pretty exciting. She's even more beautiful than when I met her. I've been going to her doctor appointments with her. It's pretty mind-blowing. I started setting up some accounts for us. I want some security apart from family funds until my folks come around, and I'm thinking of the long run, something other than office work."

Then, to offset any interruptions, Cameron called Madeline's message machine. "I'm unplugging for tonight. Robert has already called and made his feelings known. Set him up with an appointment for eight in the morning. No, make that nine, I may sleep in."

If she found what she needed, what the rest of her life depended upon, if she could make the whispers, the pleas of her nightmares stop, she'd need a breather before facing Robert. If she found anything damning to him, she would have to think very carefully about her next steps . . . about sharing the secret outside her little duel with Robert.

Cameron smiled tightly and turned to look at Hayden's powerful silhouette behind the shower curtain. He hadn't bothered to use the sliding concealing wall, but the showerhead was adjusted higher for his height. In shadow behind the curtain, his body turned as the water flowed down his back—and Cameron shivered slightly, aware that she would soon discover the answer to Phoebe's "how big was it" question.

Robert would be in full temper tomorrow, unable to impress

the Kentucky woman with the horses. She'd discover his rightful position, as the man who married an heiress, who lived on her estate, who was on an allowance, who had no power, who could not remarry—because if he did, he'd lose everything.

The balance of power was delicate: There were ways in which both Cameron and Robert could lose, and each knew the weakness of the other.

She was a part of Robert. He had created her, and she knew the workings of his mind.

On the other hand, he knew her weakest spot, what she could lose.

Cameron pulled the telephone plug from its socket and turned off her cell phone. She wanted nothing to disturb tonight, and the hours until she just might find what she'd searched her adult lifetime for—the answer to the secrets, the whispering of her nightmares, and the means to make them stop.

She needed the missing pieces to those nightmares, the images from the cellar that she'd buried away to survive. But arriving for that morning business meeting with Hayden in tow, looking as if she'd been well made—and with information about the cellar where she'd been kept—might just send Robert over that precarious edge. He just might lose it and let slip what else he knew about the kidnapping.

Cameron went to the mirror where Hayden had touched the cross and slid her finger down the golden chain. On the other hand, if she had sex with Hayden, it was her business and no one else's, a little physical release in the middle of an emotional storm wasn't her usual, and frankly, it was a little frightening—Hayden was a powerful man. Yet the challenge and determination to control him offset her fear. A rather hard attitude for a woman, but then she'd never claimed to be sweet.

"A business arrangement, no strings?" she asked, when Hayden emerged shortly after his shower, wearing only his jeans.

As he came toward her, crossing the flickering shadows, he seemed almost ominous and deadly, the hunter prowling for answers. "This whole place usually is lit up, even when you're not here. Why not now?"

Some things were just for her and no one else, to remind her that she was still human, functioning as a woman. "Tonight is private. For me . . . for you. By the way, are you sure you're finished with your girlfriend and that you don't have someone else now?"

"Does it matter?"

"Not really. I just don't like messy situations."

He skimmed his fingers along her throat, her bare shoulder, then back up to trace her ear, smoothing the small hole where her earring had been. "I see. Everything clean and neat. So we're both healthy, consenting adults?"

She smiled at that, recognizing the businessman setting contract terms, an agreement to suit them both. "Yes."

"There's no girlfriend now, no potential 'messy' situation. And I'd prefer you didn't try to leave something on my pillow, a little payment, maybe? For services rendered?"

Hayden was a step ahead of her, because that was exactly what Cameron had planned to do, everything nice and tidy—He'd be repaid with a big fat envelope of cash, and that would end any residual commitment. "Would I do that?"

"No, you wouldn't, at least not the first thing in the morning—because you're going to be out there at dawn, aren't you? If you can move."

Startled, she tensed, as if she were taking a threat. "Why wouldn't I be able to move?"

He smiled tightly, because he sensed that it would be hours before his body tired of hers, and then only briefly. Hayden moved to the aquarium, lifted his wine glass, and drank slowly. When he was finished, he turned to her, moonlight from the open windows piercing the shadows between them. "Because I'm going to be with you every minute. . . . By the way, the aquarium's temperature was set too high."

Cameron frowned, and mentally retraced her movements earlier in the day. Had she changed the temperature? She hurried to the aquarium, searched for the index card that wasn't taped to the stand, her reminder of the correct temperature. She shook her head, but the bells weren't tinkling, and fearing the whispers that came haunting her when she was upset, Cameron placed her hands over her ears. "I am very careful about that. I thought I had overfed them."

"No. It was the temperature—way too high." Hayden was studying her again, taking her apart, trying to see inside to the contrasts, the heiress people called "odd." "Take it easy. You're shaking, and you've just turned pale."

"I wish tomorrow would come now—right now," she whispered unevenly, and walked to the windows overlooking Mimosa. She couldn't remember changing the temperature—but then, she was forgetting and misplacing so many things these days.

Cameron rubbed her arms, felt the scratches run beneath her palms, and thought of the darkness, that one sliver of light coming through the boards that had formed a door, blocking her away from freedom. That place was out there somewhere in the night, beckoning to her, wanting her.

She sensed Hayden behind her, felt his heat seep into her bare shoulders. "You can tell me about it," he offered quietly.

She shrugged, accepting the loneliness of her guilt, the futility of changing the past. "I was six. It was the night of my mother's and Robert's first anniversary party, and I was taken while I slept. I was kidnapped for two weeks. They had already paid the ransom, then my mother went up in a hot-air balloon that exploded in the air, and she was killed immediately. They found me wandering and dazed in the woods after her funeral—on the day of her funeral."

"You told them about where you'd been held?"

Cameron waded through the years and the shadows, the truths and the lies. "Not just then. I guess they couldn't get anything out of me, even the investigators. I couldn't remember anything clearly, except being hungry and scared. I was under a doctor's care for a long time—years. I was pretty well isolated, away from the press and gossip. I must have been a real mess—confused. It took years to bring me back, but I had tutors—and Madeline. It was a long time before I started—"

Hayden almost spun her to face him, his hands locked to her upper arms. "Then you started to remember? What did you remember?"

No one but Robert knew exactly what had happened. Wrapped in their duel, a third party could tip the balance, either way. She just could lose—Robert knew how to pick his allies and search out their weaknesses, which were usually buyoffs. She'd known for years that Robert had made a clean sweep of the household staff and Mimosa for anyone who might question his management of Somerton. "Lay off."

Hayden tugged her to him. "And if I don't?"

"Then you'll have to come to the investors' party at Somerton House next week. It's just a little soiree—black tie, of course—to show Somerton's appreciation, and to do a little business."

"You like to take chances, ride on the edge, don't you? Testing the limits?"

Cameron had lived on a precarious edge since she'd started to remember what had happened in that cellar, where the whispers had begun. For tonight, Hayden offered an opportunity to escape until dawn.

She stood on tiptoe and rubbed her lips against the edge of his jaw. She thought of Hayden—rugged, big, intelligent, confident in who he was—compared to Robert's wealthy elegance. Her hands slid to his jeans, fingers just inside his waistband, and tugged him closer. "I'd pay for escort services, well over the going rate. Just think—a night with an heiress. Doesn't that appeal?"

Hayden's lips turned to hers, and his hands slowly moved over her breasts to slide away the towel. "Maybe I'd like that payment now."

Cameron wasn't expecting the slow exploration of her lips, the rubbing of his cheek against hers, the way his big hands pushed back her hair from her face as he studied her closely. His gaze slid downward to where their bodies touched, that thrust in his jeans resting against her stomach. Heat danced around him, that certain sensual anticipation that said they were going to make love. Then his lips were on hers, his tongue following the edge of her teeth, and playing with her own gently, as he simply held her head within those powerful rough hands. "How long has it been for you? You're shaking and hot, as if one touch—"

Could she really do this? Take a virtual stranger to her body? Despite her boldness and her plan to upset Robert, Cameron trembled at the edge, fearing to trust, to give herself. She wanted to retreat, to dress and separate herself from the man who, right now, knew more than she wanted . . .

His hands slipped down her body, strong fingers gripping her hips possessively, and then one hand lowered, his finger touching her— Cameron inhaled, caught the unexpected sensations as they hit her, tightening her inside; she arched up, lifted her arms to his shoulder, and locked herself to him. She could retreat, or she could— Against those hard lips, she whispered, "Do it."

"Do *you,* you mean? That's not very romantic."

He was teasing her just that bit, and Cameron couldn't resist returning the favor. "Oh, please, please, I'm begging you, sir, please make love to me, make me swoon with ecstasy. . . . And I've got condoms in the bathroom—an assortment. Probably something in your size. They're my ex-husband's. He stayed here a few months ago, hoping for a rematch that didn't happen. I wasn't too sure I wouldn't feel sorry for the guy and give in."

"That's nice . . . sweet." Hayden's mocking tone said he wasn't really thinking of "nice," and that suited her. He lifted Cameron into his arms and carried her to the bathroom area.

She reached to ease aside the mirror and retrieve the

package. "My, but you're such a big strong man, carrying little old me."

"And you're full of it." Hayden carried her to the bed and dumped her on it. He watched her scramble beneath the sheet and coverlet, drawing them up to her breasts. She'd been warm in his arms, the heat of desire pounding through her, but now her face was flushed with something else, and Hayden recognized it immediately. She turned away from that brief satisfied smile.

"Shy? That's a surprise," Hayden murmured as his weight depressed the wide bed. "But then, you're full of surprises."

At that, she wiggled around and produced her towel. She looked at him, challenging him, while she lifted the towel high and dropped it to the floor. "But if you'd rather not—"

"Oh, I'd rather." Hayden slowly unzipped his jeans, and let her see exactly what she was getting as they dropped. Her eyes widened, taking in his erection, and she breathed quickly, staring up at him. She wasn't saying No as her hand reached to curl around him.

Hayden's body jerked involuntarily at her inviting touch. "I guess you could call this romance," he said as he stepped out of his jeans and moved quickly, pushing the sheets and coverlet away, to lay over her.

"You're doing just fine," she said against his lips as her hands smoothed his back. "Now get busy."

"Yes, ma'am." Slowly, he eased one leg between hers, then the other, the tip of him prodding between her thighs, seeking entrance as his hands moved over her breasts, his thumbs rubbing her nipples as they peaked. And all the time, his body was moving into hers, gently, firmly, filling her. "Okay?" he whispered rawly.

She dug her fingers into his arms and waited for the pressure to ease. But with Hayden's mouth on her breasts, she felt herself tightening, fighting the unexpected current that peaked and hit her wave after wave.

"That was very effective," she whispered unevenly as Hayden watched her closely, his body taut upon her, muscles quivering in his arms, his expression grim.

"Sweetheart," he said finally. "We've just begun—"

Hayden sat watching the woman who slept soundly in the rumpled bed. Dawn was just rising in the east, slipping its fingers westward to the Somerset mansion, the lights of Mimosa glowing softly in valley shadows.

The dream catchers, leather circles of feathers and beads, caught the fresh air from the high, open windows, turning as slowly as Hayden's thoughts. He hadn't felt gentle, blood pounding in his head and elsewhere, needing relief. But he hadn't forced Cameron into anything; she'd fought to come to him, fingers digging into his back, her body arching and tightening. She'd fought against releasing herself to him, and he hadn't been satisfied with a partial accounting.

Cameron might move on, but would he erase last night? Wish that it had never happened? No.

In Cameron, he'd found more than a woman with secrets—he'd found an exciting hunger—and a tenderness—that he had to explore, some special bond that he didn't yet understand.

He frowned slightly, his feet propped on the bed as Cameron stirred, looking defenseless, a slender hand by her head on the pillow, her body curled like a child's.

But she wasn't a child . . . she took what she wanted. But for that matter, so had he, in equal measure.

A contrast of cold and hard against soft and fiery, Cameron had been sweet in his arms, flowing against him, her breath coming fast against his shoulder. In his bones, Hayden understood that making love to her had changed his life forever.

And dammit, just as years ago, she appealed to the protector in him. In her sleep, she'd cried softly, "I'm so sorry, Cammie. I won't ever forget you."

What would she do when she discovered that he was really H.J., the gardener's son? Honor demanded that he should tell her, explain to her, but once she knew his real identity, that would end everything. Cameron would close up, sealing him away—

Then, there was still that fine edge of anger riding him, because Cameron still hadn't recognized him as H.J.

Hayden ran a fingertip over his lips, and the sweet taste of her lingered there. According to the newspaper clippings and from what she had said, Cameron Somerton had been missing for two weeks before she'd been found, some distance from here. Dirty, scraped raw with briars, she didn't know who she was and had taken months to recover physically. . . . The child had been on drugs during the kidnapping and drugs were used again to keep the terrifying memories from her—she hadn't been able to identify her kidnapper—but then, she was sleeping when she was taken, tied and blindfolded, from her bed. With the exception of her birthday parties, she'd been in seclusion for years; private tutors and special doctors were her only outside contacts. Robert DuChamps had become her guardian and his rules had been strict for access to the child—protecting her, he'd said in an interview.

Cameron, the woman, a mixture of contrasts and secrets, stirred; she sighed and her eyes opened, staring blankly at Hayden for a moment.

Then she rolled out of bed, landed on her feet, and hurried by him. For just that instant, as her curved nude body sailed by him, Hayden almost reached out to snag her, to capture her for a little morning-after.

He watched her tear folded underclothing from a basket, slide into it, and tug on jeans and a T-shirt, a long-sleeve shirt over that. She quickly fashioned a ponytail, secured it, and glanced at him when she sat to pull on her pink boots. "It's almost light. Let's go."

Cameron apparently had forgotten what had run so hotly

between them just hours ago, and that nettled. Hayden rose slowly to his feet, aware that his body wanted hers, had hardened with desire. "I want to check your scratches first . . . put more antiseptic on them. Then we'll stop at my place and pick up some tools—"

But Cameron was already flying out of the door.

"Dammit." Hayden pulled on his jeans, socks and boots, grabbed his shirt, and hurried after her. He managed to catch Cameron at the edge of her fairy garden; he spun her around and hefted her over his shoulder. Out of breath and frustrated as she squirmed and cursed at him, he walked back to his house. The light slap on her rear brought immediate silence, her body taut. "We need some tools, sweetheart. It won't take long. Don't make this hard on yourself, because this time, we're doing it *my* way."

"Spanking won't do, Mr. Olson. Neither will manhandling. I am not pleased at all." The statement was wrapped in haughty elegance, but then, the lady was a well-bred heiress, wasn't she?

She hadn't been that lady last night; she'd taken what she wanted, what they both wanted. And that did a lot for a male ego. Hayden smiled and shifted her slightly, burrowing his face against her bare midriff; he nuzzled her playfully with his morning stubble and growled. Cameron squirmed, squeaked, and the sound he heard just could have been a muffled giggle. She was trying not to smile when he shifted her down in front of him, tugged her to him, and stood holding her in his arms. He slid his finger along her cheek, easing a strand of hair behind her ear. "It's the morning after, honey. Give me a break. I 'manhandled' you plenty last night. I even picked thorns from your butt with my teeth, and I've just discovered your secret."

He hadn't expected the fear in her expression, the brief trembling of her body. "Like what?"

"Like you're ticklish."

She frowned slightly and looked puzzled as though she

were trying to understand why she had laughed, when she'd just been so desperate. Hayden got the idea that she wasn't often derailed from what she wanted, and that really hiked his good mood.

"You're all woman, too," he added gently, then rubbed his lips with hers. He tasted that momentary hunger, the gentle softening in that darkness deep within him, as her body leaned into his, trusted him.

Was she starting to remember him as H.J.? Hayden held his breath and wondered what would happen next, how he could explain that as the gardener's son, he needed closure—but that everything that had happened between them last night was genuine and nothing to do with who she was.

Suddenly, Cameron's arms were around him, her body pushed against him so unexpectedly, that Hayden braced himself. Her kiss was more desperation than passion, as if terror locked her to him. "It will be all right," he said unevenly when she was finished, shaking in his arms. "I'll be with you."

The lady emerged, cautious, doubting, enunciating perfectly as Cameron asked, "You've had a lot of practice telling people things will be all right, haven't you? Your ex-girlfriend?"

"My little sister," he answered honestly. But Gracie wasn't the only one young H.J. had tried to reassure—he'd tried to make himself believe that after their lives had been torn apart. *Cameron suspected that Katherine Somerton had been murdered: "She had to die." Was his boyhood hero, his father, really a murderer, too? Was Paul Olson out early that morning to sabatoge that balloon?*

"I have to know if that is the place," Cameron whispered desperately, and placed her hands over her ears as if something were calling her, and she didn't want to hear. "And I'm afraid that it is."

"I understand. You need closure. Most people do." But Hayden was thinking about the missing ransom money,

Cameron's belief that Katherine had been deliberately murdered, and his own father's death. *Had Paul Olson really desired Katherine, enough to kill her if he couldn't have her?*

Hayden muscled open the cellar's old wooden door, the rusted hinges sticking firmly to the rough wood frame. When the door was shoved fully open, the instant movement created a vacuum, and a flurry of dust hit the bright morning sunshine, enveloping him momentarily.

The silhouette of a big man, enveloped in sunlight and shadow leaped from the past to chill Cameron, and every fear she'd held since her childhood came hurling down on her, pressing her breath from her lungs.

She had to run, to escape, but fear had locked her boots to the ground. The man had come to bring just enough food and water, just enough to keep her those two weeks. A forgotten memory hurtled at her, taking away her breath again. It wasn't two weeks; it was only eleven days—she'd only put eleven pebbles into that old glass jar.

When the kidnapper had opened the door, the sunshine had blinded her, and she couldn't see his face . . . but he had seemed so big, towering over her, terrifying the child she was then. . . . She'd cowered against the farthest wall, making herself small, his husky whisper threatening her. . . . Then twice she'd slept, drugged after eating the food that rarely came. . . . The second time, she'd awakened out there in the woods, terrified—

Hayden had turned to look at her, and it was then that Cameron realized she'd cried out. The childlike cry still echoed in the towering oaks and mimosa trees around the storm cellar, skidding over the vines and sumac brushes. Cameron couldn't define what she'd said, couldn't explain the chilling fear, in spite of the sweat she'd gotten by working through the brush with Hayden. *This place was where the whispers had begun and now they were calling her even more strongly.*

"I was wrong. This isn't the place," she lied, her heart pounding furiously, her mind locked on those eleven days of fear. . . . *But the newspapers and Robert had said fourteen days, hadn't they?*

Cameron forced herself to walk away slowly, when she wanted to run as fast as she could. She could almost feel the whispers reaching out to her, calling her back. But not now, not with Hayden so close and seeing too much. He already knew too much, and she had to protect herself. She sensed him watching her, his mind clicking across the distance, trying to unlock the puzzle she must present to him.

She had to be alone to sort through the past, that living nightmare, to silence the whispers.

"I'm so sorry, Cammie," Cameron whispered as tears streaked her face, to the child locked away in that cellar so long ago.

She closed her eyes and the image of that big man, silhouetted by bright sunshine years ago, appeared behind her lids.

The gardener had admitted he was guilty, and he was dead. Could he have somehow murdered Katherine, too?

Seven

"THE HELL IT ISN'T THE PLACE WHERE CAMMIE WAS HELD," Hayden murmured as he looked out the farmhouse window, just hours after he'd seen Cameron's startling reaction to the old storm cellar. Mimosa lay quietly in the sloping valley; on the opposite hill, the Somerton mansion caught the afternoon sun.

Using a makeshift desk, he sat at his laptop, answering the business e-mail necessary to keep Grow Green Lawn and Garden running. As a top man in research, development, and acquisitions for a growing chain, Hayden couldn't completely step away from his top corporate position; e-mail and online conferences usually sufficed when working remotely. He ran through a checklist for the Oklahoma City grand opening—but his mind swerved back to Cameron.

How could he work, actually concentrate on new developments, when his mind was constantly on Cameron Somerton? And his body had that restless, taut feel, needing more of hers? In the hours since Cameron had walked away from that crude cellar behind the farmhouse's garden, Hayden had made several discoveries. He was too close now to the trail—to the woman—who could lead him to the answers he had to have. A woman with dual personalities who had caught something inside him in those hours of lovemaking, some tenuous hold on him other than sex.

An elusive woman, Cameron was sensuous one moment, haunted by shadows the next, and the next, a tough female seasoned by life. Nothing fit when it came to Cameron Somerton, an irritating, intricate feminine contradiction of her life as an heiress.

He studied the old fruit jar, the glass bluish, and the eleven pebbles in it. He'd watched Cameron's stiff back, the way she stumbled when she could have avoided that rock, and that told him that she wasn't watching her path. But then, that stark white fear on her face, the trembling of her body, and her instant tears had already told him that this was the place she'd been held for two weeks.

Hayden had counted the pebbles in the jar. *Two weeks was fourteen days, not eleven—but then, a child, probably drugged for the kidnapper to handle more easily, could be mistaken. She could have been drugged for several days, losing track of time.*

After Cameron had gone, Hayden had brushed aside the spiderwebs with a stick and gone into the storm cellar. A gleam in a small pile of rubble had drawn him, and the prod of his stick had exposed the jar and the ribbon inside it.

Washed now, the old fruit jar with its glass lid and a wire to clamp it closed held those mysterious pebbles. Hayden shook the jar slightly, rattling the pebbles and wishing they could give him answers. "Oh, you were there, Cameron, and you aren't a good liar. Not when it comes to your kidnapping."

Hayden typed an e-mail to his mother and sister; both worried about him and what his stepping into the past could bring.

He studied the barn a distance away where Cameron had closed her windows, the ceiling-to-floor blinds and the privacy glass providing her own impenetrable capsule. Whatever she was going through wasn't sweet, and Hayden had decided to give her time to recover.

He inhaled roughly, his emotions churning. He'd become her lover, or her escape for a night, and his senses told him to go to her, to comfort her—

Cammie Somerton had that tiny scar, the little bump on the edge of her hand, and Cameron's, the adult's, hand was smooth. The pencil in Hayden's fist cracked in two, reminding him that he needed answers about his father, and tidbits of the trail all led to Cameron. She thought that Katherine had to be murdered. Why?

His time with Cameron, pushing her, would be short, because Robert DuChamps would likely recognize him, and the old antagonism would renew. The relationship between the son of a suspected kidnapper and that special kidnapped heiress would be questionable in anyone's eyes.

The sound of a revving motor drew him to his front window. Cameron's pickup had just soared down her driveway toward the main highway, tires skidding, the rear fishtailing to hit an old hedge fence post—but she hadn't stopped, hadn't checked the damage. From his front porch, Hayden watched that white pickup drive onto the highway without pausing. A state patrol car swung in behind her for a time, then veered off to a cafe parking lot. It appeared that the Somerton name afforded protection.

Hayden grabbed his binoculars and traced the pickup, until it suddenly stopped in front of the stately Somerton House. While Cameron was taking that long shower to recover from her shock, Hayden had listened to her messages and knew that Robert DuChamps was back and angry.

From what her friends had said, Cameron and Robert were clearly at war, and their meeting this morning wouldn't be sweet. Hayden ran his hand over his chest where part of him ached for her. He watched a brightly colored male cardinal flitter to the ground, the duller shade of a female a short distance away, both foraging near a hog wire fence overgrown with honeysuckle vines. Male and female, that's all Cameron and Hayden had been in those few hours away from reality.

After viewing that root cellar, Cameron had been shaking and pale, her sky-blue eyes wide and glassy with fear.

Hayden ran his hand down his jaw, the sound of stubble scraping at the silence and his thoughts; he didn't like the mix of his emotions—his body still revved, remembering hers, wanting more, a guilty contrast to his determination to use her, as the key, to get whatever information he could about his father's death.

He needed to stay near her, maybe protecting her from Robert. If Cameron were to discover his identity now, or cut him off, he needed to keep a link to her . . .

With that thought, Hayden posted a special request to his garden catalog editor in St. Louis.

"Was it you, Robert? Did you set up that kidnapping? Or did you get that gardener to do your dirty work for you? Did he put me in that hole, or did you?" Cameron demanded after she slammed the door of Robert's bedroom closed for this very private battle.

Robert was sitting on the bed and tugging up his knee-high riding boots. His black silk shirt was still open, revealing the thick gold chain resting over his smooth chest. He'd probably had it waxed in his visit to an exclusive spa—one of the pleasures that Cameron had endorsed because it meant that he wouldn't be near, giving her a breather from their ongoing war.

The pillow beside his was mussed, a woman's black lace teddy lying near it. Whoever his current "lady friend" was, she was probably local and easily beckoned.

If Cameron pressed them, the household staff would provide the woman's identity. But Cameron didn't care who the woman was, just as long as this interview was quiet. The vacuum cleaner humming in the hallway said that housekeeping was at work and the noise would shield any yelling arguments she might have with Robert. When she could, Cameron tried to spare others the hatred between them. She went to the luxurious bathroom with its quartz counters and elevated whirlpool bath, scanned the room, then checked the large walk-in closet to find no one in it.

She turned to Robert, who stood now, but hadn't bothered to button his shirt. Taller than she, he always used his height to threaten her, but it wasn't working this time as Cameron defiantly faced him.

He picked up his riding crop and tapped it against one palm. His eyes took in the dirt on her jeans, her boots, the T-shirt, covered by a long-sleeve man's shirt. "You're dressed like a tramp, Cameron. Have some pride. Try to remember that you are Katherine's daughter."

The steady tap of that riding crop was intended to threaten, but Cameron wasn't a child anymore. "Does she—the woman you're using now—let you use that on her?"

He walked closer, lifting her chin with the tip of the crop. "Jealous?"

There was always that hint of sexual interest since her teenage years, when it had become more blatant—

And when she'd started to remember, when she'd started to piece the whispering sounds of her early nightmares into the fabric of her life, her role. . . .

"Tramp," Robert said quietly, turning her face with the crop, inspecting it. "You look different. . . . Softer . . . all lit up. You looked like that after your honeymoon and for a few months while you were married to William. You spent the night with your renter, didn't you? He must be special to cause you to come out of your nunnery and fornicate with him, after just three days."

"Fornicate." How like Robert to put the dirtiest spin possible on lovemaking, Cameron thought darkly. She pushed away the crop from her face. "It was convenient and quite enjoyable. You like that special convenience with someone, a local, don't you? We're alike in that, aren't we? We take what

we want, when we want it? After all, you taught me so much, Robert."

He slapped the riding crop against his thigh. "You had those mustangs shipped from Montana, didn't you? Do you have to collect every odd damn stray thing that is discarded? Don't you know that my thoroughbreds might tangle with them?"

"*Your* thoroughbreds, Robert?" she questioned quietly. "I think my name is on the purchase papers."

Anger crackled around Robert, his face lowered to hers, his eyes burning her. His fingers bit into her wrist, twisting it. "It won't do for you to act like a tramp here, bitch. Watch it."

The pain in her wrist was bearable; she'd had worse from him. She'd learned to grow cold and to be detached when his anger flared, and now Cameron counted on those early years of experience, dealing with "her guardian." She lowered her eyes to where his fingers bit into her wrist. "Let me go, Robert. I may need you, but your days of hurting me are over. Don't push it."

She watched him debate her threat, hover on the edge of raising that riding crop and striking her. Then suddenly, Robert released his hold, finger by finger. Cameron walked to the big window overlooking the stables, the sweeping white fences of the land she had inherited. Standing in front of that window—the owner of all she surveyed—was just one of the little knife-twists, a little reminder to Robert, that she could hold her own in their duel: Robert merely resided in Somerton House as long as he did not remarry; he was a man on a leash, one with a healthy allowance, indulged in most things—a tenuous position and one Cameron could destroy—*if* she wanted to destroy her own life.

In those few inches between them, the uneasy struggle for power palpitated as if it were alive.

"Tell me what I want to know, Robert, and I just might pasture those mustangs away from Somerton House. Did that gardener kill Katherine? Let me rephrase: Did *you* pay the gardener to kill Katherine?"

His angry answer slapped at her. "Why on earth would you ask that? It was an accident. And the gardner was dead hours *before* Katherine."

But she'd caught that brief hesitation, that throb of the vein in his temple; she'd learned to read him very well through the years. "How convenient. But things can be arranged. *Were you, or were you not involved with that kidnapping?"* she demanded.

Robert's teeth flattened against his lips. "Now that would be telling, wouldn't it?"

"Just remember, Robert, that if anything happens to me, Katherine's estate will go to charities and end your grasp on her money."

Robert's face came close to hers. "When my thoroughbred arrives, my guest isn't staying in the cabins—Virginia Ulbrecht *and* her Jack Russell—are staying in *this* house."

"Not a chance. Not in your bedroom and not in a guest room. Take it or leave it. If you decide you want to challenge me on that, I'll make certain that Virginia knows who really pays for things around here."

That crop rose, quivered briefly with Robert's anger. Then he lowered it, slapping his palm. "Why don't you go back to your little honeymoon in that barn and leave me alone?" he asked tightly.

Cameron walked to the door, anchoring her hand to it because she was so angry she could have attacked him. "He was very good. I could . . . fornicate . . . like that, with him, for hours—in fact we did just that," she said, because it was the truth, and because Robert had never had her, despite his attempts to seduce her in her teenage years. "I think I have what I need from you—"

"What's the reason you came here this morning?" Robert asked abruptly. "You're usually more controlled—but then, a person as odd as you are needs to keep control, don't you? What set you off?"

Cameron managed to keep her tone level, but anger caused

her to tremble. She lifted her chin and turned to face the man who had terrified her, whom she hated for the unforgivable. "I found the place where I was kept. You probably could have told me where it was all these years, couldn't you?"

He spoke too quietly, the tone deadly. "If the gardener did it, how would I know where it was?"

Not, where is it? Not, are you sure? Not, not, not . . .

"That's something I intend to find out. I do know this: The ransom was two million, and only five hundred thousand was found on him. It would be interesting to know where the rest of the money went, wouldn't it? Take a note, Robert: If I *ever* find any evidence that you killed Katherine, or were connected with her death—I won't care what happens to me." Shaking with anger, certain that Robert knew something about the kidnapping, Cameron stepped outside his bedroom and closed the door.

Madeline was walking down the hallway, talking on her cell phone, her other arm cradling her laptop against her. She looked at Cameron and clicked the cell phone shut, tucking it in her jacket pocket. She rushed toward Cameron, her expression deeply concerned. "Fighting with Robert again?"

"How did you guess?" The question was curt and rhetorical; Cameron's mood—bristling, flushed, and shaking with anger—could be easily seen.

"Give me some credit. I recognize the signs by now. Want tea and sympathy? He's a rat, honey. You have to not let him get to you. I just wish there were some way you didn't have to put up with him." Madeline panted as she hurried upstairs with Cameron.

"Yes, well, I do. I found the storm cellar where I was kept—"

Madeline's eyes widened as they moved on to the second story. "You did? You've been hunting for years for that. How? But honey, they searched everywhere for you. Are you sure?"

"I'm sure. There are things I can't remember and things I can. That storm cellar is one that I can. The food was drugged, and someone took me out of there and left me in the middle of the woods. I remember being terrified and—then it's a blank for years. *Years,* Madeline. I lost years after that kidnapping. While other kids were having a childhood and playing ball and having overnight parties, I was too busy coping with Robert—my dear guardian."

Madeline tugged Cameron into her office—Katherine's former office, which Cameron had reclaimed when she'd first started fighting Robert, wresting his control over the estate and settling in to manage it herself. And then she'd started to scrape away his involvement with Somerton business affairs.

The older woman held Cameron, soothing her. "Cameron, he's a bastard. I'll find some way to get him out of here— If he'd only break one of the contingencies, marry someone, write an unauthorized check, or something like that. They were only married a year, but Katherine's attorneys were wise to advise her to put those clauses into their prenup."

Cameron shook her head, remembering how badly Robert had seemed to want to hit her with that crop. "He's not going to do anything to endanger his 'paycheck.' But I'll find a way to remove him from this estate if he hurts any of the horses, any livestock, any person on this estate."

"He wouldn't dare." Madeline drew away slowly and smoothed Cameron's cheek. "Honey, your earrings are missing, those cute little bells? Did you forget them and your bracelet?"

Cameron eased away. She'd been forgetting too many things, and Madeline had covered what she could, protecting Cameron Somerton, the eccentric heiress who had been kidnapped and ransomed. Hayden had removed the earrings the night before, and in the morning, her mind was on facing down Robert. "I'm changing my style. I don't know what yet, but bells may be out. . . . Madeline, do you think that gardener could have killed Katherine, done something to make her balloon explode?"

Her expression troubled and thoughtful, Madeline shook her head and frowned. "The investigation said it was an accident, perhaps a malfunction of the propane system, and something about her being so preoccupied that she may have not paid close attention to what she was doing, but the propane tanks somehow ignited."

"I'm certain that it wasn't an accident."

Madeline's eyes widened, her voice hushed. "How do you know?"

"I just do. How is the investors' dinner coming?"

Clearly upset by Cameron's statement, Madeline ran down her clipboard list. "Everyone on the guest list has responded. We're set, I think . . . caterer, bartender, string quartet. Did we forget anything?"

Cameron had forgotten so much lately.

"Order roses and plenty of them—for Katherine—and pink, her favorite color. And see if you can't come up with a swing band for a little later, will you? I know it's short notice, but it might liven things up a bit. There's a nice dance floor in the conservatory. Have the band set up in there and have some of that local minibrewery beer there and Mason's Winery has those small bottles of sampler wines so that the guests could take some home. Better yet, ask the winery to make each guest a basket of mixed wines. Those handmade split-oak baskets from that craft shop?"

"Good idea, Cameron. Support local merchants, right?"

"Investing in a microbrewery and in a winery wouldn't be a bad idea for us to consider, do you think? And it wouldn't hurt to oil the wheels for the chunk of money I'm going to ask each one to donate to my inner-city kids program—and by the way, if Virginia Ulbrecht turns up, she is Robert's guest, not mine. If there is any problem over where she stays—and that is in a guesthouse—call me."

Madeline sighed heavily as Cameron continued, "Let's just cancel any plans for breeding Jack Russells that Robert may have, okay?"

"But Robert will—"

"I don't care." Cameron leveled a look at her assistant. "I intend to start squeezing Robert out of Somerton."

"You're asking for trouble, babe," Madeline warned.

"Yeah, I know. Great, isn't it?"

An hour after going over the seating arrangements with Madeline, Cameron had returned home to kneel beneath the fairy with the rose bouquet. She placed her hand over the clamshell marking her fish. "I'm so sorry."

The slight afternoon breeze stirred the leaves above her, around the fairy statues, and she could almost feel the beckoning of the cellar, could almost hear the whispers of long ago, circling her, begging her. "I promise I will—"

A shadow fell over her and after an argument with Robert, a chill of danger shot through Cameron.

Would he dare hurt her?

Only if he had the chance.

Only if Robert didn't stand to lose his easy, luxurious lifestyle. . . .

"How's it going?" Hayden asked quietly.

Cameron swallowed the fear clogging her throat. She took her time, dusting her knees of rubble, then stood facing him. The lime scent of Hayden's aftershave was crisp against the earthy scents around them. Her image filled those black eyes, shadowed by his lashes. She could feel him waiting, wanting something, and he was too close; he'd seen too much of her fear earlier that morning.

Hayden smoothed a strand of hair away from her throat, and she thought of how he'd breathed against her, his heart pumping heavily in the aftermath of lovemaking, his body heavy and tangled with hers. Even now, she wanted to be close to him, so close that nothing else was real. She wanted to stroke that smooth, gleaming skin over his cheekbones, feel the rougher texture of his jaw, and fold herself into him where only the beat of his heart, his heat, and his strength were her world, her reality.

But she couldn't let him into her unforgivable reality, what she had done. Hayden was too perceptive and dangerous to her now, when she was riding on nerves, when she had just found the cellar where she'd been kept.

"It's over. We're done. Thanks a lot for the entertainment," she said crisply, determined to cut any tie with him, the hunter who saw too much.

When her war started full force with Robert, she didn't want Hayden caught in the cross fire; she had to protect him, and that would mean sending him away.

" 'Entertainment?' " Hayden's tone seemed more like a warning growl.

Used to acting out her games, protecting herself, Cameron shrugged. "It killed a few hours, didn't it?"

His "Uh-huh, if you say so" had a sharp, irritated edge. After battling Robert, Cameron wasn't up for arguing with another even more powerful male. "I'm asking you to be discreet. If I owe you money or anything, let me know, okay? No one needs to know about us last night or . . . or anything else."

But then Robert already knew that she'd suddenly taken a lover, didn't he? How did he know everything so quickly?

Hayden's head tilted slightly, his expression taut. "Uh-huh. So that's it, huh?"

"Sure. One-nighters happen all the time." His black eyes burned her, anger vibrating off him in waves. She'd tried to sound flip, as if the heat and the tenderness of last night, didn't matter, because if it did, she could be open to needs like every other woman.

But she wasn't every other woman, was she?

Hayden's fingertip lifted her chin. "Not with me, honey. You were into it. So was I. You were reaching out to me, and you needed more than sex. I know the difference, and you're not someone who gives yourself over easily."

She needed Hayden so desperately right now, just to hold her. Cameron lifted her chin away and folded her arms across her chest as she stepped back, using the space between them—and her lies—as an invisible wall. "You don't know me at all. I was faking it."

"You're *faking* something right now." Hayden suddenly turned and walked toward his house; the set of his shoulders beneath his shirt was taut with anger.

The cellar overwhelmed Cameron's every thought, and she needed to return, to try to remember everything. But that afternoon, after hours of prowling her barn and waiting for Hayden to leave his place, she couldn't return; he remained working in his backyard and would surely see her.

Cameron didn't want to expose her horror to him again; she needed privacy to step back into the past. If she could remember everything, face her demons, not as a child, but as an adult, then maybe the whispers of her nightmares would stop.

William Van Zandt was just the temporary relief Cameron needed.

Tall, lean, sun-bleached blond, and perfectly dressed in a navy polo shirt over his tan chinos, his bare feet in loafers, he stepped from the late-model white Lincoln Continental and stood looking at her barn. He looked every bit the playboy image, right down to the way he removed his designer sunglasses. With the Oklahoma prairie wind plastering his shirt against him, he could have been standing on the deck of a ship, rather than on Cameron's dirt and weeds.

William turned to take in the man heaping brush into a pile behind the farmhouse, then grinned at Cameron as she stood on her front porch. "What is this, lost-and-found day?" she teased.

"Hi, sweetie. You told me to come anytime, and so I did," William said as easily as though he'd only been away from her for a few hours, instead of months. "Who's the bloke with the muscles?"

That "bloke" was someone who knew Cameron had been watching him—Hayden Olson. Though he couldn't have seen through the privacy glass, periodically he'd turned to look at her window. Without his shirt and wearing his jeans, Hayden looked rugged, tough and in an obvious snit as he alternately cut brush and piled it behind the old garden.

Cameron systematically ran through the reasons she'd cut him off: Maybe he didn't like her brush-off. But then, she'd been dominated by one man for most of her life, and she wasn't taking on another—because Hayden was no sweetheart, and he was dangerous to her in every way. He was too perceptive, and she had to guard herself. She continued her reasoning; it all made sense: They'd had sex; the moment was past. He'd realize that he wouldn't want to get involved with her complications; he'd move on to someone more accommodating. And Cameron had gotten whatever fix she'd needed to continue her life. She'd spent a few hours keeping away the nightmares, and she'd definitely gotten to Robert, his jealousy obvious.

She had to focus: Scoring a hit on Robert, claiming her own power, backing him off was essential to her survival, and more important than a night with a man who already thought he had certain rights. He didn't.

But then, just because he was staring at William and her, and because she just had to show Hayden that one man was as good as another—Cameron let William sweep her into his arms and answered his steamy kiss with her arms locked around his shoulders, her body pressed tight against his. She tasted the boy she'd loved once, the friend she had now, and leaned back to laugh up at him, smoothing his hair with affection. "You're breathing hard, William," she teased.

"Now that was a surprise. May I ask why?"

"I just wanted to see if I still had it."

"Too bad I'm taken, old girl."

Inside her barn, Cameron moved away from his arms and smiled; she was certain that Hayden had gotten a good look at that kiss.

"I'd sure like to know what's going on." William held her

hand, lifted it to his lips, and applied his charming but predictable best.

"What did you bring me?"

"Mercenary," he teased, then wandered over to the window overlooking Hayden's backyard. "I've always wanted to— That chap is working rather hard, isn't he? All sweaty and dirty? Who is he?"

"A renter. Where's my present?" William always brought just the right thing to cheer her up, and she was glad for the distraction.

"It's in the car. I'll get it."

William left the house, and Cameron polished off her necessary e-mail, closing down her computer. When he didn't return, she went outside and scanned the cars, her overgrown yard, and found William talking to Hayden.

"Oh, no!" Cameron hurried inside to be shielded as she looked at the men, who seemed to be enjoying each other. William got on the garden tractor, and Hayden was obviously giving a quick lesson in running it. William tested the riding lawn mower, then, with the air of a boy delighted with another new toy, removing his shirt as he strong-armed the rototiller in Hayden's new garden.

With an air of defeat, Cameron hurried out to the car and retrieved the only thing that could be her present, a big cooler loaded with her favorites—hard Italian cheeses and sausages, crusty breads, and berry cheesecake. She looked at the men in the distance; William was too engrossed to notice her, but Hayden shot her a dark look. So he was mad; things weren't going his way, so what? He had her ex-husband enthralled, didn't he?

"This is heavy, William," she called, irritated at both men.

"Have at it, sweetie. Don't wait for me," he returned cheerfully.

"Okay, fine. Do your little-boy-buddy thing. See if I care," Cameron muttered, and muscled the big heavy cooler out of the car and onto the dirt. She struggled to drag it into the house, then slammed the door. She rummaged through the contents, sliced a piece of the berry cheesecake, then ate it as she stood watching the two men, who were obviously bonding.

Then, impatient with William, she punched in his cell phone number, watched him frown and walk to where his shirt hung from a branch. He flipped open the phone, turned to her house, waved, and grinned boyishly. "I miss you, too," she said sweetly. "Are you coming back soon?"

"Hey, you could come on over," William suggested heartily. "This guy knows his stuff. We're going to take down a tree this afternoon. I get to use a chain saw."

"Chain saws are dangerous, William. Your parents wouldn't be pleased with their one and only heir endangering himself."

"Yeah, well they're not happy with me now, anyway. Got to go. . . . Hayden wants to show me how to change the line on a weed eater—damn big suckers."

Aware that she'd lost the battle for William, Cameron sighed, "Be careful, William."

"Love ya, babe. Hey, Hayden, do you think Cameron could come over? She could help. She's a really strong girl."

In the distance, Hayden smiled at her window, and William said, "Hayden says he'd really like that."

Cameron had begun to wonder if Hayden could actually see her—he'd been able to pinpoint her location through the privacy glass. "I'll pass. I need my rest. I'm working at the bar tonight. We're kicking off our Fourth of July party. Will I see you before then?"

"Gotta go. I'm into this, sweetie. See you later."

William, her friend-brother, had forsaken her for Hayden, and that irritated. A little later, the two men had moved inside the farmhouse. William had answered her second call with a hurried, "We're changing the faucets on the sink. Man, this stuff is fascinating. Yard stuff and house repair. . . . I'm into it. Talk with you later. Hey, is it okay if we eat some of the stuff I brought? Or maybe you could cook something for us?"

"Dream on. Leave some cheesecake for me and don't forget to put it in the fridge this time." William's fascination with Hayden grated. Hayden wasn't taking the hint to stay out of her life—he was actively adopting her ex and probably priming William for information the same way he'd done with her friends.

When Cameron started her nine o'clock shift at Al's Bar, William still hadn't returned to her house. By ten o'clock, the place was busy and noisy with talk of Fourth of July picnics and fireworks displays. Phoebe was sipping her usual strawberry daiquiri at the end of the bar, brooding about Jack Morales, an ex–rodeo cowboy with no intention of settling down. Apparently, from the bruise on her cheek, Jack hadn't liked the marriage question, but Phoebe didn't want Cameron's lecture or her help.

Phoebe eyed the two men entering the double doors, then studied Cameron, who was glaring at them. Hayden met that glare impassively, then raised two fingers, signaling two beers. The little come-here crook of his index finger nettled. William and Hayden settled around a tiny secluded table, and William had never looked so relaxed.

Now *that* irritated even more, and Phoebe noticed Cameron's expression immediately. "I never would have thought you'd be jealous of your ex."

"Yeah, well, William came to visit *me*."

"He wants you back. Everyone knows that. How can you refuse to even consider that when he's so rich and good-looking? Of course, Hayden is not unappealing himself. So what's the deal with you two, after that little party at his place?"

Cameron had already recognized Phoebe's interest in Hayden. "We're off. Been there, did that. He's yours."

"Boy, you move fast when you're in the mood for a guy. Or when you're not." Phoebe studied her. "So . . . are we still friends if I make a move on him?"

Cameron popped the caps off the beer bottles; the German brand was William's favorite, and very expensive. She'd make certain that the tab went to Hayden. If he chose to come into her territory, it was only justice that he take the consequences. "Feel free. Here, take this beer to them and tell William I want to talk with him."

Swinging the beer bottles, Phoebe moved toward the men's table, her hips swaying and her red cowboy boots moving to the two-step music on the jukebox. When William came to the bar, Cameron smiled tightly and slid a filled beer mug to the cowboy at the end of the bar. "Having fun with your new buddy?"

"He's great. Knows how to fix just about anything. I could get into that really easy."

"Hate to spoil your big plans, chum, but you're the heir to a fortune. Think again. You're destined for board meetings and hoisting cocktail glasses on private yachts."

William was set to argue. "You're working here, aren't you? I wouldn't exactly call this high-class employment."

"I like the noise and the people. And I like getting paid for something that isn't attached to my heiress status. Besides that, they say I'm odd, so I take advantage of that. Sorry, hon, but you've got none of the unexpected in you."

His "Yeah" was flat and accepting. William's sullen look said he recognized the truth when it slapped him; he studied Hayden, who was now laughing and obviously enjoying Phoebe's flirtation. "Great guy. I admire him."

Then he turned and took Cameron's hand as she was wiping the bar. "Look, if you don't have the time or room for me, just say so. I'm sure that Hayden wouldn't mind—"

"But I've got the air mattress all ready for you."

"Want to play bounce?" he asked with a boyish grin. When she shook her head, William lifted his beer in a toast. "For old times, then. I'm sort of tied up anyway. The funny thing is, I never saw myself as stirring spaghetti sauce in the kitchen, or rubbing Arabella's back. I like the quiet times, just us."

"I think you like the whole deal, right? If and when she's around us, drop the pseudo-come-ons, okay? I know you're joking, but she might not."

Hayden watched William talk intimately to Cameron; they obviously cared for each other. She easily accepted William's light kiss, her hand stroking his cheek, and Hayden recognized the slow burn of jealousy he hadn't really experienced before. *Just how much did she care for William, and where would he sleep at her place?*

That was *her* choice, Hayden reminded himself as he stood to dance with Phoebe, just close enough to make his point to Cameron that this was a game two could play.

Then she upped the stakes, stepping up to the bar and doing that long-legged, sensual dance in her tight black sweater and jeans and pink Western boots. Her smug glance at him said she knew she'd gotten to him.

As he settled back to watch Cameron, Hayden ran his finger around his mug, making it whine. The lady liked to play games, but she was going to lose the one between them.

William hooted, and Phoebe wasted no time, also stepping up to dance on the bar. The music throbbed heavy and fast, and Hayden settled back into the shadows. When William took the offer to dance on the bar, between the women, Hayden realized that they'd done it before.

And Cameron was making it crystal clear that he wasn't the only man in her life. The "faking it" comment burned him. The next time, he promised himself darkly, he'd make certain she *knew* the difference.

She wasn't getting away with that "faking" comment, Hayden decided again at two-thirty in the morning as he sat on his front porch. Cameron's white pickup had just pulled into her driveway and parked beneath the plastic palm trees.

William had stayed at the bar to ride home with Cameron, and the thought of her in another man's arms wasn't pleasant. William might be about to become a father, and in love with his girlfriend, but still, he'd been Cameron's husband and—

Hayden didn't want to think about what exes did or didn't do when alone; he just knew from making love with Cameron that sex wasn't on her daily menu. And he knew that he wasn't taking her brush-off; he was certain that Cameron was the key to his father's death, and she'd intimated that Katherine's death might not have been accidental. *She had to die. . . . Why?*

As Cameron's laughter erupted, Hayden remembered her "faking it" comment. That grated—she'd been right with him during lovemaking.

Spending time with William had given Hayden a unique insight into Cameron's friendly relationship with her ex-husband. Their "accidental" meeting had been at a Hyannisport social event, introduced by none other than Robert, who had then invited William for a stay at Somerton House.

Maybe Hayden was out for a little revenge on the "faking it" comment, but whatever his motives, he wasn't leaving Cameron alone; she wasn't discarding a night of lovemaking with him that easily, not without repercussions. And there was no mistaking her reaction to the storm cellar. Hayden intended to push Cameron until she gave him what he needed.

Cruelty to a woman scarred by her childhood kidnapping? Maybe, but from what he'd seen, Cameron was holding too many answers that he wanted, and he wasn't backing away now.

When William spotted him and waved, Hayden called, "Hey, William. See you tomorrow?"

"Yeah, great. Hey, want to go out to breakfast at the cafe with us? Say 'tenish,' mate?"

"Tenish would be fine." Hayden noted the way Cameron placed her hands on her hips, glaring at him. She wasn't happy, but neither was he.

While William went inside, Cameron walked to Hayden's porch and looked up at him, her hands on hips. She stood in the moonlight, her face in shadow, the slight breeze toying with the tendrils that had escaped the knot clamping her hair, her long legs braced apart. "Stop bothering William."

Hayden didn't need to see her expression; she was all charged up and hot, and he'd gotten to her. And he intended to do more than that. "He's a nice boy that, a good mate," Hayden returned in William's jargon just to irritate her. "Tenish in the morning with you and my new mate, how much better can life get?"

Then harder, with a demand that came from his gut. "Where's he sleeping?"

Cameron marched up the steps and pushed his boots from the stone enclosure, then settled back against it, her arms over her chest. "None of your business."

If she was set to take any argument head-on, Hayden would give her one. "It *was* just last night. Your turnover is quick."

"Not so quick. Last night was last night. Hours and hours ago."

With one movement, Hayden reached for her and tugged her to straddle his lap. He caught her butt in both hands, holding her tightly against him. Maybe a little bit uncouth for handling an heiress, but then he was feeling raw. Her dance had been sensual, twisting, sliding, rubbing against William's body. Those pink boots had been beside his shoes, his hands open and low on her stomach, her butt against— "Do you dance like that often—for the men in the bar?"

Cameron's hands dug into his shoulders, bracing herself away. "When I feel like it. Leave William alone, or you'll have to deal with me."

"I'd like that—dealing with you. You're damned irritating, Ms. Somerton. Why didn't you take his name?"

"Figure it out: I'm the only heir to Buck Somerton's fortune. Mother kept his name . . . I keep it, too."

Hayden hooked his finger into the neckline of her sweater and tugged her closer. He caught her awareness, the way her lips parted, waiting for a kiss. "Most of the time you hole up in your castle over there. Then the rest of the time you're at Somerton House. What does working in that bar do for you?"

"I like the people, the noise, the music, and I sometimes get to play amateur therapist. Do you have a problem with that?"

Hayden tugged her a fraction of an inch closer, felt her breath quicken upon his lips, noted the way her lids lowered, and her intimate warmth rocked upon his hardness. He'd made his point: *She wanted him.*

And that was all Hayden wanted as he lifted Cameron to stand, then walked into his house, closing the door behind him. "Irritating, fascinating little witch," he muttered as he settled in to finish off Cameron's favorite cheesecake, and tried not to think of where William was sleeping. . . .

The sound of breaking glass startled him, and Hayden's boot trapped the rock that had rolled toward him over the shards. "That will cost you, landlady," he yelled through the broken window.

Her hand gesture wasn't friendly.

William's problem—to sway his wealthy parents into accepting his working-class pregnant girlfriend, Arabella—and the details of the investors' dinner occupied the next three days. July turned hot and dry, and Cameron was forced to delay her revisit to the cellar, something that needed to be very private with no interruptions.

Hayden had left for Oklahoma City right after a very awkward breakfast in which the two new "mates" had exchanged cell phone numbers. At one point, Cameron had returned from the cafe's ladies' room to find them in deep conversation about Arabella and her unborn child, and that irritated. When she had settled at the table, the men had ignored her and continued talking, William clearly receptive to Hayden's "Do the right thing" advice.

William had not been nearly as receptive to her identical advice. With depressing swiftness, the men had bonded.

Since Hayden was still in Oklahoma City, preparing for the

grand opening of a new store, the time was perfect for Cameron to return to the old cellar, to face that awful past, the whispers that crawled out more frequently now to terrify her—

As soon as William's Lincoln was out on the highway, Cameron called Madeline and cleared her calendar for the morning. "Anything wrong, hon?" Madeline asked immediately. "Are you sick?"

"I just have to take care of a few personal things. I'll call when I'm back in pocket," Cameron said.

Madeline was instantly alarmed. "'Personal'? Can I help?"

Within minutes of soothing her friend, and herself, Cameron was hurrying back to the old cellar—where her life ended, and where it began, where she had changed forever.

The plank door hung opened on its rusted hinges; the dark shadows filled with the past, whispering to Cameron, drawing her into a time she had forgotten for all those childhood years.

A spider hurried up an exposed shimmering web, as intricate as the patched bits of her memories: Food came, she ate, she slept. She cried, small and helpless against the door barring her from freedom.

Mommy? Mommy? Help me. I'm afraid. I'm cold, Mommy, and it's dark here. Why, Mommy? Why did they put me here? Mommy?

Cameron's growing fear tightened within her, the need to turn and run into the sunlit shadows. But unable to move, locked to this place where the whispers had begun, she stood at the doorway of the cellar, watching that spider scurry into the darkness.

She wasn't in a nightmare this time. The afternoon sun was warm upon her back, but the chill of the time she'd spent in the cellar reached inside her. This time, the darkness was real, the smells of earth and moldy wood the same as she remembered. The roots growing through the rotted board ceiling, supported by sagging beams, seemed to reach out to her. . . . Her heart pumped wildly, her face damp with sweat, her body trembling. Locked in that doorway, between the sunlight and shadows, she could barely breathe. The whispers were waiting for her, churning around her in daylight. . . .

Mommy? Mommy?

Panicked, Cameron backed away from the doorway, from the memories and the roots reaching out for her, terrifying her.

Then, bracing herself, she forced herself to take those few steps back to the doorway.

Because she had to know everything; she had to recapture those pieces of her memory lost here, where the whispers began.

Behind a stand of new sumac brush, someone else was watching. Someone who understood Cameron's fear, someone who knew everything.

Cameron was standing in front of the old cellar, her legs braced apart, her fists clenched at her side. Though the intruder couldn't see Cameron's face, her shoulders were shaking as if she were crying.

Moving slightly to one side to see better, the intruder stepped on a branch. It cracked, startling birds in the trees.

The intruder held very still as Cameron glanced around suddenly. Tears showed on her cheeks; her face was pale, her eyes huge and haunted.

The heiress who had everything was visibly afraid. Of an old root cellar?

The intruder scoffed at that, but then Cameron was known to be eccentric. After all, what kind of a woman mourned fish? What kind of woman believed every sob story she heard, shelling out money easily?

What kind of an heiress lived in a barn with gargoyles and fake palm trees and fairy statues in the back?

Hatred churned and tightened the intruder's gut, for the heiress had everything and had never worked a day in her life. *Cameron Somerton didn't deserve all her money.*

When she was in a sanitarium, she wouldn't need anything at all, but the drugs to keep her sedated.

Tripping those eccentricities of Cameron's forgetful mind had become an obsession to the intruder, and so had her money.

After five days of preparation for Grow Green's grand opening in Oklahoma City, Hayden drove back to Mimosa. The corporate detail work had been necessary, but so had removing himself from next door to Cameron and William. Then, too, Hayden wasn't exactly certain of his control where his need for answers was concerned, or his need for her.

He really couldn't afford to spend the time away from business; the grand opening was tomorrow. But according to William, the Somerton investors' dinner was tonight. Brooding about his parents' dislike of Arabella, and missing her, William had left yesterday morning, because he did not ever want to see Robert DuChamps again. "If I do, I'll beat him to a bloody pulp for hurting Cameron," William had said. "I promised the old girl I wouldn't. I want Cameron and Arabella to meet someday, so that Arabella can see the better side of me that Cameron brings out."

In the three-hour drive from the city to Mimosa in the east, Hayden had plenty of time to think. He focused on the party tonight; sparks were certain to fly—between the hostess and himself. Robert DuChamps was back in town and certain to be at the party, acting as host. Hayden's hands tightened on his steering wheel as he drove toward the Somerton mansion. He glanced at the rearview mirror and recognized his father's features, marked by his mother's darker coloring. *Would Duchamps recognize Paul Olson in his son?*

The pickup's steering wheel creaked slightly, warning Hayden that his grip had tightened dangerously with his emotions. While William did not want to cross paths with

Robert again, Hayden had picked tonight for the perfect, civilized time to warn Robert that it was gloves-off time.

On the drive back to Mimosa, Hayden had wondered how Cameron would react when he arrived. Just as he had unfinished business with Robert, he also wasn't finished with Cameron, a woman of oddities and dual personalities, who led a double life. A woman without asthma and missing Cammie's sixth finger scar and bump, a woman who didn't resemble Katherine in any way and who didn't remember H.J.

He had so many questions . . . *Had Cameron gone back to the cellar? Had she cried? Why eleven pebbles and not fourteen?*

Had Hayden's father killed Katherine? Had he really kidnapped Cammie?

Was it that mystery that drew Hayden back to Mimosa—or was it because he'd had a taste of something he didn't intend to lose—

When Hayden had arrived at the farmhouse to change his clothes for the party, her pickup was gone.

He found it parked directly in front of the mansion. The luxury cars parked in the Somerton driveway indicated that the party probably wasn't going to be casual.

In the second week of July, Somerton House was lit up. Evie was standing at the door, dressed in a black slacks suit and white gloves, greeting guests as they entered the big double doors.

Involuntarily, Hayden's gaze traced the shadowy road leading into the woods, the place where the gardener's home had been. How many times had he ridden his bicycle down that road?

For a moment, time spun away, and Hayden looked at the neatly clipped English maze. He was young H.J. again, desperately seeking his father and running through the maze. Though it was evening with stars twinkling above, Hayden could imagine Katherine's red-and-blue hot air balloon lifting slowly into the rising sun, leaving the shadows on the ground. That early morning, the big *S,* the Somerton logo, and Katherine's signature script beneath it could easily be seen. Katherine's white neck scarf had floated out of the basket—

Had Katherine Somerton's "accidental death" actually been murder?

The guesthouses were still on the estate, four in a row, lights glowing softly within. A man and a woman had just emerged from one, then stood outlined in the doorway as they kissed. They walked to the white board fence enclosing a pasture where horses grazed. Then some quirk in the evening breeze, some lapse in the crowd's steady conversational hum, some gap in the string quartet's music allowed the man's voice to carry to Hayden.

The tone was softer now, rich with a Southern drawl.

In another time, the man's voice had been hard and cutting as he lifted ten-year-old H.J. away from his father's body— Robert had been furious, his anger lashing at the boy. "You little bastard . . . get out of here."

A boy pitted against a man's strength, H.J. had refused, shaking his head as tears burned his eyes. "No, sir. I'm not leaving my dad. Give me back his note."

Robert had smiled coldly. "A confession note of a kidnapper, one who committed suicide? Get lost, boy. I'll handle this. You'd better tell your mama to start packin' her bags, because no one is gonna want her around after this. . . ."

And they hadn't. Aided by pressure and lies from Robert, Mimosa had closed its doors to the Olson family.

Determined to meet Robert again—this time man to man—Hayden quickly moved up the wide curved steps leading up to the plantation-style home. At the double-wide doors, Evie grinned and looked him up and down, taking in his dress suit and shoes. She opened one door and swept her hand toward it. "Looking good, Hayden. The party started at eight, so you're an hour late, but she'd definitely want to show you off. Go right in. You don't need an invitation.

Missed you, guy. Had fun with William, though. He's gone . . . left yesterday. He usually evaporates when Robert is around . . . hates his guts."

Inside, Phoebe did a muffled appreciative, "Wowser. You clean up good."

Hayden sampled a glass of wine from the tray she held, then sipped and rolled the slightly smoky taste on his tongue. He took in her short black dress, the red crocodile western boots, and said, "Thanks. Not so bad yourself. Having fun?"

"Nah. But the pay is great, and we can take home whatever isn't used, except the rose arrangements. Cameron likes to keep them around. Lots of pink ones in memory of her mother. Hey, that wine comes from a local vineyard—Cameron is promoting them tonight. But if you'd rather have a beer, she got stuff from the microbrewery here."

There was a party, just like this one, only with Katherine playing hostess, when young Cammie had been kidnapped from her bed while the guests had enjoyed themselves downstairs.

"The wine is fine. Thanks." His mother had dressed more modestly, serving the guests at Somerton House while, at home, Paul Olson had cared for their children. . . . She'd come home with heaps of leftover desserts and fancy dishes, tired feet, and an aching body. Paul had seen to her carefully, preparing a soak for her feet, carrying in the food from their old pickup and putting it away. Then they'd sat together on the couch as he rubbed her feet, and they talked intimately—

Was Paul Olson, a family man and loving husband, a kidnapper? A murderer?

The pieces didn't fit, just like the different facets of Cameron didn't fit.

And where was the rest of that ransom money?

"Hey, tall dark and handsome. Don't look so grim . . . it's party time." Phoebe leaned closer and whispered, "I'll be home later if you want to drop over."

"Thanks. But I've just put in a hard five days at work. I'll probably turn in early. But I'll think about it."

"You do that, honey."

The huge foyer was filled with pink roses, the magnificent crystal chandelier sparkling above the oval room, and memories swirled around Hayden as gently as the soft violin music. Hayden thought of Katherine's private rose garden a distance away from Somerton House, a tall iron fence running around them and her first husband's mausoleum. Katherine had tended the roses herself, only asking the gardener for help when necessary. A candid photograph of them, kneeling beside a rosebush, had been Robert DuChamps's only proof of Paul Olson's desire for Katherine.

Cammie had wanted to help tend the roses, but the field of pollen outside her carefully monitored world was too dangerous, and the roses never came into the house—back then.

Young H.J. had strict orders not to enter that iron fence, but he had, to pick a bouquet for his mother on her birthday.

He'd been scolded; but when his father had apologized, Katherine wouldn't hear of it, taking his mother a start of the roses for her own garden.

Hayden pulled himself back into the present and took in the small clusters of well-dressed people beyond the foyer—in the main salon, chatting while holding drinks.

"I hear Cameron's mother was a special lady," he said to Phoebe as he continued to study the house. It had been redecorated into simplicity, stripped of the heavy drapes, the ornate furniture and Big Buck's outsize, ornate chair of longhorn cattle horns. A life-size portrait of Buck, Katherine, and Cammie had dominated the main salon. It had been surrounded by paintings of western cattle drives, of buffalo on the prairie, all in gilt frames. There had been collections everywhere, those of the Texas oilman and investor and those of his Southern-bred wife, a woman who had loved thoroughbreds and racing.

Where were all those remnants of the previous owners? Could they lead to answers?

"Like mother, like daughter," Phoebe said cheerfully at his side. "Look, you're not taking me up on anything, are you? I've made it pretty clear that I'm available."

"You're sweet and good-looking—"

"Now that's a turn-down, if I ever heard one . . . just a step above 'interesting personality.' " Phoebe studied him for a few heartbeats. "Can't blame me for trying. You're right . . . Cameron is special, and you guys definitely set each other off—I saw that at the bar, the way she was trying to get to you, flirting with her ex, and the way you took it. Yeah, she said 'it was a moment,' and she's definitely bothered about something."

Hayden nodded; Cameron had been more than bothered, she'd been terrified.

Phoebe leaned slightly against him, speaking confidently. "She's special, isn't she? I don't mean the money, but how she cares for people. She bought my house and pickup for me, you know—I needed wheels for my rural route. But you just never can figure her sometimes—what sets her off, why she has those dark moods, why she won't live in a super place like this. . . . They say she's eccentric, that the kidnapping caused her to get messed up. Well, Robert sure wouldn't make it easy, I guess—gotta go."

When Hayden didn't encourage more conversation, Phoebe moved into the next room, and he returned to his memories. He remembered Cammie running up the dual winding stairways to the upper floors. He and Gracie had come to Cammie's bedroom, taking those stairs in awe—and he'd gotten another scolding for sliding down that polished banister.

Hayden studied the guests, one by one, then found Robert fawning over a woman, turning on his notorious charm. Robert hadn't aged—still sleek and handsome, the gray wings at his temple emphasizing his dark complexion and the trimmed moustache adding to his dashing appearance.

Hayden forced down that momentary rage, his mind flooded with memories. He breathed slowly, purposefully, because tonight he would face the man who had evicted his family, who had started rumors of Paul Olson's lust for Katherine, who had slapped a boy mourning his dead father, hard enough to send him to the ground.

Cameron moved between Hayden and the man he detested. She stood in the doorway to the salon filled with guests. When she turned slightly and locked on to him, the smile on her face froze momentarily, then slid away. She said something to the guest near her, then seemed to brace herself before walking to him.

As her eyes narrowed furiously and pinned him, Hayden slowly, purposely took in her simple black dress, the tiny straps crossing her shoulders. Her hair was swept into a smooth chignon, and she wore diamond earrings that matched a wide, choker-style necklace that ended in an elegant pearl drop. The hand holding an elegant champagne glass trembled a bit, setting off the twin diamond tennis bracelets. Her legs were long and bare and tanned and ended in a diamond ankle bracelet, high strappy heels, and a muted mauve polish on her toenails. She placed the glass on the foyer's polished table laden with pink roses in a cut-glass vase and put her hands on her hips.

Cameron reminded him of the chandelier overhead—dazzling in beauty and style, filled with sparkling facets, brilliant, hard and cutting, and dangerous.

"You weren't invited," she stated coldly.

Hayden lifted his glass in a toast to her, but he didn't feel like being kind. "We were almost in bed when you invited me, remember? Or have you forgotten that little bit of history? You look good, by the way."

"You're here to make trouble, aren't you? Or here for a payoff? Or maybe both? Let's go into my office, and I'll write a check. I don't have cash now, but I'll want a signed agreement that you'll be discreet."

Without waiting for his answer, Cameron turned and quickly moved up the winding stairway leading to the second-floor landing. Hayden watched her for a moment, the low cut of the back of the dress contrasting with the modest bodice, the material swaying around her hips, caressing those long bare legs. His body clenched, remembering them around him.

Eight

"LET'S CUT TO THE CHASE, SHALL WE?"

Cameron moved swiftly across Katherine's office, her heart pounding. Hayden's unexpected appearance, dressed to kill, would excite any woman—much less the woman who had already experienced the powerful body beneath his clothing.

Just the sight of Hayden, standing in the foyer, had sent ripples of awareness through her body. The lock of those black eyes on her had been relentless as she had walked toward him, her senses and her anger spiking. As Hayden had followed her up the stairs, she'd felt the weight of that stare on her body, the undeniable response within her own.

She had told him it was over and he was here anyway. Did Hayden think he had the right to interfere with the very public side of her life? Did Hayden actually think it would be that easy to announce he'd been her lover? Cameron heard the click of the office's heavy door, and a chill ran up her spine. Her fingers trembled as she reached for the hidden key that only she knew about and used it to unlock the drawer containing her personal checkbook. "How much?"

"I love it when you talk tough," Hayden stated mildly, and walked to the large windows overlooking the estate, the pastures, and the English maze. The office's muted light, the huge cream-and-mauve roses near him, did not soften those harsh features, the slash of his cheekbone, the lock of his jaw. Tall, looking tough and dangerous, he appeared a harsh contrast to the feminine office.

He ran a fingertip slowly over one large mauve-and-cream bloom, and Cameron inhaled sharply, remembering that finger tracing her nipples. Hayden's eyes darkened instantly, as if he, too, remembered caressing her body. She turned her head, shielding the hot flush of her cheeks and when her hand reached for the checkbook, it wasn't there.

No one else knew where she kept the key. Hurriedly, Cameron opened another drawer and then another, and the checkbook lay on top of the winery's brochures. She must have misplaced it after writing her latest check, one to Fancy for her mother's most recent health crisis.

Cameron fought to calm her leaping fear. She'd written the check on the day she'd first seen the cellar in daylight—and upset, she'd just tossed the checkbook on top of the brochures.

Or had she?

Hayden was standing in the shadows, outlined in the windows, his face unreadable. "Problem?"

Cameron's fingers trembled as she wrote the check, very carefully replacing the checkbook in the proper drawer. She was forgetting too many things, and just tonight had left the water running in her bathroom sink. If Phoebe hadn't come to check on her and used the toilet, the bathroom would have flooded. The incidents were small, like misplacing her address and scheduling book, usually everyday things, and the number of incidents was increasing.

"I have no problem at all. We had a business arrangement after all, no strings. And I'm asking you to stick by that and be discreet." Cameron held the check out to him. She was usually very good at protecting herself, but her voice seemed thin over the soft music downstairs.

"Used to doing this all the time, are you?" Hayden asked, as he slid his hand slowly, sensually, over the full mauve-and-cream blooms. "Having a one-nighter, relieving a little pressure, and then the check-writing–buy off scene—you as the heiress, dismissing your . . . utensil?"

He moved to her desk, and the burn of his eyes went deep inside her, where Cameron hoarded that private woman with genuine needs. "Take it," she ordered, and wished the check didn't quiver in her trembling hand.

She couldn't stand and move away; her legs were too weak. Hayden, one hip braced against her desk now, one hand on the desk, the other on her chair, blocked any escape. "If I didn't know better, I might think you didn't want me now," he murmured as that long prowling finger moved down her hot cheek to her throat.

"I have guests downstairs. Whatever game you're playing won't work."

His finger slid inside her bodice, gently caressing, just between her breasts. Those black eyes flickered, with anger and with something else. "But it's the best game, isn't it? You like that, don't you? Playing on the edge?"

"You should know. Tell me, how does it feel to score with an heiress? Did you tell your buddies and compare notes? Did you tell them you were coming back for more?" She could feel the excitement that caused her to feel like a woman stir—

"Now, that wasn't sweet." Hayden's hand slid one strap down over her shoulder, then the other, his fingertips sliding just inside her bodice, his knuckles brushing her bare skin. "I prefer to keep what happens between us private. But you're right on one account: I do need more of you. Correction: I *want* more."

Need pounded at her, the heat between them building, the tenseness of his body so close, so warm . . . On the edge, Cameron weighed the guests downstairs, the proper etiquette of a hostess, and making love to Hayden.

The thought tantalized—how furious Robert would be when she repaid him by keeping his current lover in a guesthouse, while she took hers to bed before a party. She stood slowly, checked her watch, and whispered in Hayden's ear, "Follow me."

In the hallway, Cameron glanced at one of the maids, a young thing probably already approached by Robert to be his informant. Within minutes, Robert would know that Cameron was in her bedroom with a younger man, and that would serve her need for revenge, to get some of her own back. Two needs would be met, that of revenge and her own hunger for Hayden.

Inside the luxurious bedroom, the door locked behind Hayden. Cameron turned to him, the man she needed to hold her, whom she thought of while the dream catchers spun lazily around her bed. It was only sex with Hayden, a natural appetite and one she intended to feed before going on with her life. It was all very clinical, very reasonable, she told herself.

Hayden surveyed the bedroom she rarely used; it was sleek, decorated by a professional, and held nothing of the woman inside her. He looked at the ornate four-poster bed with sheer drapes along the sides and topped by a satin canopy. Masses of pillows ran double-stacked at the headboard, a lush comforter spread over the bed, with cream satin sheets below it. The crystal perfume bottles and Cameron's makeup spread across a large vanity with a matching stool. The walk-in closet was lined with gowns and suits and shoes and handbags, all the necessities of an heiress. The bathroom was sleek, modern, spacious, and complete with a bidet.

He noted the body ball she used to ease her tense muscles at these times, when she was obligated to spend the night with guests.

He turned back to her, his hands open on her waist, caressing her body beneath the expensive fabric. "No dream catchers? Nothing to keep your dreams away? No little good-luck charms? No bells?"

He was too quick to see this room held no part of her—except the framed photograph of Katherine and Cammie beside the bed. The rest was all glitter and show, wrapped around her like a shield against the world she had to serve, that she was bound to against her will.

"I rarely use it. This dress is couture, one of a kind," she noted, unzipping the side and allowing it to flow down her breasts, leaving her standing in her diamonds, a black thong, and strappy heels. She looped her arms around his shoulder and enjoyed the feel of his hair between her fingers. She thought of the other hair on his body, that wedge at his chest and the thin trail from his naval downward.

To test his reaction, she lifted one leg high to wrap around his waist.

"Nice move," Hayden said.

"Ballet pays." He was hard against her, just perfect and ripe for the taking, and she could almost feel him push deep within her. "And don't mess my hair."

The command was meant to give her the upper hand, to test him, to push him, to find those limits.

"Take it off." Hayden's order rasped across the soft violin music downstairs and his fingers slid inside her thong, toying with the dampness there.

"I'm getting to you, aren't I?" The feeling was delicious, exciting, perfectly on that dangerous edge with Hayden. She could feel him weigh the moment, the need, the heat against something else, and she could feel herself tipping the scales.

Cameron complied, shimmying a little to toy with the moment of a female tantalizing a desirable male, then replaced her leg around his waist. She gripped his shoulders, then raised her other leg and locked it with the other. Instantly, Hayden's hands came to cup her bottom, a perfect reaction. She enjoyed that taut electricity around him, and leaned back to study his reaction.

But inside, the wildness that Hayden could give her, the pleasure of playing with him, streaked through her. He'd left her on his porch, just turned and walked away from her after seeing that she was ready—and now it was her terms. *Just how far could she push him?*

"You're really enjoying yourself, aren't you? Company downstairs, a little bit of getting back at Robert like your friends said—games, right?" Hayden asked darkly.

She placed her lips just at his jaw, whispering against that rough skin as his hands cupped her breasts, caressed them. "Tell me you're not interested," she whispered into his ear, biting it.

At that, Hayden's harsh features softened a bit as his hands ran over her thighs, then returned to caress her bottom. He held her tight, rubbing her a bit against him. "I'm not taking that damn check, and I brought my own—protection."

Cameron had always known that Hayden wouldn't take the check. She'd sensed that on some primitive level, she could trust some deep vein of honor in him. Hayden had come here tonight for her, for this, for another taste of her. It was enough, wasn't it? She'd thought of him constantly, in her, with her, the gentleness. "So thoughtful of you. I suspect you're usually prepared for anything, right?"

While his tongue played with hers, her body moistened in response, and she found herself smiling as he walked toward the bed.

"What?" Hayden asked roughly.

"I was just thinking that there's just something about a man who, obviously aroused, can hold a woman's butt, walk, and unzip his pants at the same time."

"I've always been able to multitask well." He eased down on the bed and positioned her over him. There was just that moment when their eyes locked, and the stillness of her heart settled into something soft and fluttery and feminine.

She closed her eyes, sealing in the feel of Hayden entering her, filling her gently, her body expanding to accommodate him. Hayden's hand caressed her throat, his fingers at work at the back of her neck and that tingling began—"Now you've done it . . . ." she warned.

"It sure feels like it."

He was just what she needed, Cameron decided in that one flashing instant as Hayden's black eyes locked with hers. A nice big diversion, a little something to take the edge off the night's tension. Then there was something else she had to have from him, too—the way he made her *feel* safe and feminine and desired. She pressed down on him, testing the lock, pushing him. . . . There was just that flare of his nostrils, that tense set of his body lifting into hers, and then his hand tugged her down to meet his kiss.

He was perfect to meet her on that sweet savage plane, all pretense stripped away.

Then a storm of heat swirled around them. She straddled him, his mouth at her breasts, nipping, suckling, his hands holding her bottom, Cameron's body contracted almost immediately. She cried out, holding the sensations inside her, feeling the pleasure pound at her. When they slowed, she softly collapsed upon him.

And realized that his shirt was still buttoned, his tie loosened, but—

Cameron rolled off him, her legs trembling as she stood looking down at Hayden, her arms around her breasts. Fully dressed, his trousers down around his ankles, he gave a shudder, and fought to control himself.

Lying amid her lush comforter, her four-poster bed with its drapes and ruffles, Hayden ran his hand slowly up her thigh and over her stomach to cup her breast. Because she was the only one who had obviously been pleasured, manners obligated her to say, "Thank you."

"That's all I came for, a thank-you," he returned easily.

Still flushed and trembling from lovemaking, Cameron shook her head. "You didn't come here to—"

"No. You didn't really thank me for burying your fish. I guess this will have to do," he murmured dryly.

Hayden rolled off the bed and adjusted his clothing while she watched. Stunned that she'd misjudged his purpose for coming tonight, Cameron tried to adapt from fast-paced lovemaking, the pleasure, to the reality of Hayden walking into her bathroom. She heard water run as she pulled on her dress with trembling hands; then she passed Hayden on the way to freshen her body. He took up a lot of space in the ultrafeminine bathroom, and waves of sensual heat seemed to come from him—as if he wanted to take her again. All she had to do was to turn to him—

Her need of him had been shocking, and he only wanted a thank-you? In the mirror, those black eyes followed her to the privacy area. Finished, she passed him again as she returned to her bedroom vanity to replace her lipstick with trembling hands, applying a layer of gloss. As he watched, Hayden leaned against the bathroom doorway. "You looked really good behind that frosted glass in the bathroom. What time is dinner?"

Cameron checked her wristwatch. "Right now. I'm late."

Had she really just jumped him, right here in her bedroom, a man she barely knew? Who was she? How could she do that with guests downstairs? Was she sorry? Not really.

"You're shaking. Take it easy, everything is going to be just fine," Hayden said as he bent to lightly kiss her lips.

"Easy for you to say. I have to face a whole roomful of investors." She rubbed away the gloss that had transferred to his lips, then glanced in the mirror. She studied her flushed cheeks, the way her eyes shone, and the man's hands cupping her breasts, his head lowered to kiss her shoulder. The hard prod of his body behind her said he wasn't finished.

"If you think I'm leaving now, you're mistaken." He kissed the back of her neck, just lightly. His lips and breath revved her skin, sending up those tingles that shot down low and circled and heated. When his hands slipped inside her dress, cupped her breasts, his fingers gently toying with her nipples, she shivered.

"That's not fair, Hayden, and you really won't like it. You'll be uncomfortable," she managed breathlessly as she stood really, really still and tried to pull back from a fresh ripple of sensuality—

"Let me be the judge of that." He patted her bottom, opened his hand to caress and shape it. "Let's eat."

"You're thinking about food now, are you?"

"Uh-huh. Aren't you?" he asked as if they'd never made love, as if the need for more wasn't lingering even now.

That irritated, and Cameron promised he would suffer. She turned to straighten his tie and snuggle a bit against him. "There's just one thing before we go downstairs—"

She tugged on his tie a little too hard and brought his eyes down to hers. "If you make friends with Robert, I'll kill you."

"I'm not likely to do that." His answer was too harsh and too ready, but she wasn't going to question him now.

As Cameron moved among the guests after the elaborate dinner, Hayden nursed his drink and stood in the shadows of the main salon; he noted the way Robert DuChamps played the grand host to his lady visitor.

Madeline, who also had been circulating around the room with Cameron, had briefly visited with Robert and Virginia Ulbrecht. Whatever had been discussed, Robert's temper had flashed at Madeline, and her expression had been grim. She'd looked at Virginia with cold disdain, almost with jealousy. That play intrigued Hayden, because dislike, even hatred, was definitely running between Robert and Madeline.

Cameron was playing her hostess role, smiling and laughing, and Hayden appreciated the line of her body, the way the dress clung to her. Restraining his needs earlier hadn't been easy, but almost worth it; he'd really enjoyed Cameron's little flash of anger.

And she had definitely been pushing him through dinner and later, stealthily wiggling that fine butt back against him as she spoke to other people and introduced him. Hayden surveyed the room filled with lounging, sated guests. They respected the heiress, listened closely to her, their expressions touched with affection.

Madeline was making her way to Hayden, and she looked determined. If her dark looks matched the conversation that would follow, he was in for an unpleasant experience.

On the other hand, pushing Madeline might just get him more information. As a longtime employee of the Somertons, and close to Cameron, she might have an observation that could unravel the truth.

Madeline moved close to Hayden and spoke quietly, briskly as she smiled up at him. Her brown eyes behind tinted glasses burned him, marked him as her enemy and an interfering SOB. "You look like you're having a good time."

"I am. Are you?"

"Of course. I always enjoy these parties. I wonder if we might have a private conversation in my office, please."

"Any particular reason? Cameron will miss me," Hayden said, just to start the ball rolling in his direction. Madeline was clearly protective of her chick, the heiress, which was good. Sometimes pseudomothers didn't like to move aside and if he dealt with Cameron, most likely he would somehow have to relate to Madeline.

And then, Madeline had been involved with Somerton affairs for twenty-seven years—she had information that he could use.

Robert was making his way to Madeline. He smiled briefly at Hayden, then dismissed him. Robert's hand tightened on Madeline's forearm, and she looked down at it, and then up at him. "Yes?"

"I want to speak with you."

Her "No" was curt, and she jerked her arm away. "Your *guest* will be missing you, Robert. I suggest you return to her."

Robert's expression tightened, his anger visible, but he showed his teeth in a grim smile. "I'm certain that Hayden will excuse us—"

"Not now, Robert," Madeline ordered firmly.

"I need—"

Madeline turned fully to Robert, and Hayden noted the sturdy brace of her overweight body within the poorly fitted, tight dress. "I am very busy and very tired, and I'm in conversation with Hayden now. We will talk later," she said flatly.

Robert glanced at Hayden, tightened his lips as though holding back what he really wanted to say, and recovered with a smooth, "I was just going to tell you how nice you looked tonight, my dear."

"Thank you." Madeline watched Robert walk back to his guest, stopping to socialize with clusters of others. When Madeline turned to Hayden, her expression was hard. "Just follow me."

"All right, Madeline."

Inside the large cluttered, but evidently efficient office on the ground floor, Madeline closed the door. "We don't have much time, so I'll be brief. I don't want Cameron to be involved with you. She's fragile and has to be protected. How much will it cost to get you to back off?"

The offer mildly surprised him. "Isn't that a decision for Cameron?"

"I don't want her hurt. I care deeply for her. I've practically raised her."

"What about yourself, Madeline? Did Robert hurt you?" Hayden asked softly, pushing Madeline. "He wouldn't be able to leave a woman alone anywhere near him, would he?"

Her head went back, her blond curls trembled, a definite reaction that Hayden wanted to explore. "After all, how could a woman resist all that Southern charm?"

Another reaction said he'd hit his mark: Madeline's quick intake of breath, the way her body tensed, said it all. "I detest him. But about Cameron—"

"Virginia Ulbrecht is gorgeous, isn't she?"

"She's a woman, and that's enough for Robert. How

much will it take to get you away from Mimosa and away from Cameron? I should have protected her from her ex-husband, that gold digger, but she was so—"

Hayden finished his drink and placed the squat tumbler on her desk. "Gold digger" didn't fit the William he knew, a man with wealth trying to use patience and logic with his stiff-backed parents, a man committed to his baby and the woman he wanted to marry. And William's affection for Cameron ran deep. Unless Hayden was mistaken, Madeline had just dropped him into the same "gold digger" pigeon-hole, and that grated, especially since he'd just had the heiress upstairs. "Listen up: What's between Cameron and me is no business of yours, Madeline. It's private."

Her face flushed with anger, stout little body trembling in the too-tight dress. "She has a reputation to protect, a position—"

"Discussion ended," Hayden said as he opened the door, walked through it, and closed it behind him.

He paused in the hallway he'd once known so well, bracing himself to enter the crowd in the salon. He'd learned two things: Madeline definitely ruled Robert, and she was also jealous of his women.

Could that include her chick, the heiress, Cameron? Because Robert had definitely taken in Cameron's body tonight, hungered for it, even as he courted the leggy horse breeder.

But Robert wasn't getting close to Cameron.

Not if Hayden could help it.

Robert DuChamps stood at the massive front door, playing his role as host as the guests departed, some driving away, and others retiring to the guest cottages. He smiled at the rich bastards who wouldn't be talking to him if he wasn't the pet of the deceased Katherine Somerton, if he wasn't the guardian who had raised "poor" Cameron Somerton.

And that damned overseer, Madeline, was calling too many

shots that concerned him. She needed to be brought down from her pudgy little perch, and he was just the man to do it. Even now, she was talking to guests as if she were the grand dame of Somerton House, when she was only an employee.

Robert gave his best charming smile to Virginia Ulbrecht, who was observing everything: his lowly place when he should be the master of the house, entitled to having his own guests stay in Somerton House. Virginia would stay in a guest cottage tonight, because Cameron wasn't above making her uncomfortable in front of others. But he could feel Virginia appraising him and finding him lacking. To keep her, Robert knew he had to have more substantial resources than the charm he'd already used to bed her.

At one o'clock, the dinner and dance party had ended, and Cameron stood at the other side of the mansion's double doorway. She handed out the gift baskets to the guests, smiling at them, a touch here and there, the trademark hospitable warmth that reminded him of Katherine.

But Cameron wasn't Katherine. Cameron was tough, and that was his gift to her, Robert supposed, remembering how he had formed her into the heiress draped in elegance, who as a teen had been trained in the best boarding schools—while he'd had use of Katherine's fortunes.

Robert studied the man near Cameron and automatically straightened to his full height, comparing the younger man to himself. Obviously a businessman, one used to soirees such as tonight, Hayden was tall and powerfully built, his face broad through the cheekbones, his tan settling deep within the skin like that of a man who worked outdoors. With black waving hair and black brows, he wasn't an attractive man at all, Robert decided, when compared to himself.

When introduced, Hayden's hand had been broader than Robert's and hard with calluses. Hayden hadn't smiled then, but his grip was a little too tight, and Robert's senses tingled that bit, on guard for another male poaching on his territory;

he'd noted the expensive gold watch, the custom-made shoes and tailored top-name suit. Cameron had only introduced him as "Hayden," But the man had added quietly, "Hayden Olson. I'm in business, landscaping supplies, that sort of thing."

The stillness of his expression, those black eyes locking with Robert's had sent the silent message: *This man is dangerous. He'll stop at nothing—*

But then that was a quality that Robert recognized. He was very good at using others' needs and turning them to his advantage.

They'd been upstairs—one of the servants had seen him following Cameron into her bedroom.

She'd been late to the dinner table, the guests already seated. Cameron had looked different, shining, excited, though she always had Katherine's perfect manners.

There was something in how Hayden bent his head to hers when she spoke, the way her body leaned slightly against his, the intimacy of lovers' language clearly seen—obviously for Robert's displeasure, of course. Sensuality seemed to shimmer between them, a touch here, a brush of the body there, that shared look of anticipation.

Across the heads and shoulders of the departing guests, Cameron's eyes locked with Robert's. She smiled slowly and moved closer to Hayden, who put his arm around her waist. Robert understood perfectly; she was using the man to get to him—*irritating little witch.* He returned the smile, because there was always another time to joust for power, to try tipping the other out of the game.

Then the younger man's hand slid up her arm and cradled the back of her neck. His thumb cruised the side of her throat, and the pulse in that elegant long, diamond-bejeweled throat definitely throbbed in response— Her slanted look up at him was that of a lover's promise.

But there was something familiar about Mr. Hayden Olson . . . something that nagged and couldn't be placed.

When the last guest left, Robert asked, "Would you like to

have a drink, now that's it's quiet and we can get better acquainted, Hayden?"

"No, he wouldn't," Cameron said firmly as she took Hayden's hand and drew him to the stairs.

"I guess not," Hayden said smoothly, and his smile mocked Robert, a man demonstrating that he was in full possession—or was going to be shortly. "Another time?"

"Another time." Robert watched Cameron and Hayden move up the stairs, his hand riding low on her waist.

Then she turned and looked down at Robert. He didn't hide the hatred lashing up at her, and she didn't hide hers.

"Okay, you've made your point," Hayden said, once they were inside her bedroom. "Maybe I don't like being in the middle of your little game."

"Then leave. I tried to break it off with you, but you came anyway. You insisted on staying, and now you know how it is here." To conceal her unsteady nerves after another bout with Robert, Cameron moved to the bed and tossed the masses of pillows aside, then peeled back the comforter. She felt too alive, fueled up, and revved, her senses jumping. Hayden's arrival had been perfect. Tonight, she'd won, scored a hit on Robert's control over her, had gotten the upper hand in their duel. She was taking her lover to bed—in Somerton House, while Robert's current mistress was exiled to a guest cottage.

She'd achieved dominance in Somerton House, and that was enough for now. Eventually, with enough scores, she'd force Robert away from Somerton House and every affair and every business venture. She'd cut him out and protect Katherine's and Buck's legacies. Hatred churned in Cameron, mixed with a natural high that victory could bring.

Hayden loosened his tie and tossed it away; his jacket followed, then he flicked open his shirt. "We're in a little charade, aren't we? To get back at Robert? That little show downstairs was meant for him, wasn't it?" he asked tightly. "What has he done to you?"

What hadn't Robert done? He'd killed a part of Cameron that she struggled to retrieve every day, to discover who she really was, deep inside, beneath the role she had been taught so early in life. She slid the diamonds from her ears and tossed them into a dish beside the huge rose bouquet she kept in memory of Katherine. She stripped the glittering tennis bracelets from her wrists, the signs of her bondage, one she couldn't escape.

Behind her, Hayden bent to kiss her nape, his breath causing her skin to tingle, her body to tighten. The zipper at her side slid down, his open lips traced her shoulders until the straps slid away. "So here we are. With guests in the cottages and a brunch call in the morning to see them off, I'd say you're here for the night. Am I?"

"Cook's brunch is superb. You're in for a treat."

"Always nice to know that I'm needed."

The dress slid away, and Cameron smiled briefly at Hayden's indrawn breath. "Dammit . . . you're not wearing anything under this. You were like that all night? If I'd known—"

She tried to push her smile away to an innocence she wasn't feeling. "Shocked?"

His hands were already busy, cupping her breasts, sliding down the curve of her waist to lock on to her hips, tugging her to his already hard body. "Take down your hair."

She reached to unpin her hair, shaking it free around her head before moving against him.

His hands took control of her body, lifting her to carry her toward the bed. Her body ball was impatiently kicked aside, but then she wouldn't need it to ease her tense nerves tonight, would she?

She smiled with that thought as he dumped her upon the cream sheets. "You like to push buttons, don't you?" Hayden demanded as he stripped quickly.

"You already know I have a problem with Robert—"

"And I have a problem with *you*."

Cameron gasped as Hayden gripped her ankle and lifted

her foot to his bare hard stomach. He grimly removed her diamond ankle bracelet, then flipped her over to her stomach and the diamond choker slid away.

"I don't like this—" Cameron tried to roll from the bed, to get more control, but Hayden was too quick, flattening her back, and moving over her, holding her wrists.

Above her, his expression taut, furious, Hayden's powerful arms trembled beside her as he tried to leash himself, his body already prodding hers, demanding entrance.

The moment slapped her with the raw truth: Hayden was on the edge, wanting her, just her . . . furious with her, angry with himself . . . but not enough to rape her. He'd stop at any time. She could trust him, his honor, and the glimpse into a rare man like this was something she couldn't ignore.

Cameron lifted her head just those inches and against his lips said, "Gotcha."

She ran her insoles up and down his calves, lifted her hips just that bit to enclose him. His anger and frustration eased into a humorous challenge as he bent to nuzzle her throat. "Do you? Let's see about that."

Hayden awoke when Cameron's fist hit his chest. Lying on her stomach beside him, she was threshing against unseen bonds, clearly having a nightmare.

Then she curled to her side, whimpering in the tone of a frightened child. "Let me out, please. It's dark and cold and— Please breathe . . . please don't die. I don't know what to do—"

Then, slowly, sadly, "I'm so sorry. So sorry."

Fearing to startle her awake, Hayden sought to comfort her instead as he whispered, "It's okay, honey. Come here."

"Don't want to," the petulant child said, curling tighter into her ball. "Don't want to do this anymore, Robert."

Hayden inhaled slowly and pushed away the thoughts of what "this" could be. For now, all he wanted to do was to comfort her. He turned her slowly, rocking her against him, but Cameron shook her head and whispered as if telling a dark secret: "When Robert's mad, someone pays. . . ."

"Shh, baby. Everything is going to be fine."

"Not with me, not ever. Please stop whispering." She put her hand to her ears. "Don't whisper. I'm doing the best I can. *Stop whispering. I can't stand it!*"

After Cameron eased, lying close to him as if she needed his warmth, Hayden thought of that cold storm cellar, what she must have suffered there.

Then she stirred again, and the woman in his arms started moving over him.

At four o'clock in the morning, Robert was unable to sleep and stood in front of the guest cottage, the second woman he'd taken that night sleeping soundly inside. Virginia Ulbrecht belonged to the gentler set, and it wouldn't do to relieve his temper with her.

The first woman he'd taken had served that purpose, taking only a hundred-dollar bill for the spanking he gave her—the one he really wanted to bestow upon Cameron. His fascination with spanking Cameron had begun early—

Cameron had never taken a lover inside the mansion, only her husband. But tonight, she'd taken Hayden upstairs the moment he appeared—then again, to spend the night.

The image of that big hand riding low and possessive on Cameron's hip fueled Robert's anger once again.

She was challenging Robert once more, and this time the man wasn't like William. Hayden Olson had been too keen in the business conversations, and he seemed never to lose sight of where Cameron was, mixing with her guests, the good little hostess. And that steady black stare had always come back to meet Robert's.

Cameron had come to Hayden often, introducing him to her guests. Those little looks, the way her body leaned into Hayden's, the way his hand smoothed her waist—they were lovers, no doubt about it.

"The heiress and the whore," Robert stated harshly to the sweet morning scents and to the estate that should be his, to the fortune that was rightly his as Katherine's widower.

A movement drew Robert's gaze up to the veranda of Cameron's bedroom. There, Hayden was standing, hands braced on the railing, staring at Robert with those hard black eyes. Without a shirt, Hayden's shoulders held the power of a laborer, his big hands locked on to the railing, as if they had the right to be there.

Then Cameron, wearing a man's large shirt came to stand beside him, and Hayden turned her to him, wrapped her in his arms, and lifted her, carrying her inside—

Robert tapped his riding crop against his thigh, his temper rising.

That upstart was poaching on Robert's rightful territory, having Cameron right in the same house where guests were sleeping—where he should be having Virginia now. Cameron had replaced Robert with this man, this upstart, a commoner by the look of his hands, that powerful build, and not attractive at all.

She'll soon tire of him. Just scratching a need. She knows what she has to do and what she can't do.

Robert had waited for her to grow into a woman, savoring each development, thinking it would be his hands on her, his bed she'd be sleeping in—and now she'd taken a lover to spite him.

Cameron had to be stopped.

Nine

"I'M GOING FOR A RIDE BEFORE THE GUESTS WAKE UP." Cameron hurried to draw on Hayden's shirt and her jeans. In the predawn, she sat on the bed to tug on her pink western boots.

"Now?" Hayden caressed her back and thought lazily of other things she could ride. When she'd come after him on the veranda, it was to demonstrate her sexy workout on the body ball. That had created another round of lovemaking, and he was momentarily rested and in the mood for more.

Cameron pushed an intercom button, and said, "Cody, wake up. I need you to saddle Lady Pink."

"Great," Hayden grumbled, his body already doing that tent thing. "Look what I've got for you."

"That's nice. Go back to sleep," Cameron said as she hurried out the bedroom door, closing it behind her.

Hayden debated sleep for several luxurious moments and groaned; he wished he hadn't told Cameron that her stepfather was out early. He reluctantly sighed and rose slowly to pull on his trousers—if Robert was still out there, Cameron might clash with him, and that wouldn't be good.

He paused in the foyer to use the courtesy coffee urn and select a sweet roll from the assortment there.

Outside, he slowly finished the continental breakfast as he studied the neatly clipped grounds. Then, remembering other mornings, Hayden walked slowly through the maze, the dawn cool upon his bare chest. He brushed his hand over the damp shrubs, remembering his father's caution about the hedge trimmers. Memories of his sister and Cammie, running through the maze, laughing at each other, played around him. He could almost see them, two little girls, ducking and hiding from each other, popping up and giggling at the other's surprise.

But one glance at the row of cottages, the one where his father had committed suicide caused his senses to chill, the memory of that awful morning slashing at him. . . . "Little bastard . . . you're not going to mess this up," Robert had said, throwing H.J. out of the cottage where his father's body lay—

Hayden wondered briefly if Robert remembered Paul Olson, a big blond workman; if Robert had noted that his features mirrored his father's, but that he also had his mother's darker coloring.

One thing was for certain: Robert wanted Cameron for himself and resented another man in her bed. He'd be checking on Hayden Olson, and it was only a matter of time before Cameron knew—and then the game would be on. A very serious game that Hayden had wanted for twenty-eight years, facing Robert as a man, not as young H.J.

Then suddenly Cameron's horse bolted out of the field's small stand of sassafras trees, her body low in the saddle as Robert rode close behind her. With Hayden's shirt pasted to her body, she cleared one hurdle and another, then turned to face Robert. Their horses danced around each other in the low-lying mist, their fierce argument obvious in the shadowy dawn. Cameron's chestnut mare reared, muscled by Robert's heavier black stallion. When Robert raised his riding crop, Hayden went to the fence, stepped up and over it, and started across the field.

Wheeling her horse around, her body taut and expert,

Cameron leaned forward, her hair flying around her face as she spoke to Robert.

"Come on, Cameron, back off," Hayden urged quietly, because Robert had leaned into the argument, deliberately using his horse as a weapon. But she continued to argue and back her horse from Robert's.

Suddenly, Cameron turned her mare and started for another round of jumps, an expert horsewoman, pushing the sleek Thoroughbred to the limits.

When she turned in Hayden's direction, her face was flushed and furious as if she were ready to do anything. In that instant, he knew that Cameron intended to jump the board fence, much higher and more dangerous than the others in the field.

If he moved, he could frighten the horse, and she could be thrown— Hayden could only hold his breath and watch as the mare's front hooves lifted, her powerful muscles gleaming with sweat and power as she sailed over the fence.

The horse cleared the fence. But upon landing on the other side of the fence, Cameron tumbled from the saddle—

Aware that Robert's horse was bearing down on him and fearing for Cameron, Hayden leaped up on the fence, braced one hand on a post, and swung over to the other side. She was lying on the grass like a broken doll, her face pale. Her lashes fluttered as he crouched near her, and she whispered unevenly, "Get me out of here. Put me back up on my horse and walk to the stables as if you're cooling Lady Pink down."

Fear for her pumped through Hayden as he brushed the dirt from her face. "Cameron, don't move. You could be injured."

The area around her lips was tight with pain and her hand gripped his. "Just do it. Please. I don't want my guests to see me like this. I'm fine."

"Sure you are." Hayden didn't hide his sarcasm, and glanced up at Robert, who had come to stand beside her.

"What a stupid thing to do. Is she hurt?" Robert asked coldly as he tapped the crop against his palm.

At the first tap, Hayden reached to grab the riding crop, tug it from Robert, and toss it to the ground. "*That* stays there."

Robert was furious, this time avoiding Hayden as he asked, "Are you hurt, Cameron?"

"I'm just peachy, Robert," Cameron bit out, anger flashing in her eyes. "Get the hell away from me and Lady Pink."

Concentrating on handling Cameron gently, Hayden eased her to her feet. "Anything broken?"

"She's lucky she didn't break her neck," Robert stated furiously.

Hayden looked at Robert and spoke very quietly. "But she didn't, did she? Back off."

"I'm her guardian—"

"Not anymore. I'm over twenty-one," Cameron stated firmly.

Robert glanced at Hayden's bare chest and then at the man's dress shirt on Cameron. "Do you have to scratch every itch, Cameron? And you make me keep my lady friend in a cottage, while you're at it in *my* house? How is *that* going to look to *our* guests?"

Supporting Cameron, his arm around her waist, Hayden stared at Robert coldly. "Get out of the way."

"She's irresponsible . . . someone has to take charge of her. Look at what she tried just now. She left the gate open to let my new thoroughbred out into the field with those . . . mustangs. Can you imagine what my guest must think? It's my right—"

"You can take your 'right,' and shove—"

"Don't. . . . Not now," Cameron whispered as she leaned heavily against Hayden. "I don't think I can mount. Help me up on my horse—in case anyone sees."

"First tell me that nothing is broken."

"Just my pride." She grimaced as she lifted her boot and placed it into the cup of Hayden's hands. The strain of her fall showed as he carefully eased her higher onto the mare's back.

"That temper will kill you someday," Robert stated

harshly as he swept his riding crop up from the ground. "You never listen to me, and you're getting worse—you're forgetting too many things. You forgot to close the gate, Cameron. Someone has to take charge—"

She straightened in the saddle, and the look she sent down to Robert was that of a queen to a servant. Her voice held quiet, firm dignity. "But not *you,* Robert."

Robert's anger was palpable, heating the cool dawn.

As Hayden led the mare to the stable, he glanced up at Cameron, whose face was white with pain, her lips set, tears shimmering in her eyes. "Fine, huh?"

In the stables, he helped her down carefully, and only Cameron's obvious pain kept him from giving her a dressing-down she'd remember for a long time. A teenage boy came running, and Cameron forced a smile at him. "Hi, Cody. Cool Lady Pink down, will you?"

The boy's expression was horrified. "I saw what happened. Someone left the gate open and the new thoroughbred got into the field with the mustangs. I was—"

Her hand gripped the side of a stall, her knuckles white through the skin, but Cameron smiled at the boy. "I'm fine. I must not have closed the gate. It's my fault. Don't worry about it. Thank you, Cody. Just cool down Lady Pink, then get the thoroughbred back here, away from the mustangs, okay? A trucker should be coming this afternoon for the mustangs . . . they're being relocated. Help load them, will you?"

When the boy hurried to walk the mare, Cameron shook her head and stared at the stable gate, closed now.

"I've got to get back to the house. My guests will be waking, and there's brunch to be served," she said quietly as if her mind was taking her through the latching of that gate, step by step.

"The hell with the gate and brunch. What was all that about—out in the field?"

"Family conference." Cameron started to make her way slowly, painfully out of the stables.

Hayden came to her side, placing his arm around her and supporting her as they slowly walked toward the house. "I could see that," he said grimly. "That's why you were out there early, wasn't it? Robert was mad at you, and he might have taken it out on your horse?"

"He wouldn't dare—" She turned to him and frowned. "What makes you think that?"

"You talk in your sleep, honey. You said when he's mad, someone pays. I'd say that from his looks at us last night, the guy wants you bad—and not as a stepfather, either."

Cameron almost stumbled, and he held her upright. But he didn't like the fear he'd seen in that one brief glimpse of her face— "I didn't know that I talked in my sleep. Did I say anything else?" she asked unevenly.

"Yes, you did," Hayden answered truthfully. "You wanted someone to stop whispering. You begged them. You said you were sorry several times."

Cameron's body tensed within his arm. "Everyone has bad dreams. I suppose too much rich food might explain it, the excitement of entertaining, of pushing my projects. There's a lot of stress in maneuvering a project through, wooing my investors for the new merger. I've got to do a lot more of it at brunch."

"Stress, my foot. You keep this up with Robert, and you could end up dead. He's no sweetheart."

"Not a chance. He wouldn't do anything. I'm worth too much alive," she whispered, as if to herself. "If I die, everything goes to charities."

"Why don't you just kick him out?"

"Katherine loved him. The only way he's out is if he marries, or unless he chooses to remove himself from Somerton holdings. He's free to go, but he doesn't *have* to go. In fact, I wish he would. I've tried to buy him off, but he wasn't interested."

"He hurt you, didn't he? And you enjoy pushing his buttons because of that?" Hayden asked, and when Cameron shielded her pale set face and didn't answer, he knew for certain that life with Robert as a guardian hadn't been sweet. He thought of young H.J., the rough handling Robert had given him, and knew that Cameron had taken far worse.

In the rising dawn, Cameron turned to Hayden. "I know what Robert is. He knows what I am. Stay out of it, and don't let my guests sense any more animosity, please. It would be bad enough if one of them saw us fighting. I will *not* endanger the reputation of Somerton House, or negatively influence Katherine's charity work."

Hayden fought carrying Cameron up the stairs, and he damned the pale mark of pain around her set lips. Inside her bedroom, she shook her head. "Don't. Just don't. I've had enough of arguing with men this morning. Robert will be at brunch . . . it's customary that he toast Katherine's memory. If he sees you, he might not be able to control himself, and I will not have the Somerton name exposed to more gossip. I'd prefer you left before the guests stir."

Frustration blended with anger as Hayden watched her walk slowly, painfully to the bed. Then she paused and turned slowly. Tears streaked her face as she whispered, "Please, Hayden. Do this for me. I can't take any more now."

Hayden wanted to protect her, hold her, soothe her. "You don't expect me to leave you to Robert, do you?"

"Yes," she said simply. "I do. And I'm not up to arguing with you, too. Please, Hayden. Not now."

Controlling his fierce need to protect her, Hayden was silent. "Tell me where you keep some painkillers—they're not in your medicine cabinet. I'll get them."

"I don't take them. They blur everything and I can't—" She held her breath as she eased onto the bed. "How do you know what's in my medicine cabinet?"

"Because I looked for something to use to freshen up last night, before the dinner, remember?" he lied. He'd actually been looking for asthma medications and had found none. His curiousity about how a girl with such life-threatening problems could miraculously recover as an adult had been too much.

"I think you had better leave now—please," Cameron said quietly, her face white with pain.

"Dammit, Cameron—"

"Just leave, Hayden. I can't take any more."

"If I do, you'll order up something for the pain?" he demanded because there was no fighting the tears in her eyes, the silvery trail dripping from her cheek.

"I promise."

"Then I'll wait here until you call for the pills, and you take them."

Cameron started to raise off the bed, and Hayden bent to gently push her down again. She glared up at him. "Don't you understand? I have to be on top of this game all the time. I can't take anything—"

"I'm staying until you do."

Madeline was called, and she hurried up to Cameron's room with some pain tablets. In her robe, and clearly summoned from her sleep, she stopped inside the door and frowned at Hayden. "You," she said fiercely, the single word condemning Hayden. She took in the mussed bed, the shirt Cameron was wearing, her pained expression. "I should have known."

"He didn't do anything . . . I fell while riding, Madeline," Cameron said as her eyes begged Hayden to leave. "Please, Hayden."

"My poor baby— What has he done to you? You're an expert horsewoman. He had to do something to make you fall. I knew he was no good for you," Madeline fussed over Cameron.

With a nod, Hayden left the room. But leaving her was against every instinct in him.

From the paddock where he had been walking his stallion and talking with Virginia Ulbrecht, a woman with wealth and style, a woman he deserved to bring into Somerton House as his lover, Robert watched Hayden move down the mansion's wide steps.

The men's eyes locked, and both knew there would be a time to fight for the possession of Cameron.

Jealousy rose in Robert. Cameron was taunting him with Hayden, pushing for that upper hand, for that revenge she had wanted since she was a teenager. Robert should have broken her to his hand right then, and he would still.

Cameron was clearly upset by the little misplaced things, her stupid dead fish in the aquarium, the lists she'd left in her office that no one had seen, her lost PDA, the red Miata she liked to push to the limits wasn't where she'd last parked it, the cell phone not in her bag, but left on the foyer table. All those little index cards she had pasted in her home said she was slowly breaking.

And then, when Cameron was finally tucked away in an institution, everything would be back as it should be, Robert thought darkly—it would be his way. It had been his way once before, after Katherine had died, and he wanted that power again—and after Cameron, he'd get rid of that meddling Madeline somehow. . . .

When Hayden paused, the green paddock and the winding maze between the two men, something distant nudged Robert, something familiar.

What is it? Who does Hayden Olson remind me of?

"Olson. . . . Olson. I should remember that name somehow. . . ."

Then another man's face flashed by Robert, someone from almost thirty years ago— "Paul Olson. The gardener. Had a son, black hair and eyes like his pretty mother . . . H.J.? H.J. Olson—*Hayden Olson*?"

Ten

AT THREE O'CLOCK THAT AFTERNOON, HAYDEN WATCHED THE expensively dressed woman enter the Grow Green Lawn and Garden grand opening in Oklahoma City. In the midst of a discussion with the new manager about women using electric weed eaters, and catering to star placement of them for the browsing city woman, Hayden met Cameron's furious stare.

Fine. He had work to do, and maybe they both needed a break from the tension of that morning—

Only hours after he'd left Somerton House at sunrise, Cameron looked nothing like the woman who had taken a bad fall, who was shaky with pain, who had begged him to leave.

This woman was crackling with anger, her blue eyes flashing, that lean leggy body taut with it. She'd tracked him down easily at the store's grand opening; he'd left express orders in St. Louis and at the Oklahoma branch store to identify the caller on his personal line. If it was Cameron Somerton, his orders were *not* to put her through but to relay his location. If she wanted to speak with him, she'd have to put in some face time.

She was here now and from her tight expression, the way

her eyes narrowed when she'd found him, their meeting wasn't going to be sweet. Fine. He didn't feel exactly sweet himself; when his instincts were to protect and care for her, Cameron had sent him away.

The nagging doubt that Cameron had sent him away to protect him from Robert didn't help his pride, either.

Hayden took his time with the current discussion, aware of Cameron's growing impatience. Moving in a circle around him, she pretended to be interested in a riding lawn mower, then moved to garden sprayers. She expected him to come to her, did she? Not a chance.

But he was aware of Cameron's every move and noted the tiny gold bells at her ears, the turquoise silk blouse and loose slacks, the dainty expensive heels, the tiny strap of the designer purse, crossing her breasts. A gold comb shaped like a small butterfly held back one side of her hair. The large brand-name sunglasses tucked into her blouse vee cost more than some people made in a month.

Her purse strap shifted, tightening the light fabric over her breasts and Hayden's anger momentarily slid to something else—a hard tight grip low in his midsection and a flashing memory of her opening to him, sighing softly as he entered—

What was he doing, visualizing Cameron beneath him, when he was in the middle of a business discussion? A woman who led two lives, and one of them certain to lead to the mystery of his father's death and the missing money? A woman who doubted that mere accident had claimed Katherine's life and who had lied to him about the storm cellar?

Hayden inhaled slowly, forcing himself to nod and talk with the new manager. "We'll send our own crew in for regular inspections of the plants. If you even suspect a blight or an infection, just call the office."

Eventually, Cameron moved close, smiling at the manager. "May I help you?" Leo asked, returning the smile.

"I'm just looking. What a wonderful store," she murmured coolly.

Hayden didn't want to upset the manager with what was almost certain to be an argument. "I'll take care of her, Leo. Your clerk by the birdbaths seems to be needing help."

When Leo hurried away, Cameron glanced at Hayden's JUST ASK ME badge; his name below read, "HAYDEN OLSON, V.P."

Her "Hello, H.J." carried a honey-sweet angry bite.

"Robert, I suppose?" he asked as the nickname took him back to the ten-year-old boy stunned by his father's suicide, struggling with their family's hard times.

"Who else? Did you have fun? Making a fool out of me?" The flush beneath Cameron's smooth skin was rising, her eyes blue ice, her lips tight with anger. Her fingers dug into her upper arms, crushing the turquoise silk sleeves. The huge diamonds on her tennis bracelet mixed with gold bells that matched her earrings. The tiny bells jingled their warning.

Hayden remembered removing the bells at her ears after she'd been so terrified of the storm cellar—*Stop whispering . . . please stop!* she'd cried in her sleep as she'd turned to him for comfort.

But that was just hours before she'd asked him to leave—so as not to upset Robert more—and before she'd learned that he was H.J., the gardener's son.

"Maybe we'd better take this somewhere else?" he asked, flicking one of the bells at her ears.

Moments later, on the way to his hotel's executive suite, Hayden watched the little red Miata convertible in his rearview mirror. Cameron's hair flew in the wind, her eyes shielded by huge sunglasses, but there was no missing the hard set of her lips. When he stopped for a traffic light, she shifted expertly, and pulled in tight behind the BMW's bumper. The revving motor said she was pushing for a showdown and one Hayden planned to give to her.

"You're going to kill yourself in that thing. What do you think you were doing, racing on that straight stretch?" The image of the little red sports car soaring down the street ahead of him, then pulling aside to wait for him still raised the hair on his body.

"There wasn't another car or person in sight. Can't you keep up?" she tossed back at him. "Let's get this over with."

In the suite furnished by Grow Green, Hayden pushed her inside the door and closed it behind him. He walked to the kitchenette and pulled open the refrigerator door. He bent to study the contents in an effort to give himself some cooling-off time. He was too close to getting what he wanted, the information that might lead to the real reason Paul Olson died.

Or maybe he was fighting his guilt, that he'd used Cameron to get inside the ugly past, something he was driven to understand.

He glanced at Cameron; she was working on her get-it-together thing, building up steam for a head-on confrontation, the air palpable with tension. She walked slowly around the deluxe suite, taking in the business center in one corner, his laptop open on the desk, the closed and locked briefcase, the contemporary cool furnishings, his pillow and rumpled sheet on the couch.

Sleeping without Cameron in his arms those nights hadn't been easy, and now Hayden resented his need of her, his need to protect her. He'd left her alone with Robert DuChamps, and that had grated for hours.

Hayden flipped open a beer, one of the microbrewery samplers from the guest basket. At Somerton House this morning, a woman's large handwritten note had been tucked under the basket on his pickup's rooftop. "Freebie. Phoebe. Call me anytime."

At least, he'd gotten something to remember the night with Cameron, other than her face, white with pain, as she had asked him to leave.

He inhaled sharply. In the midafternoon of that same morning, Cameron looked nothing like the woman at dawn; she'd pulled herself together into a tight, hard ball, and he had to wonder how much practice she'd had to survive collisions with DuChamps.

Hayden had wanted to hold her, to help and protect her. Cameron had turned him down flat, barring him, and that grated. They had shared a bed, but when she was endangered, she cut him out—

She turned to look out the windows to the city below; her long neck was taut, her arms crossed, and her fingers biting into her flesh. "You like this, don't you? Playing games?" Cameron asked so quietly that it throbbed across the thick carpeting.

"Look who's talking."

She pivoted, her body stiff, her eyes flashing. "Do you think I like being made a fool of?"

At that, Hayden's own anger drew him across the room in quick strides. "Okay, let's have it."

"You're the gardener's son, H.J. How much fun it must have been to have me. How you must have laughed," she stated flatly.

"Robert couldn't wait to lay that one on you, could he?"

He blocked her slap to his face, held her wrist as she looked furiously up at him. "You got what you wanted, Cameron. A man to show off, to wave in front of him. You knew he'd be jealous when you started your act at the party."

"Yes, I did."

"And that's all there was to it, right? I served my purpose, you showed off a lover right under his nose, and then you're done, right?"

"Right."

"Wrong."

"Okay. You say you can tell the difference. I admit I enjoyed myself . . . yes. It's been a while, H.J.," she said carefully, using his nickname. "But then, you didn't tell me you were the gardener's son, did you? Is that honesty?"

That slammed into Hayden. She was right: He should have told her. "Maybe not. But I didn't hide it either, Cammie."

She inhaled swiftly and the shiver running through her caused Hayden to want to hold her close. "I don't like that nickname," she said carefully. "Don't use it again."

He was too close, pushing now, detesting himself, but driven to get the answers that had waited twenty-eight years. . . . And just maybe the answers could help Cameron, too, and stop the whispers in her nightmares.

Hayden caught her face in his hand, lifting it to see her reaction to his next probe. He could be wrong, but it was worth testing her, if only to satisfy himself. "Why? Because the name really belongs to someone else? A little girl with asthma, the *real* Cameron Somerton?"

She looked as if she'd been struck, and Hayden wavered slightly. He slowly loosened his hold on her wrist and slid his thumb over the edge of her hand—where the removal of that little sixth finger should have left a scar and a bump. Cammie's life-threatening asthma would have only worsened; she wouldn't have healed completely. All the questions added up to one fact—Cameron wasn't Cammie. *Who is this woman? What happened to the real Cammie Somerton?*

Cameron tore herself away, her hands covering her ears. She was shaking now, the bells on her wrists jingling, and Hayden feared he had gone too far, too quick.

Then she turned slowly to him, her expression wounded. "Was it worth it? To make love to me? Was it, H.J.? Did you get everything you needed, the revenge? How did it make you feel, having me? As if it made everything change, made it better? Or do you have to have more, like destroying my life?"

"*Whose* life?" he asked carefully and decided to play his hunch to the fullest. The time had come to reopen the past, to find what he needed. Hayden walked to his briefcase, unlocked it, and retrieved a fat file folder. He carried it to the couch's coffee table and slapped it down. "Read this. Then we'll talk."

He ached for Cameron as she stared at the folder—as if it

could kill her. And just maybe it could. Aware that he could prove nothing, that his hunch could be wrong, Hayden watched Cameron's reactions. She moved slowly, almost painfully, and he thought of how she'd fallen, how she'd probably gone on, refusing to show pain at the sumptuous brunch, playing the gracious hostess.

Cameron slowly sat and her hand trembled as she reached to open the file, the clippings he'd collected. "You don't have to worry. I didn't put an investigator on it. It's information anyone can collect. I just happened to be persistent. I had a reason, a big one."

He watched the swallow move down that elegant throat, the way her hand came protectively to her throat as she slowly turned the pages. "There's nothing here, other than what happened."

He had to know and now, there was no going back. "I put together a few things. Our family lived there, you know. I played with . . . with Cammie. She had severe asthma, medicine and oxygen tanks a part of her every hour alive. I watched her struggle for breath when the pollen count went up, or some farmer burned brush and the smoke almost killed her. I was there when they repainted the house, and Katherine had to take her away until the fumes cleared. I was there when she got too excited, and her lungs couldn't take it. I got lectures not only from my parents, but once from Dr. Naylan, her doctor and a pulmonary specialist in the clinic her mother had started."

"He's dead now," she whispered unevenly. "I had a new doctor after the kidnapping. My asthma went away. I outgrew it."

"That was really convenient, wasn't it? Naylan was killed in a fire with all of his records, just a week before little Cammie's kidnapping. Very convenient, especially when Katherine had an accident, too. For what it's worth, I think you're right about someone murdering Katherine. The question is, did they murder my father, too?"

Cameron's voice was hollow as if she were speaking by rote, as if she were repeating what had been told to her, over and over again. "The gardener killed himself. He committed suicide, and part of the ransom was found on his body. He couldn't live with what he'd done. Robert said the gardener wanted Katherine, and she'd rejected him, and he took revenge by taking her child and her money."

"*Robert said.*" Hayden's words lashed bitterly into the silence as he remembered the gossip circling his mother, the way Mimosa cast them out, the hard life, his sister's operation—

Cameron stood slowly, her hands trembling as she smoothed her clothing, her hair. "I have to go now," she whispered unevenly.

"Dammit," Hayden cursed furiously. He was angry with himself, with Cameron, with the past, and he'd hurt her. But he was in the storm now, and he wasn't backing up. "What about that bump on your hand, the one that isn't there? The scar left from the removal of Cammie's sixth finger?"

She inhaled sharply, her eyes widening just that bit to tell him that he'd scored another devastating hit on her identity. She may have known about the asthma, but Cammie's sixth finger was definitely a surprise. Cameron seemed to brace herself, then the heiress was back, forcing a slight smile. "Medicine and plastic surgery are great inventions, aren't they? Try to keep up, Hayden. It's been nice talking with you, but I must run."

"I checked your medicine cabinet at both places—you don't take drugs for pain because you're afraid Robert will get the upper hand. And you don't take any asthma medication, and there's no puffing on an inhaler when you're stressed. You're in danger, Cameron, and you probably know it better than anyone else." He worried for her, for what could happen. Because Robert wasn't going to forget her display, her rebellion against him, and Hayden had some idea of what she'd endured as a child. "Stay with me."

Her answer was soft, her eyes sad and shadowed. "No, I can't. I have made promises that I'm going to keep. You think I don't know what he's capable of?"

"I guess you do. Look, I'm tied up here for a couple days. Stay here, with me. I'll go back with you, and we'll sort this out."

"Just that easy, hmm? Sorting out everything? I've talked to William. He certainly gave you enough information about me, enough to 'sort' everything out."

Hayden stared at her, trying to understand her reasoning. "I won't hurt you."

She raised her hand to her temple as if it ached, and the thick layer of diamonds glittered, the bells jingled—then Hayden noted the bruises the bracelet had hidden. He took her hand, carefully sliding the bracelets higher to view the bruises, the pattern of fingerprints. He didn't have to ask whose hand had left the bruises; her expression told him more than enough.

He must have shown his savage need to beat Robert, because Cameron was quick to draw away, to slide the bracelets down over her wrist. "He didn't get away free," she said. "I've learned a few things."

Rage and guilt washed over Hayden; he'd left her alone with Robert. "Dammit. He'll kill you."

"Not until I get what I want, what I have to have, what I promised someone I'd get. Besides, I told you already, if I die, the estate and everything goes to charities. Nothing will happen to me. I'm worth too much alive— What are you doing?" she asked as Hayden began unbuttoning her blouse.

"Take it easy. I just want to see the damage—" He lifted away the silk at her side, studied the large bruise and ran his hand lightly over it. She grimaced, drawing in breath. "Just fine, huh?" Hayden asked grimly. "What does the rest of you look like?"

Her hands batted against his as he slid down her pants zipper and tugged her pants down, leaving her in a beige thong. Hayden turned her, taking in the large bruise on her pale skin, the sight sickening him. "Cameron—"

She tugged up her pants and zipped them. "I took a bad fall . . . you saw it. What did you expect?"

Cameron was fighting tears, and yet bravely facing him. Hayden shook his head slightly, and understood her crisp defenses. "Tough girl. Nobody took care of you when you were a child, did they?"

"I managed. And I had Madeline. I don't need your sympathy, H.J. Now that I know who you are, that you're obsessed with your own—imagination, some screwy idea about who I am—I think it better not to see each other again."

"Finished. . . . Just like that, huh?" He stepped back and crossed his arms—because if he hadn't, he'd be kissing her, making love to her, holding her safe.

"You got it, chum," she said as she buttoned her blouse with shaking fingers. "We both got what we wanted, didn't we?"

He didn't answer, because he knew he wanted more.

But what did she want so badly? What answers to what questions? And who did she promise?

Cameron crossed her arms and angled her face up to his. "Forget about that cute little copywriting job you had me signed for. Oh, yeah. Grow Green Lawn and Garden catalog will have to move on without me working on their fall and winter tulip collection. Neat little trick . . . having someone contact me to write the copy. All a setup, wasn't it? Moving in as—"

"I never hid who I was."

"Same as, cowboy. It was all too much of a coincidence—you, the gardener's son, that meeting alone at night with no one around—that was just so you could get a good look at me, wasn't it? When you went out of the cafe, bent down between your car and mine, you put that rock in the valve—"

Okay, so he felt guilty. "You're right on all counts. I'm sorry. I wasn't planning to stop in Mimosa—ever. But I saw the heiress who had everything while my family lived in—we had a hard time."

"Apology not accepted. You bastard," Cameron said tightly, her body trembling with anger. "You lying bastard."

This time, he didn't block her slap . . . because he deserved it. "Happy now?"

She was shaking, and seemed shocked. "I've never hit anyone, except Robert in self-defense."

"There's always a first time. I deserved it—for leaving you with him. I knew what would happen by the way he looked. Too bad he didn't come after me. I would have liked that."

"You used me." As if all the air had left her, Cameron crumpled onto a streamlined couch. That tiny grimace, the way she eased her body to one side, reminded him of the painful bruises. "But then, I've been used all my life. I should have expected it."

"I don't like being placed in the same category as DuChamps, and I don't like being used either."

"Look who's talking. We both got what we wanted. We had sex. Plain old sex. Scratching an itch kind of sex," Cameron said as she slowly, painfully rose to her feet and walked to the door.

"Try again. You came back for a second helping." Surprised at how her denial had hurt him, Hayden instantly regretted the harsh reality he'd just thrown at her.

"So we're sexually compatible. I was lonely. You were having a fun time deceiving me, and I was putting one over on Robert—I admit that."

This woman knew exactly where to place her barbs and make them sting. "Sure, tell another one. We've gotten to each other, or you wouldn't be here right now."

Since Hayden had gone that far, he might as well admit the rest: "I knew I wanted you when I saw you in that Kiss Me Under the Mistletoe banner. I'm not likely to forget those elf shoes, or the way you looked at me, as if you wanted me, too."

Cameron seemed to shut down, staring at him without expression, and silence fell heavily between them. Hayden put his hands in his pockets and looked across the wide expanse of carpet and the emotional storm to Cameron. He wanted to help her, to untwist the web of problems around her. "However you're going to deal with that, we're in this now, and I'd like to see it through. I want to help. I saw your first reaction at that storm cellar . . . I held you later. I've seen how shaken you can get when you forget something, that fear in your eyes, the way your face pales. And Robert—Robert needs to be dealt with. If you really want to get to Robert, let me help."

"What do you want from me?" Cameron asked unevenly.

Hayden took a deep breath and slowly, word by word, gave her the reason, the answer he had to have. "I want you to help me prove that someone killed my father, making it look like suicide. He was found with five hundred thousand. I want you to help me find what happened to the rest of the two million ransom."

"I've wondered about that," she admitted softly.

"We sure didn't have it. And you think Katherine had to die, that someone may have murdered her. Why? Was it because she'd recognize a replacement?"

Cameron shook her head, denying his offer and his answers; she opened the door and stepped out of Hayden's life.

"Oh, I don't think so, honey," he said quietly.

Hayden Olson, the gardener's son, had developed a file, clippings, a matrix of events from the kidnapping, his father's and Katherine's deaths, to the dazed child found wandering in the woods on the day of her mother's funeral.

By eight o'clock, Cameron had been pacing her barn for hours, replaying the ugly scene with Hayden and his accusation: *Whose life? I put together a few things. I played with . . . with Cammie. She had severe asthma, medicine and oxygen tanks were a part of her every hour alive. . . .*

Cameron rubbed the smooth surface of her right hand, still surprised that Cammie had had a scar there, the result of the removal of a sixth finger. Hayden had put all the pieces together, and he wanted more—

She watched the storm clouds gather, the dark gray tinged with just a bit of green that could foretell a tornado. The wind whipped the trees, sending a hissing sound that reminded her of being in that old cellar, the sound of lungs struggling to breathe in the damp darkness with that little slit in the door, that one little ray of sunlight that captured the dirt particles, spun them around endlessly, tiny little particles of gold.

Lightning struck in the distance, interrupting that recurring image, a deadly white javelin from the sky to the earth; her windows rattled slightly, protesting the resulting thunder. The radio alert had warned of a tornado prowling the area, strong enough to rip up sturdy oak trees by their roots, destroy whole towns, then almost whimsically lift a cow into the sky and let it come down to earth safely.

A tornado could ravage anything that stood in its path, but while other people took to their basements and storm cellars, Cameron was never going into the earth again—alive. For just a moment, she was back in that cellar, the tornado rattling the door like a giant beast waiting to come in—her body was cold, despite the warm temperature, and when small branches, broken by the wind, hit the windows and the roof of her barn, a flood of chilling memories came back to her.

She'd slowly awakened to hear the sound of wheezing, the struggle for breath . . . the little girl's face had been deathly pale in the shadows, a froth of hair surrounding it like a halo. She'd looked like an angel in heaven.

Only it wasn't heaven. It was hell and the angel had died.

"You always got nervous at times like this, pacing the floor, unable to sit for a minute. I like this guy," William was saying on her cell phone, but Cameron's mind was on Robert and the way he'd toasted her at the champagne brunch.

Robert had toasted Katherine as usual, then had lifted his glass in Cameron's direction, "the replacement, our hostess," he'd said with a smile that didn't reach his eyes.

The replacement, the substitute, the survivor. Cammie, the little girl with asthma and the missing sixth finger had died.

And another girl had lived.

Who was she before she was put in that cellar? The answers wouldn't come, trapped in her mind long ago—rather, they had been locked away by those early years of Robert's brainwashing.

Cameron looked outside to the churning dark clouds and remembered Robert's cunning smile that morning.

By noon after the party's guests had departed, he'd slapped a file folder down on Katherine's polished desk. "Your lover—maybe you'd like to know just who he is. I'll wait while you read it."

"You put a detective on him?"

"I have my sources."

The printout was of young H.J.'s journey from Mimosa, through several small towns on I-44, and then to St. Louis. *We had a hard time*, Hayden had said.

His destitute mother had held several jobs, the boy taking up paper routes, then working for a landscaper, running his own business while in college, then working himself into a vice president's chair at Grow Green Lawn and Garden in St. Louis. Married once, no children, mother remarried, sister married with two children. . . .

"I knew all that," Cameron had lied to Robert, as she had struggled to absorb everything in the file folder; her hands had flattened over it, as if to seal the past from slithering out.

"The other interesting thing about H.J. is that Paul Olson was his father, the kidnapper who committed suicide—Hayden Olson is using you, Cameron, and you're too stupid to figure it out. He's got a reason for being in your bed, or he wouldn't be there."

Lightning tore through the sky again, spreading a momentary glow over Somerton House, where she'd made love to the kidnapper's son, a man who was out for revenge, having the heiress on a plate.

Bitterness and pain tore through her as William asked over the cell phone, "Are you okay, Cameron?"

The genuine concern in his voice brought her back to their conversation. "I'm fine. I think the storm is moving away now. What were you saying?"

"Mm . . . that the storms are really bad in Oklahoma. I'd really like Arabella to meet you. I was wondering if maybe we could visit—"

Automatically, she moved toward her tote where she kept her date book, ready to take a note. She dug into the bag, through the assortment of lip gloss, mascara, a bottle of ibuprofen for her bruises, the folder with her credit cards. The book wasn't there, and she hurriedly dumped the contents of the bag onto the table, foraging through them. "Sure. When?"

Lately she'd misplaced her personal checkbook . . . she hadn't parked the Miata in its usual place in the garage's arrangements of cars and trucks . . . she hadn't set the aquarium temperature right . . . she'd incorrectly assigned the seats at the dinner, a bitter ex-wife sitting next to a remarried ex-husband.

"Well, I— Arabella, too? She's in her eighth month and she's needing a little break before the baby comes. I thought a visit with you would be nice. You're on the list to play godmother, so she really wants to check you out."

Cameron closed her lids and shook her head. All she needed underfoot was an ex-husband and his pregnant girlfriend. "Sure. But here, at the barn, not in Somerton House."

"But there's plenty of room there—"

"Robert and I are in a bad patch. I don't think that would be good for Arabella now, would it?"

"The way you two go at it? No. The vibes between you two could send Arabella into an early delivery, and I do not want anything happening to her, or my baby," William stated firmly. "I've always regretted falling into that muck Robert set, but I've never regretted knowing you, how sweet you really are. I really do love you, you know."

"I love you, too." Cameron could picture William's angry expression, the one that always came when he rued his part in their marriage. "If I'm going to be the baby's godmother, I should meet Arabella. I'll put in another bed and some kind of a privacy—"

"That would be great." The boyish charm was back. "One of those sliding things you use for your bathroom. Arabella would love that."

"Oh, I guess that would be a good idea. Just let me know for sure when you're arriving."

"Great. Now I know why I love you. I'll cook. I'm a great cook. Thanks. This will be great. You always take care of everything. I know Arabella will love you. She's just super. You should see her on a go-cart track."

"Well, she won't be doing that for a while, will she, Daddy?" Cameron teased.

He laughed warmly, something that Cameron could use huge doses of right now. Obviously relieved, William ran off a list of ideas about getting a job and making a home for his wife and child, and the call ended.

"Just one big happy family," Cameron murmured dryly to herself.

She looked out into the storm and thought of young H.J.'s life, of how it had been torn apart. *We had a hard time*, he'd said. *The heiress who had everything.*

Thunder had rattled the windows again, and this time the dream catchers above her bed trembled.

She was the girl who had taken another's place. Images of Cammie's still body on that bench gripped her, and later, the dying girl's whispers had begun to haunt Cameron.

Cameron? Do I have any right to that name? But then, what is my real name?

She couldn't remember—

Out in the night, the cellar waited, taunting her with a truth Cameron had only discovered as a young teenager, years into the deception. And for all the years before that, she had actually thought she was the Somerton heiress.

Then at twelve, she'd opened a drawer one day and found the pictures of the real Cammie Somerton, and she had remembered the cellar and the girl who had died. She couldn't change her part in what had happened; it would haunt her forever. "I'm so sorry, Cammie. I couldn't help any of it."

In the shadows by the mirror, the tiny cross gleamed, a reminder of her childhood, of the role she had to play now. "My daddy gave it to me," she whispered, repeating the words she'd said so many times as a child. Words she'd been forced to memorize.

Cameron wrapped her arms around herself and thought of Hayden, his cold fury earlier that day. He had a file with all the news clippings . . . he'd actually known little Cammie Somerton, known of her life-threatening asthma, of Dr. Naylan's death, the destroyed records, of a potential cause for Katherine's suspected murder—something Cameron had already suspected herself: Cammie's mother and doctor would recognize the deception, the replacement as a fake.

Hayden had come into her life for a purpose—to resolve his own childhood trauma.

Whose life? he'd asked. Whose life was she leading? At first, Hayden had been testing her, but then he'd locked on to the truth, pushing her.

Cameron shook her head. Those first years were a blur of Robert's demands, of practicing her role, of fear and brainwashing—until she'd forgotten her real name, until she actually *was* Cameron Somerton. She'd actually thought that Katherine was her mother.

The dream catchers over her bed and near the windows pivoted slowly, turned by the overhead fans, and Cameron feared the nightmares that slipped through the feathers and beads.

She shivered and glanced uneasily at the bed Hayden had shared with her. "He was right, damn him. There's more going on between us than sex."

Right now, she needed him so much.

But she wouldn't trust Hayden again . . . she couldn't. He could unravel everything—before she got the answers she needed.

The telephone rang, and she noted Hayden's private number on the machine's digital readout. Her hand reached for the telephone, then jerked back. "Oh, no. You knew just what you were doing, coming here. Boy, I've got terrific judgment, don't I? You used me, H.J., and I'm not going to let you into my life again."

In the short space of ten days, Hayden knew more about her than was safe. And he was determined to get what he'd come after, what he'd deceived her to get.

He knew almost everything, and he could destroy her. But Hayden wanted the answer to the same question she had asked for years: *Where was the rest of the ransom money?*

Then: *Would that money trail lead to proof that Katherine had been killed?*

When the telephone rang again, Cameron turned to the night's storm outside her home, as tumultuous as her thoughts. All she had to do was to survive, to control her forgetful mind and keep her promise.

A flash of lightning highlighted Somerton House and the knoll behind it where Katherine and Buck's mausoleum stood. The pink roses would be heavy, nodding with rain. Cameron's fingers dug into her arms, the bells at her ears jingling slightly as the whispers came to slither around her. *Mommy?*

But now she wanted to hear, to remember . . . and dug into the sloping hill behind her home, the cellar waited.

While lightning and thunder strolled the night outside, Robert sat in the chair behind Katherine's desk; his muddy riding boots propped upon its gleaming cherrywood finish.

He should have recognized Hayden Olson right away, but then the gardener had been a big Nordic type, blond with blue eyes. H.J. had taken his mother's dark coloring, and now he wasn't a sniveling little ten-year-old boy crying over his dead father—he had the look of a man set on revenge.

And Hayden was Cameron's lover. She should have been Robert's, the man who created her, who nurtured her.

At first, William had been easygoing, quick to accept what Robert had told him, nurturing the romance with Cameron. But Hayden was stone-hard, and rough in comparison to Robert's leaner build, his elegant style. "Bitch," he said, furious with Cameron.

She'd brought Hayden to Somerton House as a trophy, something to taunt Robert in their ongoing little war. But that had backfired, and Robert had finally recognized the gardener's son, Cameron's lover. When confronted, she'd lied about knowing everything about Olson—but she hadn't; Cameron wouldn't expose herself to such danger if she had known.

She would have cut Hayden out of her life; she knew how to deal with trash—Robert had trained her in that, and Cameron was tough as steel, tough as Katherine had been, beneath all the smooth manners, that soft Southern style.

Katherine had kept him like a dog on a leash, and for years since she'd come to control the family millions, Cameron had done the same thing. But now, his patience was running thin.

Petal by petal, Robert destroyed the lush pink roses Cameron always kept close, a reminder of Katherine. He lifted a delicate petal high and let it spiral slowly down to the thick carpeting as he spoke to Katherine's framed photo on the desk. "Your fake little sweetheart is on the edge now. She took it hard—the gardener's son, playing her. Cameron isn't one to waste time, and her little trip into Oklahoma City was to deal with that. . . . She was shaken when she got home. How do I know? Oh, my little birds keep me informed."

He traced Katherine's soft smile, missing her a little perhaps, a genteel woman, without enough spark to keep him faithful during their whirlwind courtship or their marriage. The lonely widow had been ripe for picking, needing a man to fill the position of her husband. But then, just a month before their one-year anniversary, she'd informed him that she knew about his women and wanted a quiet divorce; Katherine offered to pay him well for his silence. She intended to cut him out of any money or decisions concerning the Somerton fortunes—while she lived.

Then Robert had known that he'd had to act. And he had. After Katherine's death, he'd had everything—until Cameron had grown up and taken Katherine's place, meting out his allowance.

Another petal fell to the pile on the floor as he said, "Just a little bit more, and Cameron will be where she belongs—heavily medicated, raving mad, where no one will believe her fantasies, and where I can do anything I want to her."

He gripped the stem, crushing it, and the thorns bit into his flesh, reminding him of how Cameron stood in the way of everything he wanted.

He opened his hand to the spots of blood and thought of the little girl who had come, dazed and wandering, out of the thickets and trees, of the blackberry briars and thorns she'd traveled through—

Then Robert knew exactly what would push Cameron over the edge.

"Since you loved that cellar so much, maybe you need a return trip to freshen your memories. Gargoyles and fairies and dream catchers aren't going to save you this time."

Just after an emotional blowup with a lover, Cameron would be ripe for an accident—something designed especially for her. Robert smiled tightly as he thought of the little girl who feared dark closets, her punishment for refusing his instructions, and of the woman who got nervous in small places. A woman with claustrophobia would want airy spaces, just like the barn she'd had remodeled.

If she thought those dream catchers and all the charms in the world could keep her from the terror of that storm cellar, she was wrong.

He smiled and placed his hands behind his head, enjoying the thought of having the upper hand once again. Because now he had the perfect idea, one that would be just enough to tip her over that precarious edge.

Taking his time, savoring his new idea, filled with confidence, Robert picked up the telephone for his local sexual fix. "Hi, sugar pie."

He yawned as he listened to the woman's whining about the time in the closet, her resulting bruises. Then, using tender promises and money, Robert arranged another meeting with her in the guest cottage in the same bed as Virginia Ulbrecht had used.

A profitable affair with Virginia wasn't going to happen, not after she saw how Cameron ruled Somerton. But Robert would take his time with his local talent tonight, building his power, and savoring his next move on Cameron . . . a return visit to the cellar.

Eleven

LATE THE NEXT AFTERNOON, CAMERON LISTENED TO HAYDEN'S message on her machine and tossed the brush she'd been using on the tile floor into the bucket. She sat back on her heels, slightly winded from a furious bout of cleaning that had everything to do with the guilt she felt deeply.

"Okay, Cameron. I know you're there. Stop playing games. Pick up."

Cameron rose to her feet and stripped off her plastic gloves. She walked to the window overlooking Mimosa and listened to Hayden speak. A flock of birds landed on the mimosa grove, causing the pink blooms to shimmer delicately in the sunlight, a contrast to the man's deep, frustrated voice on her message machine. "Look—I'm tied up here for all day and tonight, and maybe that's for the best, giving you time to cool down."

"The hell I will."

A muffled voice spoke in the distance, and Hayden ended with an angry impatient and sarcastic, "I love you, too, honey."

"So you're angry—big deal, Mr. H.J. Olson, son of a kidnapper." She punched in Madeline's autodial number. "I want Mr. Olson evicted from next door, Madeline."

"Uh-huh. I figured. Robert filled me in on who this guy really is. Bastard . . . having his little jollies with you. I've got the attorneys looking over that lease, but right now, it looks like he hasn't misrepresented anything in the papers. I could have a talk with him. I'm so sorry about this, honey. You really haven't had anyone since William, and now you end up all torn up with this guy, Hayden."

Cameron's pride went into defensive mode. "I am *not* 'all torn up,' Madeline."

"Okay, so you're not," Madeline agreed too easily. "Want me to come over for a while? I will. I don't like the idea of you, all alone and crying your eyes out over this lowlife. It's not enough that his family has the rest of that ransom money, but he has to come after you. Now, that was cold. But then, it's never enough for that kind. By the way, you didn't close the wall safe's latch all the way, so I did. And what should I do with that check to Hayden Olson on your desk?"

Cameron frowned slightly. Just after Robert's revelation about Hayden's identity, she'd put the jewelry she'd worn at the mansion into the individual velvet boxes, placing them in the safe. At the time, she'd been shaken and furious by Hayden's betrayal, by Robert's pleasure in the fool she'd made of herself.

Had she forgotten to fully close the wall safe? No one else could have opened it; she was the only one with the combination.

"Shred the check, Madeline. I know you're dealing with the investors now, taking my place and working on payroll and clearing up anything to do with the party. I don't want to bother you. I just appreciate your letting me get this out of my system. I'm mad, not hurt, got it? I'm so mad that if I tangle with Robert right now, I could really do some damage."

"So? He's only around here because of Katherine's will. If you weren't such a stickler about honoring her wishes, he'd be long gone. Men are such dogs. Take it easy, hon. Love you."

When Cameron hung up, she studied herself in the mirror. Her eyes were haunted, shadowed with hours of the sleepless night and glistening with tears. The cellar was waiting; she could feel it beckoning to her—but fear had kept her inside her home.

She was forgetting things now, and the whispers were worse, more realistic and intense as if Cammie were calling to her.

Cameron trembled, and the bells at her ears tinkled. But they and the gargoyles, the fairies and all the good-luck charms she had collected weren't stopping the beckoning of that cellar. The gold cross gleamed by the mirror, the pictures of Katherine and Cammie reminding her of her promise. . . . "I'm afraid, okay?" Cameron whispered unevenly. "What if I do go over the edge? I'm already hearing whispers, and they're getting stronger. I might not be able to do everything you wanted, Mother. I might fail. Yes, I'm really, really afraid to go back to that cellar."

After a sleepless night and a day of prowling her home, "holed up" as Phoebe had said earlier in her call, Cameron was brooding, trying to settle her fear and her need to know, to remember everything that had happened in that cellar, the little things that had been locked away in her mind. Flashing pieces of her life before the kidnapping, just tidbits, were tumbling back, too blurred to piece together.

In her mirror, all the polished heiress veneer was gone; her face was strained, too pale and vulnerable.

Hayden had known all along who she was, and he was the gardener's son. Correction: He was the son of the man who had kidnapped Cammie. Cameron laughed shakily. "What a laugh that must have been, nailing the heiress."

But Hayden hadn't been laughing. He'd come after her for cold, calculated revenge; his life and his family's had been ruined, and he wanted a little of his own back. He'd had a clip file on the kidnapping, Katherine's death, on the recovery of the little heiress. His methodical notes were extensive, a time line matrix of the kidnapping and Cameron's appearance, too close to Dr. Naylan's and Katherine's "accidental" deaths.

That was it—pure revenge, and Hayden was pushing her now, just as Robert had always pushed her.

A softer emotion slid through her, a whimsical memory of Hayden holding her close, protectively. . . . As if he cherished her as a woman, a part of him—

Well, she'd definitely been a part of him, well and good. She'd had her sexual fix, and that was that.

Or was it?

Hayden had taken too much time making love to her, and apparently enjoying it, soothing her later. But then, she'd allowed only William close to her, and their lovemaking was more like a playful game.

Hayden had dug in deep and ruthlessly, especially when he'd come to the dinner party. Maybe that was his special moment—shoving his identity in front of her guests. "Some joke," Cameron whispered unevenly.

She looked out into the late-afternoon sun, and placed her palm on the warm smooth glass. A chill shot through her, because she was really feeling the cold damp wood of that door on the storm cellar.

The desperate need to go inside it once again, to remember everything, to try to remember the gardener's face, drove her outside.

Soon she was running toward the storm cellar. Brush tore at her blouse, the pink fabric tearing slightly, just as the child's pink blanket had shredded. *Is it still there?*

If she stood inside the cellar, would the nightmares and the whispers stop? If she faced the worst, would that make her remember everything and she could keep her promise?

Standing in front of the cellar's open door, Cameron studied the shadows that her body had created; the sunlight stretched between her legs and into the darkness. Cold fear leaped in her, knotting in one tight ball around her heart, as she remembered being so small and helpless, that one sliver of daylight coming through the old door, begging it to last.

She held very still, because she had just remembered that whispers had come from *outside* the door, raw and low, so different from the childish ones inside.

Mommy? Mommy? the child had begged.

Shut up or there won't be any food, the hissing harsh whisper had ordered.

A squirrel raced across the earthen hill over the storm cellar, chattering at the human intruder.

Cameron wrapped her arms around her and backed away from that open doorway, the timbers framing the door, still sturdy after twenty-eight years. Sagging on its rusty hinges, the crude door leaned back as though waiting for her. Cameron forced herself to breathe slowly, in and out, sucking at the fresh sunlit air. "I'm not that little girl anymore. I've got to face this. . . ."

She was coming to pieces, forgetting appointments and conversations and misplacing things, and just maybe, if she could face this one yawning dark hole, step into it, she might remember everything—

Cameron backed slowly away from the cellar, but the whispers of the past began, the sucking of that air, in and out—was it hers? Now? Here? Or was it that little girl so long ago?

Taking her time, blinking back tears, fearing the memories churning around her, memories of something that had really happened, that Cameron had fought with good-luck charms and dream catchers—but they waited for her inside, calling her back.

Help me. I'm afraid. I'm cold, Mommy, and it's dark here. Why, Mommy? Why did they put me here? Mommy?

If she stepped inside, who would she be? A terrified little girl? Could she step back into the past and face her terror?

In the still, sunlit air, she was perspiring, trembling, holding herself and rocking her body. Cameron closed her eyes, fought the snaring web of fear drawing her closer to the cellar, to what she feared most of all. She had to go back, to face what had happened—

Then in one step, a bend of her head, and she stood inside. Earthy musk pressed against her, filled her senses with the terror of the past. The old benches were there, the broken shelving, the beams and planks supporting the cellar against the weight of the earth above. Roots had grown through the beams, like tiny fingers reaching out to her—

The jar with the eleven pebbles was gone. Perhaps someone had collected the jar; antique jars, scavenged from trash, sold well in flea markets. A few shreds of the blanket remained, and Cameron remembered those hard benches, lying on them, counting the pebbles, one by one, and always, the steady sound of air sucking slowly in and out, the childish whispers.

Locked in the sound of her own forced breathing, the terror of the time long ago, Cameron suddenly heard a scrape, and then the door closed, sealing her into her worst living nightmare—

She pressed her hands against her ears and still the whispers circled her. *Mommy? Help me. . . .*

The whispers curled around her, squeezed her, pushing her to the dirt floor and into the blackness. . . .

After two nights of working hard to finish at the new Oklahoma City store and driving three hours back to Mimosa and the farm, Hayden wasn't feeling kindly to the woman who wouldn't answer his telephone calls, his e-mail, or her own doorbell.

None of Cameron's girlfriends had seen her, and Madeline was stonewalling, not offering information about her employer's whereabouts. Hayden's frustration was directed at himself; he probably deserved anything Cameron threw at him. He should have told her who he was from the start; but then, he was so anxious to get his hands on her that he'd missed explaining that little bit of information. He'd never forget Cameron's stunned expression, the way her voice seemed so distant—after he'd shown her that thick, special file.

At nine o'clock in the morning, Hayden was sweaty and angry, and needed some physical release. In front of Cameron's barn, he carefully arranged mulch around the two magnolia trees he'd just planted, then bent to pick up the soaking hose to wash his hands. It was seasonally late to plant trees, and he knew the hazards of heat and drought they would face, but still, the activity helped.

He stripped off his dress shirt, wiped his hands on it, and then the sweat from his face and chest. The mud on his expensive dress shoes marked his anger at Cameron, his impatience. *Didn't she know that Robert was dangerous enough to kill her?*

Hayden looked at his palms, burning with fresh blisters; he'd dug the holes in an impotent fury, and more than once, thought about breaking into Cameron's home. Maybe he deserved a cold freeze, but at least he could try to protect her.

He studied the privacy windows and her Toyota pickup. When he'd arrived an hour earlier, the motor was cold, beads of dew drying on the hood. In the shady backyard, the dew on the overgrown weeds hadn't been marked by footprints. If Cameron had "holed up," she was doing a good job of it.

While the magnolia trees would have large creamy blooms that had reminded him of Cameron, they were a peace offering, a token of the groveling he would probably have to do—if she ever talked to him again.. One thing was for certain, he had the best possible vantage place for seeing when she came back to her barn—the farmhouse next door.

He showered quickly, then, keeping an eye on Cameron's place, he brewed coffee, checked his e-mail and message machine for a response from her. There was a clipped message from Madeline, requesting that under the circumstance, it might be better if he "found another place—perhaps a different community—all deposit fees refunded with interest and additional negotiable monies for compensation, of course, as soon as possible."

" 'Soon,' " Hayden said. "So Cameron can come back here? She's going to have to face me at some time."

He'd hurt her badly. But he'd been right about one thing—sex wasn't the only thing between them. In the space of less than two weeks, she'd become the center of his life, his fascination, and a woman he would protect with his life. Hayden sipped his coffee and stared out of the kitchen window to the quiet barn, the fairy statues in the back, overgrown with weeds, the dead plants around the house, and the two magnolias he'd just planted.

Where was Cameron? Hayden shook his head. She'd been so terrified when she'd seen that old storm cellar—

"Cameron! Dammit! No!" he said, ordering her, willing her, not to have gone back to that nightmare alone, not to face the past alone.

Hayden couldn't remember tearing out his back door, through the old garden place, and back through the heavy brush and briars to the sloping hill. But suddenly, he saw the old wooden door, closed against the storm cellar, and he cursed himself for not tearing it completely away, for not burning it— "Cameron!"

He held his breath, his heart chilled and almost stopped beating when he saw the two heavy posts had been wedged and braced securely against the door. He threw one aside and the other—and there was no sound inside as he forced the door open.

The wedge of sunlight fell upon Cameron. She simply sat on the bench, her torn palms turned upright on her thighs. Her hair was matted, tangled with debris, and her face was scratched; tears had left trails in the dirt on her cheeks.

She stared blankly at him and whispered hoarsely, "My name is Pilar. My name is Pilar, not Cameron. Is this a dream?"

Hayden held his breath. She seemed in a trance, and afraid

of approaching her too soon, he eased into the cellar and crouched beside her. One look at her injured hands caused his throat to tighten. "Would it be okay if we left now, honey?"

"I'm Pilar, not Cammie. Cammie died. He took her away."

There it was, everything he suspected, but nothing mattered now, except getting Cameron/Pilar to safety. He had to bring her back from whatever terror had left her in this dulled state. "It's warm and sunny outside. Let's go outside, okay? Can you stand?"

She nodded slowly. "I'm Pilar."

"Hi, Pilar. It's nice to meet you." Hayden had to be careful not to startle her, to snap that thin thread that bound her to reality; he wanted to carry her, but the doorway was too small. He picked a dead leaf from her hair, thought of what she must have gone through, and carefully eased his hand around her wrist, fearing for her damaged hand. Her pulse ran too slowly beneath his fingers— "Let's go outside where the sun is, okay?"

"Cammie died. He took her."

Hayden swallowed hard. *He* . . . was he the gardener? Or Robert?

She let him guide her slowly out of the storm cellar, and she blinked at the morning sunlight, staring dazedly up at him. Her voice was strained, pushed from her, and Hayden realized that she'd probably screamed for hours. . . .

"Would you mind if I carried you?" Hayden asked when she stumbled slightly as if her legs were weak.

He fought gathering her up into his arms; he could frighten her badly now, jarring her back into a hell from which she might never recover.

When she nodded, Hayden gently eased her up into his arms. "You're going to be all right now. I'm going to help you."

"No one came to help me. Ever."

That single sentence sounded thin, childlike, as she curled into him. Hayden hurried to carry her back to his house; he'd carry her anywhere to be safe. Someone had trapped her in that cellar, and he feared danger could be waiting in her home—just in case she escaped. "But this time, I came. Feel the sunshine. Everything is going to be all right."

"Robert said my name would be Cammie. He said that a lot. I had to learn so much. I didn't like the closets."

Hayden fought back the murderous rage, the need to avenge a child trapped in deceit, punished and brainwashed into playing a role.

On a path to his house, Hayden carried her through the brush, through the old gate and into his freshly tilled garden. Would she come back from the darkness unharmed? For a heartbeat, Hayden's fear turned into rage at the person who had obviously locked her within that cellar.

And that was probably Robert, the person who would most benefit from Cameron going over the edge of sanity—

Hayden suddenly realized that he still thought of her as Cameron, the girl whose real name was Pilar.

But now she was in Hayden's arms, shaking, her fingers digging into his shirt. She looked at her home, then at the old stone farmhouse, as if slowly recognizing them. He kept talking to her, pushing down his fear and his fury into one easy gentling tone. Then, almost at his back porch, she whispered, "Hayden?"

He stopped, holding her perfectly still, grateful that she remembered him, and hopeful that she was coming back from the terror. He held her closer, kissing her temple, her hair. "What, honey?"

"Don't take me inside, not yet, okay?"

He looked around for a big bold spot of morning sunshine coming through the trees. The tree stump seemed the most likely seat, and he started to lower her onto it. But Cameron locked her arms around him. "Hold me. Just hold me."

Hayden sat with her on his lap, huddled against him, her face lifted to the sunlight. Her cracked lips, the scratches on her cheeks and where her long-sleeve blouse had torn, her hoarse voice, all spoke of her terror. "Honey? You need water—"

"What day is it?"

"Sunday. I saw you Friday at the grand opening—"

"Sunday," she repeated slowly, as if turning the clock's hours in her mind. She looked at her hands, the palms torn, and shuddered. "The second week of July?"

"Yes." Hayden waited while she looked down at her body, taking in her torn pink blouse, the dirt on her jeans and pink boots. He wondered if he should tell her that the door had been braced shut from the outside, that someone had trapped her inside . . . and that someone was likely to be the person who could most profit by Cameron's instability.

"I'm dirty and I'm thirsty," she said slowly. Her voice was hoarse, but the statement was very proper and ladylike. Then, she looked up and studied his face. "You look so fierce. I must be a mess. Thank you for your concern, but I'm fine. Really, I am."

She was drawing herself back inside to the heiress's protective polished layers. Would she remember that she'd said her name was Pilar?

Hayden didn't understand what was turning in Cameron's mind, but the proper elegance of a lady contrasted what she must be feeling. He wanted to smash Robert's pampered face, but he had to remain quiet, careful of Cameron's fragile state now. "That's good. I see that you are fine. A bit dirty, but that's all," he said gently.

"You're holding me awfully tight. Let me go."

As if he could ever let her go— Hayden forced himself to release her body and slowly, painfully, as if separating him in all ways from herself, Cameron stood. Walking unsteadily, she walked toward the garden hose, and, sensing her need, Hayden moved quickly to turn on the faucet. Her scratches needed soap and disinfectant, but right now,

Cameron seemed to be finding her reality, putting herself back into life, and that was more important.

He held the hose for her as she washed her hands slowly, meticulously, as if she were washing something other than dirt from her—like a lifetime of guilt that wouldn't come off as she scrubbed harder and harder.

She studied her upturned palms beneath the stream of cold water as if trying to recognize them as a part of her. She turned her hands over, studying them. "I broke some nails."

"A good manicure will fix that," Hayden said, attempting to keep the talk light, easy, comforting. "We'll take care of that soon. I used to be pretty good at doing my sister's when she broke her arm."

"You have a sister. She was sick. Your family needed money."

"She's fine now." *Had his father been a part of the kidnapping? Had Paul Olson removed Cammie's dead body from that cellar?*

"That's good." He held the hose as Cameron bent to drink thirstily from the running water. Suddenly, she plunged her face into the water, scrubbing it. She drank again, then guided his hand to hold the hose over her head.

The cold water spilled down her. Then, hurriedly, she pulled off her boots and began to unbutton her blouse. She undressed quickly, standing naked beneath the cold running stream of water. Through the silvery sparkling veil, she looked at him. "I'd like to use your shower, if I may. But my feet are muddy . . . I'll mess your floors."

Did she remember that she'd said her name was Pilar? That Cammie had died and had been taken away?

"No, you won't. Here, lift one foot—" His floors didn't matter, but Cameron's fragile state did; her sensibilities had to be handled gently. While she braced her hand on his shoulder, Hayden bent to hold the hose with one hand and wash her foot with the other. He wrapped his arm around her and lifted her; almost as if it didn't belong to her, as if she were observing someone else, Cameron watched her foot turn beneath the spray.

"A lot of dirt happens in a person's lifetime," she stated quietly as the mud slid away from her foot. "I wish it were that easy to remove."

Hayden inhaled unevenly as he lifted her in his arms, cradling her. She studied his face and he tried not to show his fear that she might not recover fully from her terror. "May I ask you to turn off the water? I'm having a little problem with my hands," she asked.

He bent with her, turning off the faucet. "Thank you," she said very properly.

When Hayden placed her on her feet in the shower stall, Cameron continued studying him. What did she remember about Cammie? Did she remember now, as she pulled herself back into the lady?

"H.J.," she said quietly, studying him carefully.

"Yes." He waited for an eternity, or was it only a few heartbeats? Would she turn from him now?

Her eyes were clear upon him, as if she were seeing him for the first time. "I know about you. Cammie told me. She loved you."

"And I loved her." Hayden swallowed tightly and handed her a glass of water. She drank slowly, those cautious blue eyes studying him over the rim. "Do you need help?" *Pilar? Cameron?*

"No, I want to do this by myself. I've never liked small places. Would you mind leaving the door open?" She shook her head, and the shower curtain closed; water began to run, steam rose as she turned slowly behind the curtain. Hayden rubbed his hand across his jaw, then across his chest, where the tension lay like a hard knot.

Afraid to leave her alone, even for a minute, he leaned back against the sink cabinet. The woman in the shower was moving slowly, trying to reclaim herself. *Her name was Pilar . . .*

Cammie had died . . . "He" had taken her away—who was he? Robert? Or Hayden's father?

"Damn him, that gardener's son. . . . Like father, like son . . . always interfering, sticking their noses in where they aren't needed."

Robert tossed the small voice-activated recorder onto the table; it had been carefully inserted down into the cellar after Cameron had been trapped. In the quiet of his bedroom, he slashed his riding crop across the altered picture of his deceased wife and her daughter, necessities of the appearance he needed to keep—that of the loving husband and stepfather.

The frame tumbled onto the carpeting. He'd been riding his stallion around the path he frequently took when he'd seen Hayden tearing through the brush toward the cellar. "Damn him. He's going to end up the same way as his father—dead."

Very little had kept Robert from using the revolver he usually strapped to his hip when riding alone, from killing Hayden and stuffing Cameron back into the cellar to finish the job. Using his binoculars, Robert had watched Hayden carry Cameron like a child to his backyard. She's showered, naked in the sunlight, like a tramp without morals . . . like the tramp Robert used when he didn't want to play games, when he wanted raw satisfaction, to master, to overpower, to hurt.

Cameron's body had been lean, but with enough curves to fuel Robert's longtime simmering desire for her. He'd always considered her to be his property, his creation. He'd had plans for that body, for using it, making her obey him—

He picked up the tape recorder and listened again to the tape, filled with her cries, her begging, her sobs of helplessness. "She was just at the breaking point. Another few hours, maybe a day, and she'd have been in a bad enough state to use heavy sedatives, and then—"

And then, he would have his due and take charge. He'd

get rid of Madeline once and for all and it would be clear sailing. . . .

Robert ground the heel of his riding boot into the picture frame, breaking the glass, just as he would break Cameron's willpower. Then he picked up the phone and called the woman he needed to defuse his temper.

Then, relieved of his frustration, he could think coolly—

Hayden knew. Cameron had admitted everything to him, her life as a fraud, the replacement for the dead heiress . . .

After a long shower that did nothing to wash away the guilt she had for surviving when Cammie hadn't, Cameron slowly paced the small house. In the late afternoon, she wore only Hayden's overlarge cotton summer shirt—after all, what did modesty matter when he knew everything despicable about her?

And she knew even more—she knew where she'd come from, a place filled with filth and hate and no tenderness for an unwanted child.

The tea he'd brewed for her sat cooling on a coffee table as scarred as she felt now. The fresh cleaning scents and new lumber curled around Cameron, reminding her of how she could never erase those scars. A fan hummed softly in the background, and when it turned, the slight breeze stirred her damp hair, reminding her that she was still alive—and Cammie wasn't.

Thunder rolled and lightning flashed and rain began to pound the farmhouse roof and windows. Years ago, she had searched so hard for a missing girl around her age; but now she had a name for a street child that no one seemed to want or love. Fuzzy images circled her, then pictures of missing children who were never found. She heard a slurred drunken voice from the past, "I never wanted you, Pilar. Just go away. . . ."

Who was Pilar? Where had she lived? Who were her parents?

Hadn't anyone looked for her?

Did she matter so little?

"*I never wanted you, Pilar. . . .*"

The name Pilar seemed foreign, the fit unfamiliar. As a scared, neglected child, she'd slid into another's life and somewhere deep in her mind, she was still Cameron Somerton, daughter of the deceased Katherine Somerton, heiress.

But that was better than being Pilar Somebody, a street waif, raised amid terror and hunger. Any child would have taken the food a stranger had offered twenty-eight years ago—drugged food that caused her to sleep, to awake next to a dying child gasping for breath. . . . As she had listened to Cammie tell about her home and life, it had seemed so beautiful: a loving mother, all the food she wanted, and a boy named H.J. who kept her safe. Her own mother had drunk and cursed, and hadn't loved her. . . .

Pilar had no right to live; she should have died, not Cammie. . . .

She'd never gone to school . . . she wasn't on those records and probably not on others. . . .

Cameron wrapped her arms around her body and rocked, just as she remembered doing as a child, trying to comfort herself when no one else had loved her.

Pilar, her name was Pilar. . . .

She'd hunted through files of missing children for her image, the one that had been graphically inserted into one of Cammie with her mother. But she'd had no name to use when searching, no place to begin. Did she even want to find out more about her mother?

For years, she'd led twin lives, trying to discover Pilar, whom she might have been, but she couldn't find the pieces. Maybe she didn't want to know, because the pieces were ugly and cruel. She stood at the kitchen window, her hands clamped, white-knuckled to the counter, aware that Hayden was never far away, waiting for the truth that he deserved.

Rain seemed to burst against the windows, collecting and

snaking trails down it as Hayden's body came to frame hers, his hands lightly covering the bandages he'd wrapped so gently around hers. Cameron closed her eyes, remembering how he'd dried her while she stood dazed and dripping wet, how closely he bent to study her injured palms, to pick the last slivers from them, to apply antibiotic salve. Drained now, she could only stand in this small room, watching this tall, powerful man who knew everything about her, who should be calling the police even now.

Wearily, she thought that men always seemed to be holding some threat over her.

Beyond the sheets of pounding gray rain, small trees swayed in front of her barn. "I didn't plant those—"

Instead, Hayden just stood behind her, not touching, not pushing her for more. "They're magnolias. They remind me of you."

Tears burned her eyes; she knew of the beautiful fragrant creamy blooms, the glossy leaves. Wrapped in the guilt of a lifetime, weighed by it, Cameron couldn't look at him, her throat tight as she whispered, "I don't want to talk now. I never thought he would go so far—Robert, I mean."

Cameron moved away from Hayden. Cammie's affection for H.J., the boy she had loved, was something that Pilar had wanted desperately, to be cared for, and to be loved.

Cameron was everything that Robert had made her, the imposter, the changeling, the woman leading dual lives, the "odd" woman who had to keep her promise to Katherine and to Cammie.

She had to find where Cammie was buried, what had happened to that tiny body. . . . She had to discover if Katherine had been murdered. . . .

Burdened by guilt, Cameron couldn't look at Hayden and walked into the living room to sit curled on the couch, drawing the throw pillow there close against her. In the shadowy cool house with the rain pounding on the roof, Hayden stood against the kitchen doorway. His shoulder braced against the doorframe, one hand resting against the opposite side, the other hooked into his jeans. He was probably wondering how he could have touched someone so despicable. "You should eat something."

She shook her head. "Does it really matter?"

"I'd rather you ate, but then everything is up to you." Hayden moved back into the kitchen, the sound of a refrigerator door being opened and closed, dishes clattered a bit, a drawer opened and closed, and a microwave sounded.

The rain eased into a gentle hum, the storm moving away. *She could run, but could she hide from the truth?*

Hayden returned to place a bowl of soup in her hand, a glass of milk and a sandwich on the coffee table. "Peanut butter and jelly . . . that's all I have."

Cameron looked at the soup, a creamy tomato, something a child like Cammie would have loved.

But there had been no food, just scraps to keep the sickly little girl alive—

Why? Long enough to give the imposter part of Cammie's memories, her life, enough to let the imposter child slide into the role of heiress?

"Aren't you going to eat?" Cameron asked, remembering her manners, taught to her with a slap and the threat of a small dark closet. *Wait until the others eat, no matter how hungry you are, you little brat.*

Hayden nodded and returned with a sandwich like hers, only with three pieces of bread, not two. He sat in a chair opposite hers, his bare feet reminding her that he'd stood close, holding the hose while she'd tried to wash away the terror of the cellar. . . . His chest had been wet, his jeans dirty, his shoes muddy. His dress clothing had been tossed over a chair in the bathroom. Covered with mud and dirt, his expensive custom-made shoes had been carefully placed on newspaper. "You ruined your dress slacks and shoes when you planted those trees, didn't you? Because of me?"

"The shoes will polish out good as new. I had to do something when you didn't answer my calls."

Cameron mentally foraged for how to repay him, and came up with: "I don't have my checkbook, but let me know how much, and I'll see that—"

But then, she thought, mockingly, what right did she have to use Somerton money?

"Take it easy," Hayden said quietly, watching her with dark, knowing eyes. She couldn't look at him, and slowly spooned soup into her mouth. Was he afraid that she was already over that precarious edge?

"I didn't know my name until I was trapped in there . . . Pilar Somebody from somewhere. There were pictures of me graphically imposed where Cammie's image should have been with her mother. But after that, there weren't any pictures taken of me after I took her place, not for years. Robert explained that to the public as he was protecting me. Celebrities and the wealthy sometimes don't let their children's pictures be taken for that reason. I don't know how long I'd been drugged before being put in with Cammie. I don't know how many miles I'd traveled to get here. I just don't know—I wouldn't know where to begin to find where I came from.

Cameron fought the chill inside her. *For a time, from six to twelve years old, she'd actually believed that Katherine had been her mother. Then she'd wanted to paint a chest pink and had found those pictures of the real Cammie and the nightmare became a reality. . . .* "All I remember is my mother drinking herself into a stupor and that she hated me. I've tried to find myself in the missing children's pictures . . . with a name now, I could try again, but I don't know that I want to. I just remember being so hungry, and a stranger offering me food—I suppose you want to know everything."

As a child, she'd replaced her own mother with Katherine, believing for years that Cammie's mother was her own. . . . It was so much easier than the reality of an unloved child. . . .

She was so weary now, her secret exposed. His silence hung in the room, demanding the truth. "It had to be Robert—the person who trapped me in there. He has the most to gain if I flip over entirely. He would know exactly how terrified I am of small dark places."

"I wondered if you knew that was deliberate."

"A door that heavy doesn't close by itself," she stated bitterly. Then, suddenly anger and hunger set in, and she lifted the bowl to drink the soup. She placed the bowl carefully on the table. "Eleven days I was in that hole, and then I came out—rather was drugged and carried out and put somewhere in the woods. That was the day of Katherine's funeral—in the evening, after she'd been placed in that mausoleum with her husband. . . . But those first ten days in the cellar, Cammie was slowly dying . . . she'd already been there for three days. Somehow, he knew when she wasn't breathing any more, and then he came and got her."

Hayden shifted restlessly. "It all makes sense— She was so fragile. With her health problems, Cammie wasn't a sure bet to live—"

"I know—Cammie's health wasn't dependable. Robert needed a replacement, one with good lungs, so that she would live longer, and he could wring more out of Katherine's estate. Don't you think I've thought about that?" she cried.

Cameron put down the soup and tugged the pillow over her face. "I can still hear the sound of her breathing. Where are my earrings? I want my earrings!" She pushed away the pillow and was ready to stand when Hayden's hand came firmly upon her shoulder and in his palm rested her bell earrings. She hurried to put them on, shaking her head, listening to the bells, then she grasped her knees, rocking the pain inside her, back and forth, just as she had rocked the dying girl. "How could anyone do that to a little girl? He knew that she would die without her medicine, her oxygen."

Hayden stood quietly beside her. "Let me give you something to ease—"

For the first time, Cameron stared at him, not shielding her anger as it vibrated from her. "Drugs? What do you think he used to make me think that I was actually Cammie? Drugs are very effective when you're being brainwashed into thinking you're someone else, that you've lost your memory of who you really are, that your— *I actually thought I was Cammie until I found those old pictures of her—I must have been twelve or so, and they were in the bottom of an old drawer that I—*"

Hayden's mouth was tight, his eyes narrowed as his anger clashed with hers. "Cameron, do not blame yourself. You were a child."

She was on her feet now, pacing back and forth, furious with herself, with Robert. "Don't you think I've tried to find out who I was? I went through the missing children's photos whenever I could, checking the places and the dates. But I know enough about my—my mother to know that she wouldn't miss me. I was just a 'problem' to her. I doubt that she even filed on me, or missed me. I wasn't in school yet, not on the records. I don't know that anyone would have ever missed me, if my own mother didn't. Katherine moved heaven and hell to find Cammie—"

Cameron was shaking now, furious with herself as she stalked by Hayden. "I'm going to kill him. I *will* kill him. Damn him. . . . I should have done it before now, and then turned myself in."

Hayden swung her into his arms and her fists started fighting the past, but instead pounding his back. He held her tighter against him, cradling her head against his shoulder. When Cameron began to cry, the years of pain tore from her, and after a long time, she lay exhausted against him. Her voice sounded rusty as she asked, "Why here? Why did you bring me here?"

His lips moved against her temple. "Because I wanted you

safe with me. No one knows my alarm system—I installed it myself. No telling how many people know yours."

"Only my friends. . . . I'm so tired." Physically and emotionally drained, Cameron let Hayden pick her up and carry her to a bed, where the sheets smelled of him, where she was safe—for a time, until she had to reveal to the world who she really was—an imposter.

His body cradled hers, taking care of her hands, holding her wrists, his thumb stroking one, his fingers massaging her scalp as she listened to his steady heartbeat and willed herself to drift away—

In the night, she awoke to find her head resting on Hayden's chest, his hand still stroking her hair. In the shadows, his expression was grim. The small oscillating fan was in the room now, humming, cooling, lightly stirring the hair on his chest.

But Cameron could feel him thinking as something savage within him was held at bay. She deserved his revenge, waited for it, but then he asked quietly, "Do you know where Cammie is?"

"No, I've tried and tried to find her. I've hunted everywhere. Before this—I went to excavation sites at the time, to other storm cellars, to old houses, shacks, everywhere. I've tried to trap Robert into telling me."

"The fairies in your backyard . . . they were for her, weren't they?"

"Yes, for Cammie. She loved fairies. I saw them in a flea market, and no one seemed to love them—I thought she would." *When we get out of here,* Cammie had said in her wheezing slow voice, *When my mommy finds us, she'll love you just like she does me. She always says the fairies come in the night to protect me, and now they'll protect you, too, Pilar. . . .*

"Everything you do is for a purpose, isn't it? You collect odds and ends that no one wants, because that's how you see yourself—as a child—something that no one wanted. Why is that? Can you remember anything else?"

She shrugged lightly and focused on the shifting shadows on the wall, caused by the wind stirring the trees outside. Droplets of rain splattered against the windows and rattled the screens. "Food. I remember someone—a man—offering me food, and I was so hungry. He asked how old I was and I said six. I was afraid, but took the food—a hot dog, I think, and ice cream. I was a street kid from some city somewhere, and I have flashes of people yelling, hitting each other, of my mother being drunk—of being hungry, of moving into strange places. . . . There was a pretty new doll, and I'd never had anything new before and I wanted her so much. . . . Then I remember waking up with Cammie in that hole. Someone had taken her from her bed, gagged and tied her, and had put her in there three days before I came."

She shivered and continued, "I didn't realize the timing, until I remembered the jar. I was there eleven days, she was there before me, so the total was two weeks. Everything was buried inside my mind for so long—six years. And I only remembered the rest when I was in that—"

Hayden suddenly jackknifed to sit on the edge of the bed, his back to her. Powerful muscles shifted in his shoulders, as though he were bunching his fists. "So, you lead the life you think Cammie might have lived, you honor her mother's wishes—including keeping Robert around—and then, then maybe you get a little relief, by doing the things that other people might see as odd, like tending bar." Hayden spoke slowly, perfectly fitting her life together; he was the first person, other than Robert, to realize the motivations in her life. . . .

Cameron turned to her side, curling up away from him, and the tears began to brim, trailing down her cheeks. "I'll never forget her."

"The dream catchers and the good-luck charms . . . you wrapped everything around you that you could . . . and the wide-open barn, the constant cleaning, the claustrophobia, it all fits."

"Nothing ever fits. Ever."

"No, it doesn't. Except for the timing—if she was in there *before* you came, that means he *knew* he had to get a little girl in there fast—and that was you. So . . . Robert was exactly certain of the timing—if he could pull off getting her out of the house the night of the anniversary party. And that might mean he'd had help . . . he couldn't do all that by himself, and not be missed," Hayden agreed bitterly, and then his weight left the bed. "The question is who."

Cameron tensed when she heard a hard blow against a wall, as though furious with the past, Hayden had slammed his fist into it.

She lay alone in the shadows, the fan humming softly, the breeze touching her, then moving away, only to come back again. . . . Hayden had lost more than she'd ever known—a father, someone he'd loved deeply.

Hayden didn't want to believe that his father could be capable of kidnapping, but proof had been scrawled in that suicide note. "And that might mean he'd had help," Hayden had said.

Was the "help" Paul Olson?

Twelve

HAYDEN STOOD IN THE LIVING ROOM, LOOKING AT THE LIGHTS of Mimosa in the distance, the Somerton mansion on the sloping hill to the west. The storm had returned, pushed back by another weather front from the western mountains. A lightning bolt shot straight down from the rolling gray clouds, illuminating them momentarily.

He lifted the cold beer and drank deeply, working through the bog of the past, the bitterness, and what had happened to a little girl named Pilar. Because she was six and neglected, she'd simply been collected and used. *I have flashes of people yelling, hitting each other, of my mother being drunk—of being hungry, of moving into strange places. . . .*

No wonder she wanted so badly to believe that she was Cammie and that her mother was loving and kind.

Cameron came to stand behind him, and he didn't turn. "What do you want me to call you, Pilar or Cameron?"

"Does it matter now?" Her voice was thin, only a whisper.

"Oh, it matters. . . . You realize that Katherine is probably dead, and Dr. Naylan, because they could identify you immediately. Then, there's Cammie. That's three people murdered at least. And just maybe my father—Robert would have needed a scapegoat to pin the kidnapping on. Either that, or my father might have been involved in the whole mess—he was a very handy man, and he would probably know how to damage the propane system of a hot-air balloon—or the pilot light—to make it look like an accident."

Cameron's hands were still bandaged, lying soft upon his back. Then her arms circled him and her face lay against his back. "You must have loved your father very much. I'll tell the police everything I know—"

"That won't clear him. I still don't think he was involved. We need more."

"We? Your mother and sister?"

He thought about what Pilar had needed, a little girl, trapped and listening to another girl fight for life. "And you. Tell me how you knew so much about Cammie."

"That's the reason I was put in there with her, wasn't it? Cammie told me everything, the soft things, like how she loved fairies, and how her mother loved roses, but couldn't have them in the house—because of Cammie's asthma. She bought her mother a bouquet of silk roses, did you know? And then there was Robert, of course. I was in my early teens before I realized how fully that I'd been brainwashed. Finding those pictures was a shock, and it took time to adjust."

Hayden thought about Robert's need for women and didn't want to think about Cameron as a developing girl. . . . "I don't imagine he was happy when you started to remember."

Her "No, he wasn't," was too succinct, as if she remembered that particular battle and one she'd continued to fight. "When did you know? About me—and Cammie?"

"Things didn't fit right away—that first night on the highway, you had a pickup full of blooming plants. I couldn't see anything of Katherine in how you looked. But then, I wasn't positive, just uneasy with the pieces. There's a big difference between a girl and a woman, and then, things can change—modern medicine is so improved. That bump where Cammie's sixth finger should have been wasn't there—but a plastic surgeon could have reworked it. . . . Cammie's ringlets could have been straightened. . . . Whatever didn't match, could be explained, but it left me uneasy. Then, you couldn't remember me, and I knew how deeply Cammie felt about me. I'm going to get that bastard and make him pay for everything."

Hayden placed his beer aside and turned slowly to her. "But right now—"

He'd started to kiss her, but Cameron jerked away, shaking. "How can you want me now? How can you bear to touch me?"

Hayden rested his hand on her throat, felt her fast-beating pulse, and recognized her expression—guilty, and bravely ready to accept punishment. "I'm not going to hurt you."

Cameron studied his face for several heartbeats, then looked away.

Hayden turned her back to him. "He would have liked you, you know. . . . Big Buck Somerton would have admired what you're trying to do. You're keeping Katherine's memory alive, not just in a charity donation fund or on a memorial plaque, but in her house, carrying on her traditions."

"Did you know him?"

Hayden smiled as he remembered the big tough businessman. Taking young H.J. with him was just an excuse for Buck Somerton to be like any other Oklahoma rancher, sneaking away for a piece of pie and a cup of coffee with the "boys" at the Eat and Gas Cafe. "Taking the boy out for some ice cream," Big Buck had called to Katherine, his wrinkles wrapped in a boyish grin.

"I knew him. He hired Dad a couple years before he had that last heart attack. Buck Somerton was a good man."

Cameron lowered her forehead to his shoulder, her body rocking slightly. With her arms around herself, she seemed to huddle into him, making herself small. "It wasn't right that I—the replacement, a 'street brat'—lived and Cammie didn't. It isn't right. It isn't fair. She fought so hard—the things she told me about her mother, how much she was loved, how Katherine said that Big Buck, a tough oil man who'd come up with every hardship, had loved his precious little baby. He died when she was only four, but Katherine had said Big Buck doted on the both of them, that he'd given Cammie that little cross to keep her safe—the cross on my mirror, the one Robert forced me to wear."

She shuddered and held him tightly. "I think that cross somehow linked me with her and kept me safe through those first years."

Hayden smoothed her back, cupped her head, and rocked with her. "I'm turning myself in," she whispered rawly. "I'm so tired of this charade."

He didn't want to lose her, gathering her closer. "I don't think you should do that."

Cameron pushed back from him, but still held her arms around herself, her expression fierce now, tears glistening on her cheeks. "Why not? It might be worth it to put Robert behind bars. I don't care about myself."

"What about Katherine? What about my father? Don't they matter?" Hayden asked roughly, his own emotions rising with the need to protect her. He'd had enough of a picture of her "oddities" and Phoebe had worriedly remarked that everyone in Mimosa knew that Cameron was "losing it." "Would the authorities believe you?" he asked more gently. "It's been twenty-eight years, honey."

"I'd make certain you and your family are protected from suspicion, taken care of financially, before I turned myself in—"

"I don't think I like the sound of that," Hayden stated warily.

"You and your family suffered, your father was involved—maybe the kidnapper, correction: *probably* the kidnapper. Robert wouldn't want to get his hands dirty—"

His frown deepened, cutting savage lines between his eyebrows. "Wait a minute. You think I'm after a payoff?"

"Isn't everyone?" she asked dully, turning from him. "What would suit? A million? A million and a half? Two?"

For a moment, Hayden struggled against the past and leashed his anger. "Is that what you really think?"

"I think that Robert is not sharp enough to maneuver a kidnapping right under the noses of Katherine and an entire household, and guests at the anniversary party. From all the reports, the house was buzzing with investigators, and he would have little time to act on his own—to publicly leave his wife's side when she needed him most. He'd have little time to send a ransom note with a Tulsa date stamp and collect a likely substitute for Cammie so quickly," Cameron whispered softly. "You're right. I think he had help."

"Interesting. But it wasn't my father."

"You'd want to believe that, of course. You were a boy. You really didn't know him, man to man, did you? Boys are filled with ideals, looking up to their fathers, aren't they? You just said that he was handy and would know how to sabotage the gas lines of an air balloon. Maybe he did just that."

While Hayden struggled with that frustrating truth, Cameron walked to a small table, bending to study the items on a kitchen towel. She clicked on a reading lamp and the beam fell upon an old canning jar with eleven pebbles in it and a tattered pink ribbon.

She picked up the ribbon, held it in her palms, and pressed it to her face. "She loved pink. Cammie loved pink. There are still shreds of her pink blanket in that cellar. I looked for it all these years—everywhere."

Cameron carefully touched the old jar, tracing the pebbles inside. "You went in there and found these. You want revenge—"

"I want proof that my father wasn't involved and that my family did *not* have the rest of the ransom money."

But Cameron wasn't listening; locked in another time, she was crouched like a child in front of the table, taking the pebbles from the jar. One by one, she dropped them back into the jar and sealed it. She gathered the jar and the ribbon against her as she sat on the floor, rocking. . . . Then she whispered, "Was it fun having me, making love to me, knowing who I was? Your own little private joke?"

The change from a child mourning another girl to a grown woman furious with him caught Hayden broadside. But Cameron was on her feet, placing the things carefully back on the table. She turned to him, her expression furious. "That's all it was, wasn't it? I hope you enjoyed yourself."

"No, that wasn't all it was," he said, reaching for her. "We went over that at my suite in Oklahoma City."

"While you were flashing evidence in my face." She struggled within his arms, glaring up at him. "Magnolia trees, my foot."

"Yeah, silly, wasn't it?" Hayden would rather have Cameron like this, furious with him, than mentally back there in that hole, grieving over a dying child.

"You're a deceptive thug."

"So? What kind of an idiot would go back to that cellar by herself? You should have waited for me. But oh, no, you were in a snit, weren't you? Doesn't it occur to you that Robert might want to tip you over some edge, and trapping you in there might just be the thing?"

"Hey. Stop right there. I have a right to have snits. And Robert doesn't usually do his own nasty little jobs, or anything dirty or manual. And no, I do not need to wait around for you to tell me what is smart and what isn't."

"Maybe you should," Hayden suggested darkly. This one woman could nudge his temper faster than anyone alive, and his body was telling him that he wasn't immune in that respect either.

"What's smart now? I know who you are now. You know who I am—or am not. What happens now? Are you going to make love to me, or not?" she asked tightly, angrily.

"If you ask me nice." He'd give Cameron whatever she wanted now, including the need to burn away everything else by pitting herself against him.

" 'Nice.' My ex-husband is *nice*."

"Honey, don't count on me for that," Hayden murmured before he fused his lips to hers, his hands moving on that lithe body, curved against him. To prove his point, Hayden smoothed her breast, down her curved waist, her hip, then cupped her, his fingertips finding that moist cleft immediately.

Cameron's head went back, her eyes slitted, watching him as he stroked her gently. Her breath caught, her hands gripped his shoulders, fingers digging in, and she stared at him as he carried her into his bedroom. "Make this good, Hayden. And the magnolia trees were a nice touch, by the way."

"I thought so." Cameron still didn't trust him, or his motives for making love to her, but after the dramatic explosion of the past hours, the light sexual dialogue soothed that unease. Making love to her now was a necessity to reassure himself, proof that she was alive.

He lowered her to the bed, took a heartbeat to prepare, and then cradled within her thighs, slid slowly, deeply inside, locking them together. There was just that moment of tenderness skimming before the heat, a moment when she smoothed his cheek, looking up at him softly. Her fingertips cruised his eyebrows, his cheekbones, his lips, as if absorbing everything about him, storing a memory away.

Hayden did his best to ensure it was a good memory, pushing everything else away, but the woman in his arms. . . .

As a woman, she had to know if Hayden would still make love to her with the same raw hunger, that intensity that said nothing else existed.

Cameron lay quietly in the aftermath of their passionate storm, and the lovemaking felt the same; the same tenderness had followed, the lazy caresses, the little kisses to her temple and lips, the cuddling against his body. Then, clearly exhausted, Hayden slept deeply, sprawled beside her. He'd worked very hard to get to her, to make her believe that he cared—but then, he needed her, didn't he? To get what he wanted, redemption for his father?

Motives, Cameron thought as she watched the windows lighten with the gray dawn. Everyone had motives for being in her life, especially the men—Robert, William and now Hayden.

"I can hear you think, tick-tock, tick-tock," he murmured lazily at her side, turning to hold her close. He nuzzled her ear, biting it gently, his hands stroking her body, caressing her breasts.

Cameron resented that she wasn't just any woman, with a man wanting her for herself. "I thought you already got what you wanted."

The thumb brushing her nipple into a peak slowed for just that heartbeat. "Not quite," Hayden said firmly, before lifting her over him.

She could have this at least, Cameron decided, moving her hips against him, accepting that bold thrust into her body—before her life, the role she'd led, unraveled into the ugly mess it was.

Was she greedy, wanting just this bit of pleasure to remind her that she was a woman?

Hayden was kissing her so softly, tasting her, flowing sturdily beneath her. "Cameron," he whispered longingly against her lips.

In that moment, before she gave herself fully, she remembered that she wasn't really Cameron Somerton, but only a substitute, and Hayden was making love to her anyway with the same hungry passion.

After that slow easy loving, Cameron eased away, sitting on the edge of the bed. Hayden's big hand cruised her back, then slid to wrap around her wrist. "You're not going anywhere, so forget about that."

She looked over her shoulder to the man who seemed to be able to read her mind. "Aren't I?"

He sat up against the headboard and took her hand, unwrapping the bandage carefully. In the shadows, he looked tough, a contrast to his gentle care. "We need to get that bastard, Cameron."

"But my name isn't Cameron, is it? Who were you making love to, Hayden?"

That brought his head up, his expression fierce. "Who do you think?"

She studied him for a moment, that burning intensity, the set of his jaw beneath the dark stubble. He looked just as dangerous as he could be, snaring her into emotions she couldn't afford. "I think I'm going home. It's been fun, but—but do what you want, I don't care anymore."

"But *I* do." His words fell like mallet blows into the quiet, shadowy room. "I don't want you facing Robert alone."

"I'm a survivor, didn't you know? I've got nothing to lose by exposing him."

"Just your life."

"He won't do that. In our little war, I know him too well—and he knows me. He knows that I would have some insurance, a letter to the authorities stashed in a private safety-deposit box, a confession that would have the authorities checking my DNA against Cammie's—or if she isn't found, they can use Katherine's somehow."

Cameron stood and walked from the room, taking only his shirt. Naked, he rose and leaned against the doorframe in the living room, crossed his arms to keep from reaching for her, and watched as she slowly picked up the jar and the ribbon. "I'm taking these," she said.

He shrugged, because she was taking something else—a part of him. "Keep in touch," he said too tightly because she'd hurt him.

Cameron nodded, but didn't look at him. She walked to the back door where he'd placed her boots, slipped them on, and opened the door. In the dawn, she looked slender and vulnerable, a woman wearing a man's shirt, her legs long and bare. "I'm sorry about your father," she said quietly, then closed the door.

Sorry that he had died? Sorry that he was a kidnapper, who committed suicide and left a family to deal with the consequences? Sorry that he could be a murderer, too? Hayden swallowed tightly. "We're not finished yet," he stated quietly to the empty room.

Robert watched the woman ease from his bed, take the money he'd placed on the nightstand, and dress. The backwoods tramp had dreams of being his wife one day, and he smiled, mocking her. She caught the smile and thought it was for her, a special tenderness that she imagined might be love.

Pleasure built in him, because he could still charm women, get them to do what he wanted—like spying on Cameron, like helping to undo her hold on reality, like sealing her in that cellar again.

The woman was eager to please him; she was so stupid and almost like a puppy, totally devoted to him. For once, he excused the dirt caked on the heels of her red western boots. After all, when Cameron had gone into that cellar, this useful stupid woman had acted quickly, running from her car through the back bushes.

Jack Morales had caught up with her on Saturday night, before she could come to Robert, and Phoebe had gotten "detained." She had to please Morales, because through her, Robert sometimes transferred his very quiet requests and his payments to Morales.

She'd had to wait for her payment until Sunday night; then she'd come through the Somerton basement. She'd gone through the narrowed passage, along the wall that held a collection of Buck Somerton's life, including the life-size portrait of Buck, Katherine, and Cammie.

Cameron had never really explored all of Somerton House, preferring to stay within the rooms required for her role. As a child, she'd been too frightened. As a teen, on leave from boarding schools and as a college student on an accelerated program, going to summer schools, she had kept to her room; she had hurried away as soon as she could. And as a woman, she stayed only long enough to do what she must. Katherine had let the investigators search the basement thoroughly, but after she'd died, Robert had sealed the door leading to it. He'd created another hidden door within his bedroom to allow for his very private women visitors.

If Cameron would have cared enough about Somerton House and its secrets, she could have found the old door and had it reopened. And maybe someday, when that happened, Robert would have all his reasons on hand—

Hatred for a man he'd never known always ripped through Robert. He'd kept that huge painting of the Somerton family to compare himself to the dead oil man, a common burly workman, marked by weather, while Robert was sleek and suave. He was as much of a man as Buck Somerton, no matter what Katherine had said, when she'd said she was planning to divorce him—

And that was why Robert needed the woman who wore the red boots, a stupid "local" to come to his beckoning, to do everything he wanted—because she actually thought that he might love her.

Phoebe turned and smiled apologetically at Robert. "I couldn't help that Hayden came back early from Oklahoma City. Cameron told me it was over, and she was sending his things to St. Louis. I didn't think he'd be back at all."

Robert pushed away his frustration. "It was the best therapy for her."

"Are you sure?" Phoebe asked worriedly.

"I've talked with the best psychologists," he lied. "We're doing more good for Cameron than they could do in an institution. It has to do with taking the patient back to the time their trauma began—in that cellar. I do appreciate you watching her."

"I like Cameron, you know," Phoebe murmured in her wispy little girl voice, "She's been good to me, giving me my pickup and my house, and seeing that I got a good job with the post office. I don't want her to be put away someplace awful."

"There's no danger of that. You know that I take very good care of her—and of you, sugar babe. She says I don't, but then, she's odd, seeing things in her own way."

Phoebe pouted like a child, her finger twisting in her hair. "You were all over that woman with the horse."

"Just taking care of business. Don't worry your pretty little head over that." *You dumb fool. . . . There's no way you'd be acceptable in my social set.* "Use the back way in the basement, will you, sugar?"

She shivered slightly and wrapped her arms around herself. "I hate that spooky old way, all that old furniture, that chair with the horns, and that old man staring at me."

Robert didn't want to think about Big Buck, the man Katherine had worshipped, calling out his name in her current marriage bed, keeping the Somerton name when she should have been Katherine DuChamps. . . . "Get out," he ordered curtly.

"Honey?" she crooned pleadingly, but when he turned away from her, Phoebe slid from his room, using the door hidden in his wall paneling.

It closed softly behind her, and for a moment, Robert savored her terror as she hurried through the narrow basement passage and out into the path in the woods.

"Big Buck," he muttered, cursing the image of a man who was always overpowering, the man Katherine had really loved.

Cameron's sanity might be saved this time, but there would be other opportunities to destroy it.

Hayden, as her lover, might be just the trick—if he died.

And of course, he'd have to die.

At seven o'clock that same morning, Hayden watched the white pickup, a match to Cameron's, pull into the driveway of Phoebe's small, neat home. Tipped back on a porch chair and sipping his morning coffee, he didn't bother to remove his work boots from the wooden railing.

A mourning dove cooed from a high-power line, and a few feet away from Hayden, an iridescent hummingbird hovered near a hanging red container, sticking its beak into a yellow plastic flower. Hayden had already noted Phoebe's new decorative plum tree, the pear trees, all well mulched to preserve moisture during Oklahoma's burning July heat; he scanned the well-tended rosebushes and the shaded peppermint patch. Pink plastic flamingoes stood in the middle of the tiny front lawn.

Hayden appreciated the cottage look, but not the woman.

From her pickup cab, Phoebe looked at him for a few moments. Then, apparently as an afterthought, she lowered her reflective silver sunglasses, concealing her eyes, though the morning light was filtered by the trees on her quiet street. She opened the door and slowly stood. She seemed to be bracing herself and pasted a brilliant smile on her face as she walked up the cement walkway, bordered by petunias. "Hi, stranger," she said too brightly as she came up the steps.

Phoebe came to face Hayden. She leaned her hips against the railing beside his boots, and Hayden noted the torn buttonholes on her blouse, the knotted tie at her waist above her tight jeans. He noted those red western boots, the fashionable heel a little higher than usual. That heel had left very special marks on the path from Cameron's house to outside the cellar.

Her hair was tangled as if she hadn't combed it this morning; her lips were swollen slightly, and the red marks on her throat looked as if they'd come from a lover's stubble. Phoebe was holding one wrist, and Hayden suspected she didn't want any questions about the bruises there.

"I'm surprised to see you here. But it's a nice surprise," she said nervously.

"It's a real nice morning, too. . . . Been out all night?"

She tensed a little at that. "Just made a quick-stop run this morning. I was out of milk, and I like a bowl of cereal."

"Sure, I believe you. But then, I've been here for an hour, so it must have been a long run, and I don't see any grocery sack in your hand. It's going to be hard, working all day, isn't it? I mean, working at the post office, taking care to go through Cameron's personal mail when you deliver it—into her house—oh, yes, you would be one of the people she trusted, enough to give the access code to her house, right?"

"Cameron said it was a big help to her to have a friend help her sort junk mail, and since I was delivering it anyway, I do that for her."

"Except you were off on Saturday and just happened to drop by Cameron's to visit, right? A neighbor down the road just happened to see two white Toyota pickups in Cameron's driveway on Saturday. Was she home then?"

"Well . . . I just dropped by to see her—"

"Funny. She didn't see you at all. I asked." He hadn't talked to Cameron or the neighbor, but foraging for truth sometimes called for the necessity of a lie.

Phoebe trembled slightly and dug firmly into her lie. "You know she has problems, Hayden. Cameron has started to forget things. Not just once, but a lot of times. We're all worried about her. She probably—"

"I don't think so. I think you were there to check on her as always. That's what you do, isn't it? Spy on her? Well, I guess you're out of a job, because Cameron is making different arrangements. You're not delivering her mail anymore, and she'll be changing her access codes."

"She won't like you messing in her business—" Phoebe began heatedly.

"Too bad. I am."

Phoebe frowned as though circling that thought for just that heartbeat, and then she smiled slowly, seductively. She leaned back against the railing, her hands at her hips in a pose that allowed the deep vee of the blouse to partially reveal her breasts. "If you're sticking around today, I just might call in sick—I'm already late."

Hayden came down on the four chair legs and took her wrist, turning it to inspect the marks left by individual fingers. He'd seen that pattern before—on Cameron. "He plays rough, doesn't he?"

She jerked her hand back, covering it with the other. "I don't know what you mean."

Hayden scooped her silvery glasses away and Phoebe turned slightly away to shield her black eye. He inhaled sharply, fearing what Robert could do to Cameron— "You're leaving town today, Phoebe. And you're not coming back."

Fear danced on her face. "I don't know what you mean. This is my home—"

"A home Cameron paid for—right? And your pickup, too?" Hayden wondered how Phoebe could turn so easily on someone who had taken care of her.

"She's my friend— She's so odd—everyone says so. She's forgetting things and I—I support her, telling her she's okay. That's what friends are for, and Cameron needs me . . . and Fancy and Evie. They're her friends, too. They won't like you trying to bully me. I have enough of that from—"

Hayden suspected he knew exactly who bullied Phoebe, and it wasn't Jack Morales. "Friends don't lock other friends in a place that terrifies them."

She trembled slightly and looked away to the boy riding his bicycle and tossing papers onto the front lawns. "I don't know what you mean—"

"You should have changed your boots before bracing those posts against that door. And because you're *supposed* to be Cameron's friend, I'm keeping this between us—unless you make it a problem. You're leaving town quietly, Phoebe—"

"Oh, but I can't. I—"

Hayden continued slowly, clearly for her to understand. "I have a check for you, a pretty hefty one . . . consider it severance pay. You're going to pack up your things—there's enough money there to replace everything you leave—and you're going to call a real estate agent to put this house up for sale . . . this morning. I'll be with you every minute. . . . You're leaving without contacting anyone, especially Cameron. If you *ever* decide to contact her, then you're taking me on, and I don't think you'd like the consequences of jail."

Like a shamed child, Phoebe started to cry, to huddle into herself. "Is she . . . is she all right?"

"Let's just say that with friends like you, she doesn't need enemies. But yes, I think she's okay." Hayden stood to take her elbow. "You'd better fix yourself up, if you're going to make that call and sign those real estate papers. I'll help you pack."

Phoebe's expression pleaded with him. "You don't understand. I can't. I just can't."

Hayden dismissed the sympathy he'd feel for any woman in Phoebe's place—someone not bright enough, someone eager to please a man and desperately wanting him to love her; she would be easy prey for Robert DuChamps. "You can, because Cameron doesn't need to know about you spying on her or anything else. And if you stay here, you just could end up dead, because whoever is using you—and I know who—isn't going to be happy with a mistake like wearing those boots when you sealed Cameron in that cellar. So you're leaving, and you're staying alive. Got it?"

"I was just—"

Hayden reached past Phoebe to open the house door, then urged her inside. He wasn't spending too much time convincing her, because Cameron was apt to snap at any second and go straight for Robert. If she did, Hayden wanted to protect her— "Let's just get this over, okay? Before I change my mind and turn you over to the authorities?"

"But my post office job? I can't just—"

"Take your pick. I'm onto your game, and that means Robert won't stop this time with a few bruises when he finds you've been careless. Evie and Fancy probably will want to make you pay somehow—and from what I've heard, Fancy let her ex-husband have it when he played around. She sounds tough when mad, and I'd say Cameron means a lot to her, and not just for the money either. And Evie, well, Evie has a bit of a temper. Then, you could lose the sale money from the house and the pickup, once Cameron knows you're involved with Robert—she's got this nasty little temper, and she knows how to use her power to get what she wants."

Hayden nodded as terror enveloped Phoebe. "Okay, then. Make that call. Get out of town and stay safe. If you do contact Robert, Cameron, or anyone here and involved in this mess, I'll make certain that Fancy and Evie know where you are."

"But I *love* him," Phoebe wailed pitifully, and Hayden almost felt sorry for her. Almost.

In her office at Somerton House, Cameron carefully ran over the papers that Madeline had placed on her desk. The white gloves hid the damage to her still-sensitive hands.

Despite her trauma, Cameron had dressed carefully, wrapping her hair in a sleek chignon, bracing herself to talk normally with Robert the morning after he'd tried to drive her insane. It wouldn't be easy, but dressing to the elegant heiress role had always helped her maintain the control she needed to deal with him.

She wanted him out of the house while she searched for Katherine's and Cammie's things, for some evidence that Katherine had been murdered. Sharing her loves and her short life with Pilar, Cammie had mentioned several things in those ten days. Since she had been trapped inside that cellar, Cameron had remembered more, and she had never seen that big chair of longhorns or Big Buck's portrait.

Cameron had never fully explored Somerton House, but she would soon remedy that, searching every nook and cranny.

And Cammie's little body—where was it?

"I'll find you, Cammie. I promise," she whispered, and then looked to see if Madeline, who was at the opposite end of the room, pouring coffee from a carafe, had heard.

Madeline glanced at Cameron and smiled briefly. "Did you say something to me?"

"No, I was just noting the high cost of research and development."

"Cameron, you've been doing that a lot lately, talking to someone who isn't there," Madeline remarked worriedly.

"Don't worry about me, Madeline. I'm fine. I'm just balancing a lot right now, and one thing is squeezing Robert out of Somerton affairs. I want him away from the house for a few days." She touched Cammie's small gold cross beneath her elegant cream-colored silk blouse. The cross had kept her relatively safe in those first years, and now she wore it for good luck. The black slacks were loose, and tucked inside a pocket was Cammie's pink ribbon. Armed with it, Cameron prayed she would find Cammie.

The woman part of Cameron, deep inside, ached for Hayden, a man whose father had admitting kidnapping and committed suicide.

Hayden had left the farmhouse early that morning; he'd looked tough and determined, and was probably on his way to the authorities. Cameron didn't blame him; he'd lost so much. She glanced at the clock; she could only hope that she'd gotten what she needed before the police arrived, and that meant getting everyone away from Somerton House.

Madeline flipped through the papers on her clipboard and handed Cameron an invitation to visit a horse farm in Texas. "If you're looking for a way to keep him away from here and have a little peace, this might do it—a soiree down in Texas, the cattlemen's club there sponsoring it, horses, barbecue, the works, and a horse auction. Is there any special reason you want him out of Somerton House now?"

"I'd like a few days by myself to think about how I'm going to get rid of Robert permanently, and sometimes I feel as if I'm losing touch with how the house is run—though you're great, Madeline. I may think about doing some redecorating. By the way, with Robert gone, you really should take some time off, too. I appreciate you keeping tabs for me on what he's doing, keeping the estate out of potential disasters, but why don't you take a few days off?"

Madeline was sensitive to any changes in Cameron's schedule. "You usually don't like to stay here. Is something wrong? And why are you wearing gloves today?"

"Katherine wore gloves a lot. I remember a box of them when I was a girl. I thought I'd try it. Would you happen to know what happened to that box?" she asked casually. The box was old and came from Katherine's Virginia plantation family; Cammie had loved trying on the long elegant gloves that had once been worn with hoop skirts and parasols.

"Not a clue. No one wears gloves in Mimosa, Oklahoma, unless it's their gardening gloves, Cameron," Madeline stated gently, a small reminder that Cameron should consider how odd she might appear. She shook her head. "I don't think I should leave here. You've been—"

"A little off lately?" Cameron supplied gently, patiently. Her friend and an integral post in Somerton business affairs, Madeline was genuinely concerned about Cameron. "I'm just fine, but a little preoccupied because of Robert—you can understand that, can't you? You're not exactly friends with him."

"I certainly am not."

"I know. I appreciate your putting up with him, and everything you've done for me. That's why you're already scheduled for a whole week of pampering at a Mais Oui California spa—seaweed and mud body treatments, facials, every kind of massage possible, and I expect you to come home loaded with goodies, designer bags, that sort of thing. Your flight's all set. Ray is taking you to the airport in a couple hours, so start packing."

"I don't like leaving you alone," Madeline said sturdily, then she turned to Robert, who had just entered the room.

"Leaving Cameron alone?" he asked. "You're afraid Cameron might go off the deep end, or mess up your precious systems without you to keep her straight, Madeline?"

Madeline huffed up and glared at him. "I coordinate and network with a fleet of people to prevent *anyone* from 'messing up,' Robert."

Robert was in a mood to argue and upset Madeline, and Cameron moved in to protect Madeline. "That's enough, Robert."

The friction between the two scraped in the soft feminine office before Madeline handed the Texas invitation to Cameron. She left the room, but her "damned idiot" remark wasn't soft enough, and Robert glared at the door she'd closed behind her. "Why is she in a snit now?"

Cameron wondered if he felt any remorse about trapping her in the cellar. He went to the vase of light pink cabbage roses and brushed his riding crop across it. "These are damned expensive, Cameron. There are better ways to spend the Somerton fortune. You should tell the florist to stop making the deliveries."

Her hand slid to her pocket, toying with the pink ribbon there. "Indulge me, Robert. Pink is just a color that both Katherine and Cammie loved."

The intercom rang, and Madeline stated, "No sense in Ray wasting gas on a return trip. I'll just take my own car and park at the airport's long-term lot—if you're certain you want me to go."

"Have a nice time. Enjoy yourself." Cameron settled back to study Robert, the man who badly wanted her to lose her mind. How could he have allowed a child to die so miserably? How could he monitor Cammie's life within the cellar, prolonging it just long enough for her to share her life with a street brat—a substitute? How could he monitor just the right moment to remove her from the cellar? "Did you love her—Katherine?"

"That's a stupid question. Of course, I did. Why else would I marry her?"

She smiled knowingly and watched him grapple in their little deadly one-up game. He'd noted her gloves, and she'd caught just that flicker of frustration. His frustration always pleased her. Cameron handed him the Texas cattlemen's invitation. "Another auction . . . thoroughbreds, I guess. The list is included."

Robert had shown no surprise at seeing her at work this morning; he hadn't asked about her gloves, but then, he would have known how hard she would have fought to get out of that hole. . . .

He skimmed the invitation and nodded. He tossed the invitation down on her desk. "I suppose I'd have to beg to get some pittance to bid, right?"

"No. The thoroughbreds add to Somerton lands, and Katherine loved racing. You did well with the last deal from Lexington. So sorry your relationship and your idea to train Jack Russells didn't work out with Virginia." Cameron's nudge was to remind him that Virginia Ulbrecht had gotten a clear picture of his lesser role on the Somerton hierarchy and had decided to cancel their relationship.

Cameron had to get Robert and everyone out of the house for a few days; she had to find anything he may have hidden in the charade that had locked them together. He was certainly involved in the years of deceit. But only by finding exact proof that he was involved in the kidnapping and Katherine's death, could Cameron pressure him into telling her where Cammie rested.

And she had to find Cammie's body, to bury her beside Katherine, where they belonged—together. "I think Big Buck would have liked seeing horses on the pastures, don't you?" Cameron asked lightly, when her heart was beating frantically. "I'll cover your bids, Robert."

Would he take that bait and run with it? Cameron watched his expression tighten, his need to bid on the fine thoroughbreds warring with his frustration that he had to ask her for money. The nudge about Big Buck had raised Robert's competitive side, and he was definitely hooked on the idea, but wary. He tossed the invitation onto her desk. "Why? Why would you suddenly allow me to buy more horses? What is this 'go-free' pass about?"

Cameron placed her hands carefully on the desk—just in case he'd missed her gloves, in case he wanted a replay of her terror. But Robert wasn't interested, and she measured her words carefully to distract his suspicions: "I thought you might buy one for Hayden, and then we could ride together. He'd be stabling his horse here, of course."

Robert exploded, as she had expected. "You actually think that I'd allow that? Your lover's horse in *my* stable?"

"Let's not get into the particulars of who has what here, okay, Robert? You're an expert at horseflesh, and I depend on your judgment," she stated slowly, softly, treading carefully in their war—she didn't want him to suspect the real reason for his trip to Texas.

"Of course, if I'm gone to Texas for a few days, then you'd be free to bring your lover here, wouldn't you? Install him in your bed before I got back?"

She tapped her pen on the desk. Hayden had been furious with her, and a return bout wasn't likely. But Robert wouldn't know that. "True."

"Olson is the gardener's son, Cameron. He's here to get back at you. He's making a fool of you, don't you see? Why else would he want you?"

"You should know better than anyone. You married Katherine and a fortune, didn't you?" she said easily, throwing the reason back at him. "Do you want to go, or not?"

"If you move him into this house, you'll be sorry," Robert stated finally, furiously.

She couldn't resist. "I'm curious. I was a little out of touch on Saturday. Where were you Saturday?"

His smile was slow and taunting. "Golfing with friends, a tennis date later in the day. Lunch, dinner, swimming, that sort of thing. Feel free to check that out if you want. By the way, just where were you out of touch?"

"Oh, I spent most of the day—relaxing, holed-up, so to

speak. And by the way," she said, adding another nudge, "my compliments on the reproductions of Katherine's jewelry."

Robert's lips thinned beneath his moustache, and there was just that one twitch on his cheek to tell her that she'd scored a direct hit. She'd held that tidbit for years—that Robert had taken some of Katherine's better diamonds and had replaced them with lesser quality, and with fake stones in some cases.

But Robert didn't fail to give a smooth, experienced comeback. "Katherine had those reproductions made long before her death. They were for show. I have no idea what she did with the real jewelry."

"Oh, I'm sure you don't," Cameron returned just as smoothly.

"Be careful while I'm away, sweetheart," Robert murmured too softly. "I have your word on the purchase of thoroughbreds? You'll sign off on them?"

"Of course."

"We could get along better, I'm sure, if you'd always be so amenable. You can be a nasty little bitch at times, you know."

"I did learn well, didn't I?" Robert wasn't going to like what he would find upon arrival back at Somerton House, because Cameron intended to be very busy.

"She's up to something." Robert paced his luxurious Dallas penthouse that evening. Cameron wasn't answering her private line, the household staff and the farmhands weren't available. Phoebe's land-line telephone had been disconnected early that afternoon, and she wasn't answering the special cell phone that he'd given her.

Robert's anonymous call to Jack Morales, letting him know that "his woman was two-timing him with Olson" hadn't paid off yet. Famous for his fists, a knife, and a hot temper, Morales was dangerous when aroused. Robert almost regretted that he wouldn't be there to see what Morales did to Hayden—Hayden wasn't the kind of man to back down when confronted, and Morales would go for him; it would be a fight Hayden would lose.

Uneasy with Cameron's sudden generosity but eager to see the Thoroughbreds being shown in the next few days, Robert scanned his private address book, then punched in Phoebe's cell phone number. "You'd better start answering my calls. Where are you?" he demanded when the line opened. "I need you to do something for me."

"What would that be, Robert?" Hayden asked quietly, just as the door to Robert's suite opened. Hayden entered and closed the door behind him. He tossed the pink feminine cell phone to Robert. "Phoebe won't be available anymore, and if you're waiting for Jack Morales to call, he won't. Phoebe talked to him, then Jack and I had a little discussion. It seems he didn't know Phoebe was blaming him for her bruises. It also seems that his 'mama taught him to hold women in high respect,' and he doesn't like his character being defamed. I think *he's* looking for *you*, Robert."

"What are you doing here?" Robert slowly replaced the telephone, and fear raised the hair on his nape as he took in the size and fitness of the man at the penthouse's elegant bar. An ex–rodeo star on hard times and dreaming of a small ranch to raise bucking bulls, Morales could be bought off, but Hayden's flat, impassive stare said nothing could stop him.

Dressed in a black polo shirt, worn jeans, and expensive loafers, Hayden poured two bourbon neats. He held them as he walked toward Robert. "I thought we could have a private chat, man to man. We haven't done that in—oh, say, twenty-eight years, have we?"

Robert took the offered glass and downed the bourbon. "As I remember, I tossed you out of that guesthouse. You should have stayed away. But then, you came back to do the heiress, didn't you? Some sick kind of revenge? Something like the son of a lowlife kidnapper would do? Your father was so weak, he couldn't take his punishment like a man, and killed himself."

He didn't like Hayden's cool smile. "This is about my mother."

"Um. Pretty thing, as I recall."

Hayden's black eyes flickered, but his smile was cool. "Yes, she's still beautiful. She wouldn't have you, would she?"

Robert eased to his leather business satchel; the unlicensed handgun in it was small and deadly. "She had everyone else."

Hayden's arms were folded, his finger tapping the rim of the glass, his hip resting against a sofa, the picture of a man holding an easy conversation, not one packed with threats. "And Cameron. It's about Cameron, too. She doesn't like small, dark places, but then, you'd know about that—since you put her in a few closets, didn't you? A little girl then, she must have been terrified."

He tilted his head and studied Robert almost clinically. "I'm wondering if you ever dealt with a man—and I'm guessing you did. That would probably be my father. If you harmed Katherine while he was alive, and he knew it for certain, he would have called you on it."

"He was a coward!" Fear spiked in Robert, because he remembered the strength of Paul Olson slapping him, again and again, that big hand swinging, burning, methodically repaying Robert's slap to Katherine. Hayden appeared to have the same raw brute strength, barely leashed now.

Hayden put down his glass on the polished table with a quiet, deadly thud. "I wouldn't try anything now—like pulling something dangerous out of that bag, Robert. I'm not in the mood. I'm afraid you're going to have to put the damage to this room on the Somerton bill."

There was no escape—Hayden had blocked the suite door and was coming closer. "A gentleman wouldn't—" Robert began.

"You forget. . . . I'm the 'lowlife' gardener's son, and no gentleman," Hayden said as his open hand slapped Robert's face hard enough to rattle his teeth and send him back against the wall. "Isn't a slap to the face enough challenge for you? Wasn't that how it was done in the Old South?"

"I'll kill you!" Robert yelled in a rage. "I'll call security—"

"Take my advice and let's keep this little chat between us—men."

Hayden blocked Robert's blow, took the statuette from his hand, and studied the Venus de Milo replica. He set it aside. "That would be expensive to break. But then, you don't actually pay for anything by working hard—like a gardener would, do you, Robert?"

Robert rubbed his burning cheek and hated the younger man. "I'll get you for this."

"Come on, Robert. I've waited a long time for this," Hayden invited very quietly.

Fear backed Robert against the wall. Hayden's eyes were flat and cold, the air too still around him, and Robert's false bravado sounded empty in his ears. "I wouldn't lower myself to brawl with you."

"You prefer to hurt little girls and women? What do you know about Katherine's death—or my father's?"

"Nothing!"

"I think you do, and I'm going to find out just how you fit into it. If you have any part in it, I'll see you before the law does, and that meeting will not be as sweet." Hayden stepped back and smiled slightly, coldly. He turned and walked toward the door.

Robert was stunned that he'd escaped a beating that the younger, more muscular man could have given him. "You followed me all the way here, just to—"

Hayden paused, but didn't turn. "I'm that kind of guy. I want you to see me coming. See you around, Robert."

Hayden stepped outside of the elegant penthouse often used by Robert as a Texas base. He forced himself to breathe quietly, in and out, pushing his anger back and gaining badly needed control. He was good at getting details, and all of the puzzle pieces weren't in place yet. But he'd find them, just as he'd discovered that Robert had left for Texas. From a reluctant Phoebe, Hayden had learned where DuChamps usually stayed in Dallas.

It hadn't been a problem to tell the uniformed room service boy that Hayden had forgotten his ID key to the penthouse suite elevator; a hefty tip had erased any question of his identity, and he'd gotten the room key.

Hayden glanced at his watch—the three-hour drive to Dallas was worth seeing Robert's pampered face pale, the fear in his eyes, the knowledge that Hayden would stop at nothing to get at the truth.

Another three-hour drive back to Mimosa, and he'd check on Cameron. A quick call to Evie had told him that Cameron had given Madeline a trip to a California spa, and then had invited her friends over to Somerton House. Unfortunately, they couldn't locate Phoebe, but then she sometimes rendezvoused with a lover they suspected was a local married man and unknown to Jack.

Hayden had been very careful with Phoebe, a mixture of consequences and gentleness had gone a long way with her, more child than woman.

Concerned now about Cameron and relieved that Robert was no longer near her, Hayden hurried down the luxurious hallway, down the private elevator.

What was Cameron doing? Why did she want Robert and Madeline out of the house? Was she safe?

Then Hayden groaned when he saw the heavy city traffic, backed up by a bad accident that had caused others. He had to get back to Mimosa, and fast—

At ten o'clock that night, the Somerton mansion was too quiet, but echoes of her childhood, the harsh tutors, Robert's cruelty, and the ghost of Katherine prowled around Cameron.

Why hadn't she explored the huge attic and the basement

before? She'd known there was a basement area at one time. But through the years, she'd come to Somerton House only to fill her role, and she'd forgotten its existence. . . .

Madeline's privacy had been observed, her office excluded in the thorough search. Robert's room had been first on the list, and the door hidden in the paneling behind a table wasn't difficult to find—it had led down to that narrow passage and its startling contents.

With Fancy and Evie sleeping upstairs, Cameron sat in Big Buck's chair built of longhorn cattle horns and faced the opposite wall. Nearly life-size, the gilt-framed portrait of Big Buck, sitting in that same chair with Katherine behind him as he held baby Cammie on his lap, stared back at Cameron. *They'd been a family, and she had no right to take Cammie's place.*

Hayden had said that Big Buck would have been proud of her—but then, Robert had tempered her, hadn't he? Taken away any natural sweet part of her as a woman?

Cameron's gloved hands opened and closed on the big chair's arms. She turned her hands and noted the spots of blood on the white fabric. Hard work with the heavy chair and portrait had reopened the scratches.

Robert had kept the portrait and the chair for his private amusement, had he? Cameron could almost see him now, viewing the portrait, lording over it; she could almost see Robert's obvious jealously of a dead man, a man Katherine had loved. The portrait and chair would have been very private trophies for Robert's sick ego.

After Fancy and Evie had helped Cameron move the massive chair into the large room and helped her hang the huge portrait, placing other framed pictures around the hallways and in her office, they'd sat together, crowded on Big Buck's horned chair while she prowled the room.

"What a man," Evie had said, toasting the Texas oilman with her beer. "But then, Hayden's no wimp either. He's called a couple of times, just since we've been here . . .

sounds irritated and worried. Sounds like he's using his cell and calling from his car. You should have answered."

Cameron's gloved hands flexed again on the carved arms. Hayden would probably turn her in; she didn't blame him.

On the other hand, Hayden knew just what he was doing when he'd moved into her life, and as a woman, that cut went deep.

She closed her eyes and saw him again, standing in the house's foyer, looking powerful and dangerous, and something inside her ached for him, needed his arms to hold her. Cameron remembered how gently he'd treated her, his expression while tending her hands. "I don't need your sympathy," she'd said, frightened of what was passing between them.

Instead of speaking, he'd simply bowed his face into her bandaged hands. The humble gesture had startled her—it was as if he needed her, beckoning the softness in her to respond. . . . This morning, she'd questioned his motives, and he'd taken that cut deeply.

Their intimacy was over now. Both had their own truths and needs, and life had laid different paths for their lives.

Cameron focused on her absolute goals: She had to find Cammie's body, and she had to push Robert out of Somerton affairs—

At the end of the narrow enclosure and outside the basement, locked twin doors lay almost level with the ground, common to houses built in that time. Cameron had never questioned their existence; she simply hadn't cared, but now she did. "Creepy," Fancy had said, as the women used bolt cutters on the lock.

"Yeah. And someone has been using this door to get to that path out there," Evie had said. "It leads into the woods."

The massive portrait had been propped carelessly on a buffet beside the old chair with a few albums of Big Buck's and Katherine's families, then their own small one. Katherine's beautiful script labeled their pictures, including Big

Buck proudly standing by his collection of frontiersman muskets and early rifles.

None of Big Buck's arrowhead or stamp collections or the other expensive ones that were in the pictures were still in the house; she couldn't remember any of them from her childhood—but then, she didn't remember much from those blurred years, when she really thought she was Cammie.

Cameron inhaled, held her breath and released it slowly. Robert had probably sold the objects in the pictures, everything but the portrait, chair, and boxes of papers at her feet. In the shadowy light of the salon, she reached for the bottle of champagne at her side, poured it into a glass, then stood, carrying them both outside to the front porch.

"Where are you, Cammie?" she whispered to the cool, starry night, while fireflies blinked and the horses grazed in the lush fields. "I'm going to push Robert until he tells me everything—and exactly how your mother died."

A shadow moved in the trees nearby, and Cameron eased back into the pillars of the front porch. If Robert had returned, she was more than ready to face him.

A man walked slowly along the pathway as Cameron rounded the house. From behind a shrub, she saw him stop and crouch at the old basement doors.

He stood slowly and for a long time, stared at the intricate garden maze. Then he moved quickly toward one of the guesthouses. . . .

Thirteen

HAYDEN STOOD IN THE SHADOWS OF THE GUESTHOUSE, the memory of his father's body and the details of that fateful morning circling him. He was too tired, but the pictures in his mind didn't fit the details of his father's suicide—something just didn't fit. *What was it?*

He wasn't surprised to see the leggy woman standing in the moonlit doorway.

"I thought you might want this," Cameron stated as she filled the champagne glass, then crossed that moonlit triangle. As she walked toward him, he noted the sway of that curved body and appreciated those long legs in tight jeans. She moved purposefully, like a tigress on the hunt, and that secretive, pleased look she was wearing was just temporary; she wouldn't be happy when she'd discovered that he'd shipped Phoebe away from the center of the approaching deadly storm.

He took the glass, decided to skip how they had parted that morning, and downed the champagne. After a hard day and being recruited to help in a bad traffic accident with enough blood to cause him to change his clothes, he would take anything pleasant coming his way. "You look like hell, and, babe, you've been perspiring," he stated pleasantly, as he took in her pale face, the strands of hair escaping her ponytail, and then Hayden saw something he didn't like.

"A lady only glows," Cameron countered smoothly, and then she frowned. "What are you doing?"

"Hold still." With one hand, Hayden angled her face, studying the dark smudge on her cheek. Rage trembled through him, the wish that his slap to Robert's face had been more. "Did he hurt you?"

"No." The light brush of his thumb brought grime with it, and he eased a cobweb from her hair, showing it to her. Cameron followed the direction of his gaze. "I've been housecleaning."

"I thought you couldn't stand to touch anything dirty. What's the matter? Isn't household help as good as it was?" He relaxed slightly, wearily, noting the rest of her clothing—the silk blouse wasn't white anymore, the jeans torn at her thigh, the dirty tennis shoes.

Whatever Cameron had been doing, she was safe now, revved and in overdrive, despite the late hour. "How are your hands?" he asked, holding her wrist to turn up her gloved hands.

"Much better. Thank you."

His eyebrows lifted, his stare questioning her. "Those spots aren't blood, then?"

"A little. They're fine."

He looked so tired, but there was tenderness in his eyes, a softness that wrapped around her, like the feeling of coming home. . . . Cameron's heart stilled and gentled as she took the glass and filled it. She handed him the bottle, then sipped her glass and studied him coolly, but her senses told her to wrap her arms around him. He'd been traveling when he'd called—probably to Oklahoma City for business—and she regretted the way they'd parted this morning. "Rough day?"

"Bad enough. How much of this have you had?" he said as his arm circled and eased her to lean comfortably against him.

The amazing softness in the gesture, the way he rested his cheek against her head after a drink, seemed to comfort him.

Odd, she thought, that this quiet intimacy without sex . . . They'd parted in anger this morning, and now everything seemed to be just fine. Or almost. Nothing in either of their lives would ever be "just fine."

"I shared a couple of bottles with Evie and Fancy. I had a lot less than they did. They're in the guest rooms, passed out by now, I guess. We moved some furniture and celebrated a little. Where does that path from the outside basement doors lead to?"

When Hayden didn't answer, she leaned back to see his face; he was staring at the floor where his father had died. Cameron couldn't help him erase the memory; she couldn't change his father's guilt. Instead, she leaned against the wall beside Hayden and waited. . . .

"She was sweet—Cammie," he said quietly, as though memories circled him. "She loved Dad."

"I want to find her, Hayden. Could you give me that much time to push Robert?"

"Hell, I'll help you push him," he returned curtly, turning to her, violence quivering around him.

"I really do need you to help me, Hayden. What do you remember of Somerton House, the things in it? I need you to put together a picture of what was here at the time Katherine was alive."

Hayden didn't question Cameron's request and if he had, there would have been an argument, because she wasn't changing her mind now— She was going to squeeze Robert until he broke, force him to make a fatal move, and then she'd have enough proof of his involvement with the kidnapping, with the deaths of Cammie and Katherine, to turn him in—and then herself.

She had to find Cammie and give her peace.

Hayden closed his eyes and leaned his head against the wall, going back those years while his hand cruised her back, as though he needed the contact. Cameron moved in close again, this time following her instincts, stroking his cheek, the hard tension and bitter resolve that lay beneath the stubble of his jaw. If she could take away the horror that young H.J. had found, she would. But the closure Hayden badly needed might come at a cost—evidence could prove Paul Olson to be guilty.

For now, Hayden seemed exhausted, and her need to comfort him surprised her—sex was one thing, the heat and the pleasure, but the gentler emotions now between them stunned her.

Hayden leaned slightly into her hand, nuzzling it as he went back into the past, seeing the mansion as young H.J. "Collections all over the place, Buck's and Katherine's, from their families—hers came from the Old South, some horse racing trophies—I guess that's where she met Robert, through those circles. . . . I remember the basement, playing in it with my sister while Mom worked in the kitchen and Dad was in the fields. They used to send me down to get wine from the racks. Then, in bad tornado season, we all went down there. There was plenty of room to play, but Cammie couldn't because of her allergies and the stuffed animals—Buck's buffalo heads, the Bengal tiger, wolves—fascinating stuff for a boy—a record swordfish. . . . I lifted Gracie up to touch the tip. . . ."

"Collections like that would take a lot of room." *Plenty of room to play. . . .* Cameron was already picturing the stuffed menagerie piled behind the wall along the passage. *Could Cammie's body be there, too?*

"Uh-huh. The cellar ran about half the size of the house, and the wine racks filled one wall."

The narrow passageway had been crowded with furniture, but it wasn't "half the size of the house." And there were no wine racks.

Startling fear washed over Cameron: *What if she had been living in the same house, right above Cammie's body?*

"There's a passage that leads from Robert's room to the basement."

Hayden only nodded, and Cameron frowned. "You're not surprised."

"Figures."

"He probably used that way to slip out for his affairs when Katherine was still alive. I knew about the basement, but I never wanted to explore it. Even after I started to remember, I never wanted to. When I started to piece everything together, I knew that there were investigators going all over Somerton House and that they had searched the basement, so I knew Cammie's body wouldn't be there. I've only dealt with the rooms I needed to play hostess, or to do business. I should have gone over every inch of this place—"

"Cameron, give yourself some credit. You survived, and that would have been a job in itself, and you kept Katherine's good work alive. None of that could have been easy."

Hayden was still staring at that moonlit patch of oriental rug, and his grim expression said he was reliving the discovery of Paul Olson's body. "Something doesn't fit—I can't place it right now."

"What do you mean?"

He just shook his head and kept staring at the place where his father had died. Cameron should leave him . . . but she had to get him out of here, just as he'd saved her. And she knew exactly how.

"Just so you'll know that my hands are okay, and I can handle anything that needs handling." Holding Hayden's eyes, she slowly began humming a stripper song as she removed her gloves and gracefully dropped them to the rug. Adding a few bump and grinds, she began to unbutton her blouse and kicked off her shoes.

Cameron undressed slowly, took the champagne bottle from Hayden, and felt his eyes on her, just as she wanted. They were still on her as she paused at the door, as she turned to look over her shoulder at him, and crook her finger in a come-hither gesture. Her body recognized the stark desire in his; she didn't have to look back to know that he was watching as she walked from the guesthouse, around Somerton House, and toward the Olympic-sized swimming pool.

She swam the length twice before she looked up at the man who was standing with his hands in his pockets.

Hayden slowly undressed, his body powerful in the moonlight. His shallow racing dive took him far out into the pool, and he swam to the end before surfacing. At the other end, he leaned back against the side, his arms outstretched on either side of him, and stared at her.

The waves lapped softly against the pool's magnolia blossom tile, and the air between Cameron and Hayden seemed to palpitate, curling around her . . . She needed to have his arms locked around her, to feel Hayden's shocking hunger, to feel him inside her, the pounding of his body against hers, until everything else faded away. . . .

He wasn't moving, wasn't offering to come to her. Hayden just stared at her, giving her no cause to come closer, making her act on her own needs—

Cameron swam to midpool, then tucked into a dive and swam the rest of the way underwater—until she saw his legs. She started nuzzling his thighs and between them, stroking him, until Hayden dragged her up and brushed her wet hair from her face. "Sweet," he said dryly, mocking the way she had aroused him, boldly tasting him, flicking him with her tongue. "You're celebrating something, high on it. Want to tell me what it is?"

She had him now, had torn him from the past, and the hard expression of his face told her that tonight they would both have what they needed. "Are you complaining?"

Those hard lips started to curve, his hands running up and down her body, bringing her close and intimate. "Smart-ass."

But he was looking down at her breasts against him, leaning her slightly back, his hands cupping her bottom to bring her close, to watch his entrance into her body. For a moment, there was just the easy lapping of water against them as he moved her body, allowing that slight friction, in and out as her hands anchored to his upper arms.

She rose to nip at his throat, his lips, tasting the hard hot desire there as her body flowed in his hands.

Hayden caught her hair, drawing her face up to his. "You trust me like this."

Their angry parting of that morning ran between them. The statement was a question, and Cameron answered truthfully, her expression challenging him to ask for more. "This hasn't anything to do with getting back at Robert."

Again his statement, the underlying question. "This time, it's for you. Because you want me."

She wouldn't lie, or tell him that her deep and learned distrust of men had left her little else. His body moved, the deep internal thrust prompting her for an answer. "Yes. I want you."

"Then I'll have to make the most of it."

At six o'clock the next morning, Cameron stood at the doorway of the kitchen, enjoying the sight before her: Hayden was obviously cooking at the big gleaming stove, her friends groaning at the bar nearby.

"DuChamps is going to pitch a hissy fit," Evie said as she slumped on the kitchen bar's stool and held the ice bag to her forehead. She pinched her eyes closed against the bright morning sunlight.

"Oh, man, is he," Fancy agreed adamantly as she sipped her hair-of-the-dog-that-bit me champagne. She grabbed the bottle of aspirin on the kitchen bar, her hand shaking as she poured two into her hand and downed them with the tomato juice, raw egg, and hot sauce concoction that Hayden had placed in front of her. "Tell me again why we had to get up at six, when we don't have to be to work until eight? We could have slept an hour more."

Hayden grinned. "Just didn't want you kids to miss work."

"Yeah, right. And I hate cheerful morning people."

He turned back to cooking breakfast, but when Cameron entered the huge gleaming Somerton kitchen, he glanced at her. There was that brief flare of his eyes, then immediate tense heat searing her, a reminder of their night in her bed. Their lovemaking was a temporary evasion of reality, because she was an imposter and would probably end up in jail, and Hayden might be the one to put her there.

"Make yourself at home," she invited as she watched him expertly move in front of the supersized stainless-steel grill. Dressed only in his jeans, the muscles of his back slid beneath tanned skin, the hair at his nape still damp and curling from his shower, begging for her fingers through it, for her lips to capture his mouth yet again.

Cameron knew the taste and shape of Hayden's lips, the hunger they held, the raw, guttural sounds he issued that seemed unwilling to leave his restraint—restraint that she had pushed with her own lips and mouth and tongue. Evie and Fancy didn't turn to look at Cameron as she sat on the barstool, watching him. In their current state, they probably hadn't noticed the light trails on his back, the marks she'd made in her passion.

"Stop it," Hayden murmured without turning to look at Cameron.

"Yeah, the heat between you two is getting to me. On top of a hangover, it's pretty depressing, since my own love life is in the pits," Evie stated.

"I hurt all over. Moving that furniture wasn't easy. We should have waited for Hayden. Jeez, Hayden, don't tell me you're making eggs—I don't want to see them," Fancy said as she covered her eyes.

"Eat. You'll feel better," he said with a grin as he put the filled plates of food in front of the women. He bent slightly over the bar to kiss Cameron. "'Morning."

It seemed only appropriate that she offer him a slice of bacon. The intimacy of feeding Hayden was something she could really get into—if she weren't destined to be prosecuted. He lifted a glass of orange juice, and his eyes locked with hers as he toasted her and the night they'd shared.

Hayden's gaze lowered slowly to the shirt she wore—his, a way of keeping his scent with her after her shower. "I like that."

Evie's and Fancy's bloodshot, weary eyes glared at them. "Why don't you guys just take it upstairs and let us die in peace?" Evie groaned.

"Got enough food there, guy?" Cameron asked, as Hayden came to sit beside her stool, his plate heaped with food.

He smelled like soap and man, and she could have jumped him right there. And he knew it, leering wickedly at her. "I need my strength."

"This is nice. . . . I love you all," Cameron said impulsively—her friends and Hayden who was sitting on the stool beside her and digging into his plate. They seemed an odd sort of family, having breakfast together just as any family would. "All we need is Phoebe. Where is she?"

"Gone," Evie said airily with a snap of her fingers, then she winced painfully.

"Disconnected her phone, moved her stuff, left some, and asked the real estate agent to put her house up for sale," Fancy added.

"Yeah, maybe Hayden would know. His pickup was parked there yesterday morning—early," Evie murmured as she pressed the cold glass of orange juice to her forehead.

Cameron turned to stare at Hayden, her mind reeling. *Phoebe had been throwing herself at Hayden, and he'd gone straight to her after spending the night with Cameron, after their unpleasant parting.*

Beside Cameron, Hayden tensed, but kept eating. He reached for the coffeepot and, without looking at her, poured coffee into the other women's waiting cups. He filled her cup, and then sipped his own, taking his time to answer. "Don't get all worked up, Cameron," he said quietly.

"Worked up? *Worked up?*" She pushed back from the breakfast bar, studied his impassive stare and knew that he was— "You know something. What? Why did Phoebe leave like that?"

"Not . . . so . . . loud." Fancy and Evie groaned in unison.

"He's not interested in Phoebe," Fancy whispered rawly. "He's got you, and whatever he was doing there, it was probably okay—like fixing a sink or something."

Hayden glanced at the other two women and sighed. "And this was going so well, too. Cameron just said she loved me."

" 'All.' I said 'I love you all.' Family time is over. Conference, Hayden," Cameron stated curtly, and walked with as much dignity as she could from the kitchen.

Hayden took his time, pouring that necessary second cup of coffee, before he followed Cameron's long bare legs and the way her butt swayed provocatively within his shirt, into the main parlor.

He glanced at Big Buck's chair of Texas longhorns, then stopped to sip his coffee and stare at the portrait of the man who had created the Somerton empire, his wife, and their child. Then Hayden turned to the woman lounging in that big chair in the center of the room. The old red velvet upholstery had been covered with a cream silk sheet and Cameron sat cradled in it, her legs over one carved arm, her hand gripping the other arm. Blue eyes locked on to him with sizzling, angry heat. "I remember that chair," he said, and waited for the explosion.

The set look of Cameron's lips and those narrowed eyes, the tapping of her finger on that wooden arm said this conversation wasn't going to be friendly. But then, after seeing the danger she'd deliberately placed at her doorstep—a move to incense Robert—Hayden wasn't exactly happy either. With the information about the house she'd already gotten, she was armed for battle, and Robert would take Cameron down with him.

Hayden drank the hot coffee and carefully placed the cup aside. He braced himself for the upcoming battle with Cameron, then came to the large ornate footstool in front of its matching chair. He raised his foot and pushed it closer to her, jarring the big chair just that bit. Maybe he was feeling a little bit savage, a little like a disgruntled caveman, but then Cameron could bring that out in him.

"You know what this little redecorating stint will do—stir Robert into doing something rash. Making your move, are you?" he asked curtly.

"Apparently you did," she returned too softly. "With Phoebe yesterday morning, just after spending the night with me."

"Wrong," he said as softly and pushed the footstool again. Cameron lowered both legs and pushed it hard at him. Hayden ignored the jolt at his shins, reaching down to clamp her damp hair in his fist. "Jealous, are you?"

Her tight-lipped defiant expression spoke for itself.

"Would you believe me if I told you that I didn't touch Phoebe?"

"No. There's no other reason she'd leave town like she did—unless she didn't want me to know that you're as low as I thought you were."

If he told Cameron that Phoebe had spied upon her, had pushed her into that cellar and braced the door closed, she'd only have one more person betraying her.

On the other hand, Cameron had hurt him, and he was feeling nasty. "Real sweet, Cameron," he stated sarcastically. "You sent Robert and everyone else away so you could work on your little plan to kill yourself. Then you celebrated, capped off the night with me, right?"

"Not quite. I need to recover as much as I can. I'd appreciate you making a list of anything you remember. People, the staff, that sort of thing. I'll pay whatever you want. I'm putting a researcher on it as soon as I can."

" 'People' didn't want to get involved back then, and they

sure won't now. Did you ever consider the consequences of your little game of hit and hit back, one-up on whatever Robert threw at you?" Hayden looked at his hand, which was now circling that smooth throat. Just beneath her ear, her pulse beat heavily, betraying her icy expression. Her passion, her anger, and her torment throbbed around him—or was it his?

He bent down to whisper against her lips, "It always comes down to that, doesn't it? Payment? Did you even consider trusting me?"

"What do you expect from an heiress with a fat checkbook?" Her question was underlined by another silent one: *What did you expect from an imposter?*

"Something more than I got. Don't try buying me a pickup, like you bought all of your girlfriends. Give me back my shirt. Now."

Cameron's breath and her anger hissed around him. "Did Phoebe—?"

"Don't go there," he warned levelly.

He was almost amused when Cameron stood up on the footstool and unbuttoned his shirt, throwing it at him. "Satisfied?" she demanded as she stood naked above him, her flush telling him that her temper was riding her.

He slowly studied her pale body, the lean curves, the contrast of pale skin and mauve nipples, the sweep of her belly down to that small triangular patch between her thighs. She crossed her arms over her breasts, but lifted her head, challenging him. Cameron Somerton was a lady at her best—haughty, disdainful, and proud.

"No," he answered simply, truthfully and shrugged into his shirt, disregarding the buttons. "I'm not satisfied, and neither are you. By the way, your ex-husband and his very pregnant girlfriend are at your house. William called my cell yesterday afternoon. It seems you didn't want to be reached all day, and you hadn't checked your messages. I told him it would be okay for them to come ahead."

William had a settling affect on Cameron, and when he had called, Hayden had instantly decided that her ex could be used to waylay her temporarily.

"*You did what?*" She reached down to grasp his shirt. "You should have told me that last night."

Cameron's startled expression was a perfect mixture of frustration. She would temporarily have to delay her plans to push Robert. And that gave Hayden time to see who else was in this mess with Cameron's stepfather. Mimosa wasn't talking, fearful of Robert DuChamps's insidious power. But Hayden intended to find someone who would remember and would talk. *What was it about the position of his father's body that was so disturbing?*

"Your ex-husband and I get along fine. He calls . . . we talk. Guy stuff." Hayden reached around to pat her bare bottom, caressing it a little, in his own celebration—he was due. "I was busy last night, remember? I didn't have time to tell you then."

Those flashing eyes burned him as he turned; he whistled "Dixie" as he walked out of the mansion as if nothing mattered—but it did. With Cameron set to push Robert to the max, Hayden had to move faster.

In the morning sunlight outside Somerton House, the maze twisted intricately before Hayden, the thoroughbreds grazing in the field, a colt's tail high as he raced along the white board fence. Not as calm as he had seemed to Cameron, the whistled song a ruse, Hayden paused on the mansion's steps to survey the estate.

Just maybe Cameron's ex-husband and his pregnant girlfriend could keep her busy and out of trouble for a time.

Hayden's succinct curse split the soft morning air, because Cameron had immediately jumped to the conclusion that he'd had Phoebe. Now that would take a lot of doing, when all he could think about was getting his hands on Cameron and keeping her safe.

He glanced at the guest cottages, concentrating on the one

where his father had died, and that cold vise clamped around his heart. Then the crack of wood drew his eyes to the barn area, where Robert's powerful black stallion was acting up, circling a small holding corral attached to the barn. With Cody off duty, Hayden didn't want Cameron trying to deal with the dangerous horse, and he hurried toward the barn.

Inside, he started to open the double doors to the outside holding corral. Then the stallion charged from the other side and one door of the gate hit Hayden's body with the impact of a truck. The blow knocked him back against a stall and trapped him inside the barn, the big doors to the field closed, and the stallion circled inside the large barn.

He spotted and rushed Hayden, who was trying to catch his breath. Rearing in front of Hayden, pawing at the air, the stallion's hooves came down hard, barely missing Hayden, who was pinned against the stall. Huffing and nickering as he circled the barn again, the wild-eyed stallion watched Hayden hurry to open the main doors leading to the field—but it had been locked from the outside.

Hayden dodged the stallion's next charge and watched the horse return to the outside holding corral.

The big main doors had been locked from the outside; the horse couldn't run into the pasture. Keeping a respectful distance, Hayden ducked out into the small corral on his way to the main doors, and heard a small hiss followed by a small, dull thump; the stallion erupted in fury, charging Hayden again. He swung over the fence, circled the barn, and stopped when he saw the chain loosely connecting the handles of the big double doors. Hayden hurried to release them and open both doors.

The stallion raced by, and once in his field, he quieted.

In the holding corral, Hayden searched for the animal's reason for distress. A small metallic gleam drew him and he bent to collect a tiny ball from the ground. Several more pellets lay on the pawed earth, and that said that someone wanted to infuriate the stallion.

Who? Cameron? Had Robert come back to make his move?

Hayden rolled the small pellets in his palm; he scanned the mansion and grounds where someone might fire an air rifle. The pellets were too light to penetrate the horse's hide, but shot from a distance, still held enough impact to set him off. Whoever had stirred that horse had barred and locked the stallion's route to his field, and if they'd done that—they would have seen Hayden going into the barn, not Cameron.

Robert wouldn't have shot—an unexpected movement of the stallion could have cost its eye. And Robert wouldn't have wanted Cameron dead—he'd lose everything to Katherine's favorite charities.

And that probably meant that someone had been watching him stand on the front porch—

And that meant that someone was very unhappy with him, enough to serve him a sturdy warning to back off. From what? From unraveling his father's death? Or from being Cameron's lover?

Whatever reason they had, they were going to be disappointed.

"It always pays to keep tabs on my little girl." In Dallas, Robert quickly downed his bourbon on the rocks, his third since the phone call informing him that Hayden had spent the night at Somerton House and in Cameron's bed.

Hayden had almost been killed by the stallion, and Robert frowned when he thought of the metal pellets hitting his beautiful thoroughbred's sleek coat.

Furious with Cameron and the man who was now her lover, Robert hurled the glass against the wall. "So she has a nice little surprise waiting for me. She found that junk, and she's rubbing my face in it. Cameron will only go so far, because if I go down, she goes down with me—and she'll never find where Cammie is buried. She needs a dose of reality—and I'm going to give it to her. That little street brat deserves what she gets—and Olson, too. . . . Like father, like son."

Olson had somehow known that Robert was meeting a woman in the guesthouse. The gardener shouldn't have messed in things that didn't concern him—however he presented a convenient scapegoat, in the wrong place at the wrong time.

Robert recalled the blood splatter as the bullet hit Paul Olson, only a few feet from him. The pillow used to muffle the sound hadn't entirely stopped the bright red spray, but without it the sound would have drawn people too soon. And Katherine might never have gone up into the air that morning.

Sickened by the gardener's blood on his face and clothing, Robert had run to the house to clean immediately; he'd changed clothes and washed his face. And when he had come back, there was young H.J. already holding Paul's suicide note, one expertly forged, by one of the many women who had worshipped Robert back then.

"Like father, like son," Robert repeated, and flipped open his business satchel to study the thoroughbred information once more; a small horse farm, going under financially, sometimes offered good buys.

Beneath the papers was a framed photograph, a reproduction of the fake he kept beside his bed at the estate.

A black line circled the girl's head where someone had traced the almost imperceptible outline of the substitute's face.

A small, obviously reproduced and printed picture of Cammie's face lay beside it; it presented him with taunting reminders. "Clever girl, aren't you, Cameron?"

Young Cammie's blue stare locked on to Robert and seemed to follow him, just as Big Buck's life-size portrait had done—the same steady stare, accusing him wherever he walked in the room.

Robert's hand shook as he lifted a bottle of Kentucky bourbon and drank straight from it. Chilled by the whispers that seemed to circle him in the luxurious penthouse he was using as a base, Robert lifted the bottle again. He welcomed the hot burn of the alcohol, anything to take away the sounds of that dying young girl. He'd heard them from the cellar as he'd listened. . . . *Mommy? Mommy?*

Robert shook his head, put his hands over his ears, and squeezed his eyes shut. He hadn't known it would be so awful, those small lungs straining for air—and Cammie had lived longer than expected, the sounds haunting him for years. He went to stand by the window, and a child, a small girl, ran on the sidewalk below. *Mommy? Why?*

"Well, because, Cammie, your mother wanted to divorce me. I would have lost everything, and you weren't a good bet to live very long." Startled by the sound of his voice, Robert stepped back from the window and closed the blinds. When his hand wiped his forehead, it came away damp, and he cursed.

Cameron was trying to turn the tables on him, sliding into his mind and making him remember.

His hand shook as he reached for the bourbon bottle, lifting it once again. The amber liquid was smooth and aged and expensive, and that was why Cammie Somerton had to die. Naturally, the girl had to die—it was only reasonable, he justified. Everything was perfectly logical and now Cameron, the substitute, was threatening to tear everything away—and she had an ally, the gardener's son. Hayden was having her, rubbing Robert's face in it.

Robert picked up the Venus de Milo statuette and crashed it against the bar, breaking it. He tossed the pieces into the trash and hated Hayden. "We'll just have to turn up the pressure, won't we, dear Cameron?"

Did he love Cameron? She'd always fascinated him—once she'd started to become a woman. Of course, he loved her; Cameron Somerton was his creation, a part of him. It wouldn't do to kill her, or to completely ruin that struggling fine mind—before he had her. She needed to know how much they were alike.

He'd always admired strong women—but in the past, one of them had been a bitter mistake. Now, she knew his weaknesses too well, using him to get what she wanted, blackmailing him on a regular basis.

And now, he was pitted against another strong woman, his intelligent creation, a reflection of the best schools, the best training possible.

Play a game with him, would she?

Robert smiled at the thought, curious as to how far Cameron would go in their little game, locked against each other. She'd miss her lover, of course, for a time—until her mind went completely blank.

But there was still that sleek, toned thoroughbred body—and Robert intended to enjoy it.

"Sorry, Hayden, old chum. You'll have to die. Like I said, like father, like son."

Fourteen

CAMERON STUDIED THE BASEMENT WALL; THE PASSAGE WAS narrow and, if compared to the outside of Somerton House, more of the basement Hayden remembered lay behind this wall.

Evie and Fancy had taken their time leaving, and now, at nine o'clock in the morning, Cameron had to know what lay behind that wall. She held her cell phone in one hand and slid her hand over the wall, looking for some kind of opening. The flashlights she had propped behind her outlined her silhouette as it bent and stretched.

Was Cammie behind that wall? Cameron desperately had to know, and she had little time to explore. The wall had been fortified somehow, and she couldn't break through; she needed power tools, and she needed William and Arabella away from danger.

"You what?" Madeline exclaimed from Cameron's cell phone. "You found Big Buck's chair and his portrait, and you put them in the main salon? You're going to find everything Buck and Katherine had and replace them in their original place? You, Evie and Fancy, did this? Good grief, Cameron, you'll really set Robert off. He's always been jealous of Big Buck—which is insane since the man is dead. Yes, I knew the basement was there, but it wasn't any of my business what was in it—unless it leaked and contractors had to be called in, or something like that. I came to work a year after Katherine died, and I understood that the decor had been redone."

Because Madeline had alternately protected her from Robert, had taught her part of her role as an heiress, and was integral in running Somerton affairs, Cameron decided to complete her brief description of the previous night. "Hayden stopped by. He spent all night, too. Okay, I misjudged one more man, because he apparently had Phoebe, too. She left town without warning—I guess because she couldn't face me."

Madeline's silence was followed by a fast, sipping sound, then: "I'm going to need another drink . . . get me one, will you? And tell the masseuse I'll be ready in a minute. . . . Cameron, do you even know what a mess it will be to try to find those old things? Where are you anyway? Your signal is weak."

"I'm in my bedroom," Cameron lied. "I think we can do it. We've done difficult things before. We can hire an expert."

"I do not like this one bit. I had no idea you were up to anything like that, or I wouldn't have left. Think of the time something like that could consume. We could spend it better by focusing on eliminating the middlemen on that Florida Keys real estate deal."

Ice clinked, then Madeline stated furiously, "It's because of him, isn't it? *That* Hayden Olson. Cameron, you should know better than to mix with a man who is either out for your money or for some sort of sick revenge. Now everyone knows that he's the son of that gardener. I've tried to keep the lid on that, but it's impossible. How could you possibly even think of going to bed with a man like that? If you have an itch to scratch, I would think you'd be more cautious, especially after William."

Cameron was unprepared for Madeline's burst of temper. It had never been directed at Cameron before, only to

Robert. "Hayden came to find me in that cellar, Madeline. That is something I'll always be grateful for, no matter what else happens. I make mistakes, Madeline. You know that."

"You've been making too many of them lately, Cameron," Madeline stated firmly. "I knew he was trouble from the minute I saw him. This whole thing is sick, sick, sick."

And Madeline was right: Hayden had been with Phoebe yesterday morning, then last night, he'd come to Cameron. She had trusted him, even after that meeting he'd set up after the cafe, so what could she expect, after all?

Cameron studied that wall. Taking it down would have to wait until she was better prepared and had more time—and she had to get William and Arabella away from Mimosa. She moved to the flashlights and clicked them off, placing them in the tote bag that she carried up the stairs with her. "Madeline, I'll handle it. I want you to relax."

"How can I relax when I know he's hanging around you? I saw you two together at the investors' party, so did everyone else. Sex is one thing, but involvement is another. You must be careful, Cameron. . . . Where did you say Phoebe went? I can hear you better now."

"I have no idea. She just left yesterday morning." *Because she couldn't stand to face me.*

Madeline's pen started tapping, which meant her mind was working on details. "I'd like to talk with her. If she calls, find out where she is, okay?"

"Madeline, I'll handle this. She was one of my best friends."

"She was also after Hayden. He was doing both of you. If she can do that, so can Evie and Fancy," Madeline stated bluntly, and the rhythmic tap of her pen seemed faster, more demanding. "So this is why you wanted me out of the bomb you created, so you could get into trouble and have some orgy right in the mansion. I thought you cared for me, Cameron. I really did. You know how I worry. And now here you are, lying to me."

Guilt settled heavily upon Cameron; Madeline had always cared for her. "Yes, I do. I'm sorry. Please don't worry about me. I'm fine."

"Sure. Fine. Obsessed, is more like it. You got involved with this guy, and now you're paying for it. I don't like this at all, Cameron. I'm hurt."

"I'll have this cleaned up before you get back. We'll talk then. For now, just relax and enjoy your spa, Madeline." Cameron ended the call as gently as she could.

She'd hurt her oldest and best friend, and Hayden was a dog.

And she had to know what lay behind that basement wall.

Was it Cammie's body?

"Well, fine. Just peachy," Cameron said as she pulled her pickup in front of her barn four hours after Hayden had left the mansion.

Mid-July's heat was already rising, the sun burning overhead as William, a very pregnant woman, and Hayden were all in his backyard, apparently considering his garden and trees. Arabella was short and darkly Italian-looking, with flashing eyes in an expressive face and a beautiful blue-black mane of hair that almost reached her waist. She was animated and glowing, her hands gesturing. Her full smock was vivid with flowers, and her smile up at William was brilliant and loving. Apparently proud of her, he kissed the top of her head and smoothed her belly.

A lonely, aching, wistful sensation circled Cameron. They were perfect together, Arabella's rounded body leaning, fitting into the protective circle of his arm. They had created a life together, filled with emotions that Cameron could never experience. Her fingers opened and closed on her steering wheel as she pushed away bittersweet dreams that would never be hers.

She would do what she had to do, like always.

Only this time, it was to find Cammie's body and discover if

Katherine had been murdered, and nothing was stopping her.

Then William was waving at her to come to them, his beaming expression contrasting Arabella's tentative smile, and Hayden's closed, impassive stare.

Bracing herself, Cameron slid from her pickup and walked to them. With every step she took, she could feel Hayden's black eyes locked on to her, his anger shimmering in the sunlit morning.

Mad was he? After making love to Phoebe and getting found out?

For just that heartbeat, Cameron glanced toward the rear of the property, where the old cellar lay, waiting and beckoning for her. A wave of panic washed over her, pushing the breath from her. Hayden had found her there, taken care of her. . . .

For that moment in the still Oklahoma air with a male cardinal slashing scarlet through the shadows of the mimosa grove, she heard Cammie whisper her last words: *Mommy? Mommy? Help me. I'm afraid. I'm cold, Mommy, and it's dark here. Why, Mommy? Why did they put me here? Mommy?*

Cameron shook free of that memory and focused on the people in Hayden's backyard. She had a job to do, and she was too emotional now. Pride warred with pain as she thought about how Hayden had held her, so tight and close and safe, and then so desperately. All she had to do was to look at him, and her senses started heating in anticipation of when he would kiss and hold her. In a T-shirt and worn jeans, Hayden had that long-legged tough look, the set of his body tense as he locked on to her—that's what Hayden did, locked on to her as if she were a part of him, deep inside, past the sex, past what had happened years ago to bring them together.

He knew everything about her, and still, when his hands had cupped her breasts, his mouth had fused to hers, she was all over him, hungry and—that deep throbbing inside her had nothing to do with the savage anger she'd felt earlier. It had to do with the truth that she still wanted him. . . .

Then a movement through her windshield drew her to William, who was waving her to come to them.

"Great. Just great." Her plans for pushing Robert into a corner would have to wait. She pasted on a smile and walked toward them. "Hiya, William. This must be Arabella—"

Suddenly, Arabella hurried to her, enclosing Cameron with her arms and kissing her cheek. "No wonder William loves you so much," Arabella whispered against Cameron's ear. "I love you already for being so kind to him, for being his friend. I know that displeasing his family is difficult for William—I love him so much."

"I know his parents. I think they'll come around . . . give them time."

"I wasn't what they expected, and here we are, with a baby coming."

"And one that they won't be able to resist—you'll see." Cameron held very still as the soft mound of Arabella's belly thumped her gently. Stunned, she stared at William, who was beaming at them.

Hayden's cold stare said he was still angry.

The baby kicked again, a new life, precious and loved against Cameron's own stomach. Shocked by the softness within her, aware of her own potential as a woman, Cameron murmured, "Um . . . I'm glad you could come."

She had to get Arabella and William to leave . . . She had to protect them, because there would be no turning back, and Robert was certain to react dangerously.

"We were going to call you, but when Hayden said that now would probably be a good time, we didn't see any reason to wait. And you said to come anytime and bring Arabella, didn't you?" William said as he came to put his arms around both women. Arabella turned to nuzzle against his throat, as if she'd just come home to him, instead of being only a few seconds away. William nuzzled her cheek, and she giggled, cuddling close to him.

"I love this house." Arabella looked wistfully around

Hayden's backyard. "It's so perfect. I've always wanted a place like this, a place to love, that has known love. William is dying to garden . . . he said he's learned a lot from Hayden. He admires Hayden so much, almost like an older brother."

Cameron frowned at Hayden. "He's only here temporarily. I think he's getting ready to leave. Aren't you, Hayden?" she prompted sternly.

"No, I'm not," he singsonged back. "I'm enjoying myself here."

"I just bet you are. Because I don't have a rural mailbox, I had to stop at the post office and get my mail myself. It seems my personal mail carrier has left town." Cameron glanced at William, who had wandered off with Arabella; they were in an intense discussion near the fence.

"Huh. What do you know about that." Hayden wasn't apologizing for the missing Phoebe.

"Garlic!" William called excitedly as he rushed to the toolshed. "Arabella said there's garlic here. I've got to dig some. She's says it's too thick, and the heads won't make well if it isn't thinned."

"You . . . did . . . this, Hayden," Cameron said beneath her breath as William rushed back to the fence with the shovel and shrugged out of his shirt. Arabella held his shirt and pointed to different places where he began to dig. Hayden paused, turned to her, and bent to kiss her tenderly.

"Does it bother you? Your ex in love?" Hayden asked quietly.

"He's happy. That's enough."

"You wouldn't ruin that by doing anything rash, would you?"

"Like turning myself in? No, I'll just wait for you to do that little job."

"Idiot," he muttered. "I thought them being here might slow down your personal little train wreck, and we could have a chance to work on this together."

"Jerk. Think again. Rather, think of Phoebe and not my

problems. I've had enough for today. William? I'm going. Come over when you're done." Cameron turned and walked to her house, the tension at the back of her neck and the prickling of her skin told her that Hayden's black eyes followed her and that the heat of last night still simmered between them. The two magnolia trees reminded her of how Hayden had hurried through his work, planted the trees because the blooms reminded him of her, and had rushed to find her trapped in that cellar.

He'd been so tender, caring for her. He'd held her and comforted her . . . And he held the power to tear her life away, just as his had been ruined . . . He'd loved Cammie and had lost his father, still torn by that image years later . . . He'd lost more than she could imagine, while she had no right to her own life. . . .

She stopped midway between the house and barn, turned and looked back at him. Hayden hadn't moved, his eyes locking with hers.

Deep inside her, Cameron knew the truth—that Hayden was a one-woman man, and she was that woman. He'd been gentle with her, worried for her after her trauma. His concern had been genuine, and his lovemaking—well, his lovemaking had been unique, as if they weren't just feeding a need, an "itch" as Madeline had called it, but something deeper.

Dammit, they had something deeper going on than sex, and he was one step ahead of her because he had already known it.

Taking a deep breath, Cameron walked back to him. She'd know the truth when she confronted him. "You didn't make love to her, did you?" she whispered. But Hayden's pride matched hers and he wasn't apologizing for something he didn't do. "Why were you at her place?"

"I was helping her move."

He wasn't lying, but there was more that he wasn't revealing. Cameron would have to work on him, get it out of him, and she knew just how. She reached to fist his hair, bringing that set impassive face down to hers. A muscle ticked on his cheekbone, those eyes flashed, but there was nothing more. "So what are we going to do now?" she asked.

He might care deeply for her, but he was furious. "Fine time to think of that when you're all set to rev Robert, isn't it? That showdown you're pushing. It just could get you killed, you know."

"I'm asking for ideas, Olson, not chitchat."

Hayden's hands circled her waist, lightly tugging her body close to his; his forehead rested against hers. "Here's one: Let the kids have my house, and I'll move in with you. That will save you the walk over here."

"So certain of that, are you?"

"Uh-huh. Or I'd come after you."

Cameron shook her head. "I've got plans that don't include you."

"Like what?"

A powerful workman, Hayden could be through that wall in a heartbeat. Should she tell him?

"You are one cautious woman," Hayden said finally. "But then, I suppose you've had to be. I'll find out, you know—what you're hiding. Your mysterious plans that don't include me."

"Good luck."

"You hurried dinner. We should have stayed to clean up." Cameron turned at her barn door and looked up at Hayden. "We should go back and at least offer to do dishes."

"They'll manage. We were in their way. They have their own way of doing things." Hayden reached behind her and pushed open the door. He had to have Cameron and fast, his body aching. He'd been watching those hips sway for hours while he barbecued in the stone house's backyard with William. Now, Cameron's bed was just feet from him, and he started moving toward it—backing her into the barn.

"You're hustling me," she protested, as he unbuttoned his shirt with one hand and shouldered the door shut. He placed the plate of leftover barbecue on a table as he kept moving Cameron toward that bed. . . . But first—

Hayden took her face and lifted it to him. "Do you really think I'd turn you in? Don't you think I'd miss *this*? Or you, as irritating as you are?"

"I'm just asking for enough time to push Robert and find Cammie. I owe her, Hayden. I owe her everything, even my life."

"The authorities just might not believe you, honey. Did you ever think that someone was building a case against you, deliberately sabotaging you?"

Did you ever think that one of your best friends could be tied up with Robert, helping to plot against you? Jarred by the question, Cameron frowned slightly. "I don't know what you mean."

"The necessity for those little index cards everywhere, the way your favorite pen isn't in the right place, your checkbook and address book were left in various places, mail you never saw or answered?"

"That's me, Hayden. I have nightmares. I run an empire with thousands of details to remember. I'm distracted and I forget. It's overload and just that simple," she said sadly.

"But it's getting worse, and someone locked you in that cellar, probably to speed up getting control."

"That door didn't swing shut by itself. I already know who it was—Robert. Motive, Hayden. He has motives for everything, the kidnapping and for Katherine's death."

Hayden knew that the thought disturbed her; if she discovered that Phoebe had any part in the cellar imprisonment, Cameron would be shaken. She obviously didn't want to think about potential betrayal as she reached to flick on the overhead lights. "I've got e-mail to answer and business to—"

He turned off the lights. He'd had a long hard few days; the list was lengthy: Robert, Phoebe, then he'd almost been killed by a horse someone had spooked with a pellet gun. Then there was the call from Madeline this morning, the mother hen settling in to protect her chick, and then he'd played host to Cameron's ex and his girlfriend—and every minute of that time he worried about what she was doing.

"What took you so long to get here this morning?" he asked, and noted Cameron's instant sealed expression. She'd definitely been up to something very private.

"I was busy."

"Four hours of doing what?"

"Just busy. I had to see Fancy and Evie off, and that wasn't easy. I had to see that they got home okay and answer some e-mail. You know—just stuff."

"Mm. I guess you'd tell me if you'd had any other great ideas about stirring up Robert, wouldn't you?" But Hayden's only plan for the moment was to get Cameron into that bed. He intended to get what he'd been thinking about since early that morning when Cameron had showed her distrust. After all, a man deserved a little repayment from the woman whose trust mattered. . . . His lover, his lady, his woman, as Cameron currently was, and would continue, if he had his way about it.

Making love to her until she was defenseless was one way to ensure himself that he truly did have possession. The emotion was primitive, and he wasn't apologizing for the depth of it.

"Keep backing up," Hayden ordered grimly as he took off his shirt, kicked off his loafers, and unzipped his jeans.

Her eyes jerked downward and rounded. He wasn't feeling sweet; while she and Arabella had discussed window coverings for the farmhouse, Cameron's looks at him said she knew exactly what she was doing—working him up to spill his guts about Phoebe. He intended to spill something else, if he didn't embarrass himself first.

She'd deliberately left the impromptu evening barbecue to come home and shower, smelling all sweet and clean and putting on a V-cut shirt that showed her breasts when she bent slightly. Her cutoff jeans showed enticing curves, and

Cameron knew just what she was doing when she'd "accidentally" rubbed against him. Romance would come later, Hayden promised himself, but first things first.

He tugged her shirt over her head and found what he suspected—no bra, nothing but curved, soft breasts. He unbuttoned those cutoff jeans, unzipping them to find all woman.

"Now that's just not right," he muttered, staring down at that little dark nest as she shimmied out of her shorts. "Your ex-husband was over there."

Hayden knew he sounded properly indignant; he needed a minute to recover. But then, he should have expected that after she'd been without her thong at the investor's party. Cameron would have to change that little habit—it could drive him into a permanent hard state.

"Hmm. William didn't notice. You did. I guess you get the prize." Cameron circled him and started pushing him toward her bed. "Get busy, big boy."

He was too easy, a real pushover when it came to Cameron; that nettled. "Oh, so now you trust me. Enough to 'get busy.' "

"I had second thoughts. I know I hurt your feelings. You're so sensitive sometimes. I want to make it up to you."

Make it up to you. For a moment, Hayden thought of Cameron's lithe body, all toned and athletic, and that mouth, and his mind went blank. Then he recovered. Maybe he really was that fragile, that sensitive. *What kind of a manly attribute was that?* "That's it? I'm sensitive? The hell I am. You thought I'd slept with Phoebe. How the hell am I going to do that when all I can think about is getting you into bed? Like right now?"

"Don't get all huffy. Look . . . I'm sorry. Life with Robert hasn't exactly prepared me for a guy like you."

"Am I *special* then?" he asked, damning the proof of his "sensitive" nature.

"Special and sensitive." Cameron circled his shoulders with her arms and leaped upon him in one of those quick, graceful ballet movements. The momentum landed him beneath her on the bed. "I like how you do that," she said quietly, looking down at him.

"What?" Hayden realized that he'd groaned slightly as Cameron wiggled to capture him fully, sliding down tight around him; she was hot inside, wet, and slick and tight, and his mind went blank again. She wiggled a little, getting comfortable, thrusting her hips down on him—up and down, slowly. Hayden struggled to recover the thread of something that she had just said, something very important. "Like how I do what?"

She rubbed her nose against his; the playful gesture didn't distract him from the pounding need of his body. "Touch me. I just know by the way you touch me, stroke me slowly and gently, as if I mean something to you—it's an odd feeling to be . . . cherished . . . and I know a lot about *not* being touched like that. By the way you take care of me. Like the way you fell backward, careful for me. You probably took care of Phoebe, too—I mean, probably did what she needed. I think you take care of people you like—and that you just may be a one-woman man, Mr. Hayden Olson."

"Oh, I am," he said quickly, because in another minute—

"I'm that one woman, at least for now. It's a possessive, kind of cavewoman thing with me, I guess," she stated smugly as she managed to bend and suckle his nipple—and wiggle the butt he had clamped tight against him.

Hayden fought to breathe deeply, to hold his body in check, which wasn't easy. Cameron's eyes were slitted, her body clenching his intimately and she let out this little trembling sigh as she went into herself. "Thanks," she whispered heartbeats later, then kissed him and snuggled close and sweet. "I needed that—for you to hold me like this."

"Think nothing of it," Hayden whispered, blowing a little in her ear, and then rubbing that sweet spot behind it with his thumb. He smiled because she was nestling against him, nuzzling his throat, and those hips were moving again . . .

When Cameron was beneath him, smiling softly up at him, Hayden smoothed her hair back from her cheek and let the softness flow between them.

"This is nice," she whispered, her hands framing his face as he began to move slowly, surely.

They kissed softly, testing the fit of their lips, the movement of their tongues to the rhythm of their bodies, hands tracing each other.

When the storm hit, Cameron's teeth were at his shoulder, her hands digging into his back, and wrapped in her own passion, fighting and tossing against it, she probably never heard his promise, "I'm not letting you go. . . ."

When Cameron lay asleep and tangled with him, her head on his shoulder, her limp hand resting on his chest, Hayden picked it up and pressed his lips to her palm, remembering how she had been hurt as she tried to escape that cellar.

He kissed her forehead, heard her mumble something in her sleep about whispers, and held her closer.

Cameron had been up to something, and she wasn't sharing with him. But then, considering how he'd entered her life, maybe she had reason.

Hayden intended to change that.

The light slap on her butt sent Cameron flipping over angrily. "You know how I hate that."

The aroma of coffee curling around her, the cup beneath her nose, almost caused her to forgive Hayden. "We don't have much time to talk privately, so wake up," he ordered curtly. "What are you up to?"

Cameron blinked, trying to place the gentle lover of last night into the tough, determined Hayden of this morning. Dawn was creeping into her windows, and he was fully dressed, sitting beside her and holding his own coffee. The remains of his breakfast were on the plate beside him. She took the cup of coffee, sipped it while he stared at her, and came up with, "I'm not happy with you—"

"Trust works both ways, you know. I've been on the phone with my mother. She remembers the house and everything in it. She's making a list."

"Please thank her for me. I can use that."

"You can thank her yourself when this is over." Hayden leaned close, his expression hard and determined. "Use this: According to one of Mom's friends—one of the household staff now deceased—Katherine was only going for a short flight, and she needed some peace away from the turmoil of the kidnapping . . . she wanted to think clearly . . . away from Robert."

He placed his cup aside with slow precision as though he were carefully placing his thoughts in order. "Talking to my mother this morning jarred her memory—twenty-eight years was a long time ago. According to what Norah told Mom back then, Robert had insisted that Katherine take that little ride to calm herself. Norah heard everything in the house, including what was going on between Katherine and Robert, and it wasn't good. After Katherine died, Norah didn't tell the police . . . she was afraid that Robert would retaliate. She begged Mom not to tell, and she didn't. . . . But Robert and Katherine had an argument the night before Katherine decided to unexpectedly light up that balloon—he wasn't going to be bought off, and she was holding the prenuptial agreement over his head, trying for a little decorum as she got rid of Robert."

A chill lifted the hair on Cameron's body, though the bedding and room were warm. "But Katherine was in the air because she was looking for Cammie."

"Right . . . she wanted to find her daughter. But she wasn't intending to be away from the telephones very long—in fact, she really didn't want to go up that morning, afraid she'd miss that important call about Cammie. Now, that's curious, isn't it? That *Robert* would suggest she take that ride to calm herself?"

"I don't know that I'm going to like what may come

next, but go ahead, Hayden," Cameron said cautiously.

He took a deep breath, then continued, "Mom had distinctly heard Robert saying how much he hated Katherine's interest in hot-air balloons. But, according to Norah, he suggested it, very early that morning. Katherine did not want to leave the phones. Strange that her propane tanks would malfunction just that morning, the *one* morning he suggested she needed a little ride, isn't it?"

Cameron stared at him, horrified at the details of Katherine's probable murder. She slid from the bed and faced Hayden. "That accident was thoroughly investigated by federal authorities, but the basket and envelope and tanks had been blown apart. They listed it as a malfunction of the propane setup and the burners. A gas leak somehow—" she said unevenly.

"Or something could have hit those tanks, causing that explosion—say a bullet."

"Hayden! That would do it!"

He was on his feet and pacing the floor. "You got it. Just yesterday morning—when I left your house, I saw Robert's stallion acting up. When I got close, someone shot that horse with these—"

He dug into his jeans, then opened his hand to show Cameron the pellets.

She stared at them rolling in his open palm and shook her head. "Robert would never hurt that stallion, or cause it to be hurt. He's too proud of it."

"I thought that, too. But he's desperate now, Cameron. A man does many things when he wants to hold on to what he considers his—and that would be you and Somerton money. He had to have someone help him during the kidnapping . . . maybe he has someone now. A pellet gun couldn't hit that tank, but a high-powered rifle could. I checked—the tanks sat right beneath Katherine Somerton's signature script, the big *S* logo above it. . . . No one could miss either one of those from the ground. Now what are you holding back?

What took you so long to get here yesterday morning?"

Cameron was shaking, her body cold. She had wondered about Robert's method of killing Katherine, but now the likely details of the heiress's death were clearly adding up to murder. "It's too early to wake William and Arabella. Would you please take a note over to them while I dress? I need to show you something. You'll need tools."

"No more bells, Cameron. I want you to wear this for good luck, something from me to hold you safe. You're not losing your mind, honey. You just happen to be someone in the line of fire," Hayden said grimly as he wrapped a bracelet around her wrist and closed the clasp. A miniature gold gargoyle lay against her skin. The pink tourmaline eyes caught the light, twinkling at her. Gold and obviously expensive, a little barbaric, yet feminine, the bracelet seemed to warm instantly. Uncertainty trembled in Cameron; it was the mark of Hayden's possession, to show the world that she was his. *How could he want her? The woman who had led a lifetime of lies? An imposter?*

"It's beautiful. But I have nothing—"

"You have yourself. It's one of a kind, just like you."

His face was just a blur through her tears, her body trembling, her throat tight with emotion. "I don't care what happens to me. I'm going to prison, Hayden—"

"The hell you are. They don't let you wear something like that bracelet in prison, do they?" he asked harshly. "Would I give you something like that—if I even thought you were headed into a cell with a too-friendly roommate?"

Cameron tried for a smile that wobbled. "Thanks," she managed humbly.

"That's better. That's my girl."

The musty air seemed to burst through the hole Hayden had created by punching a crowbar through the drywall and cutting away a section of a two-by-four. Filled with mold and dust, the cloud surrounded Cameron, and she cried out.

Instantly concerned, Hayden turned to her. "Okay?"

"What if Cammie is in there? I couldn't bear knowing that I'd slept over her for years."

"You just concentrate on—" Hayden kicked out more drywall and stood back as something crashed inside the area he'd just broken through.

When Cameron's flashlight caught the head and bulky horns of a stuffed water buffalo, she started to laugh. It was a nervous burst of energy that Hayden seemed to understand. "That's good. Keep it up."

"Do you think she's in there?"

Bracing his hand on a heavy old buffet, Hayden put his boot through the hole and pushed at the head, which slid away slightly. Crouching, Hayden flashed the light inside the hole. "That head is blocking the way. I'll have to open more."

Cameron's hand touched his shoulder as he stood. "Please be careful. I don't want anything to happen to you."

"So that means you care, right?" he asked briefly, then noted the tears in her eyes, luminous in her pale face.

When she simply leaned against him, her face pressed to his throat, her body trembling, Hayden held her tightly. "Maybe," she whispered softly, and moved away.

Hayden smiled briefly; he decided "Maybe" was as good as he was getting in the way of promises and affection just then, and went back to work.

Fifteen

IN HER BARN'S HOME OFFICE TWO DAYS LATER, CAMERON lifted her wrist, studying Hayden's slightly barbaric, beautiful gargoyle bracelet. "You're not losing your mind, got it?" he'd said firmly.

The bracelet was physical proof of his confidence in her, something she had to hold on to—because Hayden's troubling suggestion that someone might be actively trying to unhinge her, and his description of what *might* have happened to cause Katherine's murder, had never left Cameron's thoughts.

Cameron sat at her computer, scrolling through the list Sophie had sent by e-mail, a growing composite of items she remembered being in Somerton House.

Cammie's body hadn't been in the closed section of the basement. It had been filled with Buck's safari kills, his American buffalo, and a stuffed donkey—items too large to move easily. Trophies of all kinds lay in boxes, ones marked with his name and Katherine's, mementoes that couldn't be sold without raising interest. Only a few dusty bottles of wine had remained on the floor-to-ceiling wall rack, and they had been of lesser grade; Cameron could imagine Robert celebrating his good fortune with the best bottles.

Cautious about pushing Robert too much right now, with William and Arabella near, Hayden had convinced Cameron that they should seal the basement area as it was, concealing the intrusion with a chair on top of that heavy buffet.

Cameron stood and frowned at the computer screen. The lengthy list was growing daily, and Robert must have made a fortune selling the contents of Somerton House. But what had happened to the rest of the two million? From Hayden's curt and bitter description of their life after Paul Olson had died, the Olsons certainly hadn't used it.

In her backyard now, Cameron listened to Hayden's and William's voices, the rumbling man talk somehow comforting her. The sounds were steady, not rasping and dangerous such as the whispering *outside* the cellar where Cammie had died. Cameron frowned slightly, trying to place that low, rasping sound, one she'd heard somewhere, sometime before—

Was Hayden's suggestion true? Had someone been deliberately planting her missing items in different places?

The notion nagged at her, and she turned it: Robert certainly did not have access to Cameron's private home. But with the code to the barn's security system, Phoebe would have access to everything inside it. *Was it possible she'd helped Robert?*

What had Sophie said? That Robert had actually pushed Katherine into taking his suggestion when she really didn't want to leave the phones? That *one* morning? And with the Somerton logo pinpointing the location of the tanks, they could be detected easily by someone on the ground, aiming a rifle.

Hayden had given a brief description of how, as a boy, he'd seen that hot-air balloon rise into the sky—Katherine had been wearing a flowing white scarf, so her location within the basket could be easily pinpointed, if a shooter wanted to hit the tanks and not the woman. . . .

Cameron pushed herself to remember, her hand wrapped tightly around the gargoyle on her wrist. *I have to remember everything*. "Where are you, Cammie?" she whispered.

She stared at the little gold cross on the mirror, the framed pictures beneath it, the ones she'd used to scan and place in Robert's satchel, beneath his pillow, and in the envelope with his allowance. In later years, Cameron had been very careful to hand Robert his allowance personally, just a little reminder that she, too, held trump cards and would play them if necessary.

"Cammie," she whispered, drawing the old pink ribbon through her fingers, winding it around them. "Where are you?"

Katherine's hot-air balloon had exploded in midair . . . on the one morning that Robert suggested she lift up . . .

Katherine and Dr. Naylan had both died. . . . Hayden's file was exact and a sample DNA comparing mother to daughter could prove Cameron as an imposter. However, Katherine and Naylan would have instantly identified the replacement child, some street waif who was afraid that the dream would be taken away from her if she didn't do as she was told. But then, little Pilar had actually believed that she was Cammie for years—until she found the photos of the real child-heiress with her mother. Then the whispers had started to make sense. . . .

Was Robert really capable of killing Katherine? Of letting Cammie die without medical aid? Cameron remembered his harsh treatment of her, and the answer came back. Yes, certainly. He was capable of marrying a lonely widow, of having women right under her nose. And Katherine was preparing to divorce him.

After the kidnapping, Katherine had been wrapped in the desperate search for her daughter, and then she'd died—according to the federal investigators, her crew had gone over the balloon and tanks with their usual intensity prior to her ascent.

But somehow, the propane gas had leaked . . . and a bullet just could have caused that explosion.

With a sigh, Cameron stood, stretched, and surveyed

Mimosa and the Somerton estate in the distance. She glanced at the tiny pink tourmaline eyes of the gargoyle and stacked up facts.

From what she already knew, there had been too much press and too many investigators around during the kidnapping. Robert hadn't left the town, or the estate; Cameron had checked his schedule long ago. If Cammie had been taken from the cellar the night before "Cameron" emerged the next day, there would have been enough confusion to hide her somewhere. But where? The whole area had been thoroughly searched.

Sophie had loved her first husband, and Paul Olson had loved her. He hadn't even looked at another woman, but according to Sophie, he had more than once protected Katherine from Robert simply by appearing at her side.

That was believable, because while Robert might hurt a woman, he wouldn't do it with a big man looming beside her. And Paul Olson had been frustrated that Katherine would put up with a man like Robert.

Yet, Robert had had help—he couldn't have pulled off the kidnapping *and* maintained appearances at the anniversary party *and* managed trips to the cellar with investigators installed in Somerton House and watching everyone's moves. *Who had helped him?*

With those facts tumbling through her mind, Cameron opened her back door and looked onto her shaded fairy garden.

My mommy says . . . the fairies come to take care of us while we sleep, Pilar. I'm going to sleep . . . and the fairies will take care of me. . . .

Then: *Shh, someone is outside. Can you hear what they're saying? Why won't they let us out—I need my mommy!* Cammie had called to the person outside the cellar.

Cameron remembered a low, harsh whisper: *Shut up in there, you brats! I brought food. . . . If you don't want it, just keep whining. . . .*

The door had opened and a giant of a man had stood there in the night, his flashlight blinding the girls. *Get back....*

Cammie's face had been too pale, her breathing labored, her face damp with perspiration—

That man was big enough to be Hayden's father, and he'd killed himself. Or had he? If Katherine and Naylan had been killed to cover the exchange, was it possible that Paul Olson had also been killed?

The sound of a weed eater cut into her thoughts. William turned the machine off, then turned to wave and grin back at her as he walked toward the farmhouse. Cameron absently returned the wave but took in the clearing the men had done around the statues. Her picnic table was now near a new privacy fence, blocking the view to the farmhouse. A double hammock had been placed near it, sheltered beneath the mimosa tree in full pink bloom. In mid-July, the air was sweet and fresh, seeming to capture and hold that one perfect moment.

Oblivious to her, Hayden was standing beneath a sparkling waterfall from the hose over his head. At odds with the delicate blooming mimosa behind him, he looked rugged and male and delicious. He lifted his face to the water, angling and shaking his head. The water streamed down his body, gleaming on that black hair, onto his chest, dampening the strip of his shorts, revealed just above his jeans' sagging waistband.

Fascinated, Cameron stepped onto the back porch, and then, grinning, he turned to her. He seemed so boyish now that it was easy to picture him as that ten-year-old boy whose life had been torn apart. *Was it possible that he was right? That his father wasn't involved in the kidnapping or his own suicide?*

It was only a moment in time, in that sweet July air, Cameron reminded herself, because her DNA wasn't like Cammie's, and because there was no future in her affair with Hayden. The bond was momentary—

The blast of cold water caught her in the face, taking away her breath, and while she was stunned, it poured onto her T-shirt, plastering it against her. "Hayden! That's freezing!"

"You were thinking too hard," he returned. Then Hayden's grin changed to that intense sensual one as he stared at her breasts. He kept the spray on her, slowly running it up and down her body. She hadn't bothered to put on a bra, and pasted to her breasts, the damp cloth revealed peaked, dark nipples.

By then, Hayden had tossed the hose aside and was in full stride, moving purposefully toward her. His tight hot look shot straight down her body, immobilizing and jolting her into one simmering ball of hunger.

"Oh, no you don't," Cameron said, because she wasn't going to make it easy for him. She laughed as she started to run toward the farmhouse.

Hayden caught her with one arm, gathered her back to him, and nuzzled that spot behind her ear while his hands were busy cupping her breasts. "Miss me? Couldn't stay away from me?"

She wiggled her bottom against him and smiled when he groaned. "No," she lied. "You got me all wet. That water was cold. . . . It's daylight here, Olson. You can't have your way with me here."

"Mm, I'm working on it."

"Tell me about your ex-wife and your girlfriends." *Had he played with them like this?*

He lifted his head and stared blankly at her. "Now?"

"I picture a little homemaker type, the supportive corporate wife, kids, the whole baking-pie-in-an-apron picture. Had your favorite chair ready when you came home, did she? Put your feet up while she brought you a drink, then hurried to set a lovely dining room table?"

Hayden shook his head. "You just love making my life difficult, don't you? I've had a few relationships and enjoyed them—but nothing clicked. As for my ex-wife, she's remarried with a houseful of kids. She sends me a Christmas card with their pictures. I send her a poinsietta from Grow Green. We were both too young and moved on, and I'm busy here, if you hadn't noticed."

"Oh, I'd say so," Cameron whispered unevenly because he had slipped one hand down inside her capris, cupping her as he dragged her backward, still nuzzling that spot behind her ear.

The image of pie-baking other women slid away as Hayden growled hungrily against Cameron's throat. She couldn't help laughing, twisting within his hold, the nuzzling more playful than sensual. When he spread his shirt over the picnic table, then bent her over it, sliding down her capris, she smiled, "Olson, you're kidding. We've been—Ohh . . ."

The hard blunt heat slowly entering her body, stretching her femininity, the big hand reaching around her belly to stroke that sensitive nub said he was serious.

Cameron held on to the picnic table and let herself fly.

Later, snuggled against Hayden in the double hammock, lazing and sated, Cameron listened to his heartbeat and dozed. "Thanks," she whispered.

"Mm? For what?"

"For the nice time."

He cupped her chin and lifted her face to his, brushing her lips. "We're having more than a 'nice time,' babe."

"It isn't nice when you wake me up with a slap on the butt."

Hayden smiled and nuzzled her hair. "You know how to carry a grudge. Just remember that there are other ways I wake you up."

Their play was only a temporary respite, because nothing was keeping Cameron from facing Robert, stirring him up enough to tell her what had happened. "We've got to get William and Arabella away from here. Robert closed the deal on the thoroughbreds, and he'll be back soon."

"I know. I'm working on it."

Cameron was silent for a moment, her hand smoothing

his chest. Hayden, as a confidant who knew everything about her, was more than her lover. When she exposed herself and the crimes to the world, she would miss him terribly. "My nightmares are getting stronger."

"Mm. Getting locked in that cellar would do that."

She shook her head. "No, it's something else. Something I can't remember, and it's just on the edge of my grasp. It's a voice, not Cammie's, but someone else's—a raspy voice I can't place. I've heard it before."

"Robert," Hayden supplied grimly.

"Probably, but not quite." With a sigh, Cameron lay close and soft against him, the summer breeze cooling them, the sound of William and Arabella chatting in the garden.

Cameron and he needed this time, Hayden thought lazily, time to regroup and let her memories stir to life. She was enjoying William and Arabella and the relief had seemed to relax her slightly. And that gave Hayden time to work on his theory that Madeline was a little too close to Cameron—for a reason. And Cameron wouldn't like that theory—that Madeline was somehow involved with the secrets of Somerton House.

Hayden's thumb stroked the gargoyle bracelet. Meant to keep Cameron safe, it was also a mark of his possession—something to warn Robert off. He wanted Cameron badly, but he'd have to go through Hayden to get her. The bracelet was certain to set Robert off, if not the portrait and Buck's horned chair.

And there was no stopping Cameron; she was primed to deliver the information of Katherine divorcing Robert to him, and jump-start their war.

"Your father was murdered," Cameron stated suddenly.

"I know. When I was at the guesthouse the other night, looking at the floor where Dad had died, something seemed wrong. I couldn't place it until I was putting this bracelet on your wrist, thinking about which hand you used the most. Then it clicked. The gun was in his left hand, the bullet wound entry from the left. He used his right. Yes, I'd say he was murdered. Mom never saw him or the pictures they took; otherwise, she would have spotted it right away—but then, no one was listening to us at the time."

He'd never forget the helpless frustration of being that ten-year-old boy . . .

Cameron moved over Hayden suddenly, and the hammock tipped, tumbling them to the ground. She laughed and lay on top of him, cupping his jaw with her hands. There was soft damp grass beneath him, and a woman he wanted above him. How much more could a man ask?

William studied the tomato plants that Hayden had taught him how to "cage" and prune. "Arabella wants a lot of tomatoes. She wants to can them. . . . I like gardening, and so does she, and we want our family to eat healthy. . . . My folks will get over this, once they come to know her—they'd better, because they are not going to make her uncomfortable again. Cannot tell you how furious I was when they suggested *to Arabella* that she was out for my family's money."

"They'll come around. After all, she's the mother of that little Van Zandt, isn't she? Their only grandchild? A lot happens to soften the heart when a little one is coming," Hayden suggested.

"I should have played the whole thing another way—but there we were, pregnant," William said cheerfully, proudly. "I do think the folks are coming around though, softening a little bit. Mother actually called and had a civilized conversation with Arabella."

While William continued his plans to leave "stuffy offices and social business parties," Hayden's mind was on Cameron. Since she had decided she needed time in Somerton House's office early that afternoon—before Robert returned—Hayden had been uneasy. Robert hadn't left the horse farm, and Madeline was still at that California spa. Or was she?

Without question, Cameron trusted Madeline; she wasn't going to like Hayden's suspicions.

He looked at the Italian herb starts that he'd ordered sent from Grow Green; the scents of basil and oregano blended in the afternoon air with that of lemon-citrus-scented geraniums that he intended to use in Cameron's fairy garden.

His gaze moved to Cameron's backyard and the makings for a koi pond stacked in one corner, the aquatic plants that he'd ordered standing in the plastic pool. Nearby were the bricks for an outdoor Santa-Fe-type kitchen and walking stones for the paths.

Hayden stripped off his leather gloves and considered the birdbath with the fountain coming from a concrete fairy's pitcher. Laying out the design for the garden behind the barn and planning the outdoor kitchen had kept his mind busy—because he knew that Cameron was up to something, and she wasn't sharing exactly what.

"I feel much better—physically and mentally—when I'm active and working in a garden, or doing handyman stuff, repairing things," William was saying. "I just don't know how much that sort of thing pays."

Hayden had to get Cameron's ex-husband and his pregnant girlfriend away from the explosion that was certain to happen. "There's offsets. When you don't have to pay a gardener, or a handyman, you save money. You can make it on your own, William—and provide for a family—with less money than you think. If you think you want to try getting into the gardening business, there's a position open at Grow Green— You'd learn from the best."

William stared at him. "You mean it?"

"Sure. But we're needing someone at Grow Green right away. Should I make that call?"

"You bet. How soon can we leave?"

"Where are you, Cammie?"

Katherine's pink and red roses swayed softly in the late-afternoon breeze as Cameron pruned the bushes, placing the remains into a basket. Somehow the task brought her closer to the wonderful woman who had been Cammie's mother. The world seemed to have stopped, shadows softly draping the mausoleum, and everything was so still, as if waiting for the explosion when Robert returned.

Madeline had been furious with Cameron for setting him off. "He's a dangerous son of a bitch, Cameron. No telling what will happen now. You're pushing him too hard now. Wait until I get back, please. I don't want you hurt and—"

"And?" Cameron had asked. When Madeline had avoided the question, Cameron had asked, "Did he hurt you, Madeline?"

"I can handle myself. It's you that I'm worried about. You're like my own daughter."

"Then stay away and stay safe. Please, Madeline. I have to do this, and nothing is going to happen to me—you know the conditions of Katherine's will."

"It's Hayden, isn't it? You're living with him now, aren't you? Cameron, he's just out to get revenge," Madeline had worried. "I'm coming home. The hell with this spa."

"You stay there. That's an order. I don't want you hurt."

Now, with the delicate fragrance of the roses circling her, Cameron watched Robert's black Lincoln Continental speed up the Somerton driveway. He must have seen her, because the car's tires squealed to a stop. Robert slammed out of the door and started trudging up the path to the mausoleum.

Cameron braced herself for the encounter and placed her basket of clippings on a bench; she held her pruning shears tightly in one hand—from Robert's angry expression, she might need them for defense.

He jerked open the ornate iron gate, stalked through it, and stood facing her with his hands on his hips. His pampered face was bruised and bloody, one eye swollen shut, his expensive white tennis outfit spotted with blood. She almost laughed at the two rolls of cotton stuck up his nostrils. "Have a nice time socializing in Texas, Robert?" she asked calmly, while her stomach was clenched with nerves—apparently their war had already begun . . . and he hadn't even seen the portrait or the chair yet.

The stench of alcohol bit into the air as Robert yelled, "Hayden just beat the hell out of me. I'm going to have him charged and put away."

"I'll have a fleet of attorneys on that before the ink is dry, Robert."

He leaned toward Cameron menacingly. "You'd protect that son of a bitch after seeing what he did to me? The man who raised you?"

Someone else had obviously beaten Robert; the blood was fresh and bright on his shirt, and Hayden had been at the farmhouse with William and Arabella—apparently they were leaving for St. Louis. On the telephone, Arabella's bubbling excitement about William's upcoming "internship" at Grow Green hadn't mentioned Robert's appearance. And Cameron was grateful that Arabella hadn't experienced Robert as his true self, an arrogant bully. "That's a lie, Robert, and I can prove it. You'll have to do better."

His hand gripped her wrist painfully. Then he noted the bracelet biting into her flesh. "What is this thing?"

"A gift . . . from Hayden."

"It's ugly. I don't have time to—" He started dragging her toward the gate. "Listen, you little witch, I'll deal with you later, but right now, I need you to come down to the house to write a check to me. Is Madeline back? You could call her and tell her—"

"I've asked her to stay away for a while. I'm redecorating."

Cameron moved quickly. She came down hard on Robert's foot, and surprised, he released her. She gripped the shears tightly, and the two faced each other, locked in the war that had gone on for years. "I'm not a little girl any longer, Robert."

She glanced at the other man coming into the enclosure, an angry one. "Hello, William."

"As if I'd believe that—" Robert raised his hand to slap

her face, and another man's hand gripped his wrist, stopping the blow.

"That's enough, Robert," William stated softly.

"You'd better keep out of this, playboy," Robert sneered as he tugged his hand away.

"It looks like you're having a bad day all the way around, because you're not hitting Cameron." William placed his body protectively in front of Cameron's.

"Who's going to stop me?"

"Me."

Cameron's instincts told her to protect William. But she also knew that her ex-husband needed to face Robert down; William needed to clear away that part of his past.

Robert's wild mocking laughter stopped abruptly, ended by William's fist. "That felt so good," William stated cheerfully.

Hunched over, Robert gripped his nose, blood seeping through his fingers. "You broke my nose. I'll—" The remainder of his threat slid into silence as he stumbled toward Somerton House.

"I've waited for years to do that."

"My hero," Cameron stated shakily.

"I just came to say good-bye for a time. I'm going to try really hard at that internship Hayden has arranged—with pay and housing—not office work either, but fixing up the greenhouses, learning about bulbs and such, that sort of thing. Arabella will have a little house and a garden and whatever those employee benefits things include. . . . But maybe I shouldn't leave, after all."

William eyed Robert warily. "I should stay and get that brute out of your life," he added dramatically as he rubbed his fist.

"But Arabella and your baby need you. I'll be fine, William."

"And there's Hayden, of course. He'll keep you safe—I wouldn't want to spoil that, a man taking care of his own. He's helping Arabella pack now and making arrangements,"

William reasoned. "I want to know if I'm needed, though, you understand? You'll call? Promise?"

"I've always loved you, William, Of course, I'll call, and I want to know every detail of how Arabella is doing—and you. I'm quite safe," Cameron lied, because she didn't want William involved in the dangerous collision that was certain to come. And she wanted to keep Hayden out of the line of fire. "I have a favor to ask—"

"Anything."

"I don't want Hayden to worry about me. Please don't tell him that Robert is back. He'll be passed out soon, and I need to collect some papers from my office."

Hayden would be furious, but she knew Robert's moods well. After an obvious beating and enraged, Robert was ripe to push now—careless with his words—and she wasn't waiting for Hayden.

After she'd convinced William that she would be safe, he left, boyishly eager for the experiences his new life would bring. "You'll be all right, William. Your parents love you, and you're all going to be very happy."

Then Cameron turned her mind to what she had to do, before Hayden came looking—she had to face Robert before he started on his hidden bottle of absinthe.

Bracing herself for the confrontation and what she might learn, Cameron momentarily remained on that bench. She tried to wrap around her the peace of this place, where two people who loved each other deeply lay together, for eternity. Birds chirped in the trees, a squirrel tearing down a tree trunk, the pink cabbage roses nodding in the slight breeze.

The breeze caused the tree limbs above her to sway, and the sound of the leaves seemed like a whisper: *Mommy?*

"I know, Cammie." Above, the gray clouds were gathering, the air heavy and damp.

Cameron lifted her face to the gentle raindrops. She listened to the sound of them hitting the hard, dry ground, the marble mausoleum, and pattering softly in the leaves. The rain would clean and allow life to travel on as it should, just as William and Arabella would with their child.

She listened to the echoes of whispering inside her head, the child and the man's. "I'll find you, Cammie, and I intend to prove that Robert murdered your mother. Then you'll be able to rest. After that, what happens to me doesn't matter."

The wind had risen, the rain pelting her as she moved toward Somerton House. Angry and drunk, Robert would head for his shower first. He'd meticulously care for his wounds, trying to avoid scarring to his face, and then he'd start on the absinthe. His recovery from the strong liqueur would take days; Cameron had to get to him before the secrets he knew would be sealed again.

Bracing herself for the collision, Cameron entered Somerton House.

Cameron listened to Robert's footsteps as he hurried through the foyer and into the main salon. Showered, his facial cuts dressed carefully, and dressed only in his satin robe, he stopped when he saw her sitting in Buck's chair, the bottle of greenish, licorice-scented absinthe in her hand.

"I suppose you want this. Too bad." She noted his hunger for the strong drink, then she lifted the bottle high and let it fall; it shattered on the marble tabletop beside the chair.

"I'll kill you," Robert said quietly as he slowly looked at the chair, then the portrait of the Somerton family.

When Robert turned back to her, the surprise she had expected on his expression wasn't there. But now she didn't care what happened to her, only the truths Robert was holding. Not entirely defenseless, Cameron lifted one of Robert's antique dueling pistols. "It's loaded. You've used it yourself to show off. At this point, I don't care what happens to either one of us. I care only about the truth."

Robert's surprise was almost comical, and Cameron savored it, too, before she placed the pistol back into its velvet case. "You won't do anything. You know what it would mean if I die. That's why you've been trying to make me think I was losing it, isn't it? So you could put me away and gain control of Somerton again? I'd be alive, but probably with mush for a brain, right? Once the drugs got to me? And for the record, Robert, you really shouldn't 'medicate' a small child that much."

Cameron dove into pushing him and watching for tiny cracks in his control. "What happened to all the money from the things you sold, Robert? What happened to your share of that two million—after you killed the gardener? And just how exactly did Katherine die?"

The lightning storm stirred outside Somerton House, thunder rolling as the lights flickered and died.

Then Robert was coming for her, stopped by the nudge of that pistol against his chest. "It doesn't matter how they put me away—even for murder," she reminded him. "And now, I *know* the gardner was murdered."

He stepped back quickly, his hands raised. "Take it easy, Cameron. You know how you've been lately."

"Do I? Forgetting things? Is that how I've been? Maybe you had a hand in that. Let's start with whoever gave you a beating you probably deserved, and it wasn't Hayden—and why you need a sizable check. The money for the thoroughbreds has already been transferred—I checked. So you need that check for something else, and someone else treated you to that facial. That sounds like payoff money. Why?"

Cameron carefully placed the pistol aside and picked up her checkbook. "You're in such a hurry, Robert. You told whoever it was that you'd be back with the money, didn't you? You need me for this, don't you? Madeline isn't here, and you're really not good at forgeries."

"God, I hate you. I have to have that money, Cameron. Now."

She waved the checkbook, taunting him. "All you have to do is to tell me why."

Robert spat the answer: "Jack Morales. I've got to get that check to him."

"Jack Morales? Phoebe's rodeo boyfriend?" Suddenly, Cameron thought of the times Phoebe had entered her home, sorting her mail, doing her a favor. She thought of all the times that only Phoebe would have special details to relay to Robert. Phoebe would have access to Cameron's home, to her aquarium, to her computer and files and could misplace things easily—

The thought sickened Cameron. "Nice. Real nice, Robert. He found out that she was two-timing him—with you. She's taken off, and now he wants blackmail money, or your hide. Ah. That's it, isn't it? Jack is very good with his knife, and your precious pretty face just could get a scar or two. What's the matter, Robert, did Phoebe get Jack to do a few dirty little favors for you, and now he's made that connection?"

Then Cameron asked quietly, "What else did Phoebe do for you, Robert? Tell me, or I won't write this check."

Sixteen

WILLIAM HADN'T BEEN A VERY GOOD LIAR.

After hurrying William and Arabella away from danger and into their new life, Hayden pushed his pickup to the limit, the windshield wipers working furiously. The heavy gray clouds had darkened the early evening too soon, made worse by the heavy rain.

He hit a fast-moving stream on the state highway, and his truck fishtailed slightly before he brought it under control. Every moment Hayden struggled with that big limb, clearing it off the Somerton driveway so that he could get to Cameron, Hayden pictured her facing down Robert.

Hayden was already out of his truck and running up the Somerton House steps when he saw a movement, a woman outlined by a flash of lightning.

Bent against the wind, Cameron was heading down a familiar road beside the cottages, one Hayden and his family had traveled many times. The road led to the gardner's house where they had lived.

The doors of Somerton House swung open and Robert stood outlined in the light. In a billowing shirt and tight riding pants, he looked almost comical, as if he were the last

Southern gentleman defending the plantation. *If he'd hurt Cameron—*

But Robert was no gentleman; his curses streamed hot and furious into the storm as Hayden hurried after Cameron.

Running, slashed by the wind and rain, the woods' leaves blowing against him, Hayden saw his old home—and Cameron bend toward the door. It opened and she moved inside. . . .

He had to see that she wasn't hurt— His heart racing, Hayden pushed himself through the distance. When he passed through the open door, he noted a big key ring dangling from the door's lock. Then, in the jumbled shadows of stacked barrels, boxes, and stored lawn equipment, he saw Cameron; she was hunched into a ball on a big wooden box, holding her knees.

Hayden knelt beside her, noting her damp clothing. She was shaking, locked in an emotional chill far deeper than her damp clothing. He picked a few leaves from her tangled hair, smoothing it back from her cheek, damp with tears.

"Hi," he said gently, fearing for her, for what she had gone through with Robert. Hayden sat beside her, then glanced around the old house, used for storage now.

"This was your house, wasn't it? Before your father was murdered?" she whispered.

He nodded, concerned by Cameron's stark expression, her face pale and haunted in the shadows. A bolt of lightning lit the open doorway and dirty windows, then thunder rolled, rattling the glass. In that moment, he remembered another time, the warmth of the house, the smells of the kitchen, and the roaring laughter of his father. Then he turned to the woman beside him, her words echoing in his mind: *"Murdered", not "committed suicide." . . . Was that what Robert had just told Cameron, upsetting her? The murder of Paul Olson?*

"Every time it rains, I hope Cammie's body will somehow be found," Cameron whispered. "Every time, I hunt for her all over again, in the same places."

"I know, honey." He ached for Cameron, who had been tempered into a role that had weighted her with guilt.

Trembling beside him, Cameron was in no shape to be questioned about anything, including the strong scent of licorice around her. He put his arm around her, drawing her into his warmth. "It was Phoebe," she said quietly, turning her face up to him. "Robert used her to spy on me. You found out, didn't you? Why didn't you tell me? *Did you know that she was the one who locked me in that cellar?*"

Cameron shrugged free and stood, angrily facing Hayden. But then, it was a night of anger and storms, Hayden decided as he stood slowly to face her. "I found out and asked her. She thought she was helping you stop having nightmares. She swallowed that fool therapy idea that Robert had pitched to her."

Her hand slashed the air between them. "Don't give me that. She did Robert's dirty work for him, misplacing things, and she took his beatings. Oh, no, it wasn't Jack Morales beating her. She was having Jack, too, but she was in Robert's bed all the time. She was the go-between, getting Jack to do Robert's dirty work for him. And Jack never suspected—I just wrote Robert a big fat Somerton check to get all that information."

Just then, the door slammed shut and the sharp smell of gasoline slid into the musty room. "I guess Robert wants to finish the job," Hayden murmured as flames danced outside the windows.

He opened the door and flames swept inward. As they stepped back, an explosion sounded at the back of the house and Hayden noted the boxes of chemicals. "We've got to get out of here before this whole place explodes."

Black smoke hovered above Hayden and Cameron as they circled the living room, stacked with boxes and barrels. Flames danced at the windows of the bedrooms. Holding his hand and coughing, Cameron was Hayden's only concern.

The kitchen window above the sink was the only way out, and Hayden pulled Cameron toward it. He broke the glass, and the remaining shards as well as he could and lifted her up. Cameron crouched in the window, turning to him. "Git," he ordered, in a term she'd once used on him.

"Not without you."

"Honey, you're blocking my exit."

When she leaped out, Hayden followed and landed on the ground. Cameron hadn't backed away from the burning house; instead, she had waited for him, grabbing his hand as they ran from the house. Hayden lifted her over a stack of workman's cement blocks just as the windows' glass shattered and flame burst through them. Winded, Hayden and Cameron crouched behind the cement blocks. Rain slashed down, lightning lit the sky, and thunder crashed, and then, the next explosion hit, seeming to burst the walls of the house open.

The sound of a revving motor turned them; the rear lights of Robert's Lincoln were shooting away into the night.

"He's not getting away with this." Hayden had just taken a few running steps to get to his pickup when Cameron's body hit him from behind, her arms around him.

He turned to her desperate smudged face, her hands gripping his shirt. "Someone will see that fire and the rural firemen will be here soon. I want you with me. Don't you dare leave me now, Hayden. I'm not done with Robert—I don't have what I need from him."

"You'd let that bastard go?" he asked incredulously.

Her fists tightened and she shook him. "He's delivering a check to Jack Morales. You should have told me about Phoebe. You were there that morning to get her out of town, because you knew exactly what she had been doing, right?"

"Would you have believed me?"

Cameron straightened her shoulders, her head lifting; she was back to the heiress in charge—cool, tough, and determined—stepping into the role of getting what was best for Katherine Somerton's honored memory. "Probably not. I think you were trying to spare me, Hayden, dear. But I can take my bumps as they come, and you are not leaving me now."

"So I'm needed then. *You* need *me,*" Hayden pressed.

"You could say that," she said, as the fire engines whined in the distance. "I do not want any problems with this fire, Hayden. I will not have this mess come out before I'm done with Robert. I'm not dragging Katherine's name through the muck, and I haven't found Cammie yet. Stop cursing and looking at me as if I really am losing it. All I'm asking of you is that you stand by me."

"Cameron—" Hayden began and then frustrated, glared at her. "You ask a lot. You could really get your butt in a sling over this."

"I want a lot. And if my butt gets pinched, I'll keep yours safe. And I always keep my promises."

Those black eyes searched her face, then Hayden smoothed her hair back from her face. "If that's your story about the fire, we can try. You're a mess, by the way."

"So are you." *No wonder Cammie had adored H.J. As a man, Hayden was everything a woman could want. He wasn't running; he was sticking and supporting her—standing right beside her when she needed him. A good guy, Hayden really deserved someone normal, those kids and a home. . . .* Cameron shivered; she had no idea what "normal" was.

Hayden was running through the scenario they would present to the firemen: "I was here. We tried to stop the fire, got it? You were set to destroy the house anyway, but the lightning did the job for you—"

"Yes, dear. You're my hero. Oh, and by the way, I had a tracking device installed on Robert's car. Just a little protection for myself. I need my laptop from the barn to track him, but you're not going anywhere now. You are *not* leaving me. Wherever Robert is, probably delivering Jack's check, he isn't here, and that's good enough."

Hayden held Cameron to him as the fire engine roared

toward them. "Dammit. I hate it when you do that, play sweet and cute, then come up with something beautifully sneaky. Our little game has to change. You're going to have to let me in on what you're doing at all times—and I mean *every* minute from now on."

"I will. Just do this for me. No one must know that Robert just tried to kill us."

As the fire engine slowed near them, coming to a full stop, Cameron whispered urgently, "Please do this for me. For Cammie."

The fire chief was running toward them now, and the pulse in Hayden's forehead was pounding, his jaw tightening, the blazing firelight gleaming on his cheekbones. "Protecting that bastard goes against the grain, Cameron. And it's only temporary, because when I get my hands on him—"

"Ms. Somerton?" the fire chief asked, as rain slashed against them. A short sturdy man in his forties, Norman Rufin, shook his head, and rain spun from his helmet. "I'm afraid there's not much we can do at this point but keep a safe perimeter."

Cameron squeezed Hayden's big hard hand and stepped in front of him. If anyone had to lie, it would be her. "I was going to have it emptied and torn down. I guess the weather took care of that for me. Lightning must have struck it. It was already burning when we came out of the main house. I should have called, but we were busy trying to stop it. . . . Please, the rain shouldn't let the fire go too far. Just let that old house burn and keep your men safe—there were old lawn mowers and gas cans in there and some chemicals used for maintenance."

She sensed Hayden bristling behind her, warring with his own honor and truth.

"I'll vouch for that," he murmured slowly, and she caught the reluctance and the darkness in his voice. Hayden breathed just once, heavily, and she leaned back against him, reminding him to remember his promise to stay beside her.

His arms came around her slowly, his body taut behind her, and Norman was quick to take in the protective stance. "And you are?"

"He's—" Cameron began.

"Hayden Olson. I hold Ms. Somerton in very high regard," Hayden stated firmly, his gallant phrasing slightly surprising Cameron.

"I see that. I heard about you, Olson. You rented her farmhouse, didn't you? Several of my men worked with you on that place and have good words about you. . . . She's a sweet girl, that," Norman said as he glanced back at the burning building. "We're lucky to have her carry on her mama's good-work traditions. Better get her out of this storm. My men will handle it from here on. We could have used that old house as practice—if you were going to remove it anyway."

"How did you get here so fast?" Hayden asked carefully.

Norman eyed his men at work. "We had a call that someone had seen lightning strike the Somerton House—just glad it was that old house instead. Hey, John! Get back—let it burn. . . . She says there's gas and chemicals in there!"

Hayden reached to catch Norman's arm before he hurried away. "Someone called? Who?"

"Dunno. The storm knocked out the station's regular phone stuff. Roy Stephens took the call at his house and rounded us up by the tornado siren," Norman called over his shoulder.

"Inside," Hayden ordered, his arm almost lifting Cameron off her feet as he made his way up the front steps. He pushed open the door and hauled her inside. "Stay behind me."

"Robert isn't here—"

"Would you shut up?" Hayden's hand gripped Cameron's as he led her through the first-story rooms.

Cameron had enough and pulled back from Hayden's tight grip. "I told you he wasn't here," she said tiredly. "He just wanted to frighten me. He wouldn't actually let me die. That's why he called the firemen."

Scowling, Hayden leaned down to her. "Yeah, well, you just never know, do you?"

"I know Robert," she stated firmly. "You're irritated because we almost—repeat, almost—got killed. Stop shoving me around, Hayden. I've had enough of everything, including men bossing me. That includes you. You could *ask* me to be quiet, not tell me to shut up. That is just so rude."

He stared at her blankly and his curse was short and cutting. Then he sniffed, glancing around the foyer. "What's that smell? Licorice?"

Cameron dreaded his reaction to the scene with Robert. "Absinthe. The bottle broke. I haven't had time to clean—"

Hayden was striding into the main salon and shaking her head, Cameron followed. He stopped beside the big chair, studied the broken bottle, and then turned to her. His stare was hard and furious. "Explain."

She briefly relayed the argument with Robert.

"You just couldn't wait, could you? And by the way, William can't lie. It's so nice to know you trust me—"

"The timing was right—"

Hayden shook his head as he glared at her. "You little—"

"Don't. Just don't. If you call me an idiot now, I'll hit you." Exhausted, Cameron wasn't ready to take on Hayden's anger. "Jack Morales beat Robert to a pulp, and then William stood up to him. Not a very good day for Robert, and he'll be nursing his bruises with a bottle. He'll be back. He always comes back."

"Do you possibly have any other way to track Robert's car here?" he asked too patiently after a deep breath.

Too volatile now, Cameron tried to control her frayed temper. This one man could really push her to the limits, even when she was exhausted. Somehow, Hayden could find any remaining nerves and scrape them. "No. I understand you're angry—"

"Damn straight. You almost got killed, and you didn't want me around, did you? While you faced down Robert? I don't know who's more the idiot, you or him."

"I said not to call me an idiot." Now, Cameron strained to leash her own anger, returning his patient tone. "No one has the password for my laptop, and I use it for the tracking program . . . I like to know when he's in my area. He isn't here in Somerton House, Hayden, and that's all that matters now. He had to get that check to Jack Morales before midnight, and he's holed up somewhere drinking himself under."

"You know that for a fact, do you?" Hayden demanded.

"Yes. I know every one of his habits. I've studied them for years."

They stared at each other, unmoving, barely breathing, because they were both alive, they'd escaped. . . . Then Hayden tugged her against him, his kiss hard and furious. Cameron understood his need as his hands traveled her body quickly, assuring himself that she was safe, because her own were just as busy. She enveloped herself in Hayden, gave him everything, demanded everything, the heat rising between them—

"We can't," she whispered desperately against his lips.

"We can't?" His hands were unbuttoning her blouse, caressing her breasts; his body thrusting heavily against her thighs.

Trembling, assured that Hayden was safe, Cameron shook her head and tried to smile up at him. "Well—I think it would only be appropriate to invite the firemen in for something to eat and to thank them all properly. They did leave their homes in this storm to help—"

Breathing hard, Hayden still held her tight, his hand cupping her breast. "Don't tell me. You want to clean this up and have me go out there and invite them in for sandwiches and soft drinks."

"That would be so nice of you. Could you, please? Honey? Sweetheart?"

"Dammit."

When the last of the firemen had left Somerton House, Hayden closed the door firmly. He made the rounds of the house, cleaning up a bit, and noted the key ring, which had been returned to Cameron, in the kitchen. On his way to the front door and the house alarms, Hayden dropped the key ring on the foyer table, where it was certain to be found. Then he began setting the alarm carefully, according to the code Cameron had given him.

The honking, banging, and yelling outside the door caused him to inhale slowly and shake his head. He opened the door to find a white pickup parked behind Cameron's, the doors open, the motor running as Evie and Fancy rushed past him. "We heard about the fire. . . . Where is she?" they asked in unison.

Apparently, from the blue face masks they both wore and the partial corn rows in Fancy's hair and the jumbo curlers in Evie's, they'd heard about the fire during a girls' night beauty session. Both wore men's shirts over shortie nightgowns. A cotton ball was stuck between Evie's toes, her flip-flops decorated with rhinestones. Both women's fingers were separated, their hands held up and away from their bodies.

As a man with a sister, mother, and an ex-wife, Hayden understood immediately. "She's just fine. . . . Upstairs. Must be hard to drive that way—just after a fresh polish job."

"You have no idea," Fancy muttered, as the two rushed up the stairs.

The feminine squeals upstairs sounded immediately, and Hayden cautiously went to turn off the pickup's ignition, taking the key and locking it. In the house, he finished tapping in the alarm sequence. Resigned that he was the only male in a house of excited females, Hayden went to the kitchen and scouted for food.

Minutes later, he balanced a tray of sandwich makings, chips, and a six-pack of beer, carrying it into the bedroom. "Food," he said simply as he placed the tray on Cameron's vanity table.

Her eyes locked with his. The slinky black robe had opened partially down her body to reveal curves that set Hayden's senses humming. She was slowly stretching backward over her body ball, easing away the tension of the night. As she rocked slightly, the black robe fell away from her thigh and revealed a smooth butt that Hayden wanted to grip; he could almost feel those slender feminine muscles of her thighs against his—

"Thanks for the food, Hayden. Too bad Phoebe moved away. We could have had a party," Cameron added, clearly to warn Hayden that Phoebe's part wasn't to be shared.

He understood and smiled tightly. "Are the girls staying over?"

"You know, we should," Fancy said as she slathered peanut butter onto bread. "Where is that damn Robert, anyway? Jack Morales was asking about him earlier, where he was."

"That no-good. Robert, I mean. Jack, too," Evie muttered around a mouthful of cheese and crackers as she bent to carefully ease that cotton ball from between her toes.

"Are the girls staying over?" Hayden repeated to Cameron as he stretched out his palm to take the cotton ball. He tossed it into a small expensive tray on the vanity table. He folded his arms and glanced at the two women devouring the food and ignoring everything else. Then he locked on to Cameron, driving his message home. "It might be a good idea."

She frowned slightly, clearly understanding that Robert just might want to take his frustration out on one of her friends and that for tonight, they should be protected. She rolled to her side on the giant ball and faced him; she rocked slightly on the ball, considering him as she did her leg-lift thing, her eyes lowering to the telling bulge in his jeans. The robe slipped again and revealed her breast. Hayden could just see a portion of her nipple, one he wanted to taste badly, as she said, "We don't know yet. They're worried about me. But I'd like them here."

Instantly, Hayden decided three things: One, tracking Robert with Cameron's laptop would have to wait; he wasn't leaving Cameron tonight. Two, Cameron trusted him to keep them all safe. He decided that was an improvement from hours ago, when William had lied for her. Then three, he hated that body ball; if she wanted to roll on something to ease her tense muscles, it should be him.

"What's that licorice smell?" Evie asked.

"Licorice," Cameron said flatly, as Hayden nodded and left the room.

He settled downstairs, waiting for the women's excitement to slow and for Cameron to make them comfortable in the guest rooms. In the muted light of the salon, Hayden sat in Big Buck's chair and ate a thick roast beef sandwich. It was something that Buck would have shared, that sandwich and a beer, with the women settling in upstairs. It was a time for man talk. The portrait of the Somerton family seemed to stare at Hayden as he recalled the long, exhausting night.

Before the firemen came inside Somerton House, Cameron had somehow showered and dressed, and looked fresh as if she hadn't been dragged through a gamut of emotions and locked in a burning building. In a pink blouse and jeans, she had played hostess, thanking the firemen and promising to donate a hefty check to their rural association. Only the brief times that she had come to lean against Hayden said that she needed him with her, and those moments took away some of his unease about their relationship.

She wouldn't like that he had just called the Mais Oui health spa where Madeline was supposed to have been staying. Tight on their security, the spa wasn't giving out details of their clients, but Ms. Fraiser was "unavailable for calls." And that meant that Madeline could be anywhere—relaxing in a mud bath . . . or close enough to lock the stallion in the same barn with Hayden, to use an air rifle on that horse, incensing him.

It wasn't likely that Robert would hurt that horse—and that left Madeline.

The defection of one trusted friend was one thing, but Madeline had been almost like a mother. Cameron would defend her, and Hayden had to move carefully. *Wrongly accusing Madeline could cost him Cameron.*

Big Buck's eyes seemed to lock with Hayden's, and it seemed only right to carry on a conversation with the portrait. "Protect the women, circle the wagons, right, Buck? I'd really like to kill this guy, you know. I tell Cameron what I suspect, and I could lose her. She took the news about Phoebe hard, and Robert probably really enjoyed that part."

Cameron had heard two distinctly different whispers in that cellar: one inside from a dying child and the other unrecognizable outside the door . The man at the doorway had been huge and terrifying. *Who was that man? Robert?*

Buck's stare denied that: *Hell, boy, skunks like him usually pay to get their dirty work done.*

And just where was Madeline? Hayden asked silently.

Better round her up, boy.

"You can come up now, Hayden," Fancy singsonged from upstairs. "We're going to the guest room."

"Finally. Good night, Buck. Thanks for the advice." Hayden made his way slowly up the stairs, uncertain how to face the woman he'd called an idiot, a word that was certain to arise. So which came first, laying down the law to his woman, telling her not to make a move without him nearby? Or the lovemaking he needed to reassure himself that she hadn't been hurt, that she did care for him?

He stopped at her bedroom door and frowned. *Cameron had better be right about Robert—that he would be holed up somewhere, nursing his bruises, and away from her.*

The real question was: Where was Madeline? And how

would Cameron react to what Hayden suspected—that Madeline somehow had played a part in the whole mess?

Taking a deep breath, Hayden prepared himself to be stern with Cameron, and turned the doorknob, pushing open the door.

One look at her, naked and bent over, opening the sheets of her bed, and Hayden knew that sex would have to come first—that first cleansing of the emotions and dangers of hours before, the heated bonding of their bodies washing everything else away, but that Cameron was safe and breathing in his arms.

He could frighten her, taking her with the force of his needs, and Hayden closed the door slowly behind him.

Cameron watched Hayden slowly remove his smoke-scented clothes as those black eyes pinned her, his expression grim. Then he turned, the muscles of his back, butt, and thighs were rigid with tension as he walked into the bathroom.

Hayden was angry, of course. His dark mood was apparent through the hour or so of the firemen's thank-you reception, but he'd never left her side, obviously protective. There was always that big hand on her waist when she came to him for comfort, that strong arm circling her.

But now, Hayden was very delicate, nettled that she wanted to keep Robert safe—long enough to admit his part in Katherine's death and tell where Cammie's body had lain for all those years.

Tears burned Cameron's eyes, the reaction of finally letting her guard down, of keeping the whole truth of the night from her friends—that Robert had closed them in a burning building.

The sound of water, running in the shower, irritated, and Cameron realized her lips were trembling. Hayden should have come to her immediately, held her in his arms and they'd be holding each other safely by now, in the aftermath of lovemaking. Well, what the hell was Hayden doing, taking a long shower when she needed him to hold her? She wrapped her arms around herself, remembering his "idiot" comment. She longed for a "honey" from him; she felt weak and deserted.

Just then Hayden stalked out of the shower, still drying himself. He threw the towel into a delicate chair with enough force to topple it. "Okay, I've had it."

In another minute, she'd be crying uncontrollably in pure reaction to the horrible night. He wasn't noticing that she'd taken off her robe, that she was waiting to be held and cuddled against the strong body she adored, that she needed him, breathing safely against her. Yes, it was true—Cameron Somerton, seasoned fighter, substitute heiress, needed her lover to cuddle her and call her "honey."

Cameron braced herself and swallowed and asked softly, "Had what, dear?"

He blinked at her tone, then said roughly, "It's been a long night, that's all. We'd better get some rest. Tomorrow will be a long day."

Cameron did the only thing she could do—hurried to him and wrapped her arms around him. "I'm so glad you're safe," she whispered unevenly against his throat.

Hayden's arms were instantly around her, his face rough against hers as he bent to kiss her hard, the perfect kind of open-mouth/slanted to fit/devouring kiss that she needed, to know that nothing could stop him from making love to her. Or cuddling her later. Her feet were off the carpeting as he carried her backward, tumbling onto the bed with her.

The moment was savage, perfect, hard and blazing, Hayden pinning her to the bed, his hands trembling as they smoothed the length of her body. When her hand wrapped around him, he tensed and held his breath as she drew him to complete her. Those black eyes closed momentarily as he slid deeply, his hands beneath her bottom, lifting her.

His eyes were open, her reflection in his pupils, as he began to kiss her gently, small little caring kisses that trailed across her damp lashes and across her cheeks. She reveled in the pulsing of that vein in his throat, the fresh smell of him, the thrust of his body against hers. She reveled in his demand that she meet him fully, pit herself against him, and cried out as his lips and mouth found her breasts. Then she was flying into the fire within her. . . .

Hayden's breath seemed to explode everywhere around her, and his muffled shout was guttural, drawn from deep inside him.

When she finally opened her eyes, he was still braced above her, his expression tender. His hands smoothed her damp hair from her face and on to the pillow. "Feel better?"

"Much. I need you, you know."

His smile was knowing, his kiss light and soothing. "More than that body ball?"

"Oh, you're *so* much better. Thank you for standing by me tonight. I know it wasn't what you wanted and that it was very difficult for you."

Hayden rolled to the side, taking her with him, their bodies tangled, and everything settled quietly into place: He was breathing beside her, his chest rising and falling beneath her cheek. He did that little kissing her forehead thing, his hand running up and down her arm, soothing her. On her side, Cameron snuggled close. There was a lot to Hayden, but she did her best to gather him up safety against her. Exhausted, she listened to his heartbeat slow, gave herself to his gentle stroking hands, and tried not to think about what might have happened in the fire. She tried not to think about Phoebe and Robert.

She tried not to wonder what kept Hayden awake. . . . But everything could wait until the morning.

Seventeen

"IT'S GOING TO STORM ALL DAY, RAY. THE CREEKS ARE START-ing to flood, and the weather is expected to get worse in the next few days. That 'low-water' bridge over the creek will be covered soon and dangerous. No sense in your men doing this now. The cleanup can wait," Cameron instructed the chief maintenance man of the Somerton grounds. After a hard morning of fielding concerned calls and visitors, answering insurance questions, Cameron needed silence and a catnap.

"It's a 'gully washer,' okay." Ray hunched beneath his plastic raincoat and peered at her through the raindrops falling from his hood. He glanced up at the lightning bolt fingering into smaller ones across the dark-afternoon clouds, the crack of thunder followed seconds later. "I saw your girlfriends leave earlier, and Hayden made me promise to stay while he went to the barn to collect something for you. . . . Robert isn't here now. I would have thought he'd come back as soon as he heard about the fire. Are you sure you'll be all right?" Ray asked.

Assured that Ray and others would be staying with Cameron, Hayden had gone after her laptop in the barn. The wind plastered her poncho against her, and she held the hood firm. "I'm fine. I think Robert is still out of town, and I just need some peace and quiet for a few hours. It's been quite a day."

Just where was Robert? He had a lot of answering to do.

More than likely, he was holed up somewhere, licking his bruises and drinking. It might be days before he pulled himself together, got his stories straight, and returned to Somerton. However long it took, Cameron was determined to get what she wanted—

She watched Ray's pickup, marked with the big *S* logo, drive into the sheets of gray rain. Madeline had called, the returning lightning storm breaking up the lines, but Cameron had managed to reassure her friend that she was safe and well.

The mausoleum on the hill seemed to beckon to Cameron, her place of retreat and peace that she badly needed. She locked the front door with the key ring she'd taken from Madeline's desk the previous night. Then Cameron set out to visit Katherine and Buck.

Heavy with rain, the roses were nodding, the dark clouds churning overhead as Cameron entered the gate. She sat on the bench, her arms around her body, the rain streaming from her hood. "What you must have suffered, Katherine. I just hope it wasn't that bad for you. But then, you were going to divorce Robert, weren't you? You must have had good reason. He even used one of my best friends against me, and I can only imagine your life with him. No wonder you had to try to find some momentary peace after Cammie was kidnapped."

But Katherine had wanted to stay by the telephones, to be there for any word of her missing daughter; she had only gone up in her balloon after Robert had basically pushed her into it. That big S *logo would have defined the resting place of those propane tanks for a shooter.* Was Hayden's scenario possible? Was that how Katherine had been murdered?

The wind circled Cameron, slipping through the leaves around her, and she could almost hear the eerie whispers again: *Mommy? Mommy?*

Cameron sat for moments, absorbing the quiet sense of peace that Katherine must have given every one around her.

Walking slowly back to Somerton House, Cameron unlocked the door and entered, shaking free of the wet poncho and removing her muddy shoes. With a sigh, she decided to return the key ring to Madeline's desk and turned to walk down the hallway to her assistant's office. The scent of licorice lingered, bringing back to Cameron the ugly scene with Robert, the realization of how Phoebe had betrayed her.

In the shadows of Madeline's office, Cameron slid open the desk drawer, ready to drop the keys—

Dislodged from the rear of the drawer, the edge of papers appeared; Cameron was to have signed them. . . . Madeline had said she'd placed the papers in Cameron's office for signature. Holding her breath, Cameron shook her head, she'd never seen them. The answer was simple: Madeline had been mistaken.

Housekeeping cleaned Madeline's room, but one of her quirks was that she was very territorial about her office. After her "discussion" with Robert, Cameron had only entered the office the night before to get the key ring. She hadn't noticed the papers then.

Cameron signed and dated the papers, her proxy vote for a corporate matter, and pulled them forward to place on the desk. But something at the back of the drawer held them tight. Using a letter opener, Cameron worked to free a small leather case, the familiar one—her PDA that had been missing.

Madeline must have found it and— Cameron decided to write a note to that effect, and pulled open another drawer for a memo pad. And stacked beneath it were invitations to the investors' party, the special ones Madeline had said she'd placed on Cameron's desk, but they had gone missing and had to be replaced. . . .

Cameron rummaged through the files in Madeline's desk drawer—investments, addresses, and then a file folder marked GOAL. Carefully lifting it out, Cameron turned on the desk lamp and opened the file. Clipped articles from psychiatrists and psychologists explained different modes of the unstable mind, the medicines and therapy used to control patients. The brochures for institutions listed costs and conveniences. *It appeared that Madeline's "goal" was a big one—to put the Somerton heiress into an institution and gain control of everything.*

Cameron shook her head and leaned back in the desk chair to collect herself. Were all these things just coincidence?

Have you ever thought that someone might be helping you forget? Hayden had suggested quietly.

There was Phoebe, of course. But Madeline? Was she involved? She'd have access to Cameron's barn, and to every part of her life—Cameron's foot touched something on the floor of the kneehole, and Cameron crouched, reaching to tug from its hiding place the camera she thought she'd misplaced.

Kneeling, she held the camera, remembering how Madeline had said she'd seen it last near Cameron's laptop in the barn. "Oh, Madeline. . . ."

A shadow blocked the light from the hallway, and Cameron looked up at the woman wearing a long raincoat and slacks, and standing with her legs braced apart—a woman holding a gun on her. "Housekeeping isn't supposed to do my office. And I thought you, above all others, respected my privacy," Madeline said very softly.

The dangerous lowered rasping tone chilled Cameron. From her position on the floor, she might have been at a child's level, looking up at a small woman, and thinking her to be a large man—the man with that strange, chilling whisper. "Hello, Madeline."

"Just place the camera on the desk and get up slowly," Madeline ordered, and the gleam of her revolver followed Cameron as she stood. "Let's go upstairs, shall we?"

"Of course, anything you say." *Madeline's rough, low voice was that of the person outside the cellar twenty-eight years ago—it hadn't been a man's voice, but a woman's!* The woman who had befriended the substitute child, who had protected her, was also involved in the kidnapping and probably Cammie's and Katherine's deaths. All the pieces started tumbling into a pattern, fitting neatly.

Battered by memories, hurt by the defection of a woman who had been the closest thing to a mother that Cameron had ever had, she gripped the stairway banister, anchoring herself to the reality and the unforgivable.

At the top of the stairs, Cameron turned slowly to face Madeline and found the hard face of a killer. Madeline's eyes were slitted behind her glasses, her short permed hair frizzy with rain, the lines hard around her tight lips. Her plastic rain boots were caked with mud, and she wore a long black raincoat. The small revolver gleamed in Madeline's hand as she indicated Cameron to move to her bedroom.

But Cameron had to know: "How long were you waiting out there, for everyone to leave?" *Had Madeline helped Robert set that fire?*

"Long enough. I parked in the usual place—out there in the woods, then circled around when everyone left. I never took that plane ride to California because I knew you were up to something. I know how to use this, Cameron. Don't test me. I'm an excellent shot."

Good enough to hit the mark of that balloon's propane tanks with a high-powered rifle? Cameron's stomach was clenching with all the bitterness of betrayal as she remembered all the skeet shoots, the way Madeline had hit her mark with deadly precision. She would handle an air rifle with ease, hitting Robert's stallion and endangering Hayden.

With Cameron's every step, the reality of Madeline's being involved with the kidnapping and death of Cammie seemed more possible.

Why hadn't she seen the greed and the cruelty sooner? Had she been such a fool?

A motion from Madeline's small revolver indicated that Cameron should move down the hallway; instead, she stood very still, facing the other woman. Terrified for Hayden, she asked, "Where is Hayden?"

"You should know. He's collecting your laptop, isn't he? So you can track Robert's car? That was really very funny—that you would use 'Cammie' as a password—how stupid of you. I enjoyed playing with that program, keeping track of him, too. But Robert was furious when I told him just lately, Cameron—or should I say *Pilar*?"

Click. That rough low voice had called the child to the car, luring her into eating the food—*Your name is Pilar? Come here. Come get into the car and you can have all this to eat. There's a brand-new doll for you, too. . . .*

Cameron's body went cold, because she knew that it had been Madeline who had drugged her, who had brought her to the cellar. "I'm stronger than I look. I lift weights and work out," Madeline had said once, when they were moving furniture.

Now Cameron feared for Hayden. *Was he alive?* "Where is Hayden? And where . . . is . . . Cammie?"

"Don't worry, your lover will be along. Boy, you can pick 'em, can't you? If there was anyone you should have stayed away from, it was that gardener's son. Paul Olson deserved what he got, for interfering in— Get into your bedroom, and then we'll chat."

"The gardener found you that morning, didn't he? He told his wife he was checking on a hose, but he found you in that guesthouse with Robert, didn't he? And that was why he had to die?"

"Couldn't have timed it better. That gardener already suspected Robert of being involved in the kidnapping, and he was trying to get proof. You see, he was worried about Katherine, that she might be in danger. He was right. We needed a patsy, and there Olson was. Bang." Madeline smiled tightly, coldly. "Get into your bedroom."

Cameron moved slowly, her blood chilled by Madeline's cold admission. *The gardener had been murdered—a* "*patsy.*" In the bedroom, Madeline motioned her into a chair. "Sit. We're going to have to wait a little while."

While Cameron sat, overwhelmed by the reality of her living nightmare, the past and the danger to Hayden now, Madeline shrugged off the raincoat. The strap crossing her stout body held a bag, which she removed carefully and tossed to a table.

She glanced around the room, taking in the unmade bed, the tray Hayden had prepared, the empty chips bags and cans of beer. "I know about Robert's precious little bottle of absinthe. He was very angry about that, but the place still reeks of it—which is just perfect for what is going to happen. There will be witnesses who will testify that this house smelled of it last night—it will be easy to convince them that you secretly drank it."

Cameron's fingers tightened on the arm of the chair. "Where is Robert?"

Madeline shoved several of the crystal perfume decanters from the vanity table and reached to pull on the drapery of the four-poster's canopy until it sagged. Keeping the gun on Cameron, she knocked over a chair, then poured stale beer onto a brocade pillow on the chaise lounge. "What a fight you must have had, before you killed Hayden," Madeline said cheerfully as she walked back to her bag and flipped it open.

She carefully placed a small bottle and a hypodermic on the table, then a bottle of greenish liqueur. "Not as easy as stuffing drugs into food for a hungry six-year-old, but effective. Especially combined with an absinthe binge after killing your lover. You have no idea how much Robert is going to rave over wasting his beverage of choice."

"I smelled it often enough as a child and later."

Madeline's plans didn't matter now, only the answers that Cameron had sought for years. "You let Cammie die, didn't you? You could have saved her, and you didn't. What does it feel like to let a child die, Madeline? To have her beg for her mother and deny her that?" she demanded.

"I know how she begged and sniveled. That had to be monitored somehow, and I was paying very close attention to my investment by listening—the same way that Robert listened to you in the cellar. Technology is wonderful, recorders, mikes, all that so helpful. When the search began for Cammie, I just volunteered. I pretended to hunt for her on that old deserted farmland myself, clearing it with the authorities, and that kept the dogs away." Madeline swallowed and momentarily turned pale, as if she, too, had been deeply affected by Cammie's pleading.

Cameron inhaled, storing away that brief insight into Madeline's negligible humanity. Madeline had never liked to hear about Cameron's nightmares, about the whispers. . . . "Why did you try to kill me last night? You know if I died, the estate—"

Madeline slashed her hand aside, cutting Cameron short. "I only saw Hayden going into that house, not you. You were coming along so nicely, until he turned up. You were getting frazzled, thinking you'd misplaced everything, that you'd forgotten appointments—"

Cameron had to hear the words: "*You* killed Hayden's father, didn't you? Not Robert?"

"Well, he had to die, and Robert certainly didn't have the guts to do it. There we were with Cammie's body and something had to be done, and fast. He didn't want to touch Cammie—she was dead then, all neat and wrapped in a plastic sack, ready for disposal. After I shot Olson, Robert almost vomited—he was terrified of the blood. Some big strong man he is."

Cameron had to know which had actually caused Katherine's death. "And it was you who shot the balloon's propane tanks, right?"

"It was a clean shot. After the explosion, that gas must have gone everywhere, because there were flames all over, dripping onto the ground. A high-powered rifle with a scope is a marvelous thing. Hitting Katherine would have caused problems. I had to wait until she was in just the right position in the basket—this after taking care of Cammie. I had to move quick, I tell you. And so did Robert—a coordinated effort for success."

Lights flashed twice on the window's glass, and Madeline smiled tightly. She moved to the window, drawing the drapes aside to stare out into the storm. "Good. Here come Hayden and Robert, of course. Oh, did I tell you that the house phones are out? We don't want anyone to interrupt our little get-together."

Hayden was alive! Cameron forced herself to breathe quietly, because if she could, she would jump Madeline, and just maybe Hayden could escape—

Madeline stared at the vase of pink roses, then knocked them to the floor. "I hate these things. Everlastingly hate them . . . in every room, ordering them, paying the florist's monthly bill. I suppose after you're locked up, I'll have to pay someone to take care of those at the mausoleum, too. Absolutely a waste of money. After a while, no one will notice that it's nothing but weeds out there, and that this place isn't cluttered with them. Oh, you have no idea how slowly the years have passed, how much time I've put into this whole plan, how much I'm going to enjoy Somerton money."

"You probably have enough of it stashed away now, don't you?"

Madeline smirked briefly. "Of course."

"*You're* the reason I couldn't get rid of Robert. He's afraid of you."

"To say the least. He knows what I'm capable of. Do you really think he could put all this together, the timing, the kidnapping? He's no mastermind, Cameron. I called the whole thing, 'Operation Clean Sweep.' Cammie wouldn't have lived long without her mother's care and devotion, and the girl was too fragile to put away like you're going to be. So Katherine had to die—because she was getting rid of Robert. That was when *I* knew we had to act, to keep our investment."

Furious now and forgetting her previous caution, Cameron started to rise, to jump Madeline, but that dangerous revolver pointed toward her. "Back off."

"Didn't you feel anything when Cammie died, Madeline? A child dying isn't a pleasant sight. Do you remember how she whispered at the end, just those little gasps of breath? Let's see . . . it sounded something like this: *Mommy?*"

Behind her glasses, Madeline's eyes widened; she trembled, her face paling. "Shut up."

The echo of those words swirled around Cameron. *Shut up, you brats!*

Cameron sat back in the chair, seeing everything clearly now, just as clearly as she heard the sound of the front door slam shut. "You were Robert's mistress, weren't you? The woman that Katherine discovered he'd had before they were married—and after? And just a year after she died, he brought you into Somerton House for good, as a bookkeeper and then as a manager and someone to pacify your little investment—me. And that's why he hates you so much, isn't it? Because you—"

"Because I had the brains, and he didn't. Because I had the *guts* he didn't."

Cameron could hear her heart beat, but everything within her had gone cold and still at the enormity of what had happened twenty-eight years ago.

At the death planned for Hayden and her.

Then she realized that the racing beat of her heart was actually the approaching footsteps of the two men.

With Robert's handgun pressed into his back, Hayden entered Cameron's bedroom.

"Hello, babe," he forced himself to say calmly when his heart had stopped racing with the fear that she might already be dead. She was pale and evidently shaken, clearly terrified for him as she noted the bleeding cut on his forehead, the duct tape Robert had used on his wrists while

Hayden was momentarily unconscious. With his hands taped behind his back, there was no way he could hold Cameron. But he noted with satisfaction that Cameron had gripped the gargoyle bracelet with one hand, and that meant she was holding on. . . . "I'm fine, honey," Hayden said quietly.

Hayden had been hurrying, anxious to return and protect Cameron, secure that she was in the company of her girlfriends and Ray. Now Hayden damned himself for being careless. "Robert had a little reception party for me at your place. By the way, I thought your girlfriends and Ray would still be here."

He knew then that Cameron had sent them away—because she'd known that Robert would come back to her. Her former guardian and Cameron were locked in a duel that would only end when one gained full control, and she was determined to push him for answers.

"Here's your little toy. I wondered how you could know when I was here and when I wasn't." Robert threw the tracking device that had been installed into his car at Cameron; she deflected it easily.

Madeline's order was sharp: "I don't want any bruises on her, Robert."

"You old witch. You really should have gone to that spa—you need everything in it and the entire list of what a plastic surgeon can offer. But that isn't enough to make me want to touch you again. I want Cameron. I promised myself I'd have her first, before she goes to La-La Land. I want her to know what's happening, that she—"

"Bastard. I've put up with your whining for years. Get in here and close the door." When the men moved into the room, she said, "Good. Hayden, you really shouldn't have come back. That was a fatal mistake. You see, in her 'self-medicated' state, after drinking absinthe, Miss Cameron Somerton is going to blow a hole straight through your head. She has a motive, after all. You are the gardner's son."

Madeline looked out at the storm raging beyond the windows, the crash of thunder rattling them. "Your clothes are wet, Hayden. Yes, I suppose your clothes would be damp from the rain," she said as if weighing the pieces that would suit his murder. "You ran an errand for her and when you came back . . ."

She continued in the same crisp, businesslike manner she'd used to describe Somerton business affairs to Cameron: "That would fit . . . you just went outside for a breath of fresh air, and when you came back in, Cameron was waiting for you—with this revolver. Oh, yes, it's Katherine's little pride and joy—she used to clean it herself. It was one of the things that Robert gave me, when we were—courting. Katherine's jewels were beautiful, too, but of course, I had to 'market' them. The diamonds were old and untraceable, quite nice."

Then Madeline seemed impatient to get started with her plan. "Move back, Hayden . . . there, against the wall. It'll take a moment before Cameron's shot takes effect. She used to like drugs as a child, in those months and years after the kidnapping. She'll be just as easy to control now. Robert, get that bottle of absinthe."

Hayden met Cameron's terrified stare, and tried to reassure her with a slight nod. With a shift of his eyes, he drew hers to the body ball at her feet. If she could use that, distract Madeline for a heartbeat, he'd rush her and Cameron might have a chance— He had to keep Madeline talking, because she clearly liked to demonstrate her intelligence.

"Hayden, sit down. Over there, on the bed. Replacing the mattress set will be a lot cheaper than refinishing the floor and carpeting to remove bloodstains. We had to have the floor in the guesthouse completely refinished when your father was so messy."

Hayden tensed at the image, but he moved slowly, watching for any chance to rush Madeline. He ached for Cameron, whose brief shattered expression told him everything—how devastated she was by Madeline's betrayal. "Robert filled me in. I know Dad was murdered, and so was Katherine—and how."

Her expression changed to grim determination, and that terrified him—Cameron was set to make Madeline and Robert pay, and she wasn't stopping because of a gun. All those finely tuned muscles, that lean body were primed to strike. "Watch it, honey," he advised softly.

But she was focused on Madeline; Cameron was clearly building for a moment that could shatter any hope of escaping death. Or insanity.

"He had everything put together, the questions, not the answers," Robert was saying, apparently to compete with Madeline's superior intelligence. "I found a file in his briefcase . . . clippings, notes. We'll have to take care of Cameron's laptop and that briefcase right away—probably his laptop, too. He wanted to follow the kidnapping money trail, what happened to the rest of that two million, Maddie—"

Enraged, Madeline's revolver turned to him. "I told you: Don't ever call me that again."

Obviously aware that she would shoot, Robert cowered momentarily. After all, he'd seen Madeline kill, hadn't he? Cameron's foot was slowly nudging the body ball closer to her. If she could distract them for one moment—

But Cameron didn't look like she'd run. She looked like she'd fight to get what she wanted—revenge for Cammie and Katherine. Her hand wrapped tightly to that gargoyle bracelet, as she asked, "You took the rest of the money, didn't you, Madeline? After killing the gardener?"

"Of course. I had to have money to live on until the flurry died down, until Robert could openly bring me into Somerton affairs. What was I supposed to do? Live in that backwoods trailer forever? Keep meeting him in the woods? He thought he'd hit it big with Virginia Ulbrecht, too, but she saw right through him. So sorry, Robert." Madeline's cheerful tone mocked her former lover.

There might never be another chance to get the answers that Cameron had to have—because if Hayden could, he was killing them both. "Who is Cameron? I mean, who is Pilar? Where did you get her?"

Madeline and Robert both laughed. Then Madeline said, "Funny. That's what she always wanted to know, too, didn't she, Robert? Sweet little Pilar really was hungry that day. Amazing how fast she went to sleep after eating. She's from the Irish part of town—had to be from the same-looking stock as Katherine. I'll tell Cameron everything just as she's going under. I heard somewhere that they remember their last major traumas with astounding clarity. It'll make the doctors even more certain that she's off her rocker."

"Where is Cammie's body, Madeline?" Hayden pushed.

Madeline smiled coldly, as if enjoying a successful coup. "They'll laugh at that one, too. She's with her mother, of course. I put her there after her mother's funeral, but she spent time right in the Somerton basement."

"I see . . . the day that I was found, everyone's attention was turned to me, right? And no one was watching the mausoleum?"

"It was perfect. Couldn't have timed it better. 'Cammie' emerged at sunset, still a little dazed by the drugs, but okay." Madeline's laughter cracked across the room. "The kid thought she was really the heiress—for years."

Cameron's eyes closed as if she were finally complete, as if her lifelong quest had ended. Maybe, through the years, Cammie had been calling her to that peaceful retreat, just waiting for her. . . . Then she said politely, "Thank you, Madeline. That was thoughtful of you to put Cammie with her mother and father."

"I thought so. She was going to end up in there anyway, the way her health was going. We just helped it along. We've wasted enough time—"

"Mommy? Mommy?" Cameron whispered softly in a

childlike voice that she'd heard in her nightmares for years.

Hayden tensed, because he'd heard her whisper the same words while tossing and fighting her nightmares. Playing illogical games with Madeline now was too dangerous. He tried to distract Madeline, to get Robert to turn on her: "Robert, do you actually think Madeline is going to let you live? You know too much. With you out of the way, she'd have complete control of Somerton."

"Don't listen to him, Robert," Madeline ordered quietly, but Robert's expression was easily readable—the possibility that she might kill him had already occurred. Robert's gun swung to Madeline. "Don't be an idiot, Robert. We'll both be sitting pretty after this. You can play the grand host, without interference. I've never liked that role."

"Mommy?" Cameron whispered eerily. Obviously startled, Madeline tensed, her free hand shaking as it rose to her throat, her face pale.

Her reaction seemed to be what Cameron had wanted, because she rose slowly and moved in front of Hayden. He was instantly on his feet, trying to nudge her out of the way. "Don't do this, Cameron."

"She won't shoot me, Hayden. I'm their meal ticket. Bullet holes won't do, just like they wouldn't do for Katherine," she answered, before focusing back on Madeline, "You never liked to hear about my nightmares—the little girl whispering, did you, Madeline?" Cameron asked softly. "For years, I thought that was my voice, and then I knew it hadn't been. *Mommy?*"

"What's happening, Madeline?" Robert asked desperately. "What do I do? You can't shoot her—"

"Mommy?" Cameron's childish voice slid into her adult tones. "How did it feel when you listened to her struggle for air? It's not long-distance, like shooting a high-powered rifle to murder someone, is it? But then, you needed her to tell me the little-girl things, didn't you? Those special little things about her life. Did you like to listen to those?"

"Cameron—" Hayden warned softly. But then Madeline seemed to cower; her hand shook as the revolver lowered. . . .

"Mommy? Mommy? Help me. I'm afraid. I'm cold, Mommy, and it's dark here. Why, Mommy? Why did they put me here? Mommy?" Cameron continued softly.

"*Shut up!*" Robert yelled. "Madeline! Get on with it!"

"Mommy?"

Madeline visibly shuddered, and Cameron started moving toward her, the woman who had been her most trusted friend. "You're not getting away with this, Madeline. You're going to pay for killing Cammie and her mother."

"Get back, Cameron," Robert ordered fiercely.

Fearing for Cameron, Hayden tried to push past her, to slam into Madeline.

Instead, Cameron turned to him suddenly, "Hayden, I—"

Then, already in motion and unable to stop, he collided with her, sending them both to the floor. Scrambling to his feet, he saw Madeline run out of the door.

But Robert's handgun was still aimed at them. He looked confused and uncertain as he moved toward the door. "Madeline? Come back here. What do I do?"

At Hayden's feet, Cameron was crawling toward Robert, and his gun wavered, aiming at her. "You shoot her, and you've lost everything, Robert," Hayden stated carefully in a bid to save Cameron's life. "She can't testify against you, or she'll be sending herself to jail. You're better off taking your chances away from here."

Cameron was crouched now, coiled and ready to spring as Robert's gun pointed to her, then to Hayden, then back again. Fierce with anger, her low tone ricocheted around the room. "Don't interfere in this, Hayden. He's not going anywhere. I don't care what happens to me. He's going to pay—"

In that instant, Robert's fear of the woman he had mistreated for so many years flared. He stepped outside the door, closing it behind him.

Hayden knew exactly what Cameron would do—run after

Robert—and he stood in front of the door, blocking it. "Cut this tape, Cameron. Then we'll get them together."

She furiously tried to shove him aside. "They're getting away!"

"I'm not letting you kill yourself. They've got guns, Cameron. Madeline is an expert shot. Use your head. If we're killed, Madeline and Robert may not have all of Somerton, but for a while they will have the means to empty your accounts and take everything."

With a defeated groan of frustration, Cameron turned to hunt for a scissors. "We're losing time," she muttered as she began cutting through the layers of duct tape. "I hope you're happy."

"No, but you're alive. Don't complain."

"You're so frustrating."

"But you love me," Hayden pushed, because in a few short hours they'd escaped death twice. That caused a man to see things in a different light—like living with Cameron was something he wanted to do every day.

"Maybe. But I see why your ex-wife divorced you."

"We weren't ever in a situation like this. And there's nothing wrong with me," he stated logically.

"Try again," Cameron said, as they hurried down the stairs.

"I told you to use the body ball as a distraction—if you had to do anything at all. Or we could have turned them against each other—but oh, no. You *just* had to do things your way. My pickup is outside—we'll take that."

They hurried through the rain, and Cameron leaped into the pickup. She scooted across the bench seat to the passenger side and fastened her seat belt. "You didn't *tell* me anything. And if you did, I don't like taking orders—"

"We need to change our mode of foreplay as I age, dear."

"Is that what you think, you—?"

Hayden was busy with his seat belt and starting the pickup. "Uh-huh. It's all foreplay. By the way, the next time you decide to get yourself killed, I'd rather it wasn't because of me. But now I know you love me, so there's no going back."

She stared blankly at him for a minute. "Dammit."

"How very unladylike of you, dear." Hayden revved the engine, the headlights lasering into the slashing rain as they raced down the estate's curving driveway. "They're driving Madeline's red Porsche. We won't be able to catch that thing, once it hits the highway. That low-water bridge was covered when we came in—getting across that may slow them down."

Beside him, Cameron held on to the seat, her face pale in the light of the dashboard. "They just can't get away."

"They won't, honey." Through the torrents of rain, the windshield wipers clacking rapidly, Hayden spotted the taillights of the Porsche—and pulled quickly to a stop. He grabbed the battery lantern from the pickup bed and shot the beam down into the rushing water before them.

The creek previously beneath the low-water bridge had become a roaring, tumbling river, covering it.

In slow motion, the dangerous water caught the red sports car, slowly tumbling it into the main depths and rolling it. Eerily, the front and rear lights continued shining momentarily beneath the frothing dark water. Snagged briefly by an uprooted tree that had fallen into the water, the vehicle seemed to pause in its journey.

Then, too pale to be tree limbs, two bodies bobbed up beside the car, soon to be carried away by the rushing water.

Holding Cameron's hand, Hayden followed the creek bed, taking care to stay away from the muddy edge as it seemed to fold into the rising water. They moved through trees, brush, and mud, and the steady, pouring rain. Periodically, the lantern's beam caught those strange pale limbs—human limbs, catching a bit now and then and tumbling through the water.

"They're dead," Cameron stated hollowly, as Hayden's light caught the upturned sightless faces of Madeline and

Robert, their bodies tangled eerily in a tree's roots, just as their lives had been. "We should—"

"They'll wait. It's too dangerous now." Hayden gathered Cameron's shaking body against his, grimly sheltering her as best he could while she cried.

He'd been right: Madeline and Robert hadn't gotten away.

But now, he had to protect Cameron from herself, from the guilt of the innocent child-substitute, the survivor. . . .

Eighteen

"I CAN'T LEAVE THEM THERE."

Cameron drew back from Hayden. "Whatever they've done, I just *can't* leave them out there like that."

Hayden stared at her as rain slashed down between them. Cameron was soaked and chilled, her hair plastered to her face. He tried for logic. "Now, honey. Be reasonable. These creek banks can cave in at any time—and lightning could hit. You need to get inside. . . ."

Cameron was staring at the bodies, the water frothing around them. "They could wash away and get tangled up somewhere. It could be days before they're found. We've got to do something. Whatever she was, Madeline was the only one to show me kindness when I was growing up. The *only* one, for whatever reason, Hayden. I'm not leaving her—or Robert. We've got to get them out."

He took her arms and shook her gently. "Honey, after what they did to you—were planning to do—they don't deserve anything."

Her eyes had locked on the bodies. "How can we get to them?"

Hayden quickly scanned the rushing water, the Porsche that could roll downstream toward the bodies at any time, the creek banks crumbling into the stream. "Not from this side—"

"The other side, then? Your truck could make it across the bridge, couldn't it? And maybe down that dirt road on the other side?"

Hayden took a deep breath. "Maybe. But—"

Her eyes begged him, her fists gripping his shirt. "Please, Hayden. I just can't leave them—"

"Dammit." *Cameron wasn't budging. . . .* He took a careful look at the tumbling water, gauging the bridge beneath it. Then he took Cameron's hand and started running toward his truck.

Inside, he put it into reverse and started backing up to the mansion. Cameron gripped his arm and asked, "You need things, right? To help them?"

Hayden stopped in front of the mansion. "You get Robert's extra car keys. I'll get some rope from the service building."

"Keys?"

"Just get them—and a bottle of bourbon."

Cameron stopped on her way out of the pickup door and shook her head. "Now is no time to—"

"I'm having a bad day, okay?"

Moments later as his truck started cautiously over the bridge, Hayden tried to concentrate on driving, but that was difficult with Cameron crying softly beside him; she was still absorbing the harsh reality of those deceitful years, of Madeline's deadly treachery.

"We're not turning down the service road that runs along the creek," she stated unevenly as they drove through the heavy rain and storm. She gripped his arm and turned to him. "Hayden, *where are we going*?"

"We'll come back for them, don't worry."

"But they could be—" Cameron stared at the deserted highway in the sheets of rain and at Hayden's face. "We're going to my place, aren't we?"

"Would you just let me handle this, dear?" he asked tightly. *They only had so much time, and if his idea worked, Cameron would be safe. . . .*

"But—" She leaned forward, peering into the rainy night as Hayden pulled off the highway and onto the road leading to her house. He drove to her place, turned around, and came back to park near the stand of mimosa trees. "Why are we pulling in here?" she asked.

He nodded to the black Lincoln parked just inside the grove and took the keys from her. "That's why. That's where Robert parked when he walked up to your house and waited for me. I was in too much of a hurry and didn't see his car until we came out in my truck. Just back this thing up and follow me— You can drive a stick shift, right?" he asked.

"I drive mine, don't I?" Cameron's indignant tone said she'd taken that comment as an insult, and that meant she was picking up the challenge, which was Hayden's intention.

"This truck has a whole lot more power—maybe you'd better drive the Lincoln, and I'll—"

For an answer, Cameron's elbow nudged his ribs. When he got out, she settled into the driver's seat and put an expert hand on the gearshift. "Give me a break. I just want to know what you're doing."

Hayden reached across her to grab the bourbon bottle, and Cameron scowled at him. "*Now* is no time to—"

He slammed the truck door; he missed the rest of whatever Cameron was going to say, and he was certain it was an argument. But the headlights traced his path to the Lincoln, and when he started it and started reversing, his pickup backed up, too. She reversed slowly, swinging into position to let him out. "Good girl."

The big Dodge's headlights followed the Lincoln down to the end of the road, where it met the highway. Hayden pulled over to the side, stopped the car, and ran back to his truck. "Keep the motor running, Cameron," he ordered.

"What the hell are you doing, Hayden Olson?"

For just that heartbeat when his hair lifted at the back of his neck and fear ran through him, Hayden was certain his mother had caught him—although she'd never used "hell," the tone was the same. He was certain that there was a course for women somewhere, some nefarious school, that taught them to use that exact, hair-raising tone—to remind men of their mothers. Then he hurried to complete the task, opening the liquor bottle and splashing some onto the Lincoln's upholstery.

When he returned to Cameron, nudging her over so that he could drive, she just stared at him. "I don't know you at all, do I?"

He set the truck in gear and headed onto the highway. "I have to have some mystique, don't I?"

Cameron was still staring at him. "I do not believe what you just did."

Hayden pressed her hand on his thigh, then concentrated on driving through the rain, the water filling the highway. "Robert was a known drinker. He'd been drinking tonight when he collected me. . . . He was just too drunk to drive through this storm, and Madeline—on her way home—gave him a ride. They just didn't make it."

"Do you realize that you could be put in jail for tampering or obstructing or something?"

"Uh-huh." Hayden took a cell phone from his pocket and tossed it into her lap. "*Now,* you can call for help. We're going to need it."

But Cameron had scooted close to him, in the light of the dashboard, her expression was softly concerned as she touched his forehead. "You're bleeding."

"Oh, well, hell yes."

She gently smoothed back his hair. "Does it hurt?"

Hayden stared at her, trying to dissect that tender look. "You're quite a guy, Hayden. But it won't work. I'm still a fake," she murmured. "I don't want you involved in this."

"Do we have to go through this right now? Make that call, Cameron."

"You're very bossy, you know. And I am *not* your employee. I really would prefer that you didn't use that tone."

Cameron punched in some buttons and her voice trembled. "Ray? There's been an accident. We need help."

She looked at Hayden as she spoke to Ray, "It looks like Madeline tried to cross the bridge in her Porsche, and Robert was with her."

They had just driven down the muddy service road to the location of the bodies, when a big farm pickup pulled in behind them, then another and more. With headlights cutting into the slashing rain, men came running toward them. Ray pulled a rain poncho over Cameron, but she barely noticed as she watched Hayden wrap the rope around his waist and toss the other end to Ray.

"They could wait. They're not going anywhere," Ray called after peering down at Robert and Madeline.

With her fingers pressed to her lips, fear for Hayden almost stopping her heart, Cameron huddled in the chilling rain. She watched the rescue of the bodies, the two main people in her life until Hayden. "Hayden, if you get hurt, I'm never going to forgive you," she called into the night as she held a flashlight beam on him.

His face lifted and stared into the beam, his expression blank. For the second time that night, he had that expression as though he'd been caught in some misdeed. Then he shook his head and continued down the muddy bank and waded into the water. Fighting the current and working furiously, he managed to tie ropes around Madeline, then Robert.

When he finally stood, muddy and wet on the bank, Cameron ran to him, holding him tightly. "You're everything to me," she whispered desperately, kissing and running her trembling hands over his face. "I'm so glad you're safe. I didn't know it would be so— I put you in danger. . . . I—"

"Hush, honey. Not now." Exhausted, Hayden stood and held her as she watched the bodies loaded into the back of Ray's pickup.

"Is she all right?" Ray called, as the men prepared to drive away.

"She's okay," Hayden returned.

But he wondered; Cameron seemed so empty, so lifeless. "My head does hurt," he said quietly.

Instantly she turned to him, concerned and back in the ball game. "Does it? You should see a doctor—"

He made a mental note that male fragility sometimes worked on the female psyche. Sometimes it was okay to be delicate. "All I need tonight is you. But we've got to clean up the mess at Somerton House before someone finds it."

In her bedroom, Cameron methodically replaced the perfume bottles and straightened her vanity, while Hayden did what he could with the canopy and drapes. Carefully replacing the hypodermic and drug back into Madeline's bag, Hayden met Cameron's disbelieving look. "She would have done it, you know."

"I still can't believe it."

Cameron collapsed onto the bed as if all the breath had gone out of her. She looked as if she couldn't take another step, as if she was still trapped back in the moment that Madeline had turned on her. Hayden took the bottle of absinthe to the bathroom sink, pouring it and liquid soap down the drain. When he returned, Cameron was sitting staring at the doorway and he feared her going into shock— "Cameron . . . honey?"

"Now we know where Cammie is," she whispered finally. "She was there all the time. That's why I felt so peaceful when I visited. She was trying to tell me that all along. That she was with her mother and father."

Cameron badly needed rest before tomorrow—to be up to answering questions and playing her role as grieving heiress. She was soaked, muddy, shivering, and so pale, still trapped in the darkness that Madeline and Robert had created, trying to make sense of it all—

Hayden looked out at the dying storm, the lightning moving away. As fast as that creek had risen, it would subside quickly, too. He had to get her out of the house . . . and it was definitely time for a little more play on his new male fragility. "Do you have some aspirin at your place? Maybe something to clean my cut? Cameron, honey, I'd really like to go to your place if I'm going to get any sleep tonight. I don't think I can do that here."

Her eyes swung to him—they were blank at first as though dragging herself back from another world, then she shook her head. In that heartbeat, she was on her feet and hurrying to him. Tucked tight against him, her body trembling, Cameron whispered, "I'm so glad you're not hurt, dear."

He smiled because the lady was still a lady, no matter how muddy, how tired, how brave, and Cameron was definitely never boring. But Hayden needed time to convince her that he needed her, that she had a life waiting ahead of her— They just needed to be careful—if he could convince her to see things his way. And for that, he needed her out of Somerton House. "Let's go home and take care of me, shall we?"

On the way to her home, Cameron stared at Robert's car. "I'll call the accident details in, as soon as we're inside," Hayden stated quietly.

In her barn, Hayden placed that very careful call—that they'd seen Robert's car parked near the highway. Hayden "supposed" that Robert must have stopped by Cameron's and had some kind of car problem, and he must have been collected by Madeline on her way home.

Meanwhile, while he was speaking, Cameron's hands shook as she worked to remove Hayden's wet, muddy clothing. When he finished the call, she urged him into the shower—in seconds she stood, wrapped in his arms, the water streaming over them. Her body felt as if it would never warm.

"You're shaking, honey. It's all over."

"I keep seeing them—" She eased back to check his cut, exploring it gently. "It's not deep. I think it just needs a bandage." Cameron took one quick look down his body, and then she turned him. She smoothed his back as if she had to touch every inch of him to see that he was alive and uninjured.

Cameron urged him around again, and Hayden understood, returning the favor and inspecting her.

He poured shampoo into his hand and began massaging her scalp gently. "Everything is going to work out, honey. We're safe."

If we can just get through the next few days. . . . She was so pale and shaking, her eyes haunted. Usually so self-sufficient, Cameron now seemed helpless, her eyes brimming with tears. Fearing for her, Hayden began soaping her body, using his hands as if she were that child long ago, who had badly needed attention.

Then he concentrated on getting her away from the last awful hours and protecting her. "We're going to have to be very careful now, Cameron."

"Yes," she answered hollowly. "They should have a proper funeral. I'll see to that."

He gently washed her face, using his hands to turn it up to him. "I'll help you make arrangements. I'll be right with you every minute. We have to be careful with what we say. I don't think we should answer any phone calls tonight, so I'm going to turn off the message machine, okay?" *Come on, Cameron, stay with me. We can do this together.*

"I know . . . we need the rest. Tomorrow will be a hard day."

In that warm water, the shower tingling a bit, Cameron held his wrists as if anchoring herself to him; the gesture reminded Hayden how she'd fought for so long—alone. She'd learned to distrust early, but now he was asking for her complete trust. Hayden kissed her lightly, nuzzling her face. *He had to keep her mind off those bodies and focused on moving through tonight, minute by minute. . . .* "You know what I'd really like?"

"I'll take care of that cut."

"I'd like that. And I'd like a long soak in this tub and a beer, just to come down a little. Maybe a little to eat, too. How about you?"

"I'm not hungry," Cameron said, as he gently eased her

out of the tub. "I was so terrified for you when you went down that bank and into the water. What if I'd lost you?"

"That's not going to happen. Fix me something to eat, okay?"

Cameron dried quickly and left the bathroom area. Hayden watched her pull on a T-shirt and move into the kitchen area; she seemed to be moving automatically, her mind locked on the night. But Hayden's thoughts were running quickly: *He had to keep her safe . . . but Cameron was a long way from agreeing to what he wanted.*

He ran water into the tub and settled down to collect his thoughts—and his plan for keeping the woman he wanted safe. Cameron returned with a sandwich and a beer—now, if he could just get her to eat something. . . . Hayden leaned his head back on the tub, closed his eyes, and murmured, "Eat that for me, will you?"

"But I'm not—"

"Halfsies?" Hayden reached over to take his half of the peanut butter sandwich. He ate it with his eyes closed, following it with a beer, which he shared with her.

"I don't know how you can just sit there and relax like that," Cameron said as she sat on the edge of the tub and placed her hand on his chest. The last dangerous hours swirled between them again. "It's good to feel your heartbeat—solid, steady, like it won't ever stop."

"It's not going to. I'm here for the long haul, honey, right by your side." Hayden drew her hand to his lips, kissed her palm, and closed his eyes. As she carefully treated the cut, he planned how to keep Cameron safe in the next few days.

"Bastard," she said fiercely, dabbing a little bit too hard. "Robert was a bastard. He hit you."

Hayden decided to take advantage of her anger. He took her wrist, staying her momentarily. "Don't let him ruin the rest of your life, Cameron. Think about making your own life, away from this. . . . With me. Or without," he added, because she'd been forced into a life slot that had taken its toll; after keeping her safe, all choices were hers—but Hayden hoped she'd choose him. "Live for yourself, now Cameron. This is your chance. Take it. Be free."

"It's wrong. It's not how it should be. I've waited a long time to be able to clean up everything—to tell what really happened—and now is the time."

"It's right—for you. Give yourself a chance, honey. Make your own life. Your own choices."

"Hayden, I can't just dismiss what I've done for all these years—taking Cammie's place."

"But think of all the good that you did, continuing Katherine's work, keeping Big Buck's business ties—they both would have been proud of you."

"It's wrong."

"Don't you think the Somerton name and honor has had enough problems surviving? You did that, Cameron, you kept Katherine's and Big Buck's honor. You come out now, start a ruckus by admitting that you're not Cammie, and the news explosion will wipe away everything. By admitting you're not Cammie, think of the people you'd hurt."

Cameron frowned. "What do you mean?"

"Think back to how many donations you've made in Katherine's name . . . how much business you've conducted in Buck's. All that will be scrutinized, and a mass of lawyers will pick at the bones of everything they loved and built. Don't do that, Cameron. Don't destroy what they built—what you've continued and enriched. Katherine wanted everything to go to her charities, make that happen—the right way before the vultures move in. You're the only person who can do that. Keep the estate the way they built it—put clauses into the contracts to keep it safe, keep the scholarships safe and monitored. Then excuse yourself slowly, methodically, turning everything over the right way. See that Big Buck's business interests are turned over to the best people. You can do it."

"But—"

"But if you turn yourself in—everything they built is going to be torn apart until it's nothing."

"You actually think the news media won't be nosing in every corner of my life? This is too big, Hayden."

"Do it slowly. The right way. It's the perfect time—with the death of . . . your best friend and your stepfather, you can say that you've been deeply affected and wish to leave public life."

Cameron shook her head. She finished slowly, thoughtfully, moving away carefully to stare at herself in the mirror. Hayden knew she was weighing truth and honor—against a potential new life away from her role as heiress.

In bed later, he lay holding her, the dream catchers slowly turning above them.

It was a long time before either slept.

In the morning, Hayden was up early, fielding calls to reporters and smiling briefly at one's surly reference to "the heiress's guard dog." Hayden studied Cameron as she called the funeral home, making arrangements for Robert and Madeline, "small, private graveside services."

He left for a short time to get his briefcase, and paused in Cameron's backyard. He burned the file he'd collected for years in the new pottery chiminea. When the paper was ashes, he turned to the woman on her back porch, and she said, "That won't erase what's happened."

He walked to her. "It's a good start. *You* could have a fresh start, Cameron."

But Cameron was looking past him, past the fairies that had guarded her, toward the old cellar, and Hayden waited and feared her reaction.

"I didn't hear anything last night," she said quietly. "The nightmares didn't come. I didn't hear the whispering."

Hayden held her close. "Cammie is at peace now, Cameron. You did that—gave her what she needed. She'd want you to go on, to make the life you'd never had—one of your own."

"I don't know that I can."

Hayden tipped her head up to his. "Hey. You've got me, don't you?"

But Cameron didn't smile at his attempt at light humor. She just rested close to him.

Two days later, while Cameron dressed to play the role of the grieving Somerton heiress, to receive a small party of mourners in the Somerton salon, Hayden lounged on the bed and read the newspapers. The headline read: ROBERT DUCHAMPS AND EMPLOYEE VICTIMS OF RECENT FLOODING. Beneath the headlines, the story read:

> Madeline Fraiser, a twenty-seven-year employee of Somerton, was returning to the rural estate after a short vacation when she and her passenger, Robert DuChamps, widower of Katherine Somerton, were killed by floodwaters. DuChamps's vehicle was found on a side road near Cameron Somerton's barn-retreat, where he had gone to collect business papers.

No mention of Robert's drinking said that gentler forces were at work behind the scenes. Hayden frowned slightly: Somehow Cameron had managed to keep the Somerton name intact as always. No mention had been made of Robert's reason for being with Madeline.

The article continued: Robert was catching a ride to the estate with Madeline when they attempted to cross that dangerous low-water bridge. Another article, GRIEVING HEIRESS SEEKS SECLUSION, focused on Cameron, her kidnapping, the tragic death of her mother, and now her stepfather and her very good friend and assistant, Madeline Fraiser.

Hayden folded the papers away and found Cameron staring at herself in the mirror. Still stunned by Madeline's treachery, the truth about the deaths of Cammie and Katherine, Cameron seemed very close to releasing a very different story to the press. On edge now, the next few hours would be very difficult for her. Hayden stood and walked to her at the vanity. He placed his hands on her shoulders, and met her reflection in the mirror. "You're not doing it."

"I have no idea what you're talking about."

"You're not going downstairs to announce that you're really *not* Cameron Somerton. You're still in shock and trying to adjust to what happened. Now is not the time to make big decisions—give yourself some time to consider the consequences of tearing apart everything that Katherine and Buck built. If you think Cammie watched over you as a child, think of her now. She wouldn't want you to have even more trauma, not the girl who tried to comfort her at the last."

Cameron shook her head, and the pearls in her ears gleamed. "I have no right—"

He tilted her face back to him and stroked those pale cheeks with his thumbs. "Oh, you have a right. You paid a lifetime for it. I am a vice president, you know. I didn't get there without having a plan, and confidence that it would work. For once—could you just let me handle things?"

But Cameron wasn't arguing; she smiled slightly, sadly, as she stood and smoothed her black dress, Katherine's pearls at her throat and ears. The gargoyle bracelet flashed on her wrist, and Hayden hoped that it would keep her safe in the next few days. "Do I look all right?"

He gripped her shoulders, shaking her slightly. "Do this for yourself, Cameron. We can pull it off."

She shook her head. "I'm just so tired of everything."

He folded her into his arms, rested his cheek against her head, and worried for her. "Just don't do anything rash, okay? We'll get through this. I want to lie beside you tonight and know that you're safe. I want to wake up in the morning with you in my arms. That's not too much to ask, is it?"

Cameron held him tight, her face damp against his throat. "You want me to go through this whole charade—bury Robert and Madeline, then turn everything over to charities as Katherine would have wanted. . . . Then walk away—just like that? With you? After all I've done?"

"It will be more complicated than that, but then you've been running this empire for years. You can manage a handoff." Hayden smoothed her tense back. "I can read the headlines now—GRIEVING HEIRESS WALKS AWAY FROM SOMERTON EMPIRE. And honey, all you did was to protect Buck and Katherine Somerton's legacy from Robert and Madeline."

"Why didn't Madeline shoot me? She's an excellent shot—I was coming after her."

Hayden nuzzled Cameron's hair and rocked her against him. "I think that at the last minute, she saw someone she'd grown to love—she wasn't expecting it—and it shocked her."

"What a crock of—" But Cameron snuggled close to Hayden, and he wasn't letting her go.

He smiled briefly; they might never know the real reason why Madeline didn't pull that trigger. "We'll get through this together, honey. Give yourself some time to think about what I've said. Only you can unravel this the way Buck and Katherine would have wanted. I knew them both and they would have been proud of what you've done already."

That night, as they lay together, Hayden smoothing her arms and breathing safely beside her, Cameron wondered if what he proposed—a new life, her own—could happen. She really should—

"Don't even think about it," Hayden grumbled sleepily as he held her closer. "Think about this—"

Their lovemaking was sweet, a slow reassurance that each was alive. Each taste, each touch reaffirmed the tenderness between them. "I want you like this every day and every night. Understand?" Hayden asked as he held her later, tight against him.

She did, because she wanted him as badly.

After Robert's and Madeline's services, Hayden stood at the gate to the Somerton mausoleum as Cameron sat quietly on the bench. She mourned a mother she'd never known, a child who shouldn't have died so cruelly.

Cammie had always been there for her, giving Cameron peace, the strength she needed to face every day as a substitute heiress. Cameron held herself, rocking on the bench and grieving. "I'll never forget you, Cammie. Never."

When Hayden came to sit beside her, his arm around her, Cameron leaned against him. "It's quiet here. It's always been so peaceful. I should have guessed."

"You could come back—to visit with her."

"How? I'll either be in prison—or if you get your way, I'll be off somewhere, leading a different life."

Hayden latched on to her second "different life" comment. That meant Cameron was slowly wondering about her life away from Somerton. An heiress couldn't just drop out of sight; the change would have to be slow and thorough, sealing away the past—if they were to have the future he wanted.

His fingers toyed with hers. "When you're setting up the clauses on this place, put one in that Grow Green has the contract on keeping up the roses and garden here. You'd look really cute in a pink ball cap and bib overalls and digging in the dirt. You'd have to wear big sunglasses, of course. Maybe a wig."

Cameron smiled slightly, teasing him. "You're just after that big fat contract."

But Hayden was serious as he turned her face to his and brushed his lips across hers. "Uh-huh, that's it. And I'm after you, of course. I want you with me, Cameron—"

"It's not even my name, Hayden. Nothing about me is real."

"*Everything* about you is real. Come on, Cameron. Give us a chance."

Could she really do as Hayden wanted? Start a new life with the man she loved so much? Walk away from everything she'd done? "What about your father? Don't you want his name cleared?"

Hayden's cheek lay against hers. "I don't think for one minute that Dad would want your life to be ruined to clear his name. I'll handle this with my mother and sister, but that's enough for us. We loved him, knew what he was, and that stands. He'll always be with us, in our hearts. He always said, 'Do what's right,' and I don't think raking up the muck from the past is right."

Exhausted by sleepless nights and guilt, Cameron simply rested against Hayden's strength. Then she watched the butterflies on the pink roses, causing the big blooms to bob slightly. She looked up at the clear Oklahoma sky and felt the hot, burning July sun upon her face. *Could she really put everything behind her, and walk into a new life? With Hayden?*

The next day Cameron was at Somerton House, working "in seclusion." The gates to the estate were closed, preventing curiosity seekers and press access to her, and Hayden had returned to the farmhouse to catch up on necessary business.

But when that white pickup barreled up the driveway and tires screeched in front of his house, he braced himself. Moments later, Cameron threw the morning newspaper down on Hayden's makeshift desk at the farmhouse. "I suppose you know about this?"

Hayden briefly admired her sleeveless, short dress, and the cute little flower sandals. Fancy's and Evie's midnight beauty-therapy session had ended up with his toes wearing the same shade of pink polish as Cameron's—which was okay, since no one was ever going to see it. Besides, every man should experience a pedicure once in his life. He looked up from information on Grow Green's newest potential acquisition to the headlines of the paper: HEIRESS MEETS CHILDHOOD BOYFRIEND.

Hayden settled back to look up at Cameron, then grabbed her and held her on his lap. "I might. What of it?"

"You're putting your butt on the line, Olson."

He kissed the side of her throat. "You like my butt. You'll have to keep it safe."

"That's blackmail. You're involved in this—whatever—up to your eyeballs. If I open up this mess, you'll be involved, too. You're just trying to stack the deck . . . influence me into seeing things your way."

"I know," he agreed easily. Then, he tried for logic and hoped that she would buy it. "Honey, our involvement, our relationship to each other, was bound to come out sooner or later. The Somertons have had too much news coverage, and those news hounds aren't going to let anything go. It's better just to flop everything out on the table and get it over. I thought it was a cute 'heartwarming' story—childhood friends become lovers—"

"You didn't actually say *that,* did you?"

"I simply implied that the past was past, and that I had long-term plans for you when you recovered from grieving. I expect we'll be pursued a bit, but that will die down. It is a Romeo and Juliet story, after all."

"To whom? Whom did you talk to?" she demanded.

"Fancy is now dating that newspaper reporter. He was there at the salon yesterday. I was just trying to help her out with him. An inside story would do that. She could end up married again because of me."

When Cameron groaned delicately and closed her eyes, Hayden brushed her breast with his thumb. He studied its peak, and added, "But I have more immediate plans right now."

She inhaled and slid from his lap. "So do I. . . . Oh, not that. Hayden, I haven't been having nightmares. I haven't heard any whispers. I think what you propose might just work—if done in the right way. You are definitely right about me being the only person to unravel the Somerton business and estate in a way that would protect it as Buck and Katherine would have wanted. I can do it."

"So what are your immediate plans?"

Hayden breathed quietly as Cameron slowly hiked up her dress, just enough to reveal she was entirely—his. Then she straddled him. "Olson, you're right about the people that could be affected by my admission. I've got to protect them. The grieving heiress goes into seclusion idea just might work."

"So your immediate plans are this?" he asked as his hands smoothed her bottom.

"You're all about confidence, aren't you?"

"Ask me later," he said as he tugged her head down for a long, hungry kiss.

Late that afternoon, in Oklahoma's searing late July heat, Fancy and Evie stood with Cameron as Hayden leveled the cellar with a bulldozer. In the aftermath, shaken by memories of that frightened child inside the darkness, Cameron simply sat on a log, huddled into herself, her arms around her knees, and cried. Hayden stopped the bulldozer, climbed down, and walked to the women's log. "Scoot over, girls," he ordered gently. "This is a man's job."

Evie's eyes sparkled with humor. "Yeah. A man with pink toenails."

"Tell anyone, and you die."

Then Hayden sat beside Cameron on that log, his arm around her, his body rocking hers. Cameron's voice was only a whisper against his throat when she said, "I'll do it. I'll really try."

"You do that. I'll be right with you."

"Try what?" Evie and Fancy asked.

"I'm leaving the heiress business. Checking out. Adios."

Cameron's tone was uneven, and Hayden understood her fears.

Her friends stared at her. Then Fancy said, "Good for you, hon. You need a new life."

"Yeah, we didn't want to say anything, but you get all depressed when you've got Somerton stuff on your mind," Evie stated.

Cameron turned to them. "Meanwhile, I'm loaded. And you can have anything your little hearts desire—big stuff, like your own beauty shop, or a business you want—like a big house for your mother to stay with you, Fancy, and a full-time nurse to watch her. Think about the big pictures, lifetime stuff—I'll take care of it."

While Evie and Fancy were ecstatic, the Somerton board of directors weren't happy.

Katherine's favorite charities were.

By the end of July, Cameron's attorneys were working furiously to sort the Somerton empire—disposing of businesses, property, and donations to charities kept her busy. It would take years for Somerton's board of directors to establish another corporation, removed from the Somerton family and playing fair with investors. But Cameron would no longer be involved in decision-making, or the corporation, after disposing of her shares. With funds designated for perpetual upkeep, the mansion would be kept intact, pink roses everywhere. Soon to take full possession, Katherine's favorite charities would use it for a showplace and fund-raising.

After the flurry of objections from corporate people, they realized that Cameron Somerton, heiress, had made up her mind. She was exhausted by public life, wanting her privacy. The recent events had caused her to realize how short life really was and that she wanted what every other woman wanted—her own life. The heiress was set to give up an empire, her wealth, her status—but then, she'd always been a little "odd," after all. Upon the deaths of her stepfather and her dear friend, Ms. Somerton had decided to retire quietly into private life, the burdens of managing the empire unappealing.

At the estate, while trying to help Cameron unravel her heiress role, Hayden leaned back from his laptop screen; his eyes burned from hours of prowling through old newspaper stories. Twenty-eight years ago, a little girl named Pilar had been taken from an Irish part of some city—but where?

Cameron came to stand behind him, her hand caressing his back as she placed a glass of iced tea beside him. It was "sweet tea," made with sugar in the Southern mode.

"I don't really care about where I came from, Hayden. Someone should have loved that little girl, Pilar, and they didn't. The way my mother drank, she's probably dead now, and I'd really prefer to think of myself as Katherine's other daughter. If my feelings change someday, I'll deal with it then. Is my real identity important to you at all?"

He ran his thumb over the gargoyle bracelet Cameron continued to wear; he wondered about getting earrings to match. "Not if it doesn't matter to you."

She slid into his arms. "It doesn't. The question is, who am I going to be, if and when I can manage totally to slide out of here?"

"You're really good—you can. And what's wrong with the name 'Cameron'? That would be a way to keep Cammie with you, to remember her, wouldn't it? She never used it—it's yours."

"I guess it would keep her close, and I can't entirely leave her out of my life. She may be resting now, but she'll always be a part of me." She looked down at his notes. "Phoebe? You've been keeping track of her?"

He tossed the notes into the trash can. "She won't be back now that Robert is dead."

"But I want to talk with her—I have to. She was my friend."

"Dammit. You can't fix her, Cameron."

"But you can—honey."

"Dammit."

Nineteen

AUGUST CAME IN HOT AND DRY, BUT ROSES AT THE MAU-soleum bloomed lush and pink. Cameron would sit there many times, feeling the stillness and the peace, the whispers silenced forever.

The Somerton heiress remained secluded, managing her "disengagement" from business duties and her family's wealth and obligations. Working at her side was Mr. Hayden Olson, who was personally overseeing the quiet purchase and return of the Somerton collections.

Cameron watched the dusty white pickup pull to a stop in front of the house. She'd given clearance to Ray's man at the front gate to let the pickup enter the estate. "She's here," she said to Hayden, who was busy negotiating the return of a collection of muskets and early firearms—reportedly something that Andrew Jackson's men had used in the Battle of New Orleans.

He ended the call and nodded, then moved silently, purposefully out of the office to go downstairs.

Cameron watched Phoebe get out of the pickup and stand looking up at the office's second-story window. Moments later, Hayden ushered Cameron's former friend into the room. "Hello, Phoebe," Cameron said as she took in the other woman's thin body, ragged appearance, and fearful expression. "Sit down, please."

"Hi." Phoebe wasn't used to seeing Cameron in her powerful businesswoman-heiress role and was visibly frightened, her hands gripping the chair's arms.

Cameron thought briefly of Robert, trying to intimidate her, his riding crop in hand. She thought of how Phoebe might have suffered, a woman easily misled by a certain kind of experienced, knowing man—such as Robert. Hayden had settled against the wall, his arms crossed, his legs braced. It was a protective stance Cameron had seen many times in the past two weeks. She thought of Phoebe dancing on the top of the bar in her red boots; she thought of Phoebe laughing and flirting.

Nothing remained of that Phoebe in this worn, fearful woman.

"I'm so sorry!" Phoebe cried out suddenly.

"I know you are." Cameron came to lean against her desk. "You need a new life, Phoebe, and new skills. You need to know that you can stand on your own and that you don't need to lean on anyone else, that you are smart enough to do what you want—"

"But I'm not. I'm a follower, Cameron. You know I—"

Hayden inhaled impatiently, the restless, disbelieving sound ricocheting in the office. Cameron looked at his grim expression as she spoke to Phoebe. "Hayden has come up with an idea. Everything is your choice. Hayden likes to let people make their own choices."

"I heard he was the gardener's son, the one who kidnapped you and killed himself," Phoebe began furiously. "He's just after your money. Men are like that—they use women."

Cameron swung her cool gaze around to Phoebe. "But haven't you heard that I'm not going to have any money? I'm leaving everything about Somerton."

Phoebe's eyes rounded, and she glanced fearfully at Hayden. "What do you want with me? Are you going to turn me in?"

"No."

"Then what? You're so mad at me," Phoebe whined, and began to cry. "I just wanted to make Robert happy. I thought he loved me—"

"I know. You like to make men happy because you're afraid that you don't know what's best for yourself. But you do—if you stop and think, Phoebe. As for the cellar and your shutting that door—I think that part may have all worked out for the best. But it certainly wasn't easy on me—the cellar is gone, by the way. And after today, I never want you to contact me again."

Phoebe sobbed quietly, her hands in her face. "I had a good thing going. Friends—I miss them. You got my job at the post office for me. . . . I was on my own and didn't have to— Oh, I ruin everything."

Cameron thought of the little girl in Phoebe who needed the same comforting as another little girl long ago. She ached for her former friend and hoped that somehow Phoebe would reach out for a better life. "If you choose to do so, you can go to college, Phoebe . . . expenses paid. The only provision is that when your grades show you aren't putting an effort into it, or any tutors you may need say you aren't trying, the funds will be cut. I only ask that you really try. I'm offering you a way out, Phoebe, a start for a new life. You'll have to watch yourself very carefully, try to change who you were—"

In the shadows, Hayden stirred restlessly, and Cameron knew her decision nettled him as she continued. "People can change; so can you. That means, no men and no bars and no drinking. You take this deal, and it means studying really hard and walking into new experiences every day. You're going to hurt and cry and be terrified. And the only person [illegible] have to depend on is you. . . . But if you want it badly [illegible] you can do it."

Hayden moved forward with a portfolio and dropped it onto Phoebe's lap. Then he moved back into the shadows and crossed his arms, his expression unreadable.

Phoebe stared at the portfolio as if it were poisonous.

"It's your enrollment, Phoebe. You can start college right away. You're really smart, and you should have no trouble with the classes—but again, that depends on you. I'll personally select your clothes and have them sent to you—a new life calls for new clothes. I'll be integrating matters for a long time with a business manager, and his name is in there. All you have to do is to reach out, Phoebe," Cameron said gently.

"Can I go now?" Phoebe asked in her childish voice.

Cameron's instincts told her to soften, to guide Phoebe through life; but Phoebe would have to adjust to many things in the future, and just maybe gain confidence in herself. Or not. The choice was Phoebe's alone. Cameron smiled and hugged the other woman. "Sure. Have a good life, Phoebe. Don't ever come back to Mimosa and don't contact me."

Phoebe was crying, clutching the portfolio close to her as she hurried from the room and downstairs.

From her office window, Cameron came to watch Phoebe drive away. Hayden stood behind her, his hand resting lightly on her waist, and Cameron realized how many times he touched her, in that comforting way, to let her know she wasn't alone—even when he didn't agree with her decisions. . . .

She turned simply to look at him, this man who meant so much to her.

"I know why Katherine loved Buck so much," she said, moving into his arms. "He was a really good guy, like you."

"I thought you said I was a good guy," Hayden said in August's second week as they drove from the airport in St. Louis to his mother's home. He looked at Cameron, whom he'd just collected. She was sitting on the passenger side of the car, her arms folded across her chest, her frown locked to him. There had been a hungry kiss when she'd first gotten off the plane, but after that first bliss of being reunited, she'd been silent and brooding.

"I don't like this," Cameron stated abruptly. "You caught me at a weak moment. . . . Stop smiling. You—you set up that bathtub-candlelight scene, the romantic music, a movie you knew would make me all soft and wilty, and you cooked dinner. How could any woman refuse a man who had baked a pie and was wearing nothing but a frilly apron?"

Hayden deftly handled the BMW in city traffic and took her hand. It was cold with fear. He laced his fingers with hers, warming them. Taking care of Cameron was something he did with an intensity that sometimes shook her independence. "You'd been working so hard. I thought it was a nice little touch at the end of the day."

"Then, when I was all—you know—you asked this *one little favor.* Some favor. I'm set up to face the woman who paid dearly in this whole mess."

"It's important to me, Cameron. To her, and to you, I think." The bridge between the past and their future together included his mother and Cameron's acceptance that she was moving into a new life—with him.

Those sky-blue eyes looked at him, and he ached for the sadness there. "Does she know about me?"

"She knows you're the woman I'm seeing and that I'm going to keep seeing. She knows your name is Cameron Somerton. She knows I want to change that to Olson. It's a good generic kind of name." Hayden held his breath as Cameron digested the meaning of his words; he hadn't mentioned marriage, but now the idea was on the table.

Cameron stared out at the passing traffic without a reaction.

So much for an enthusiastic Oh, Yes, I'd love to.

Later, after a dinner with his family in which Cameron had acted polite and friendly, but tense, they entered his apartment.

Hayden placed her travel bag on the floor and turned her around, kissing her hard. Maybe it was the wrong approach to get the attention of a woman who seemed to be set to draw away from him—but it was the best he could do at the moment.

When she could tear her lips away, Cameron said, "She knows. Your mother *knows* that I'm not Cammie."

"She knows how much good work you've done for Somertons' and Katherine's charities. She knows that you're trying to return the mansion to what it was, for a showplace in Buck's and Katherine's memory. She knows that—we're together." Hayden realized that though Cameron was moving through changes, there would always be moments of doubt, of guilt.

A brief description of what had happened had made his mother cry, but she understood everything; Sophie had gotten the closure she badly needed—Paul Olson had been innocent of any crime, and had only tried to protect Katherine. Sophie ached for the child Pilar and for Cammie, but she also understood that Cameron had no choices but the ones she would make now—for a new life, and probably with Hayden. Gracie would be told, and Hayden had no doubt that she would feel the same as his mother; the man they had loved was held deep in their hearts, and that was enough.

And Hayden intended to make Cameron's doubting moments disappear.

On the other hand, he was frustrated. Somehow, he'd expected more of a reaction about changing Cameron's name to Olson. A man's ego deflates pretty quickly when the woman he's intended to marry him discards the first introduction of the idea.

Cameron studied him. "You've got that peeved look. You're upset. Why?"

"You first." She could do anything she wanted with her new life, go anywhere, but he intended to be with her. Maybe she had different ideas. And she was definitely getting too good at spotting his "sensitive" side.

Cameron moved close to him and wound her arms around his shoulders. "You look so delicate now—that fragile look. What's wrong, honey?"

"Oh, I just had some crazy idea. Not worth mentioning really."

"Really? What was it?" She moved slightly, hitched up her skirt a little, and lifted her foot up to his shoulder, resting upon it.

The sudden move had completely erased his thoughts. Hayden looked down at that long leg, and that heavy heat shot low in his belly. He smoothed her leg, enjoyed the curved length, and ran his hand up to cup her bottom. He lifted her slightly and started walking into his bedroom. "Ballet?"

She was kissing him, doing the cute little flicking tongue-tip thing that she could do when they— "It pays to keep in shape. I love you, Mr. Hayden Olson."

He needed a moment for that statement to sink in. He stopped carrying her and put her down; Cameron's leg slid from his shoulder, and she stood watching him as she slowly undressed. Hayden wasn't able to speak, to move, and Cameron looked away, her arms around her breasts. "You're not obligated to return the . . . the, what I just said. Please don't feel that—"

Hayden took a deep breath and began undressing. He might not be able to speak just then, his throat tight with emotion, but he had other ways to tell Cameron that she had his heart. . . .

He stood before her as he was, just a man wanting a woman in every way.

She moved into his arms as if coming home. . . .

In the stillness of the night, Cameron listened to Hayden's heartbeat, the sound of his breathing, slow, regular, in and out. . . . He'd told her that he'd loved her in so many ways, but most of all in the gentle, cherishing way he touched her.

This time, their lovemaking carried with it special promises of tomorrows.

Hayden tensed slightly, just that tiny shift of his tall body tangled with hers, and Cameron knew he was awake, fearing that she'd awakened in a nightmare, that the terrifying whispers had gripped her.

"It's so quiet," she whispered, as Hayden gathered her closer.

"Cammie can rest now. She's sleeping, thanks to you," he said quietly. "You've been wanting to do something special for her. I thought maybe we could change the landscaping at the—where she is. We could move those fairies over, set them properly. She'd like that."

"Yes, she would." Cameron listened to the night, waiting for the whispers.

But she heard only the quiet beating of her heart, where Cammie would always be.

Epilogue

One year later

AT SUNSET, WILLIAM AND HAYDEN SAT ON THE DECKING OF Hayden's new St. Louis home. After one of his barbecues, they watched the women meandering through the garden-in-progress. It was a calming time, when summer seemed to stand still with the sound of women talking quietly. William proudly cradled his sleeping toddler and was evidently flourishing in his new married life, his internship, and work. His parents wanted to enjoy this grandchild, and the coming one, and were gradually abandoning their rigid stance about his "low" occupation as a gardener.

William had that touch, a real green thumb, and he was an asset to Grow Green. Hayden felt proud, almost like a father himself. Cameron's ex had emerging qualities that any man would admire.

However good William was as a gardener and fix-it man, Cameron's ability to nurture plants was, as yet, sadly lacking. She stood and looked at a dying plant while she spoke to Arabella. Arabella nodded, but her gaze met Hayden's in a way that said she understood why the plant looked poorly.

Hayden shrugged and smiled back at Arabella. It was a tropical that wouldn't do well in the shade of a Japanese maple tree, but Cameron had been so enthusiastic about planting it that Hayden hadn't stopped her—at the time, he was enjoying the way her bottom wiggled.

Paul Olson would have enjoyed Cameron's attempts at gardening; he would have loved her, too, and he was at peace now—that was something that Hayden knew for certain. He sighed and leaned back, his arms across the railing, his feet propped up on an opposite wooden bench and simply enjoyed his life.

Cameron was dressed in a cute little vest and tight black pants that showed off the butt Hayden planned to enjoy after their company departed. She hugged Arabella and patted her "baby-bump."

Hayden slowly scanned the Japanese garden-in-progress—simplicity at its best, a little bridge over a koi pond, aquatic plants, and stone paths. He smiled a bit at Cameron's ideas for "lots and lots of roses, and flowers everywhere." Hayden shrugged again; the cluttered look went well with simple, if given a chance.

He studied Cameron as she pointed to the stones for the walkways and indicated the places they would be laid. After a hard day at the office, Hayden really enjoyed his own hands-on garden and whatever Cameron brought to the experience of hands-on-in-the-garden.

In the year that Cameron had worked to "disengage" herself from Somerton and moved into a new life with him, there were times she'd brooded over the past. But the dark times were lessening, and she seemed to be enjoying herself—here, with him. And as vice president of Grow Green, Hayden had gotten a part-time, top-notch, catalog copywriter. He'd really enjoyed giving her that first small check, Payable to Cameron Olson. Her enthusiastic reaction had been to buy him dinner with it.

Hayden inhaled the fragrances of the night again—the toddler sighed, and the women went inside. Country music began, a little heavy, a little fast-tempo for his mood, but hey—the night was sweet and still, and he had everything a man could want.

Then he turned to the two women in the doorway of the house: one, shorter and pregnant again—and the other lean and leggy, obviously giving dancing directions to the beat of the music. Arabella tried, but shook her head and walked to sit beside William.

His arm around her, William noted Cameron's body moving to the beat, her finger crooked at the men. "I guess that's for you, old man. I'll just sit here with my woman and see if you can keep up."

Hayden shoved himself to his feet. "All I can do is try, mate."

He moved toward where Cameron was doing her swaying, leggy dance, her hands moving over her body. Arabella's giggle didn't stop Hayden from taking one of those hands in his as Cameron slowly danced around him.

He stood still, letting her do a little bump and grind against him, her body behind his, her hands moving over his chest, her lips to his ear. Hayden held out his other hand, and she took it, whirling out, away from him, and then back close and friendly, undulating her bottom against him.

He shrugged a little at William's bawdy laughter as Cameron circled him again, leaned back against him, and lifted her arms high. When she looped her hands behind his head, her bottom swaying to the music, Hayden held her still—because any more and he wouldn't be able to hide his special little present for her.

As Hayden stood still, occasionally extending his hand to

take Cameron's, or placing his hands on her waist as she moved against him, Arabella was laughing with William.

But Hayden was only seeing the promises in those sultry blue eyes, the sensual way Cameron licked her lips after kissing him.

Looking up at him, Cameron's arms circled his neck, and she lifted that long leg, then the other, to circle his waist. "Having trouble keeping up?" she asked with the cute little smirk that meant it was going to be a long, busy night.

"Ballet," Hayden explained hoarsely to William. "I'm getting good at it."

As William and Arabella made their laughing departure, Hayden carried Cameron to the door in just that position. "Night, people," she called to them, as he shut the door and stood holding her.

There was that brief time when they just stood, looking at each other, and the past moved away; this man was worth every moment of the journey. "I love you, Hayden," Cameron murmured against his lips.

She smoothed Hayden's rugged face, those black eyebrows, the ridges of his cheekbones, his lips. This man had come into her life, shaken her world, and moved her into a different, new one.

He'd stood by her in the worst of moments and had shared the best.

His hand was always there to hold hers; his shoulder was always strong and safe beneath her weary head as she dealt with periodic small Somerton issues.

Cameron smiled as she traced his lips with her fingertips. Those were the times that matter—not the yelling when she accidentally spoiled his "landscaping" by adding a few touches of her own. There was that yin yang thing—little sensitive male issues that needed to be tended, his preference for plain iced tea, when she liked hers sweet, the sugar added as it was made, not a spoonful later.

Hayden was hers in every way, kind of a possessive ownership thing, this wifey-business—and most enjoyable.

Now was the time she came softly to him, the man she loved . . . when the night was sweet and long and silent, made just for them and all their tomorrows.

Next month, don't miss these exciting new love stories only from Avon Books

Tempting the Wolf by Lois Greiman

An Avon Romantic Treasure

When an ancient warrior finds himself in Regency England, trouble is bound to follow. O'Banyon enjoys mixing with fashionable society, just as long as he doesn't allow his passions to overtake him. But when a mysterious miss wins her way into his heart, he must risk everything for this one chance at love.

Return of the Highlander by Sara Mackenzie

An Avon Contemporary Romance

All Arabella wants is to study and write about the legendary Maclean in peace and quiet. What she *doesn't* want is to actually meet the centuries-old Scotsman! But now that he's appeared, nothing will ever be the same again . . .

From London With Love by Jenna Petersen

An Avon Romance

Meredith Sinclair has perfected her flighty, popular personality with the *ton* in order to hide the truth: that she is a highly-trained spy. Now, as she investigates suspected traitor Tristan Archer, Meredith knows she must risk it all to embrace a passion that overwhelms all reason.

Once Upon a Wedding Night by Sophie Jordan

An Avon Romance

Nicholas Caulfield is desperate to marry off the scheming miss who is after his family's money. But the more he gets to know her, the more confused he becomes. Will he be able to forgive the past . . . before it's too late?

Visit www.AuthorTracker.com for exclusive information on your favorite HarperCollins authors.

Available wherever books are sold or please call 1-800-331-3761 to order.

REL 0706

Sink Your Teeth Into More Delectable Vampire Romance From *USA Today* Bestselling Author

LYNSAY SANDS

"Lynsay Sands writes books that keep readers coming back for more."
Katie MacAlister

Now available

A QUICK BITE

0-06-077375-8/$6.99 US/$9.99 Can

Lissianna has been spending her centuries pining for Mr. Right, not just a quick snack, and this sexy guy she finds in her bed looks like he might be a candidate. But there's another, more pressing issue: her tendency to faint at the sight of blood…an especially annoying quirk for a vampire.

A BITE TO REMEMBER

0-06-077407-X/$6.99 US/$9.99 Can

Vincent Argeneau may be the hottest guy PI Jackie Morrisey's ever met, living or dead, but she's out to stop a killer from turning this vampire into dust, not to jump into bed with him.

Visit www.AuthorTracker.com for exclusive information on your favorite HarperCollins authors.

Available wherever books are sold or please call 1-800-331-3761 to order.

LYS 0506

Don't look over your shoulder, you never know who might be there . . .

Romantic suspense from

CAIT LONDON

FLASHBACK

0-06-079087-3/$5.99 US/$7.99 Can

Rachel Everly has returned to Neptune's Landing to sleuth out the person responsible for her sister's tragic death.

HIDDEN SECRETS

0-06-055890-0/$5.99 US/$7.99 Can

An unsolved murder, a fateful accident, and a strange disappearance. Marlo Malone senses that these are somehow connected to Spence, the charismatic man she cannot resist.

WHAT MEMORIES REMAIN

0-06-055588-2/$5.99 US/$7.99 Can

Two people won't allow Cyd Callahan to keep the past buried forever. One is Ewan, who is fascinated by this woman. The other is a faceless predator determined to make Cyd pay for her "sins."

WITH HER LAST BREATH

0-06-000181-X/$5.99 US/$7.99 Can

Maggie is running from frightening memories, but Nick Allesandro won't let her forget. He knows someone is out to get Maggie ... and he must stop the killer before it's too late.

WHEN NIGHT FALLS

0-06-000180-1/$5.99 US/$7.99 Can

Uma Thornton has always kept the secrets of Madrid, Oklahoma ... until her safety is shattered by a shadowy murderer. Can she trust Mitchell—who claims he wants to protect her? Or is he as dangerous as he seems?

Visit www.AuthorTracker.com for exclusive information on your favorite HarperCollins authors.

Available wherever books are sold or please call 1-800-331-3761 to order.

CLO 0406

DISCOVER CONTEMPORARY ROMANCES *at their* SIZZLING HOT BEST FROM AVON BOOKS

Flashback by Cait London
0-06-079087-3/$5.99 US/$7.99 Can

The Boy Next Door by Meg Cabot
0-06-084554-6/$5.99 US/$7.99 Can

Switched, Bothered and Bewildered by Suzanne Macpherson
0-06-077494-0/$5.99 US/$7.99 Can

Sleeping With the Agent by Gennita Low
0-06-059124-2/$5.99 US/$7.99 Can

Guys & Dogs by Elaine Fox
0-06-074060-4/$5.99 US/$7.99 Can

Running For Cover by Lynn Montana
0-06-073483-3/$5.99 US/$7.99 Can

Sighs Matter by Marianne Stillings
0-06-073483-3/$5.99 US/$7.99 Can

Vamps and the City by Kerrelyn Sparks
0-06-075201-7/$5.99 US/$7.99 Can

Almost a Goddess by Judi McCoy
0-06-077425-8/$5.99 US/$7.99 Can

Silence the Whispers by Cait London
0-06-079088-1/$5.99 US/$7.99 Can

Visit www.AuthorTracker.com for exclusive information on your favorite HarperCollins authors.

CRO 0406

Available wherever books are sold or please call 1-800-331-3761 to order.

PROWL THE NIGHT WITH
RACHEL MORGAN AND

KIM HARRISON

DEAD WITCH WALKING

0-06-057296-5 • $7.99 US/$10.99 Can

When the creatures of the night gather, whether to hide, to hunt, or to feed, it's Rachel Morgan's job to keep things civilized. A bounty hunter and witch with serious sex appeal and attitude, she'll bring them back alive, dead . . . or undead.

THE GOOD, THE BAD, AND THE UNDEAD

0-06-057297-3 • $7.99 US/$10.99 Can

Rachel Morgan can handle the leather-clad vamps and even tangle with a cunning demon or two. But a serial killer who feeds on the experts in the most dangerous kind of black magic is definitely pressing the limits.

EVERY WHICH WAY BUT DEAD

0-06-057299-X • $7.99 US/$10.99 Can

Rachel must take a stand in the raging war to control Cincinnati's underworld because the demon who helped her put away its former vampire kingpin is coming to collect his due.

A FISTFUL OF CHARMS

0-06-078819-4 • $7.99 US/$10.99 Can

A mortal lover who abandoned Rachel has returned, haunted by his secret past. And there are those willing to destroy the Hollows to get what Nick possesses.

www.kimharrison.net

Visit www.AuthorTracker.com for exclusive information on your favorite HarperCollins authors.

Available wherever books are sold or please call 1-800-331-3761 to order.

HAR 0406

AVON TRADE... because every great bag deserves a great book!

0-06-052228-3
$12.95

0-06-088536-X
$13.95 ($17.95 Can.)

0-06-088229-8
$13.95 ($17.95 Can.)

0-06-089005-3
$12.95 ($16.95 Can.)

0-06-089930-1
$12.95 ($16.95 Can.)

0-06-077311-1
$12.95 ($16.95 Can.)

Visit www.AuthorTracker.com for exclusive information on your favorite HarperCollins authors.

Available wherever books are sold, or call 1-800-331-3761 to order.

ATP 0706